Never let facts get in the way of truth.

—J. FRANK DOBIE

THE DEVIL'S BACKBONE

BILL WITTLIFF

The Devil's Backbone

Illustrated by JACK UNRUH

University of Texas Press, *Austin*

THE PUBLICATION OF THIS BOOK
WAS SUPPORTED IN PART BY
THE UNIVERSITY OF TEXAS PRESS
ADVISORY COUNCIL.

♾ The paper used in this book meets the minimum requirements of
ANSI/NISO Z39.48-1992 (R1997) (Permanence of Paper).

LIBRARY OF CONGRESS CATALOGING-IN-PUBLICATION DATA
Wittliff, William D., author.
    The devil's backbone / by Bill Wittliff ; illustrated by Jack Unruh. —
First edition.
        pages   cm
    ISBN 978-0-292-75995-4 (cloth : alk. paper)
1. Families—Texas—Fiction. 2. Texas—Fiction. 3. Epic fiction.
I. Unruh, Jack, illustrator. II. Title.
    PS3573.I933D4 2014
    813'.54—dc23   2014007075

doi:10.7560/759954

For My Grandchildren

SLOAN   TEGAN   LEIGH   WADE

And For My Pal

OCHO

THE DEVIL'S BACKBONE

OH LISTEN HERE

Papa said, it was still a wild and wooly Country back then. Why it wadn't nothing to hear a Panther scream in the night or to have to go run a Bear out a'the corn crib with a stick or a Pitchfork and ever once in a while, he said, you might see some poor o'broke down Inyin passing through with a raggedy o'bundle cross his back headed down South to Old Mexico or somewheres else. This was in the 1880s and Papa was talking about the world along the Blanco River in the Hill Country of Central Texas. Old Karl, my Daddy, wadn't much on anybody just setting round, he said, not if they was old nough to work. And old nough to work, Papa said, started bout the time you could get round on you own two feet So, he said, ever morning at Sun Up Old Karl'd lift me and my Big Brother Herman up on this o'Swayback Horse we had name a'Molly and send us off with the Cows to make sure they didn't stray moren a mile or two from the House while they was grazing. Soon as we was gone a ways we'd climb down off o'Molly, Papa said, and just walk along with the Creatures chunking rocks to keep em from taking directions of they own. One day we heard Something stomping round in the Brush over yonder. Something big. Maybe even moren one Something. I said What's that yonder, Papa said. Herman said It's Something gonna eat you up. I was just a little Boy but I knowed when my Brother was a'teasing me so I said No they ain't nothing in there gonna eat me up. Herman said Well go look you don't believe me. So I picked up a rock and walked over there to the Brush. I don't hear nothing I said, Papa said. Well go on in there and take you a Look you little Sissy Baby Herman said. I throwed my rock instead then took off a'running when here come two big o'Longhorn Bulls a'charging out a'the Brush right on me. Up a tree me and Herman went fast as we could go, Papa said, them Bulls just a'hooking at us. Then they went to bellering and snorting and kicking the ground up and all our Cows run off in ever which direction and they wadn't one thing we could do bout it from up that tree. After a while them Bulls went a'walking on off but fore

*Old Karl, my Daddy, wadn't much
on anybody just setting round . . .*

1

we could get down out the tree here come this Cowboy a'riding up on his Horse and wanted to know why in the Hell we was messing round with his Bulls and what the Hell was our dam Cows doing on his land anyhow. No Sir this ain't your land here, Herman said, it's everbody's land. No not no more it ain't the Cowboy said, Papa said. He said he had it all leased up from the Govment now ever Inch of it and we better run go tell our Daddy to get his Live Stock off his Land fore he decided to take the whole dam Bunch in somewheres and sell em for his trouble.

We run right on home, Papa said, and told Old Karl what the Cowboy said. He give us each one a good Whupping for letting his Cows run off like that then took down his Big Gun and said Well I'm gonna go see bout this. A couple a'days later me and Herman come up on them two Longhorn Bulls at a waterhole. They was both dead with a bullet hole in they Heart, Papa said, what Herman said was a case a'the Lead Poisoning.

OUR DADDY WAS A HORSE TRADER

Papa said, Old Karl'd rope Wild Horses out a'the Cedar Brakes long the Blanco River til he had him a good little bunch say bout thirty forty head then me and him'd loose-herd em from this town to the next Trading and Selling as we went and Camping long the way. Sometimes we'd be down to maybe just a Horse or two, he said, Other times we might have us moren a hunderd but Old Karl wouldn't turn for Home til he sold or traded away ever last Horse we had save o'Molly who pulled the wagon. That'd take months on some trips, Papa said, and I did all the Choring long the way while Old Karl set back and smoked on his pipe. Do this Do that Get over here Get over there Hurry it up Hurry it up That's how it went Morning Noon and Night, Papa said. I wadn't no bettern some o'Slave to my own Daddy on them trips and they wadn't no fun in it at all. Except when they went through a town. Then Papa would sit on the tailgate of the wagon and make faces like he was a Loonie at the Town Boys on the boardwalk as Old Karl drove past. Then them Town Boys would jump and come a'running after the wagon a'throwing rocks at me, Papa said. Big rocks, he said, rocks that'd put a Knot on your head. But that was what I wanted, Papa said, cause one or two a'them rocks would always go right over me and conk Old Karl on the back a'his noggin and then Oh he'd go to yelling and cussing and shaking his fist and sometimes jump off the wagon and go to chasing them Town Boys down the street and I'd cover up my face with my hands so he couldn't see me a'laughing like I sure nough was a Loonie.

OLD KARL NEVER MADE HIM A HORSE TRADE but what at the end he didn't get him a little To Boot—a little something extra, Papa said. Sometimes it might be another Horse, or a few dollars, or maybe even the other fella's hat or his pocketknife. It was a matter a'pride, Old Karl said. No it wadn't, Papa said, it was a matter a'Greed but I didn't never say nothing to Old Karl bout that.

One time, Papa said, Old Karl was in the Saloon cross the street having him a Bowl a'Beans, all the Boot he could get off a'some old hard-headed Dutchman he just traded out a'fourteen good Horses. They was two Men at the bar Old Karl knowed was a'watching him. He seen em watching him a little while ago too when he was out on the street trading that o'Dutchman out a'his Horses.

Get ready to cough tonight he said when he got back over to the wagon where I was keeping the Horses. Oh oh here comes Trouble I said to myself, Papa said.

First thing Old Karl done when we made us a camp down the road that day, he said, was to have me dig a deep hole. Then he dropped his Money Sack down the hole and I covered it up. What you got a broke leg, Old Karl said. Now run go get some wood and set me a fire on top of it and I did, Papa said. That night we was setting there in front a'the fire eating our suppers when here come somebody our way through the Brush. Yeah, Old Karl said, here they come. I coughed, Papa said. Old Karl reached over and give me a thump on the back a'my head. You better do bettern that he said. I coughed again, Papa said, then went to wheezing like I couldn't even catch my breath. That's when them two Men from the Saloon stepped up in the firelight. Seen your Fire, the one with the Double Barrel Shot Gun said. What concern is it a'yours we got us a Fire or not, Old Karl said and give me a look to get a'going with the coughing So, Papa said, I went to coughing again. What's wrong with your Boy there. the Other Man said. He was a Cowboy wearing a Hat so big I couldn't even see his face, Papa said, but I sure did like that Hat. He caught him the Pox or something, Old Karl said, and I went to coughing again, Papa said. The Man hefted up his Double Barrels. You got some Money on you ain't you, he said, a smart o'SonofaBitch like you. I was coughing right along, Papa said, but drawing it out now so I could hear everthing was being said. I had me some Money, Old Karl said, but I spent it all on a Doctor in town for this Boy here. Go dig in they pockets and see, he told the Man in the Big Hat. I coughed. No Sir I ain't gonna take money might help a Sick Boy even if he got some, the Big Hat Man said. Let's just ride on off from here.

But the Shot Gun Man raised up his Big o'Gun, Papa said, and said You and that Boy take your clothes off ever stitch and throw em over here to where we can see you got Money on you or not. I won't do it, Old Karl said. I won't take my clothes off for you nor any other Man no matter you shoot me or not. Them two didn't know what to do, Papa said. Well just have em turn they pockets inside out then and lets go, the Big Hat Man said. Old Karl give me a swat. You heard what he said he said, Papa said. I turned my pockets inside out. So did Old Karl, he said. They ain't got nothing, the Big Hat Man said. Well then they a'hiding it somewheres else round here the Shot Gun Man said. Old Karl put another big stick on the fire. I wish I did have some Money on me he said, Papa said, I'd buy me a Gun and some Bullets and shoot you two SonsaBitches deadern a god dam Anvil with it. Well Yes Sir maybe you would and maybe you wouldn't the Shot Gun Man said then lifted up his Gun at us and give both hammers a cock back with his thumbs. Now Jack, the Big Hat Man said, put that thing down fore you get you self in the kind a'trouble you can't no way get you self back out of. And what kind a'trouble would that be, the Shot Gun Man said. Why this kind a'trouble right here Jack, the Big Hat Man said. And then Oh the Shot Gun Man seen in the firelight the Big Hat Man was a'pointing his own Pistol at him and it was cocked too but we never even seen him pull it out his pants or cock the hammer back neither one, Papa said. You wouldn't shoot me the Shot Gun Man said, we're Friends ain't we. Yes Sir I am the Best Friend you ever had in your Life Jack, the Big Hat Man said then aimed his Pistol up at his Heart and said And I'm a'gonna be the Last Friend you ever had too you don't move them Gun Barrels off a'that little Sick Boy there. Shoot the Son-ofaBitch, Old Karl said, and no man the wiser. But the Shot Gun Man seen the Pickle he was in and said I didn't mean nothing by it and pointed down his Shot Gun and then off they went back in the Brush where they come from in the First Place, Papa said, and Old Karl said Why ain't you coughing like I told you to. Cause they gone now that's why I said, Papa said. Old Karl Snaked his Eyes at me and said For all you know they a'setting right over there behind that tree yonder just a'watching to see if you really sick or not. They see you ain't they liable to come back over here and shoot the both a'us just for the Hell of it. Then he reached over and give me a good hard slap cross my face, Papa said, and said You ever give one god dam thought to that. No Sir, Papa said, but I am now.

*M*Y MOMMA WAS A CRIER

Papa said. Her o'Granpa John Crier come down here to Texas with the first White People ever did come and then everbody else come on down behind em with the same idea, he said, and that was to take some Land off the Mexkins however much they could get. Oh them First Ones was as rough and tumble a'Bunch as any you ever did see, Momma said, and a little Loonie too to think they could make em a Living down here where just bout everthing they was either bit you or stuck you or tried to yank your Feathers off. Oh she said, Papa said, they was People went Chained-to-a-Tree-Mad at the Horrors a'them old times. But not us, she said. Oh No Sir not us. We jumped in Texas all Hands and Feet right up to our Chin and when word come down the Mexkins was a'riding up from Mexico to take Texas back why Granpa John and my Daddy Andrew got right up from the Supper Table and took down they Guns and lit a shuck to San Hacinto to be with o'Genral Houston and the Boys when the Fighting commenced but first thing happened was some Crazy Fool ordered Daddy to the Baggage Detail back in Harrisburg but he run off from there early next morning to be with his Daddy John over at San Hacinto and wadn't no surprise he did Momma said, Papa said, cause after all Great Granpa Honor Crier his self done limped through the Froze Ice and Snow with Genral Washington to whup those Sissies in they white britches and another thing, she said, was given the Family Motto was Blood Follers Blood it was just Fore Ordained that come Hell or High Water my Daddy was gonna be in on the Fireworks when the Texas Boys caught o'Sanney Anney taking him a little Siesta with some o'Gal in his tent and sent all them other Mexkins a'running and a'jumping and a'hollering cross the Country for they very lives.

Course, she said, if the Boys had a'lost that fight her Daddy Andrew and her Granpa John and everbody else too would a'got stood up against a near wall and shot to rags for they trouble. Instead they was all Heroes after that and Heroes for the rest a'they lives and Heroes still—all cept my Daddy, she said, who went a'running and a'whooping and a'shooting longside all them others but who the official papers said No he was back in Harrisburg on the Baggage Detail the whole time it took the rest of em to bobtail the Mexkins. We got us a big laugh out a'that Papa said his Momma said, cause Daddy Andrew had the proof he was at the Battle right there tween his legs everday. What she was talking bout, Papa said, was a Mexkin Saddle he pulled off a'some dead Mexkin's Horse right after the Fight that had Brass Nails and shiney Nickel Conchos on it. The same one he give over to Momma when she married our Daddy against his Caution and said If you ever find that Man unsatisfactory you can ride this pretty Saddle back to here and we be glad to see you Darlin.

OLD KARL'S IDEA OF A WIFE
was somebody to Cook, Wash, and Wait on him, Papa said, but Momma didn't fit no bill. She carried two pistols, smoked her a crooked pipe, and could shoot then skin a Buck Deer fore it ever drawed last breath. But Oh she was tender when it come to Horses, he said. Catch one a'us Boys mistreating a Horse even o'Molly and she'd kick you halfway to Georgia and back. Old Karl on the other hand wadn't tender bout nothing on this earth. Not one thing, Papa said. For sure not no Horses.

Amanda came down to the pens one morning when Old Karl was trying to break a Little Bay Mare with an ax handle and a rope. For her part the Little Bay Mare tried to bite him, kick him, run him over, kill him, but Old Karl was a veteran at such sass and gave her a good lick of the ax handle for each of her efforts. Papa and Herman got down to the pens just in time to see Amanda step through the rails and jerk the ax handle out of Old Karl's hand. What the god dam Hell you think you a'doing, she said. You gonna kill her you keep a'hitting her like that. Yes by god I will kill her if she won't gentle, Old Karl said and raised up his hand for his ax handle. Momma whacked him cross his fingers with it, Papa said. Oh she was Red Hot Mad, he said, they both was but they was mad at each other all the time anyhow so this wadn't nothing new. Give me that Stick here, Old Karl said. Momma wadn't about to. That ain't how you gentle a Horse and you dam well know it, she said. Be dam I know it Old Karl said and reached for the ax handle again. Momma stepped back. I can gentle this Missy pretty as you please and don't need no dam Stick to do it, she said. Old Karl's face went Red as a Beet he was so mad, Papa said. The Hell you say Old Karl said and reached for the ax handle again. Yes, the god dam Hell I do say Momma said, Papa said, then reared back with the ax handle to hit him again if he went to grabbing for it. Old Karl give her the Snake Eyes but he didn't want to get whacked with that ax handle again. Be dam you can gentle that Horse, he said then spit and walked on off.

Amanda waited until he was gone then picked up the far end of the rope and ever so slowly, ever so carefully led the Little Bay Mare out of the pens and down to the Creek. She was still panicky and shied at everthing, Papa said, but Momma led her out in the Creek bout belly deep and started whispering to her. She told her she was sorry she'd been bad mistreated and told her that nobody would ever hit her like that again. No not ever again, she said. Not ever again. Not ever Not ever Not ever again. It was like some o'chant, Papa said. Like some o'Inyin chant. Nooo Not ever Not ever Not ever again. Nooo Not ever Not ever Not ever again. In a few minutes the Little Bay Mare put her head down and drank.

Amanda petted her neck and cheek then scratched her between her ears and splashed water up on her back and in her face. The Little Bay Mare watched her but accepted it. Nooo Not ever Not ever Not ever again she crooned, then waved for the Boys to come on in. Herman wanted no part of it, but Papa skinned his pants off and jumped in.

Amanda patted the Little Bay Mare's back and said Here climb on. Before Papa could say No, Amanda grabbed him around his waist and hefted him up. Oh the Little Bay Mare exploded, Papa said, bucked and pitched and just went to raising all kinds a'Hell and I went a'flying off in the Creek but Momma waved me back on. Didn't hurt you none, didn't hurt her none neither, Papa said she said. She'll be too tired to buck here in a minute, won't even want to no more and she won't be hurt one bit. Momma was right and it was fun too, Papa said. Amanda helped him back on. He was laughing now then laughed some more when the Little Bay Mare threw him off into the water again. Then Herman jumped in with his clothes on. In just a minute we was taking turns getting bucked off in the water and just couldn't stop laughing. Even that Little Bay Mare was having fun, Papa said, evertime she'd buck one a'us off Why she'd come back over and just stand there til Momma put the other one on. After a while she stopped her bucking altogether and we could ride her all over the place. It was the first time I ever seen Momma really laugh, Papa said. The last time too.

Old Karl was sitting out on the front porch smoking his pipe when they came back up to the pens from the Creek with the Boys riding double on the Little Bay Mare. He didn't like seeing the four of them together like that. It made him think they'd taken a side against him.

Amanda had just drifted off to sleep that night when she heard the crack of a rifle shot coming from down at the pens. She knew what it meant. I did too, Papa said.

I RUN DOWN THERE TO THE PENS at first light next morning, Papa said. The Little Bay Mare was dead on the ground just like I knowed she was gonna be. I couldn't help myself and just stood there and went to crying, he said. Well what'd you reckon you was gonna find Momma said from over yonder by the shed where she was saddling up Precious. No I knowed what I was gonna find when I heard his Big Gun go off, Papa said. Yes Sir, Momma said, I knowed that little Missy was dead when I seen she wadn't gonna bend to him. Then she swung up in the Saddle her Daddy give her that he'd just walked off with after that Battle at San Hacinto the one with the brass Nails and Shiney Nickel Conchos on it. Hand me up my sack there, she said. Papa picked up her cloth sack. It had her clothes in it. I knowed she was leaving, he said. He handed it up. She was looping the drawstrings over the horn when Old Karl stepped through the fence rails, Herman trailing along behind and looking scared. Where you think you a'going off to this morning on that Horse, he said. You the last Man on this earth I'd tell that to, Amanda said. But I will tell you this one thing I ain't a'never coming back. She gave him a long cold look. You're a hard Man, Karl, she said. And mean And god dam you to Hell if you don't

Well go on and go if you don't wanna be married to me no more, Old Karl said.

work at being both the same way another Man might work at a job. Well go on and go if you don't wanna be married to me no more, Old Karl said. Hell I won't miss you. Old Karl reached up and grabbed the bridle. But you can leave this Horse right here where you found her, he said. By god you ain't a'takin her. Momma put her hand on one a'her pistols and her face went cold as Froze Ice, Papa said. This is my Horse and you'll take your hand off a'her you SonofaBitch or I'll leave you dead on the ground same as you did that Sweet Baby yonder, Papa said she said. Old Karl got him a better hold on the bridle and give her his Snake Eyes. You better watch you self out there Manda, he said. You don't never know what might come up at you in the middle a'the night in this Country round here. Momma cut her eyes at him for the warning. I reckon you'd be the one to know bout that, she said, then of a sudden Precious bared back her Teeth and struck out to bite him like some o'Rattle Snake might do and Oh it surprised Old Karl so much he let out a Holler and fell back on his Bottom, Papa said, and when he did Why Momma touched her heels to Precious and galloped on off not even bothering to blow me or my Brother Herman a kiss Goodbye. And that just bout broke my Heart in two, he said.

NO SOONER'D MOMMA GONE ON DOWN THE ROAD Papa said, when Old Karl told us Boys to hitch up o'Molly and drag that god dam little Mare's body off out in the Brush somewheres and set it to fire fore it got to drawing flies and stinking.

I cried all day long, Papa said, and so did o'Molly but Herman just clomped his mouth shut and never let out one Peep bout it. That night Old Karl told us we was gonna have to make our own suppers from now on out and our breakfasts too. That suited us just fine, he said. We didn't wanna be round him no moren we had to.

Next morning Old Karl was gone and not one word bout it, Papa said. We gathered us up some Chicken eggs and had us a breakfast then went swimming in the Creek but they wadn't the same fun in it as was the day before with Momma and the Little Bay Mare. Herman said he didn't wanna live here no more anyhow and was thinking he might just run off from Home and go live in a town somewheres and was Papa gonna come along with him. Papa said No I wanna be here when Momma comes back. You're just a stupid little Boy, Herman said. Our Momma ain't never coming back. Papa started crying and said Yes she is too. Maybe when you're an Old Man with a long grey beard Herman said. Maybe then. Papa put his face between his knees and started sobbing. Oh hush, Herman said. That ain't gonna bring her back.

That night Papa dreamed he saw his Mother standing out there in front of the house. In his dream Papa waved to her But, he said, she just give a scared look back over her shoulder to the Woods like maybe they was something bout to get her then run on down the Road in the Dark. Papa always believed he really did see his Momma that night, that it wasn't a dream at all, that she'd come back to say she loved him and that she'd be back one day. But they was another part a'me, he said, that thought No maybe Momma'd come back to say Goodbye Forever.

O LD KARL STAYED GONE FOR DAYS AND DAYS Papa said, and we got to thinking Well maybe he ain't never coming back at all and feeling pretty good bout it Then all of a sudden one morning there he was setting at the kitchen table drinking his coffee when we come in. We didn't say nothing, he said, we was afraid he could read our mind and tell we wadn't really all that Happy to see him back, Papa said. Go do your chores, he said. Yall got work in the field today. Papa wanted to ask him had he seen their Momma or heard anything from her but he knew he better not. You sure was gone a long time, Herman said, we been a'missing you. Old Karl give him the Snake Eyes like he was accusing him a'something or other. I come and go as I dam well please Old Karl said, Papa said, and neither one a'you got a god dam thing to say bout it neither you hear me. We just stood there, Papa said. Herman knowed he should a'just kept his mouth shut. You hear me. Old Karl said. Yes Sir we hear you we said, Papa said, then run on down to the Barn to gather the eggs and milk the Cow.

We spent the rest a'the day hoeing weeds in the field, Papa said. I wish he'd a'drowned his self in the River fore he got back, Herman said, or got kicked in the head by some o'Mule and his Brains knocked out. I wish it too, Papa said. We said things like that back and forth all day long, he said, but when we got back to the house at suppertime Why here come Momma's good friend Hattie Choat a'riding up in her wagon.

Old Karl was sitting on the porch smoking on his pipe. Well there Miz Choat, he said, what is it you want to come a'riding all the way over to here. I know Mandy run off and left you I know that, Hattie Choat said, she stopped at my place and told me so. By now me and Herman was standing over there by the Well more or less in between em, Papa said. Well you know she ain't here then don't you, Old Karl said. Yes I do know that, she said. And I don't reckon she's ever coming back neither do you. I ain't got all day for you Miz Choat Old Karl said, Papa said, tell me what you want then git on your way. Last thing Mandy asked me to do for her, Miz Choat said, was to take these two Boys here Home with me and put em in School where they can learn to read and write and I told her Yes Mandy I will surely do it. Papa almost cried he was so happy to hear their Momma had been thinking about them. They need em a haircut too, Hattie Choat said. They look like a couple a'wild Inyins. Now you boys go roll your clothes up and let's get a'going, she said, it's gonna be way past dark by the time we get back Home as it is. Then she looked over at Old Karl again, Papa said, and said If you wanna argue about it Karl let's do it now. But you better know this. I'm a'keeping my Word to Mandy and they ain't just a whole lot you can do about it.

Old Karl pulled on his pipe. I'm gonna want em back here fore long, he said, ain't no Farm I know of can just run its own self. They gonna need something to ride back and forth to School on too, she said. Old Karl didn't like it but he said they could take Molly that o'Swayback Horse down there in the pen but he wanted her back too here shortly same as us.

HERMAN RODE O'MOLLY

and I rode up on the wagon with Miz Choat, Papa said. I asked her Did my Momma say where she was a'going to. Miz Choat said Mandy said she had Family over in Fayette County and she was thinking a'going there cause her Daddy'd said he'd always be glad to see her once she got shed a'Old Karl and now she had. How far is that, Papa said. Maybe two or three days depending on if you a'Horseback or a'walking and how fast, she said. But don't you get no ideas, you're too little to be a'going off somewheres just on your own. You and your Brother both. Besides, Miz Choat said, if she'd a'wanted you to go with her she'd a'took you long with her. It almost broke Papa's Heart again to hear that. Why wouldn't our Momma want us to go with her, Papa said. Because your Momma didn't want to make your mean o'Daddy no maddern he already was, she said, cause she was afraid he'd come after you and your Brother both with a Gun or a Strap or something if yall was to run off and leave him like she did and they just wouldn't be no saving you from him then.

*M*IZ CHOAT AND HER HUSBAND

gave them a good hot supper and a nice bed to sleep in when they finally got to their Farm over by Fischer. I hoped I'd see my Momma in my Dreams again that night riding that Saddle with the sparkling Conchos on it but No, Papa said, I dreamed a'finding Arrowheads long the Blanco River just like me and Herman did when we was really there. In my Dream they was Arrowheads everwheres you looked Some even hanging off a'trees like Wild Plums and I filled my pockets up then took off my hat and filled it up too. Oh I worked all night long a'gathering up them Arrowheads, Papa said, but when I come awake next morning Why they was all gone and I seen I'd worked all night long for nothing. After breakfast Miz Choat sat them down in a chair under the big tree out in the front yard and gave them haircuts so they wouldn't look like Heathens when she sent them off to school riding double on poor o'skinny Swayback Molly. No fighting, she yelled after them. Yall be nice.

Papa didn't want to go. We never been round no other Children before and I was scared to death, he said. Herman said Just Hush bout it. They probably ain't gonna let you in the School anyhow. Papa said No you Hush. Then we went to shoving each other back and forth on o'Molly and yelling No you Hush No you Hush at each other and in a minute we strayed off the road and had to double-back but School was already In by the time we got there.

They walked into the Schoolhouse holding hands. The teacher called them up to his desk. One at a time, he said. But I wadn't bout to let go a'my Brother's hand so we went up together, Papa said. What's your name, the Teacher said. Herman, Herman said. The Teacher looked at Papa. What's your name, he said. I just looked at him, Papa said. I asked you what's your name you little Monkey, the Teacher said. I squeezed my mouth together hard as I could and shook my head No, he said. The Teacher looked over at Herman. Can your little brother talk or is he one a'them Mutes you hear about. No he can talk, Herman said, but once you get him to talking you can't hardly never get him to stop. Alright then, the Teacher said, just give me his name and he don't have to say not one word long as he's here. When they got to their desk Herman frowned at him and whispered If you don't be good they gonna send you back Home to our mean o'Daddy.

At recess Herman got into a fight with three other boys over behind the Schoolhouse. Papa jumped in and tried to help but got a bloody nose and puffed-up ear for his trouble.

When they got home after school Miz Choat took one look at Papa's red nose and swollen ear and said Why you been a'fighting ain't you. Papa squeezed his lips shut and shook his head no. I didn't want her to send me back Home to our mean o'Daddy, he said. Yes you have too, Miz Choat said. Papa looked at his feet and started crying. Yes I thought so, Miz Choat said. Herman thought it was funny that his little brother was in trouble and giggled. Miz Choat gave him a look. You're the Big Brother, she said, didn't it never cross your mind you're supposed to be a'looking out for your Little Brother. Don't you know that's what Big Brothers are for. Papa frowned at Herman the same way Herman had frowned at him back in school. Maybe if he don't get no suppers tonight he'll look out for his Little Brother better next time, Papa said. Miz Choat turned her look on Papa. And maybe if you don't get no suppers tonight you won't be such a little Smarty Pants neither huh, she said.

HERMAN GOT IN ANOTHER FIGHT THE NEXT DAY Papa said, and another one the day after that. Pretty soon he was fighting Fights ever single day and starting to grow him a Mean Streak, Papa said. Why he'd go to fighting bout nothing, he said. If we got to School early nough he'd pick him a Fight even fore the Teacher rang the School Bell. Herman was getting to be like some o'Bully, Papa said. At first Papa'd jump in and try to help him fight but he was smaller than the other boys and always took a licking. After awhile I started hiding from my own Brother cause I didn't want no more Bloody Noses, Papa said. But I felt bad about it. Herman did too.

One day when we was riding home from School on o'Molly Herman said Where was you today when I got in that Fight. I run off, Papa said, I didn't want me no more Bloody Noses. You saying you wouldn't take no Bloody Nose for your own Brother, Herman said, that what you saying. Yes I done took all the Bloody Noses I want, Papa said. I don't want no more. I can give you a Bloody Nose my self any time I want to, Herman said, And I'll tell you what else he said, Papa said, I'm gonna give you one ever time you don't help me in a fight. No you ain't, Papa said. Yes I am, Herman said, so it don't matter if you help me in a Fight or not cause you gonna get you a Bloody Nose out of it either way. Oh I was bout to cry at what he said, Papa said, but then Herman said You cry bout it and I'm gonna give you a Bloody Nose for that too. So I dried it up, Papa said.

A FEW DAYS LATER ON THE WAY TO SCHOOL Herman slid off o'Molly and handed the reins up to Papa. You go on, Herman said. I ain't a'going to School today. We got to, Papa said. Miz Choat'll skin us alive if we don't. You go but I ain't, Herman said. Papa didn't know what to do. The Teacher's gonna wanna know why you ain't there, Papa said. Just tell him I'm sick, Herman said, Just tell him I got the Shits or something. The Shits, Papa said. I can't tell the Teacher you got the Shits. I can't say that. Yes you can, Herman said. Just lean over close and whisper He's got the Shits in his ear. You say He's got the Shits in his ear and he won't never ask you another thing bout it. I'll meet you right here after School, Herman said, then walked on off in the Woods with his lunch pail.

I climbed down off o'Molly at the Schoolhouse, Papa said, and here come this big o'Farmboy Herman been a'fighting off and on. Where's your o'dumb Brother at he said. I'm gonna whup him good today. Papa looked around to see several other boys gathering around. He's sick, Papa said. He ain't coming to School today. The Farmboy gave Papa a little push. I don't believe he's sick, he said. I reckon he's just scared to fight me ain't he. The Farmboy was half again bigger than Papa, but Papa gave him a push back. Who'd be afraid to fight you, you dumb Jackass, Papa said. The Farmboy gave Papa another push. So what's your big Brother got that he can't come to School. You sure it ain't just a bad case a'the o'Fraidy Cats. The other boys started laughing and pushing Papa. Yeah, they taunted. The Fraidy Cats. Papa was desperate to defend his brother. No he don't. He's got the Shits is what he's got, Papa said. The Shits. The o'Farmboy hooted. Herman's got the Shits. The Shits. the boys laughed. The Shits.

The Teacher rang the School Bell and I thought I was saved, Papa said, but then we went in and the Teacher called the Roll. When he got to Herman, Papa stood up and said He ain't here. Herman's sick today. What's wrong with him the Teacher said. Papa was afraid he was going to ask him that. I need to come up there to tell you, he said. Well come on up here then, the Teacher said. We don't have all day long to call the Roll. It was all the other boys could do to keep from laughing when Papa walked up the aisle to the teacher then leaned over and whispered Herman's got the Shits in his ear. What's that you say the Teacher said, Papa said. Speak up, I can't hear you. Herman's got the what. The Shits, the big o'Farmboy said loud nough for everbody to hear. Herman's got the Shits. Then everbody just fell down on the floor a'laughing, Papa said. Even the Girls. Herman's got the Shits they'd whisper to each other then laugh til tears went to rolling down they Cheeks. Herman's got the Shits. Herman's got the Shits . . .

HERMAN HAD JUST STEPPED OUT OF THE WOODS when Papa rode up on the o'Swayback. Well he said. Well what Papa said. Well did you tell the Teacher why I wadn't in School today. Papa nodded. What'd he say Herman said. Uh he didn't say nothing, Papa said. See I told you he wouldn't, Herman said. Papa nodded but couldn't bring himself to look Herman in the eye. What's wrong with you Herman said. I feel sick Papa said. You ain't got the Shits have you Herman said, then went to laughing like it was the funniest thing he ever heard.

Papa asked him what he did in the Woods all day. Herman said Nothing much Just walked round and threw some rocks in the Creek then seen a Buck I figgured might a'been a ten-point. You gonna go play in the Woods again tomorrow, Papa said. Herman said he didn't know yet but he sure might. I think you should, Papa said.

But the next morning Herman didn't rein up at the place where he'd gone off into the Woods the day before. Oh no, Papa said to himself, he's coming to School. I thought you was gonna go back in the Woods today, Papa said. You know like you still got the Shits. Naw not today, Herman said. But I sure might have the Shits again next week. Maybe once ever week he said. Uh oh, Papa said to himself, This is gonna be bad.

And it was. No sooner had they tied o'Molly to a tree when a couple of girls walked by. Hello Herman, one of them said, how're you feeling today? Then they giggled and went on. Herman didn't think anything of it then he looked over and saw a cluster of girls watching him from the front steps of the Schoolhouse. They were giggling too. You feeling better today Herman one of them said then they all laughed. What's wrong with those stupid Girls, Herman said. Papa shrugged But I wanted to go down a hole some-wheres, he said. Then here come that big o'Farmboy and some other Boys. Everbody was watching from all over the place, Papa said. The Farmboy stopped and give Herman a good look up and down like he was a Doctor or something. Well Herman he said, Papa said, you don't look so bad for some-body who had em a big case a'the Shits all day long yesterday. Everbody just went to laughing, Papa said. Girls and all.

Herman jerked Papa over behind a tree and shook him. What's going on here, he said, what's going on. Oh he was mad, just fit to be tied, Papa said, so I told him, told him everthing they was to tell. Herman looked over and seen everbody laughing. His face fell down like melting wax, Papa said. Ev-erbody's laughing at me, Herman said. They all a'laughing at me ain't they. Then his eyes went to swimming, Papa said, and he run off in the Woods where couldn't Nobody see him crying.

*I*T WAS ALMOST DARK
by the time Papa found Herman skipping rocks down Cotton Mouth Creek. I'm sorry you got your feelings hurt, Papa said. I bet you was laughing at me too wadn't you, Herman said. No I wadn't, Papa said. I promise. Herman reared back and skipped another rock sidearm all the way across the creek and into the trees on the other side. I'm going to China first chance I get, he said. Papa had to squeeze his mouth shut to keep from crying. You ain't

gonna just up and run off on me like Momma did are you, he said. Herman made like he was gonna throw a rock at him. Dry it up you little Titty Baby, he said. I don't wanna hear nothing bout it.

The next morning Miz Choat gave them their lunch pails and they went down to the pen to saddle the o'Swayback. It wadn't much of a saddle, Papa said, just an old hull with a leather strap to hang on to. Papa climbed on then scooted up so Herman would have room to climb on behind. You go on, Herman said. I'm just gonna walk today. No you come on with me, Papa said, but Herman reached over and give o'Molly a little slap on the butt. Go on now, he said and Papa went on off to School. He rode a ways then looked back over his shoulder to see if Herman was following along behind. For awhile he was Then all of a sudden he wadn't no more, Papa said. He was just gone, he said, Not hide nor hair of him nowhere in sight. Papa wadn't surprised. I knowed Herman was still hurting at what happened the day before, he said, and wadn't never coming back to School ever again in his whole Life.

CHRISTMAS WAS COMING and Papa hoped his Momma would come back with it. One night when it was his turn to help Miz Choat wash the supper dishes he asked her Did she think his Momma was coming back at Christmas to see him and Herman. Miz Choat said they wadn't no way a'telling but it'd be nice if she did. Mandy's always welcome at my table, she said. Anytime at all Don't even have to be at Christmas. Papa asked her where she thought his Momma was. Honey you don't wanna dwell on that, she said, it's just gonna make you Sick. Papa said he was getting to think she didn't care nothing bout him and Herman anyhow. He said I don't think she even remembers our names no more. Miz Choat said No a Mother don't never forget her own Children. Not never, she said. Then she sat down at the supper table and cried in her hands. Papa didn't know why she was crying but just naturally patted her shoulder to comfort her. Uh, he said. Uh Uh. Miz Choat looked up at me the tears just a'running down her face, Papa said. Listen to me, she said. I want you to remember this. You and Herman always got you a Momma right here. Even if it ain't the one you started with. And I always got me a Boy too, even if it ain't the one I started with neither. She reached out to hug me, Papa said, but I stepped back. I already had me a Momma and she was the only one I wanted and no other. Miz Choat knew she'd said the wrong thing. I'm sorry Honey, she said, I just got to missing my own little Boy. Her Heart just broke then, Papa said, just broke in a bunch a'pieces and she started crying in her hands again. Papa felt disloyal to his own Mother but he stepped over and hugged Miz Choat anyway. We didn't say nothing, Papa said, we just stood there Her a'crying and Me a'hugging her.

PAPA WENT LOOKING FOR A CHILD'S GRAVE the next day after school. He found it in about five minutes. It was between the back of the field and the Creek in a stand of oaks. I didn't really have to look for it, Papa said. I just kind a'walked straight to it. The gravestone said GILBERT LEE CHOAT and under that it said OUR LITTLE BOY and then under that was the two dates. Papa did his subtraction and decided Gilbert Lee was four years old when he died. I wondered what could a'happened to him, Papa said. Did he get a Snake Bite or did he get kicked by a Horse or come down with a Fever or a Cough or what? Maybe a Panther come a'sneaking in through the winder one night when he was sleeping and grabbed him up or a Bear. They just wadn't no way a'telling, Papa said.

Papa looked past Gilbert Lee's grave and saw the Creek just running along peaceful as you please down below. He imagined Mister and Miz Choat had taken him down there to the Creek many a time so their little Boy could splash and play in the water. It made Papa smile to think of that—but it made him sad too to think that Gilbert Lee was dead now and would never splash and play in that Creek ever again. So Papa went down to the Creek and picked up a couple of rocks from under the water and put them on Gilbert Lee's grave. I guess I just wanted to do something that'd remind him of all the Good Times he'd had splashing round in the Creek, Papa said.

That night Papa dreamed he was fishing in that same Creek. Somebody said Having any Luck. Papa looked over and saw an Old Man with a beard sitting next to him. No not yet, Papa said. What you a'fishing for anyhow, the Old Man said. I don't know, Papa said, just a'fishing. Best to know what you a'fishing for, the Old Man said. Otherwise you liable to catch just bout any o'thing at all. Papa got a bite and lifted his pole to see what he had. It was a

Skunk. See what I told you, the Old Man said then smiled and scuffed Papa's head. Papa liked the Old Man. It was like I'd been a'knowing him all my Life, he said. Now what you wanna catch next, the Old Man said. A Possum. Papa said No not no Possum. Well what then, the Old Man said. Papa thought about it a minute. How bout a Catfish. he said. One with Whiskers. the Old Man said. Papa said Yes Sir one with Whiskers. And maybe he's a'wearing some old Hat too, the Old Man said. How bout that. Okay, Papa said. Can you see a Catfish wearing an old Hat in your head now, the Old Man said. Papa closed his eyes and he really could see a Catfish wearing an old Hat in his head. Look you got a bite, the Old Man said. Papa opened his eyes and raised his pole and up came a Catfish with Whiskers wearing an old straw Hat like the Farmers wear And he was smoking a crooked Pipe too, Papa said. You like him a'smoking that Pipe. the Old Man said. That was just a little joke I played on you. They both laughed. It was all so real, Papa said, Like that night when I dreamed I seen my Momma out there in front a'the House.

You gonna be down here at the Creek again tomorrow night, Papa said. No you ain't my Job the Old Man said. Then, Papa said, he pointed cross the Creek to where a bunch a'other People say eight or ten or maybe even moren that was standing there just a'shimmering like Heat Shimmers in the Summer. You they Job, the Old Man said. Who are they, Papa said, I don't believe I know a one of em. Why sure you do, the Old Man in my Dream said, they your Friends. You got a lot a'Friends over there on the Other Side a'the Creek. Why pretty much everbody got Friends over there cept maybe not your o'Daddy. I reckon next thing you gonna tell me is you don't know who I am neither, the Old Man said. Papa shook his head No. No Sir I don't believe I do know who you are neither, he said. The Old Man smiled and gave Papa a nudge. Oh yes you do too know who I am he said. Why just this afternoon you brought me some wet rocks from down in the Creek and put em on my Grave as a favor. Then, Papa said, I looked cross the Creek to where some other Shimmery Person come a'walking up way back behind all them others to where I couldn't see they face but for a minute there I thought Why that's my own Momma ain't it but then No I seen they wadn't riding no Horse and I knowed my Momma wouldn't never go nowheres on this Earth less she was a'riding Precious and that Mexkin Saddle with the Sparkling Conchos on it her Daddy took off that dead Mexkin's Horse at San Hacinto and give to her for a Present. And that's all I remember bout that time he said.

20

*T*HE NEXT MORNING PAPA ASKED MIZ CHOAT
Did she know anything bout Dreams and what they meant. Well, Miz Choat
said, One time I dreamed my Little Boy was an Old Man with a beard. I almost fell over when she said that, Papa said, cause that's how I seen him in
my Dream too but I didn't say nothing. Did that scare you, Papa said. Yes it
did, Miz Choat said. At first. But then o'Jeffey told me it was just Gilbert Lee
trying to show me he was still alive but just not here no more. She was bout
to cry, Papa said, so I told her I was sorry I made her Sad again. She said No
that's okay don't worry bout it I cry all the time anyhow. Papa said Who's
o'Jeffey? O'Jeffey Benders, Miz Choat said. She's the only one I know round
here really knows anything at all bout Dreams and such. Over yonder in the
Colony she said and pointed down the road. Papa knew about the Colony.
That was where the Ranchers around there had set some land aside for the x
slaves to live on after the War was over so the Ranchers'd always have some
Workers handy when they needed em.

O'Jeffey's a big woman, Miz Choat said. You wouldn't want her to go
a'setting on you.

*P*APA WAS SCARED
to go down to the Colony just by himself so he told Herman he'd do his
chores for him for two days if he'd go with him. Herman wanted to know
what he wanted to go down there for anyhow. Papa said Just cause. We was
bout halfway to the Colony then Herman said Just cause why, Papa said,
so I told him Just to see o'Jeffey Benders. Who's o'Jeffey Benders, Herman
said. Just somebody, Papa said. Just somebody who? Herman said. Just
somebody I wanna talk to bout Momma, Papa said. What about Momma?
Herman said. Papa wadn't about to tell him About if she was coming back or
not someday so he pulled up and said Why don't you just go on back Home
where you belong. Herman slid off o'Molly. You still gotta do my chores for
two days, he said. I know it, Papa said, then went on down the road.

They was some Shacks scattered round and some Pens and some Sheds,
Papa said, just like everbody else had but just maybe not nearly so good.
People come out from wherever they was to see a White Boy ride by but I
was too shy to look back. And maybe a little too scared too, he said. Then he
saw a Boy about his own age building a cookfire out in front of an old shack

and reined up. Me and that Black Boy just looked at each other, Papa said, like a couple a'half wit Mutes who couldn't talk. But Papa finally worked up his courage and said o'Jeffey and the Boy jiggled his thumb toward the shack behind him. Wadn't that something, Papa said, rode right up to o'Jeffey's. I always had the knack a'getting where I was going even when I didn't know where that was. Papa walked over to the front door and peeked in to see a Big Woman sitting way back in the shadows. She was so big I just froze up at the sight a'her, Papa said. I couldn't even remember what I was doing there. Now what you want with o'Jeffey, she said. I just stood there like a Knot on a Log, Papa said. I couldn't think a'one single thing to say. Was it something bout you Momma, o'Jeffey said. Now I was really struck Dumb, Papa said. How'd she know that. But I nodded back, he said. Step you self on in here then, she said, I might gnaw on you a little but I ain't gonna eat you up. Papa shook his head No. I wadn't bout to go in there, he said. Matter a fact it was all I could do to keep from a'running off down the road like my Pants was on Fire. You Momma huh, o'Jeffey said. Papa nodded. What you wanna know bout you Momma, she said. Papa just stood there. Just anything that come to me huh, she said. Papa nodded. Well let's see who here this morning o'Jeffey said then closed her eyes.

In just a minute she was turning her head this way and that, Papa said, like People was talking to her from all over the place and even up there on the ceiling and out the winder too. What's that, she said, What's that you say. Then things like Yeah I hears ya . . . Slow down Slow down . . . You. You get outta here We ain't a'talking bout that . . . Oh poor baby . . . No No No aw my goodness No . . . Stop it Everbody talking at once Stop it I say . . . Oh lawdy . . . Oh lawdy lawdy lawdy . . . Yes well . . . Yes well I knows it . . . Yes yes I knows . . . Yes Life jumps Yes it do Oh Yes Sir it surely do . . . Oh my yes yes yes . . . No no no can't tell him that . . . Oh no no no won't tell him that No . . .

Then she started whispering to somebody but I couldn't hear the words, Papa said. I didn't understand none a'it anyhow. Then o'Jeffey opened up her eyes and looked at me. You go on now, she said, you too little for me to be telling you any things. Papa just stood there. Go on, o'Jeffey said, Go on now. Papa just stood there. No you too little, o'Jeffey said, you come back when you growed up an I tells you then. Papa just stood there. Hon you can stand there like some o'rock til Hell freeze over but I ain't telling you noth-

Step you self on in here then, she said, I might
gnaw on you a little but I ain't gonna eat you up.

ing You too little, she said. Papa just stood there. O'Jeffey shook her head, I never seen anythings like you, she said. Okay I gives you one question. One question you hear. One question. Papa nodded. I couldn't decide what to ask her, he said, I wanted to ask her so many things. Ask it Hon, o'Jeffey said. Ask it if you gonna ask it. Papa said Is my Momma gonna come see me and Herman at Christmas Time. She cocked her head like somebody standing right behind Papa was talking to her. You ask me is you Momma gon come see you at Christmas Time. Well, o'Jeffey said, Yes She Is—an No She Ain't.

*I*T WAS A DOUBLE ANSWER Papa said, and I didn't have no idea what to think. But the Yes She Is part was the part he'd wanted to hear more than anything in the world so he decided he'd just believe that part and forget the No She Ain't part.

It was after dark by the time he rode up to the house on the o'Swayback. Miz Choat was waiting for him out on the porch. Herman said you went down to the Colony, she said. Papa said Yes I did. Lord Boy I don't know what to do with you Just go a'riding in there like that Wouldn't think you had a lick a'sense, Miz Choat said. You see o'Jeffey. Papa nodded. She tell you about your Dreams, she said. I didn't ask her bout my dreams, Papa said, I ask her Is my Momma coming to see me and Herman at Christmas Time and she said Yes She Is. O'Jeffey said Mandy's coming to see you and Herman at Christmas Time. She said that, Miz Choat said. That's what she said, Papa said. Miz Choat just stood there like she didn't know what to say, Papa said, then she said Oh Honey I don't know about that. They was something bout the way she said it made me think she didn't believe it for a minute, Papa said, but I'd already decided my Momma was coming to see me at Christmas Time and I wadn't gonna hear nothing different. Well that's what o'Jeffey said, Papa said, she said Momma's gonna be here at Christmas Time that's what she said. Miz Choat could see Papa was desperate to believe it and that he was on the verge of tears. Well Honey that'll be nice if she does, she said. That'll be so nice. Just then Herman stepped out of the house behind her. You better go do your chores he said, Papa said, yours and mine both.

CHRISTMAS EVE MORNING

Mister Choat took Herman and me out to the pasture to chop a Cedar Tree, Papa said. Herman found one right away but it was just a little one and I wanted a big one so when Momma came she'd say Why who found that big o'beautiful Christmas Tree for me and I'd say Why I did Momma. Mister Choat didn't have any patience for them arguing back and forth about it so he went at another one altogether with his double-bladed ax. About three seconds later, Papa said, here come this big o'Blue Norther just a'whupping in with a Freezing Rain to boot and us there just in our shirtsleeves. You could barely stand up in it, Papa said. Even Mister Choat had to hold his hat down on his o'ball head with both hands. Well ain't this a fine Hidy-do, he said, I ain't never seen nothing like it in all my Life.

By the time they got home with their Christmas Tree the whole world was covered in a thin sheet of ice. I mean Ice just everwhere, Papa said, and it was cold nough to already be freezing the water in the Horse trough. Wooo don't that cold wind just perk you right up Miz Choat said when they got inside. Freeze you right up is more like it, Mister Choat said and gave her a little Christmas hug. It made me feel good to see that, Papa said, but I had something else on my mind. He grabbed his coat and headed for the door. Now just where you think you're a'going Young Man, Miz Choat said. It's Christmas Time, Papa said, I'm gonna go watch for Momma coming down the road. Miz Choat caught him at the door. Not out in this weather you ain't, she said and started pulling at his coat. Papa stepped away from her. Yes I am, he said. Now listen to me, she said, No you ain't. Something come a'bubbling up in me from way way down, Papa said. I guess it was my Declaration of Independence. No Miz Choat, I said, Yes I am. Miz Choat could see there was no talking him out of it. Well, she said, button your coat up good then and keep your two hands in your pocket so your fingers don't freeze up and fall off.

That Norther all but blowed me off the porch when I went outside, Papa said, but I found a spot in the corner and kind a'hunkered down there where I could watch the road. Oh it was cold. Cold Cold Cold, he said, and Herman put a pot on his head and made faces at me in the winder too but all I cared bout was seeing my Momma coming down the road on Precious. Papa sat there all morning. At lunch time Miz Choat pushed the door open and said You come on back in here now and warm yourself up while I fix you a good hot bowl a'soup. I'm watching for my Momma, Papa said. I know it Honey but you gotta eat, she said. Papa shook his head No and Miz Choat brought him a glass of hot milk instead.

By mid-afternoon the Norther had blown itself on further South and Papa went walking up the road thinking he might run into his Momma coming his way but No they wadn't no sign a'her, he said. Then he noticed that every leaf on every tree and bush was carrying on its face an exact duplicate of itself in ice. Papa peeled one off. It was like a perfect little glass leaf, Papa said. You could even see the ribs. He peeled a few more off then ran back to the house to show Miz Choat. She liked them too. They almost look like Crystal Leaves don't they, she said. What's Crystal, Papa said. She told him it was a very special glass made in a very special way and only Kings and Queens and Presidents could afford to buy it. Queens. My head just went Pop with a idea when she said that, Papa said. He grabbed a big mixing bowl and headed for the door. Hey where you a'going Miz Choat said but I was already out the door and gone, Papa said. He spent the rest of the day gathering ice leaves off the trees to make a Crystal Road for his mother to ride in on that Christmas Night. Oh I gathered em by the hundreds, by the thousands, by the thousands and thousands, Papa said. Then I poured em out a'my bowl on Momma's Crystal Road and run back to get me some more. You wouldn't believe how long it was to go just a foot or two.

When suppertime came Miz Choat opened the door and told him to come on in and eat something, that he was going to dry up and blow away if he didn't but Papa shook his head No and kept working. I just wouldn't quit, Papa said, even when Herman come out and told me they was gonna lock all the doors and winders so I couldn't never get back in again if I didn't come on in right now. Papa told him he didn't care if they did and kept gathering Crystal Leaves until it was past dark and he couldn't even feel the ends of his fingers anymore they were so cold. But Momma's Crystal Road was finished, Papa said. It went from the Big Oak tree down the road all the way back to the Yard Gate and I could just see my Momma riding in on it and just a'smiling cause it was so pretty. Then he sat down on the front porch to wait. Ever minute was like an hour Ever hour was like a day, he said, but I was so sure my Momma was gonna come riding down her Crystal Road a Mule couldn't a'pulled me off that porch. Miz Choat come out and put a blanket over my feet and give me a little kiss on my cheek but all she said was

I was so sure my Momma was gonna come riding down her Crystal Road a Mule couldn't a'pulled me off that porch.

Oh Honey then went on back in. The Moon come up and Momma's Crystal Road started twinkling like them Nickel Conchos on her Saddle. I took it for a sign she was almost here, Papa said, and one or two times I thought I seen somebody coming a'Horseback down the road kicking up Moon Sparkles off them Crystal Leaves but I reckon it was just my eyes a'playing tricks on me. And then I guess I just went off to sleep, he said.

*T*HE RISING SUN WOKE PAPA UP the next morning. He looked over and saw somebody all wrapped up in a blanket was asleep right beside him. I thought it was Momma and my Heart just went Boom Boom Boom, Papa said. But then I pulled the covers back and Why it was just Miz Choat. Did Momma come. Papa said. No I don't believe she did, Miz Choat said then raised up and looked yonder toward the road. Well wait just a minute, she said. What's that there. Papa stood up and looked too. He could see something was different, he just couldn't see what. I run out to the road, Papa said, and they was Horse Tracks coming right down the middle a'Momma's Crystal Road. Then they stopped in front a'the house and kind a'shuffled round a little like somebody a'Horseback was standing there looking at me a'sleeping there on the front porch. It was Momma. I knowed it was Momma, Papa said, my Momma come to see me and Herman at Christmas Time just like o'Jeffey said she would But then them Tracks turned and went on back up the road again. I follered em, Papa said. I follered and follered and follered em til little by little they just faded on away to nothing and you'd a'never thought Momma had ever been there at all.

Papa decided that was the No She Ain't part of o'Jeffey's answer.

*E*VERY NIGHT AFTER SUPPER Miz Choat would give Herman a dancing lesson. She taught him how to do the Put Your Little Foot, the Two-Step, the Polka, and the Waltz. She'd just hum or da-da-da whatever tune it was and away they'd go across the room, Papa said, bumping the Table and Chairs and whatnot where evers they went. She tried to teach me too, he said, but I didn't want no part of it. Well what you gonna do come New Years Eve and ever other Boy is up and dancing with some Girl in Fischer Hall, she said. I don't know, Papa said, but I ain't dancing with no Girl.

Fischer Hall just set out in somebody's Cow Pasture, Papa said. It was like a big o'Barn with a wood floor to dance on and People come from miles and miles round to Dance out the Old Year and Dance in the New. It was the one thing Mister Choat looked forward to all year long and the Choats just never missed. Mister Choat was what you called an Up and Down Dancer, Papa said. He just sort a'bobbed up and down in one place and didn't never slide round the floor to the music like everbody else. Miz Choat said A Mule couldn't kick him a inch either way. But Herman, Papa said, Herman was just a natural borned Dancer and couldn't nobody hold him back once the music got going. Away he'd go with his o'Hiney sticking out and his elbows just a'flapping like some o'Duck and all them other Dancers'd just give him Bad Looks and get out his way if they could. Watch him, Miz Choat'd say to Mister Choat when Herman whirled by. Watch Herman, she said, see he knows how to dance. But Mister Choat stayed an Up and Down Dancer for all his Life, Papa said, and she never could break him a'the habit.

I was too shy to dance, Papa said, but I went over and stood close as I could to watch the Band play they Instruments. I'd never even seen a Band play before and it was really something to me, he said. I'd stand there and listen to how each Instrument added its own special sound to the Tune. It was like a bunch a'Creeks running together to make one big River and I started kind a'bobbing up and down to the Music the same way Mister Choat danced and didn't even know it. I guess you'd have to say I got lost in the Music and I told myself Someday I'm gonna be one a'them fellas with a Horn to my mouth. Then somebody almost knocked me over with a poke in my back. I turned round and Oh it was Old Karl a'standing there. Where's your Brother at, he said. I just looked at him, Papa said. I couldn't make it work in my head that my mean o'Daddy was a'standing there in front a'me. It was like he just dropped out a'the Blue. Where's Herman at, Old Karl said again. Papa pointed out to the Dance Floor where Herman was dancing away with some girl two or three years older than his self. Tell him to git over here, Old Karl said. Papa could see Herman was having a big time with the Girl so he said Well let him finish his Dance first. But Old Karl stepped right out on the Dance Floor and grabbed up Herman by the back a'his shirt and jerked him away from the dancing Girl then give him a push over to me, Papa said. You Boys run go git in the Wagon We're a'going home, Old Karl said. The Music stopped. People started looking. Mister Choat stepped up. What're you doing, he said. Time these Boys come home, Old Karl said. A Farm don't just run itself. I ain't a'going, Herman said. Old Karl give him a look, Papa said. What'd you say, he said. I said I ain't a'going, Herman said, and I ain't. Old Karl grabbed him by the front a'his shirt and pulled him right up close. I guess you'll do what I tell you to do, he said. Herman was bout to cry, Papa said, getting treated like that in front a'all them People and that Girl he'd just been a'dancing with too. Somebody said That Boy just told you he ain't a'going and he ain't if he don't want to. Old Karl looked over to see Mister Choat taking his coat off. They both a'going, Old Karl said, and you got not one god dam Word to say bout it. Mister Choat handed his coat to Miz Choat like he was ready to fight about it and he was. I reckon we gotta talk about it first, he said. Mister Choat was just a little Scrawny Man and I knowed Old Karl would eat him up and spit him out, Papa said, so I said I'll go with you. Just leave o'Herman here. He don't know how to do nothing anyhow. Miz Choat was crying. Oh Honey you don't have to go neither if you don't want to, she said. No, Papa said, I want to. I'm tired a'that School ever day and I don't see I need no more of it. I told you Boys to go git in the Wagon, Old Karl said. No I ain't a'going, Herman said. I looked over and seen two a'them Horn Men in the Band putting they Instruments down to the floor. You don't have to go nowheres you don't want to Son, one a'the Horn Men said. They was ready to fight bout it too, Papa said, I could see that. So I took a'hold a'Old Karl's sleeve and said Come on let's go. Old Karl give the Horn Men a look to lock em in his head then give Mister and Miz Choat his Snake Eyes and said You stole a Boy from me tonight and you better know it's gonna come back on you here one day. Old Karl gave Papa a push toward the front door. Git, he said. Miz Choat reached out to give me a goodbye hug, Papa said, but I ducked out from under it so I wouldn't go to bawling then went on out the door fast as I could go. The last thing I heard was Herman saying Don't worry I'll take good care of a'o'Molly.

PAPA DIDN'T WANT TO SIT BY OLD KARL

so when they got to the wagon he climbed over the tailgate and jumped in the back on a pile of hay. Wadn't a second later, Papa said, but what I felt Something roll out from under me then a Hand come a'reaching up through the hay and give me a hard push away. Hey I said. A Mexkin giving me a Bad Look poked his head out a'the hay where he'd been sleeping, then another one. Hey I said, they's two Mexkins back here. Let em sleep, Old Karl said, they gonna need it. And you too. Old Karl give a Pop to his whip and off we went. Well I guess here's how the New Year begins, Papa said he said to himself. Herman's in the Dance Hall just a'dancing away and I'm out here a'setting in this Wagon with Old Karl and two Mexkins.

Papa scrunched up in the corner between the tailgate and the side-board and tried to go to sleep but just as he was about to drift off one of the Mexkins tooted under the hay. Then the other one did too, Papa said. It turned out they was Brothers and couldn't one do something without the other one follering suit right along behind Didn't matter what it was. They names was Pepe and Peto and I'd a'had to paint one of em Red and the other one Blue to tell em apart, Papa said, but Boy Hidy they could work. They could do just bout anything with they hands. Build a Fence, Clear a Field, Plant a Crop, Slaughter a Hog, Braid a Rope, Rob a Bee Tree, And it didn't take much to feed em on neither, Papa said. Old Karl'd just give em a sack a'Beans and some Corn Meal and they'd make do on that and whatever else they could catch be it a Squirrel Coon Possum Armadilla Bird Snake or any-thing else that Walked Crawled Squirmed or Flew by. It was a Rough Life I reckon, Papa said, but they didn't know no different any moren I did.

It was way into the New Year by the time Old Karl pulled up at the Farm. He showed Pepe and Peto where they was to sleep in the Barn then told Papa to unhitch the wagon and give the Horse a drink a'water then he could go sleep with the Mexkins after that he said, but Papa said No he wanted to sleep in the House where he always did but Old Karl said No, if you don't wanna sleep with the Mexkins you just gonna have to sleep out there on the front porch. Well why's that, Papa said. Why can't I sleep where I always sleep? Cause they's somebody else a'sleeping in there now that's why, Old Karl said, and I don't wanna hear no more bout it.

OLD KARL THREW A COUPLE OF BLANKETS
out the door and Papa made himself a pallet on the front porch. I tried to sleep but I was so Homesick for my Momma and now my Brother both that I couldn't do it so I just laid there a'looking up at the Stars. They made me think a'the Nickel Conchos on my Momma's Saddle like everthing else that sparkled did and I got to thinking soon as I'm big nough I'm gonna just go a'walking off down the road to find her. Fayette County that's where Miz Choat said she might a'gone, Papa remembered. Just two or three days away she'd said, depending on if you're a'riding or a'walking. Two or three days didn't seem like a long way to walk Not to find my Momma it didn't, Papa said. On the other hand two or three days was a long time. He'd get hungry and thirsty and he'd hear things at night. Things that might jump out a'the Dark and get me Maybe even eat my Fingers and Toes off, he said. It was scary just thinking bout it. Then he remembered Gilbert Lee's Lesson of the Catfish which was to always make a Pitchur a'what you wanted in your head first then here it'd come True like catching that o'Catfish wearing the Hat. So now, Papa said, I started making Pitchurs in my head a'me walking off down the road to Fayette County but I couldn't get no furthern the Big Oak Tree in my head cause I didn't have no idea in the World a'where Fayette County was at. I almost cried thinking I was trapped here forever with Old Karl and them two Mexkins and Whoever it was a'sleeping in my bed, Papa said. Then he started thinking that Miz Choat knew where Fayette County was and all he had to do was go back to her house and she'd tell him the direction. I had me a plan now, Papa said. I'd walk back to the Choats. I'd do it in my Head first, he said, Then I'd do it on my own two Feet.

SOMEBODY TOED ME AWAKE
even fore the o'Rooster crowed, Papa said. He rolled over and looked up to see a tall skinny woman standing over him with a butcher knife in one hand and a long gut of sausage in the other. Run git me some farwood, she said. We don't have no Boy Holidays round here. Papa just looked at her. Old Karl made Snake Eyes whenever he was mad at somebody or bout to clobber em, Papa said, but this one here was born with hers and they didn't never change no moren her long pointy nose did or her two ears that grew flat on

her head to where you couldn't hardly see em sticking out. Who're you, Papa said. I'm your new Momma, she said. Papa shook his head No. No you ain't, he said. No Sir you ain't. Yes I am long as I'm here, she said. Can you say Gusa? Papa just looked at her. Lona Gusa, she said, That's my name. Papa didn't say anything. You don't wanna call me Momma you call me Miss Gusa whenever you got something to say to me you understand that, she said. I didn't like her, Papa said, so I decided to be as much Trouble as I could. Tell me again what I'm supposed to call you, he said, I can't remember that far back. I'll go get your Daddy and you tell him you can't remember that far back, she said. Miss Gusa, Papa said. Good that's settled, she said. Now run go git me that farwood like I told you and don't go peeing off the front porch here no more neither where somebody's liable to step in the puddle. You gotta pee you go round behind the house where everbody else goes. It embarrassed Papa to hear a woman talk about such private things but he didn't know what he could do about it.

Papa gathered some firewood and took it to Miss Gusa then went down to the barn to do his chores. Pepe and Peto was setting there cooking tortillas on a piece a'tin they had set over a little fire, Papa said. Soon as they seen me they rolled up they tortillas and gobbled em down fore I could tell what they was eating in em but I already seen the Chicken Feathers and I knowed. Come on, I said, we got our Chores to do then pointed at each thing we had to do and said Look we got the Chickens to feed Look we got the Eggs to gather Look we got the Cow to milk Look we got the Hogs to slop. Come on let's get a'going I said, Papa said. But they just kept chewing on they tortillas like they didn't understand no English. Yall come on, I said, We ain't got no Mexkin Holidays round here. Pepe threw a rock at me then Peto did too so I went on and did the Chores without no help from neither one a'them.

The Sun was just barely up, Papa said, and here I was already wanting to go back to bed on the porch so I could start walking down the Road to the Choats in my head.

OLD KARL COME DOWN TO THE BARN and wanted to know Why in Hell the Wagon wadn't hitched up and the tools loaded so we could get on out there to where he wanted the Brush cleared for a new field. I said I didn't know Why, Papa said. Well you better Know Why here fore long, Old Karl said, it ain't nothing to me to run go get another Mexkin or two somewheres if you don't wanna work. Or eat, he said.

Old Karl rode us out to the Brush in the wagon then left us there with our tools and a jug a'water. Pepe grabbed him the Grubbing Hoe and went right at it. Peto grabbed him the Double-Blade Ax and did the same. That left the Shovel for me to dig the roots out with and what made it bad was I was Barefoot and it hurt like all get-out to push the Shovel in that hard dirt with just my bare foot, Papa said, and it wadn't long and there I had blisters running all up and down the bottom a'my feet from my heel to my toes. I finally tore my shirt tail off and made me a pad and that helped some but by then it was too late and I knowed when them Blisters popped it was gonna hurt for days and weeks and maybe longern that. Pepe and Peto thought it was funny to see me bite my lip ever time I stepped on the Shovel to dig a root out and I wished a Snake'd jump up from somewheres and bite one of em so I could grab they sandals off they feet when they was fooling with the bite. But what a Snake didn't never do, Papa said, a Stinging Scorpion did do. Pepe reached under a big flat rock to lift it off a root he was trying to get at with his Grubbing Hoe and a brown Stinging Scorpion big as a biscuit reached out from under the rock with his Stinger and give Pepe three quick stabs on the back a'his hand. Oh Pepe he just went to jumping and a'hollering all over the place, Papa said, and his hand swoll up so big it looked like he was swinging a bucket round. That was my chance to laugh at him same as he had at me and I Hoohaaed and slapped my knee and just carried on til Peto give me a Bad Look for laughing at his Brother and I quit.

Old Karl come to get us in the wagon long bout Sun Down. He didn't say nothing when he seen Pepe's big fat hand, Papa said, or me a'limping round on my feet neither one. Course I didn't expect he would, he said.

Papa ate his supper out on the porch that night and thought afterwards he might go walking off down the road toward the Choats in his head that night like he'd planned to do. But I was so tired and my Blisters hurt so bad, Papa said, I just couldn't do it.

with my feet a'hurting something awful and my Blisters puffed up so big it was like walking round on Balloons to get anywheres, Papa said. But off I went a'walking down to the Barn on the sides a'my feet like some poor o'Begger you might see hobbling down the road somewheres, he said. He found the leather awl in the tool chest then lit a lantern over by the corn crib and sat down to pop his blisters with the awl. Then right away here come Pepe and Peto to watch, Papa said. I tried to shoo em away, he said. Go on away, I said. Go on get away from me But they just squatted down right there in front a'me. I don't think they was a thing in the World they liked moren me a'hurting, Papa said. I touched the point of the awl to the lantern fire to burn off the Tomane, he said, then went to a'stabbing at the biggest Blister but the skin was so thick there the awl wouldn't go through. Pepe and Peto laughed and Peto made little poking motions with his hand to get me to poke harder and I did, Papa said, then went to groaning cause it hurt so bad and course Pepe and Peto just fell over laughing at that and I tried to shoo em away again. Go on away I said, You Mexkins git but No they wanted to see the whole thing even if it was a'killing me. Papa poked at the blister again and this time the awl went all the way through the skin And now out come all this Blister Juice and tears just went to running down my face and I started rocking side to side on my Bottom it hurt so bad. Pepe and Peto just laughed and slapped each other on they back like they never had so much fun in all they life. I had nough of em, Papa said, so I put my hands up under my arms and started flapping my elbows like some o'Chicken and going Puck-puck-pa-kuck Puck-puck-pa-kuck and they took off like somebody just lighted they Pants on Fire cause now they knowed I knowed they been a'stealing Old Karl's Chickens and cooking em to roll up in they tortillas and the last thing in this World they wanted was for him to land on em for it.

One by one Papa popped his blisters then made himself a crude pair of sandals out of some harness leather he found in the scrap box. They wadn't much but they was bettern nothing, Papa said. Then I did one more thing, he said. I tied the Grubbing Hoe up under the wagon to where Pepe and Peto couldn't see it.

Old Karl rode them out to the field in the wagon just as the sun was coming up. He pointed out a dozen or so mesquites they'd missed the day before then pulled out a match and said he wanted them to pile everthing

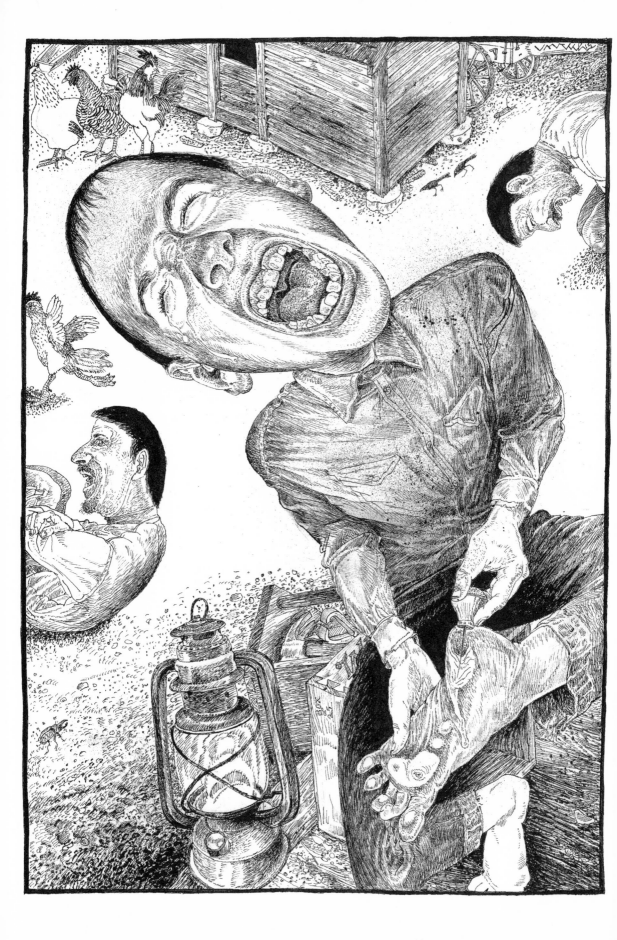

up they'd already cut down and everthing they were gonna cut down today and get it all burned up ever single stick of it by the time he got back at Sun Down to pick them up in the wagon.

Papa held his hand out for the match. I wanted Old Karl to give me that Match, he said. It'd be like him telling them two Mexkins I'm in charge a'things round here I'm the Big Boss and they better do what I say do from here on out. But Old Karl handed the match to Pepe instead and said No you just keep on a'doing what you been doing Hell you don't know nothing bout setting no Brush on far. Then he said Grab up your tools out I got other things to do today and climbed back on the wagon.

Pepe and Peto reached in the wagon for the Grubbing Hoe and the Double-Blade Ax but what they found was the Double-Blade Ax and the Shovel. They seen how that Shovel ruined my foot the day before and didn't want no part of it, Papa said. Then they seen me take the Grubbing Hoe out from under the wagon where I had it hid and seen I tricked em. Pepe kind a'come at me to take it away but I give him a couple a'Chicken Puck-puck-pa-kucks and a little flap a'my elbows to remind him I could tell Old Karl bout them stealing his Chickens anytime I wanted to and Pepe went off with the Shovel and not another word.

I WORKED THE GRUBBING HOE ALL DAY

Papa said, and was glad to do it. Pepe and Peto took turns on the Shovel and it wadn't long and they was both limping around same as me the day before that Shovel being such a regular Crippler. Course I was glad to see em hurting and a couple a'times I thought it'd be good to see o'Peto get him a Scorpion bite same as his Brother had but he was careful and smashed ever one he seen fore it could stab him with his Stinger.

We cut Brush and made a big stack a'what we cut as we went along. Fore long it got higher'n me, Papa said, but then Pepe couldn't find the Match Old Karl had give him to light it afire. Oh they was scared what Old Karl was gonna do at them losing his Match, Papa said. They eyes started bug-ging and they went to running round all over a'looking for that lost Match. I'd see a little stick off over there somewheres and I'd point to it and say Is that it Is that it and one of em'd run over there fast as he could go to look

I don't think they was a thing in the World
they liked moren me a'hurting . . .

but No it wadn't never no Match and then I'd point to another little stick over there somewheres else and say Is that it Is that it and here one or the other'd come a'running again. But after awhile they wouldn't pay no more attention to me at all but kept on running round all over the place a'looking for that Match. Then I seen a little stick way over yonder that really did look like a Match and I said Is that it Is that it but they didn't pay no attention to me now so I walked over there and sure nough it really was Old Karl's Match. I reached down to pick it up then I seen tween my legs Pepe was a'coming over to take a look his self so I stepped on the Match with my foot to cover it up just when he got there. Dunde he said, something like that. I pointed to a little stick over there that didn't look no more like a Match than some body's big fat Pig did. Is that it I said, Papa said. Pepe spit at my foot and went off a'looking somewheres else. Papa picked up the match from under his foot and stuck it in his pocket. Wadn't long and here come Old Karl in the wagon, Papa said. Why in Hell ain't that Brush pile burned up yet he hollered. Pepe and Peto looked at they feet then at the Brush pile then way up yonder at a Buzzard in the sky then at a Rock then just ever-wheres else but not at Old Karl they was so scared a'him. They done lost your Match ain't they I said, Papa said. Lost my Match, Old Karl said. You lost my god dam Match. Pepe and Peto scooted over against each other to take the Storm together. That's when Papa reached down in his pocket and came out with Old Karl's match cupped in his hand where nobody could see it, then he dropped it on the ground and eased away a few steps with Old Karl still a'going at Pepe and Peto. How can you lose my god dam Match, he yelled, Hell it's long as your god dam peter. Wait a minute, Papa said. Wait a minute, here it is right here ain't it. He waited until all three were looking then reached down and picked the match up off the ground. Well god dam, Old Karl said to Pepe and Peto, can't find a god dam Match and there it is a'setting right here in front a'you. God dam. God dam if that don't beat all, he said. Don't worry, Papa said. I'll go set that pile afire right now. But Old Karl said No here gimme that god dam Match I already told you you don't know nothing bout setting no Brush pile on far. Then he grabbed the Match out a'my hand, raked it cross the bottom a'his boot and touched it to the pile and Whoosh up it went in fire and smoke so heavy you couldn't hardly see Pepe and Peto a'standing over there holding hands with each other like a couple a'little Baby Children.

THE BLISTERS ON PAPA'S FEET STILL HURT

but not so bad as the new ones on his hands did from working the grubbing hoe all day. He went down to the barn and popped them with the awl same as he'd done the ones on the bottoms of his feet the day before, but this time Pepe and Peto didn't hurry over to watch. I give em a couple a'Chicken Pucks anyhow, Papa said, just for a little Reminder. Papa got his supper off the stove then went out to eat it on the front porch again. I hadn't said not no ten words to Miss Gusa since when I got there, he said, and didn't plan on saying many more but I was missing somebody to talk to especially Herman and Miz Choat. Course Herman never said much anyhow but Miz Choat was a regular talker and would carry on bout just any o'thing at all. Oh she was so good to me and I missed her, Papa said, so I got to thinking I better go on and get started walking back to the Choats in my head.

Papa laid down on his pallet, pulled the covers up and started walking in his head. I got to the Big Oak Tree in just a second, he said, then took off a'walking on down the road. The Stars come out and then the Moon did too and I could see the road stretching way out there in front a'me in the Moonlight just pretty as you please and I thought Boy Hidy it ain't gonna be no time at all and I'm gonna be back at the Choats. But then I seen somebody just a'shimmering way off down yonder in the middle a'the road and I stopped to get a better look and then I seen they was two or three more Shimmery People a'standing there too and then four or five or six more and maybe even moren that all just a'standing there shimmering and they looked like they might be them same People that was standing cross the Creek that night down there at Gilbert Lee's Grave. Hey I said, Papa said, what yall doing down there but they didn't say nothing back So then I said Well what yall want with me anyhow I ain't done nothing that I know of but they just kept on a'standing there a'shimmering So now, Papa said, I said Shoo, Yall go on Yall a'scaring the Pants off a'me here but No, he said, now they just set down in the middle a'the road like they was waiting for me to come on but I had bout all a'them I wanted in one night so I run on back to my pallet on the front porch fast as I could in my head and went off to sleep.

THE BRUSH PILE WAS STILL KICKING OFF SPARKS
when Old Karl rode us out there next morning in the wagon with our tools, Papa said. Then he showed us how far we had to go in ever direction to make the new field and I thought Well I'm gonna be some Old Man with a long gray Beard fore we ever get the Brush cleared that far. But Pepe and Peto just nodded and went on at it. Papa said he figgured they knowed they was already looking at the rest a'they Lives strapped to a Grubbing Hoe or a Double-Blade Ax and just couldn't see nothing different from now on out no matter how long they lived—or where. Papa, on the other hand, was working on a whole new future in his head now And they just wasn't no part of it had me clearing Brush for Old Karl the rest a'my Life neither, he said. No Sir I was gonna walk back to the Choats and Miz Choat was gonna give me a direction to Fayette County then I was gonna walk over there and find my Momma then me and Momma was gonna ride double on Precious back to the Choats and get o'Herman and Molly. Course by then Momma'd have got a Horse for each one a'us, Papa said, and then the three a'us and o'Molly'd ride off to one place or another to start a New Life without Old Karl or Miss Gusa neither one. That was the future Papa saw in his head and he liked thinking about it so much he almost didn't see the Rattlesnake coiled up right there barely a step in front of him, but he yelled and jumped back just in time and fell on his Bottom. Then here come Pepe and Peto just a'running, Papa said, and they started chunking rocks at that Snake and Oh wadn't but a minute and they had him Bloody all over and then Pepe scooped him up in his Shovel and pitched him over on top a'what was left a'the Brush fire. Oh listen, he said, that o'Snake just went to squirming and turning and striking at them burning hot coals but they wadn't nothing he could do but just set there and sizzle. I didn't like no Rattle Snake, Papa said, but I sure did feel sorry for that one.

That night Papa went walking off down the road in his head again thinking he just might see the Shimmery People again But when I got to where they'd been a'setting in the road the night before, he said, they was all gone. I just kept on a'walking, Papa said, then after some time I looked over yonder and seen some o'Cows with the Bar T burned on em and I couldn't believe I'd walked all the way over to o'Mister Ed Tinker's Farm bout four miles from the House where I started but there I was.

PAPA WOKE UP THE NEXT NIGHT

with something licking on his face. At first I thought it was a Panther or a Bear, he said, or maybe somebody's o'Dog but No then I seen it was a Coyote. A Coyote was just a'setting there a'licking on my face and I didn't know what to do so I just went dead right there where I was on my pallet and didn't move nothing but my two eyes. I knowed Coyotes ate up pretty much everthing they could catch specially Sheep and Goats and little Calves and Chickens but I didn't have no idea if they went to eating on little Boys like me or not. I thought they most likely did and wished I had me Old Karl's Big Gun to shoot him down with, Papa said. Then the Coyote sat back and Papa saw in the moonlight he was missing about half of one of his front legs. I figgured he got it caught in somebody's trap and had to chew his own Foot off if he wanted to get away. That happened all the time, Papa said. Wadn't nothing to find a trap with just a bloody Foot left there in it and I thought that must be Something Awful to have to chew you own Foot off to get away so I reached out my hand to pet him cause I felt Sorry but he moved back and wouldn't let me do it. Then we started to looking back and forth at each other just natural as you please then we smiled at one another too and I thought Boy Hidy here I am a'setting out here on the front porch with a wild Coyote and then my very next thought was Why I got me a Friend here ain't I First one I ever did have and my Heart just blowed up on me to think such a thing, Papa said. Course I knowed it couldn't be, he said. What People done with Coyotes was shoot em same as you would a Snake. Shoot em and hang em over a fence cause sometime that'd bring Rain and everbody was always needing Rain. Papa decided he didn't care about all that and again reached out to touch the Coyote So he'd know how I felt about him, he said. And I guess I wanted to know he felt the same way bout me too but he shied away from my hand then jumped off the porch and hobbled over to where his Wife was waiting for him at the edge a'the Brush with one a'Old Karl's Chickens locked up tight in her mouth. Then he give me a little smile over his shoulder, Papa said, and they run on off in the Woods together to eat that Chicken.

PAPA CALLED HIS NEW FRIEND

Mister Pegleg because all he had for one of his front legs was a stump and Papa worried he wouldn't have much of a chance if something was to get after him. But what scared me most, Papa said, was here we already got two Mexkins stealing Old Karl's Chickens and now we got Mister Pegleg and his Wife a'stealing em too and I knowed wouldn't be long and Old Karl'd wanna know where all his Chickens was a'going and Oh then here he'd come with his Big Gun. Papa thought if Old Karl caught Pepe and Peto stealing his Chickens he'd give each one of em a lick or two and a good cussing but not much moren that cause he was already working em near half to death and wouldn't wanna run a couple a'good Workers off over a few scrawny Chickens. But, Papa said, I knowed he'd shoot Mister and Miz Pegleg dead on sight for the same thing then hang em over a fence somewheres or skin em one and nail they hide to the side a'the Barn. Tween the two, he said, I wanted Mister and Miz Pegleg to get all the Chickens they could eat and them Mexkins to go a'hunting for they suppers somewheres else beside the Chicken Coop. But course, Papa said, I knowed you couldn't no more get them two Mexkins to quit stealing Chickens than you could kick a Skinny Dog off a Fat Bone.

The good thing was Mister Pegleg'd come to visit ever two or three nights. He'd just lay there on the porch with his chin on his stump, Papa said, and look at me with them Yellerbrown Eyes he had and I'd just talk away at him. I told him bout missing my Momma and my Brother Herman and bout walking back to the Choats in my head. I even told him I was gonna try and be a Horn Man and play in a Dance Band some day when I was big nough. He listened to ever word I said, he said, even when he was looking off to the Barn where his Wife was at. That's how they made they living, Papa said. Mister Pegleg'd keep a Look Out for anything Bad a'coming this way while Miz Pegleg was down there at the Barn biting a Chicken right under Pepe and Peto's nose. I stayed scared they was gonna get caught one a'these nights and knowed I ought to run em off to keep em safe, he said, but I was so glad to have me a Friend I just couldn't do it.

Boy Hidy here I am a'setting out here
on the front porch with a wild Coyote . . .

PAPA GOT BLISTERS ON TOP OF BLISTERS
even with wearing his own hand-made sandals. And Old Karl never even heard of a pair a'work gloves, Papa said, least not for me and them Mexkins. If you wanted to eat you just had to learn to make do with whatever you had, he said. That's all they was to it. It was the same for Miss Gusa. Old Karl worked her hard as he did us. Once or twice I heard him a'hollering at her so loud I had to stop walking in my head and come back to my pallet, he said. One night he yelled at her Just Get Out. Just go on and get out I don't want nothing more to do with you or that Baby neither one. That's how I found out she was gonna have a Baby, Papa said. Poor Miss Gusa started crying and said Where would I go. I got no place in the World to go and then Old Karl said back to her I don't give a god dam where you go Just go. But Miss Gusa was still there the next morning when I took the eggs up to the house from doing my Chores, he said. I wanted to tell her I was sorry bout her Troubles with Old Karl but fore I could say one thing bout it she said What's wrong with them Laying Hens they don't lay no more eggs'n this here. Course I wadn't bout to tell her we was getting less eggs cause we had less Hens a'laying em so I said Well Miss Gusa I don't have no idea Why and then she said Well it might be we got us a big Chicken Snake down there in the Chicken Coop somewhere eating all the eggs fore you can gather em up. I liked it she thought a Chicken Snake was getting the eggs and said Yes I think I seen one down there, Papa said, a great big one. A Chicken Snake'll crawl right in the nest under that o'Hen and go to eating her eggs even while she's a'laying em, Miss Gusa said, did you know that. Papa said No I never heard a'nothing like that in all my Life but course, he said, everbody in the World been a'hearing that since the day they was borned. Old Karl rode me and the Mexkins out to the field in the wagon after that, Papa said, and we went to clearing Brush like always.

WE CLEARED BRUSH RAIN OR SHINE
ever single day, Papa said, then burned it up in piles. I don't know how many Snakes Pepe and Peto put in the fire, he said, but it was a bunch of em and all kinds too not just Rattle Snakes. Sometimes we might accidentally scare

up an Armadilla or a Jackrabbit and they'd run straight into the fire and get theyselves burned up. Why would they do that Papa asked himself but he didn't know.

Papa stayed away from Pepe and Peto as much as he could, even going way off over there somewhere by himself to eat his cornbread lunch. They just treated me Bad ever chance they got, Papa said. I guess it was cause that's how Old Karl treated me and they didn't wanna be no different. Oh well I thought, he said, I can always go a'walking off in my head if I don't wanna be round em. And then one day while he was grubbing Mesquites roots he did. Just all a sudden I was a'walking down the road to the Choats and I looked over and Why there was all them Shimmery People a'standing cross the road in front of this big o'Rock Bluff that went way up high. I looked round, Papa said, but I didn't have no idea where I was at cause I never seen this place before in my Life. They was Caves all up and down that Rock Bluff but one had this o'Cedar Tree a'growing out it like the Cave went way way back in there somewheres and that's the one them Shimmery People was a'pointing at. What's in that hole up yonder I said, Papa said, but they just kept pointing up at it like they was something Special in that one they wanted me to see. But I got this Bad feeling, he said, and said No I don't wanna see what's in that Cave now Yall just leave me alone. But they just kept a'pointing up at it then went to giving me a sign with they hands to come on over there and take a Look. No, I said, I ain't coming over there They's something Bad in that hole and I don't wanna see it or know nothing bout it neither one. Then they went to pointing at something way down there on the ground under that Cave and I looked at it a minute then Oh I seen it was somebody's dead Horse. And then of a sudden I was back in the Field clearing Brush with Pepe and Peto again and didn't have no idea what to think bout what I just seen.

PAPA TOLD MISTER PEGLEG ABOUT IT the next time he and his Wife came to steal another one of Old Karl's Chickens. I told him some day I'm gonna have to find that Cave up there on the Bluff then climb up there and see what's in it, Papa said, even though I don't want no part of it or that dead Horse down there on the ground under it neither one. Mister Pegleg turned his head and listened to ever word I said, Papa said, and I tried to read his thinking on it and what I got back over and over and over again was Yes you do Yes you do Yes you do.

Course I already knowed that so I started drawing pitchurs in my head a'everthing round that Cave so I'd know it when I seen it again, Papa said. But what I didn't know was that when I finally did see it again Oh I wished I'd a'Never.

MIZ PEGLEG DISAPPEARED NOT LONG AFTER THAT Papa said. And then Mister Pegleg did too. I was worried sick somebody'd gone and killed em both, he said, and couldn't hardly sleep at night for thinking bout it. Then late one night when the Moon was full Papa saw a little movement toward the Brush on the other side of the road in front of the house. It was Mister Pegleg with a fat hen in his mouth. He didn't even look back at me, Papa said, just hobbled on off in the Brush fast as he could go. Uh oh I thought, Papa said, Uh oh what happened to Miz Pegleg that Mister Pegleg is the one a'stealing Chickens now and him with just only three good legs. I wanted to tell him Stop it right now Mister Pegleg, somebody gonna catch you for sure hobbling round the Chicken Coop on just three legs and a stump like that, Papa said, but ever few nights there'd he go a'hobbling off in the Brush again with another one a'Old Karl's Chickens in his mouth.

It went on like that for weeks with Mister Pegleg just a'grabbing Chickens fore they could even let out a squawk to wake Pepe and Peto. I don't know how in the World he done it, Papa said, he was ever bit good as them two Mexkins at stealing Chickens. Maybe even good as Miz Pegleg'd been, he said, but I didn't have no idea what might a'happened to her She was just gone. Gone forever, Papa said, and I knowed it must a'just broke Mister Pegleg's Heart to lose his Wife same as it done me to lose my Momma. I wanted to tell him Yes I know xactly how you feel Mister Pegleg but he was always in a hurry to get off with a Chicken and didn't have time to come up on the porch and talk to me no more. Oh and that broke my Heart too, Papa said.

COUPLA THREE-FOUR NIGHTS LATER

Papa woke up to a big commotion down at the barn. Oh you would a'thought the World was coming to an end, Papa said. Things was just a'crashing all over the place and Pepe and Peto was a'whooping and a'hollering to beat the Band. But what turned my Blood to Froze Ice, he said, was I could hear Mister Pegleg just a'screaming and a'howling and a'crying bove everthing else and I knowed in a second what was a'going on. Papa jumped off the porch and ran to the barn Fast as my two Feet could take me, he said. You'd a'thought somebody was after me with a Chinaberry Switch I run down there so fast. I throwed the big double door open and seen right off they had Mister Pegleg cornered tween the Corn Crib and the Horse Stall and was just a'going at him Pepe with the Pitchfork and Peto with the Double-Blade Ax. Oh poor Mister Pegleg he was total helpless and just a'screaming and a'snarling and a'crying all at once and bleeding all over his self to where you couldn't hardly see nothing but Red Red Red. I hollered at them Mexkins to Stop. Stop, I hollered. Leave Mister Pegleg alone you Mexkins he ain't done nothing to you. But they just kept a'going at him with that Pitchfork and Double-Blade Ax like I wadn't even there. Then Pepe give Mister Pegleg a stab in his chest with the Pitchfork and Blood just come a'squirting out everwhere like water out a pump and Mister Pegleg fell down on his side and went to biting at the holes and crying like a poor little Lost Baby and I was all the time a'hollering Stop Stop Stop Stop. Then I seen Peto rear back to swing the Double-Blade Ax to finish Mister Pegleg off so right quick I grabbed up the Grubbing Hoe and took a chop hard as I could at his Foot and he let out a yell and I seen in the lamplight his Big Toe just go a'flying off somewheres in the Dark and now him a'jumping up and down all over the place and a'holding his foot. Oh I was Mad, Papa said, I mean just crazy blood-bubbling Mad and whatever door it was in me that'd kept the Bad Me locked up in there all my whole Life before was wide open now and the Bad Me just come a'running out a'swinging and a'chopping at Pepe and Peto with that Grubbing Hoe with everthing I had in me. Oh they went to stumbling backwards to the wall with they hands up in front to guard they face and just a'jabbering and a'begging but Oh they wadn't no Quit in me and I tasted Copper in my mouth and knowed Oh I'm gonna kill em both for what they done to Mister Pegleg. I would a'done it too but of a sudden here come Old Karl through the Barn Door with his Big Gun. What the god dam

Hell going on down here he said, Papa said, and Pepe and Peto just went to jabbering like two crazy Loonies and pointing over to the dark corner where Mister Pegleg gone down a'crying. Old Karl grabbed the lantern up off the post where it was hanging and give it to Pepe. Shine that light, he said, then raised up his Big Gun and cocked it. Oh and then I could taste that Copper in my mouth again, Papa said, and I locked my jaw down tight as I could and got ready to swing my Grubbing Hoe again. Oh listen here to me, he said, I was gonna murder my own Daddy to keep him from shooting Mister Pegleg and certain it was I was gonna do it. But then Pepe shined the light and I seen Mister Pegleg was gone Just a little trail left there in the dirt where he dragged his self off a ways then got to his three feet and hobbled on out the Barn Door and I had to catch myself to keep from crying at the Joy of it. What critter was it. Old Karl said. Big o'Coon, Papa said, after a Chicken I reckon. Coon, Old Karl said. All that ruckus from a dam Coon. Old Karl took the lantern and went over and put the light on the tracks in the dirt then pulled Papa down to his knees beside him and pushed his face right down to the tracks. Them look like Coon tracks to you, he said. Papa said Yes they surely do. Old Karl gave him a slap across his head. Them look like Coon tracks do they, he said again. Maybe Bobcat tracks Papa said. Old Karl gave him another slap across his head. That one bout took my ear off, Papa said. I don't know what it is I said. I can't read no tracks. It was a god dam Coyote eating my Chickens was what it was Old Karl said then looked over at Pepe and Peto and said Coyote Coyote and they nodded back then Pepe shined his teeth and made a bunch a'stabs this way and that in the air with his Pitchfork to show Old Karl how he'd got him. SonofaBitch is good as dead then, Old Karl said. Just crawled off out there in the Dark somewheres to die now I reckon, he said, they just ain't no coming back from a Stabbing like that is they.

P APA WAITED UNTIL OLD KARL PUT OUT HIS LAMP in the house then jumped off his pallet on the front porch and ran out into the Brush to look for Mister Pegleg. I was already crying at what I knowed I was gonna find a'laying dead out there somewheres, Papa said, but No I couldn't find hide nor hair a'my Friend Mister Pegleg nowheres at all. Well

Oh poor Mister Pegleg he was total helpless and just a'screaming and a'snarling and a'crying all at once . . .

49

I thought, he said, maybe he ain't as dead as I thought he was. And then I thought if he's alive he's hungry cause Pepe and Peto went at him fore he could get him a Chicken for his suppers.

Papa went back to the Barn. Pepe and Peto was setting there the lantern tween em, Papa said, Pepe a'trimming off what was left a'Peto's Big Toe with the tin shears and Peto just a'crying at the hurt and Oh tears just a'running all down his face and it made me smile, he said, to think o'Peto gonna be hobbling round just like Mister Pegleg from here on out for the rest a'his Life without that Big Toe a'his. Then I went over to get a better look and they was so surprised to see me they scooted back on they Bottoms. Oh I could see they was scared a'me now, Papa said, so I kicked a little dirt at em as a Warning not to fool with me never no more. They looked up at me, they dark black eyes a'shining back the lantern light and I knowed they hated me even moren they did Old Karl. I didn't care, Papa said, I hated em right back. I had just only one Friend in the whole World and these two here done everthing they could to murder him and maybe did I didn't know for sure. The one thing I did know for sure, Papa said, was that if Mister Pegleg was still alive out there somewheres I wadn't gonna let him starve to death so I went over to the Chicken Coop and grabbed up one a'Old Karl's big fat Hens and wrung her head off right there for Pepe and Peto to see then went out in front of the house and left it under a Mesquites Tree where Mister Pegleg could find her if he hadn't already died and could still get round. After that Papa went back to his pallet on the front porch But I couldn't sleep a wink, he said, for worrying bout Mister Pegleg and not only that but too that I got so mean and ugly down there in the Barn with my Grubbing Hoe I didn't even know who I was or what I was doing no more and I thought Oh No Oh No I got some great big part a'Old Karl Blood in me and I don't know how in the World I'm ever gonna get it out.

*E*VEN BEFORE DAYLIGHT

Papa went to see if the chicken was still under the Mesquite Tree where he'd left it for Mister Pegleg the night before. No it was gone, Papa said, course everthing that breathed went round hungry in that part of the Country and who knows what might a'grabbed it up to eat. He hoped it was Mister or Miz

Pegleg though but I couldn't say for sure either one of em was even still alive, he said, but I made a promise to my self I was gonna feed em best I could ever couple a'days anyhow to keep em from taking any more chances down there in the Chicken Coop. Oh I worried about em night and day, Papa said.

Old Karl left them at the field just after sunup then drove off to Blanco to buy some coyote spring-traps at Bindseil's Feed and Hardware. By god this'll be the end a'the Chicken Stealing round here he said. No, Papa said to himself, it's just the beginning a'the Chicken Stealing round here and you might just as well throw your Coyote Traps in the Creek for all the good they gonna do you when I want a Chicken. I didn't worry bout Pepe and Peto telling on me neither. After last night, he said, they didn't want no part a'me long as I was in reach a'that Grubbing Hoe. Specially Peto he couldn't hardly even walk with that missing Big Toe a'his. He soaked the Stump all night long in a bucket a'Coal Oil then tied it up with a piece a'his shirt he'd a'soaked in that same o'stinky stuff. Wooo you could smell him a'coming a mile off. And that turned out to be a good thing for me, Papa said, cause later when I was grubbing with my hoe I smelled his Stump foot a'coming up behind me and I turned to have a look and Why there was Pepe and Peto a'standing there with a live Copperhead Snake scooped up in they Shovel. I knowed they was gonna set it down on the ground behind me so I'd step on it when I wadn't looking and get me a bite or two. It scared me so bad to see that Snake sudden like that Why I just naturally come straight up with my Grubbing Hoe and whacked the bottom of they Shovel and that o'Copperhead Snake went a'flying out the Shovel right at em. Oh they jumped and took off a'running fast as they could go Peto just a'screaming and a'hollering cause his missing Big Toe hurt so bad with ever step. They didn't bother me no more that day Papa said. I reckon that was bout the only Trick they had in they bag.

That night Papa took his supper off the stove and went out on the porch to eat. But I didn't take but a bite or two, he said. I waited til Dark then went out and left the rest of my suppers under that Mesquites Tree for Mister Pegleg.

I knowed my Walking Off in My Head Days was over for a while too, Papa said. I just wadn't gonna walk off nowheres in my Head or on my Feets neither one long as they was a chance Mister Pegleg might still be alive and out there somewheres.

HERE'S BOUT HOW IT WENT AFTER THAT

Papa said. I took to stealing least two Chickens a week then I'd wring they heads off and leave em out there under that o'Mesquites Tree for Mister Pegleg to find. In tween Chickens I'd leave him most a'my suppers. Then first thing ever morning I'd go out to take a look and ever morning whatever I'd a'left there the night before'd be gone. Oh I hoped Mister Pegleg was the one a'getting it or Miz Pegleg one, he said, but Miz Pegleg'd been gone so long I didn't have no hope for her.

Pepe and Peto stayed mean as ever, Papa said. Wadn't nothing to find a Stinging Scorpion in my lunch pail, one time even a big o'long black Centipede which was scary cause where ever a Centipede bites you will rot right off and nothing to do bout it no matter was it your arm or your leg either one and don't matter how long you soak it in a bucket a'Coal Oil neither. Oh Pepe and Peto they had moren one Trick in they bag after all and for ever one they went to pull on me I'd go to pointing at Peto's missing Big Toe and grin like some o'Possum. They didn't like it but what could they do I was too smart for them two Mexkins and they knowed it.

One night Miss Gusa came out on the porch just as Papa was about to go out to the Mesquite Tree with Mister Pegleg's supper. I know what you're a'doing, she said. I seen you more times'n once. I wadn't a good liar, Papa said, but I said I don't have no idea what you're a'talking bout Miss Gusa. Oh yes you do, she said. You're a'feeding your supper to Somebody hiding out there in the Woods. When she said Somebody I knowed she didn't have no idea bout Mister Pegleg so I said Well you are right I am. Who is it then? she said. I can't tell you he wouldn't like it Papa said. Want me to talk to your Daddy bout it, she said. Papa knew he was in a pickle and the only thing he could think of was how a pickle tastes so he said His name is Mister Sour like a pickle. Is he out a'that Henry Sauer bunch over yonder at Smithson Valley, she said. Papa said No I don't think so but I don't know. What's Mister Sauer want round here, Miss Gusa said. He's hungry is all, Papa said, just going round the Country looking for a bite to eat. Miss Gusa wanted to know if he was a nice man. Yes ma'am Papa said, Nice as you please. Miss Gusa's eyes started tearing up, Papa said, then she leaned over and whispered to me Wonder if Mister Sauer'd take me long with him. Tell him I'd keep him fed night and day and that's a Promise. Papa didn't know what to say. I don't see him that much, Papa said, he just grabs up his suppers and goes on off. Well when you do see him ask him for me will you, Miss Gusa said, Ask him if I can go with him when he leaves this part a'the Country. I don't wanna raise no Baby here. Well, Papa said. You know what I'm a'gonna do. Miss Gusa said. No, Papa said, what. I'm gonna cook up a extra suppers ever night and you just take it to Mister Sauer out there in the Woods somewheres okay. Well, Papa said. Just be our secret tween us, she said, okay. Papa knew he was about to step off a steep cliff but he nodded anyway. Okay, he said. And then when you do see Mister Sauer you tell him them suppers is all from me and I wanna go with him when he goes okay. Okay, Papa said. Make sure they good suppers though. Okay, Miss Gusa said, I will. Then she went on back in the house, Papa said, and I thought to my self Well if this works me and Mister Pegleg both gonna be fat and happy. And if it don't work, he said, well then I sure nough am gonna be in a Pickle.

*B*OY HIDY MISTER SOUR GOT TO BE AS REAL to Miss Gusa as you and me a'setting here, Papa said, and I had to tell stories to a fare-thee-well to keep them suppers a'coming. And I did, he said. She'd sneak out to the porch and I'd just go to telling her all kinds a'things. She asked How's Mister Sauer make his living and I said Well he was a Begger and didn't have to make no living. She asked Is Mister Sauer a handsome man and I said he was cept for one ear got blowed off in the War when he was a'holding Robert E. Lee's o'Horse at some battle or another. She asked Where was he a'going when he left these parts and I told her Up to Fayette-ville to see his Momma. And from then on out, Papa said, pretty much ever answer I give her was more me a'talking for my self than me a'talking for some Made-up Man like Mister Sour. Does he have some Friends up there in Fayetteville, she said. No just one Friend in the whole World and he's sickly right now, Papa said. Where's he at, Miss Gusa said. This Friend a'his. Some-wheres round here, Papa said, but Mister Sour don't know where or he'd run go help him. I was bout to cry, Papa said, thinking bout poor o'Mister Pegleg out there in the Brush somewheres with all them stab holes in him. Mister Sauer sounds like a Good Man to me, Miss Gusa said, wanting to help his Friend like that. I knowed I was gonna cry if I said another word, Papa said, so I just nodded and looked way off out yonder somewheres. Then Miss

Gusa wanted to know if Mister Sauer had him a Wife somewheres, Papa said. Yes he did but she run off on him one night and he ain't seen Hide nor Hair a'her since, Papa said. Oh Lord that Dear Man, she said. No Wife. Papa thought it was sad too But a'course I was really talking bout Mister and Miz Pegleg, he said. Well, Miss Gusa said, you tell Mister Sauer I am a Good Woman and wouldn't never run off and leave him like his Wife done. I said I would, Papa said, then she went on back in the house fore Old Karl even knowed she been gone.

Ever time I seen Miss Gusa after that she looked like she was up in a Dream somewheres, Papa said, like maybe she was a'building some great big Secret Life in her head for her and Mister Sour to live in. And all this time Miss Gusa's belly was a'getting bigger and bigger and Old Karl got to where he wouldn't even hardly talk to her no more, he said, cept to tell her to run go do this or that.

ATE ONE NIGHT I JUST COME STRAIGHT UP wide awake on my pallet, Papa said, and they was little lights just a Sparkling everwhere in the Brush out in front a'the house. First thing I thought was Oh them are the Nickel Conchos on my Momma's Saddle and Momma's setting out there on Precious. But No they was too many of em and they was spread too far apart to be on no saddle. Then the next thing I thought was I guess the Stars just dropped down out a'the sky and is a'looking for a place to settle in the World but No some of em was going up and down both and I knowed No them couldn't be no Stars. Then I said Oh them're Lightning Bugs first ones I seen this Spring and that was in fact what they was and Oh so pretty and just a'twinkling away everwheres you looked. Then I thought I seen something coming out a'the Brush tween them Sparkles and I looked some more and then Oh Why I couldn't believe my eyes cause coming right out a'the Brush with them Lightning Bugs a'sparkling all round his head like a big o'twinkling Hat a'Lights was my o'Friend Mister Pegleg his self. Oh Mister Pegleg was alive and here again. Oh my Friend Mister Pegleg. Oh and I wanted to run over there to him and hug him and pet him but No I knowed he wouldn't have it so I just smiled at him cross the road and he smiled back at me and I just kept a'whispering to him Oh Mister Pegleg Oh

Mister Pegleg Oh Mister Pegleg and course I was just a'crying away and best I could tell he was too. Then guess what Oh here come another surprise. Miz Pegleg she come a'stepping out a'the Brush right behind Mister Pegleg and all this time I'd a'thought her Dead and Gone Forever but No there she is right here in front of me now. Oh and my Heart just went to jumping and I thought Well I seen everthing now. And then Mister Pegleg he went back in the Brush and I thought Oh no Oh no he's gone again, Papa said, but No then here he come on back out again in just a minute and Oh. And Oh now he got two little Coyote pups a'follering long behind him. Oh look at em. Look at them little Fellas just a'rolling round and a'snipping at each other and Oh tears just a'running down my cheeks and it don't bother me one bit to say it, he said.

Papa knew now why he hadn't seen Miz Pegleg in so long. She'd been off having her babies somewhere and had had to leave the chicken stealing to her husband. And if Papa hadn't left food out there in the Brush for them every night the whole family would've starved to death and left not a trace on the earth of their ever having been here at all except in his heart..Oh I wanted so bad to run away from there and go live with Mister Pegleg and his Family, Papa said. I could just see myself a'sneaking in Barns and Houses at night and stealing Chickens and Pigs and Eggs and Bread and Pies and just whatever we needed to get along on and I didn't have no problem with me becoming a Thief and a Out Law to do it. Then I looked over my back and there was Miss Gusa just then a'stepping up to the winder to see everthing. I guess Mister Pegleg seen her too cause right away he nosed Miz Pegleg and they Babies back in the Brush and when they was bout gone he raised up his head to me and just stood there with them Lightning Bugs a'twinkling all round him like he was on fire then he give me this long look and then Oh here come the tears just a'running down my face again cause I knowed Mister Pegleg was a'saying Goodbye. Goodbye to you Forever that's what he was a'saying and I guess I blinked cause of a sudden them Lightning Bugs scattered in ever which direction and then Mister Pegleg just wadn't there no more and they wadn't nothing left anywheres in the World but the dark dark night and I said to myself I'll never see my Friend Mister Pegleg ever again. Not ever Not ever Not ever again, Papa said.

And I never did, he said.

MISS GUSA WAS WAITING FOR ME

with a bad look when I come in the house from doing my Chores the next morning, Papa said. And Oh she was fit to be tied. There ain't no Mister Sauer is they she said, and I don't reckon they ever was one neither huh. No, Papa said, I reckon I'm the only Mister Sour ever was or ever will be. She made Mean Eyes at me, Papa said, then slapped me so hard I tooted like a pack mule and my hat flew off. That's for a'lying to me, she said, and getting my hopes all up. My eyes was watering so much from the slap I couldn't hardly even see her and my ears was just a'ringing. What'd you say, I said. You been a'feeding some dam o'Coyote out there ain't you, same one been a'eating up all our Chickens like they was Sugar Candy ain't that right, Miss Gusa said. He was my Friend, Papa said, and ain't nothing you can do bout it. Tell your Daddy is what I can do bout it, she said. Well don't forget to tell him how you was the one cooked up all them suppers he was a'eating, Papa said. Oh she just really went to steaming then. You're a little Smarty Pants ain't you, she said, I ain't never seen the likes a'you in my Life. And don't forget to tell him you was planning to run off somewheres with Mister Sour too, Papa said. You gonna tell him bout that. I was wrong bout you, Miss Gusa said. You ain't just a little Smarty Pants you the very own Devil his self ain't you. I don't know if I am or I ain't, Papa said. You are, Miss Gusa said, I know it now. Then she turned to look somewheres out the winder and went to shaking her head back and forth and saying I'm lost I'm lost I'm more loster'n poor o'Jobe, Papa said. Papa didn't know what to do so he just stood there ready to jump in case she decided to slap him again. Then she turned and looked at him. They was big tears in her eyes, Papa said. This still just tween you and me, she said, okay. I reckon, Papa said. You better reckon, Miss Gusa said, less you want your Daddy to tan your hide for feeding them Coyotes. And mine too, she said. She looked so scared for me and her both I nodded and said Okay, Papa said, then I went on out and got in the wagon with Pepe and Peto and in a minute or two here come Old Karl to drive us on out to the field with our tools and whatnot.

WE'D CHOPPED AND HOED AND BURNED
most all the Mesquites by now and was just starting to clear the thorny
brambles that growed along what was gonna be the fence line, Papa said.
Them brambles was killers, he said, and us there only in our sandals which
maybe helped the bottom a'your feet some but didn't do nothing to save
the top of em or your ankles neither one. Oh them thorns hurt, Papa said.
It was like a'walking through a field a'straight razors your feet just a'getting
butchered up so bad with ever step you took. Course I had the Grubbing
Hoe so I'd hoe me out a place to step on fore I ever stepped at all and that
saved my feets a time or two, he said. But poor o'Pepe and Peto they was
all but crying from the cuts and scratches them thorns give em all up and
down they feet and wadn't nothing to do bout it cept smear on more Axle
Grease which we all three did on our cuts ever chance we got. Worse thing
I ever seen though, Papa said, was when o'Pepe got all tangled up in the
thorny vines and one of em got wrapped round his leg and then when he
went to get it off it went round his arm too all the way up and then Oh Boy
Hidy them thorns give him a cut or a poke ever time he moved. Oh he was
a mess, Papa said, blood a'running everwheres all over him til Peto finally
got them brambles cut off him with his knife bout half a foot long. After
that Pepe and Peto went to whispering back and forth to each other all day
til Old Karl come up in the wagon at Sun Down to fetch us Home. Let's
go he said, Papa said. But Pepe and Peto just stood there a'looking at him
then shook they heads to say No we ain't a'going. I said get in the god dam
wagon, Old Karl said. What the Hell's matter with you two. Pepe and Peto
raised first one foot then the other to show Old Karl how tore up they feets
was. I didn't dare do the same cause I knowed I'd get a good whupping for it
and was surprised they didn't. Well what the Hell you xpect, Old Karl said,
you ain't working out on a god dam desert somewheres. Peto give Pepe a
look and Pepe said Za Pa Toes to Old Karl, something like that, Papa said.
I didn't have no idea what they was talking bout but whatever it was made
Old Karl maddern a basket a'wet Snakes and he said No god dam Za Pa Toes
now git in the god dam wagon. But Pepe and Peto didn't budge not one inch
neither one of em, just stood there a'looking back at him. I'm gonna tell you
just one more time Old Karl said Git in the god dam wagon. They didn't but
I did Papa said, even if he wadn't even talking to me. Old Karl made ready
to drive off then give Pepe and Peto another Snake Eyes. Yall coming or not

god dam you both to Hell, he said. They give each other a look then just turned round pretty as you please and went to walking off. Old Karl let em go a fair piece then said god dam Mexkins to his self and hollered All right god dam you, Za Pa Toes. And then Pepe and Peto come on back and got up in the wagon with me and away we went, he said, them two just a'grinning at each other the whole way Home like they was just two happy Possums going off to a Birthday Party somewheres.

OLD KARL COME BACK FROM BLANCO the next day with a load a'Bob Wire to fence round the new field and two pairs a'Shoes for the Mexkins but none for me, Papa said. Oh them Mexkins was happy. They chunked they old sandals away then just went to marching round everwheres in they new Shoes with they knees a'going way up high like they was a couple a'Soldiers in Robert Lee's Army a'the South fore the yanks whupped us with they Bag a'Tricks. It made me so mad seeing them Mexkins in they new Shoes I got my back up and went right over to Old Karl and pulled on his shirt tail to make him look round at me. What the Hell you want, he said. I said Where's my new Shoes at, Papa said. Old Karl said I didn't get you any they cost too much money. That ain't right, Papa said. I do the same work as them two Mexkins and you didn't buy me no new pair a'Shoes same as them. That's right, Old Karl said, I didn't buy you no new pair a'Shoes. Now just hush up bout it There ain't one god dam thing you can do bout it and then he give me his Snake Eyes. Papa took a step back so it'd be hard for Old Karl to hit him if he took a mind to. Well there is too one thing I can do bout it, Papa said. I can leave. Oh and now Old Karl really did give me the o'Snake Eyes, Papa said, and he would a'hit me sure if I a'been in distance. Well listen here to me you little SonofaBitch, he said, if you do leave don't you never come back here ever again in your whole Life cause I won't have you step in my sight. I was bout to cry, Papa said, cause I knowed my mean o'Daddy meant ever word he was a'saying but I meant ever word I was a'saying too so now I give him my own Snake Eyes and I said Okay I won't never come back. Even if I hear you are sick and dying I won't never come back Not even to stick you down in the Ground when you fall over dead.

And then I turned round and went a'walkin on up the road toward the Choats like I been a'doing all them nights in my head, Papa said. And the only thing come to my mind was Well here I go and the last thing I seen was Pepe and Peto just a'standing there in they new Shoes laughing at me and a'waving Bye Bye.

P APA WALKED AND WALKED AND WALKED then it started getting dark And then I went and walked some more yet, he said. I might a'got a little scared but the Coyotes started a'yipping all round and I figgured it was Mister Pegleg and his Family and Friends a'looking out for me. Oh I was homesick for Mister Pegleg best Friend I ever did have, Papa said, but wadn't no help for it. He kept walking. He'd walked this road so many times before in his head and he knew every twist and turn of it so it wasn't any surprise to him to see Old Man Hugo Schmidt's house just up ahead. O'Man Schmidt and his wife Miz Schmidt was both just skinny as a hair off your head, Papa said. People said they was too tight with they Money to buy Foods and too lazy to grow they own. Light was coming from the window so Papa stood out in front of the house and said Hello the House Hello the House. In a minute Old Man Schmidt stepped out his door with his Squirrel Gun and said Vot you vant. I'm just a'walking down the road here a'looking for a place to sleep tonight, Papa said. Who's dot out dere Hugo, Miz Schmidt said from somewhere inside the house where Papa couldn't see her. Old Man Schmidt looked out at Papa. Who's dot out dere, he said. I'm Old Karl's Boy, Papa said. Old Man Schmidt gripped his Squirrel Gun and shouted to his wife It's dot Old Karl's Boy. Ja, Old Karl's Boy. Miz Schmidt said then poked her head out the door to take a look at me, Papa said, so I tipped my Hat and said How you Miz Schmidt, been a'getting any Rain lately. Vot's he vant, she said. He vants somevhere to sleep, Old Man Schmidt said. Oh she didn't like that one little bit, Papa said. She took a step back in the house. Nein not Old Karl's Boy, she said, not here Hugo Nein Nein Nein. Vhy ain't you home in your own bed, Old Man Schmidt said. I run off from my Home, Papa said, and I ain't a'never going back neither. I'm a good worker for a Boy my size, be glad to work for you for just my suppers and a place to sleep tonight. Nein Hugo, Miz Schmidt said, not Old Karl's

Boy Nein. I do all the vork round here myself, don't need no help, Old Man Schmidt said. Thank you anyhow, Papa said. Ja vell goodnight to you then, Old Man Schmidt said then locked the door behind him to keep me out. It didn't surprise me they was scared a'Old Karl, Papa said, pretty much everbody round there was and me too.

Papa went over to the Horse trough and was just cupping out a drink of water with his hands when he heard somebody say Psst Psst from over there in the Dark somewheres. It scared me so bad I like to a'jumped outta my pants, Papa said. Then Psst Psst Psst here it come again then Somebody come out from behind a tree a'pushing a Wheel Barra but I couldn't make out the face in the Dark but I seen that Wheel Barra ever day a'my life so I knowed who it was so I said Why Hello there Miss Gusa what you a'doing out here in the Wilderness with Old Karl's Wheel Barra.

*M*ISS GUSA HAD ALL SORT A'THINGS

in the Wheel Barra. She had Matches and a Quilt and a Pan a'Bread and I don't know what all else but it was nough you could a'set sail to China on it if you a'had a mind to, Papa said. We went on down the road a'ways then got us a fire going and pulled off a piece a'Bread and I asked her why she'd up and left Home. She said, Papa said, that after I walked off Old Karl jumped on his Mexkins for having such a good time a'parading round in they new Shoes and rode em out to the new field to push them spools a'Bob Wire off the wagon. I knew he'd be a'coming at me next for one thing or another, she said, and I just didn't want no more of it. Why come at you, Papa said, you ain't done nothing. It's just in him to come at me that's all, Miss Gusa said. I don't know but what God His Self put it in him when he made him. Course I guess I egged him on a time or two myself, she said. What'd you do to egg him on, Papa said. I called him a sorry o'Turd one time but you too little for me to be a'talking like that round you and I won't say it again, Miss Gusa said. To his face, Papa said. Yes o'Black Turd right there straight to his face, she said. Whoops there I went and said it again didn't I. Must a'made you mad, Papa said. Miss Gusa put her hands round her belly. He wanted to hurt my Baby but let's talk bout something else okay. Where you a'going anyhow, Papa said. I don't have no idea in the World where, she said, just a'going til, til I guess I don't know what. Papa told her he was going to the Choats. He said they were nice people and his Brother Herman lived there with them. Then he told her she might could live there too. She got tears in her eyes when I said that, Papa said and then she said Oh no I gotta keep on a'going or Old Karl gonna get me. I felt a little chunk a'Ice run up my back, Papa said. And then I said, You don't really think he's gonna come after you do you. Why yes I do and you too I reckon, she said. I hadn't even thought a'that, Papa said, and it near took my breath away to think it now. What's he gonna do he catches us? he said. Miss Gusa shook her head. No Telling, she said, just ain't No Telling. Papa was really scared now. Well, he said, I don't wanna be nowheres round here when he finds us. No and not me neither, Miss Gusa said, but if I know Old Karl he ain't a'going off no wheres til he gets his Mexkins a'working on that Bob Wire fence so I reckon we still got us a little time to get on down the road a'ways.

*W*E TOOK TURNS PUSHING THAT

o'Wheel Barra down the road, Papa said, and we wadn't neither one a'us shy bout keeping a look out should Old Karl come a'riding up behind us neither. Tell me some more bout the Choats, Miss Gusa said. I gotta be somewheres when my Baby comes. When's that Papa said. It's still a good ways off, she said, least a month or two. You think it's a Boy or a Girl, Papa said. I don't care neither way, she said. Be glad to have a Baby Boy, be glad to have a Baby Girl. Wanna feel it kick. Here set your hand right here. Oh no not me, Papa said and put a little more space between them as they walked along. Miss Gusa laughed and said Don't be silly it's just a little Person in there same as you. Not if it's a Girl it ain't, Papa said. Miss Gusa laughed again and I seen she wadn't the Person I thought she was. No I guess that's right, she said. Well which ever it is gonna be your little Half Brother or Half Sister one or the other you know it. What, Papa said. They got the same Daddy as you but not the same Momma. That makes em a Half to you, Miss Gusa said. Papa had trouble understanding it. Whoever's a'coming is just a Half that what you said, he said. To you they's just Half, she said. To everbody else they just be the same as anybody else in the World. I don't believe a word of it, Papa said. Miss Gusa laughed when she realized what was confusing him. No no she said, Half in name only, not half a person if that's what you a'thinking. Oh, Papa said. Yeah, Miss Gusa said, I reckon you was thinking bout just half a Brother. Oh I can see that now, she said. A little half a Brother a'walking round on just half a leg and a'grabbing things with just half a hand. And just looking round with a half a eye, Papa said. And a'listening just outta half a ear, Miss Gusa said. And just a'smelling half a'some o'Skunk, Papa said. They were just laughing away now. But I guess the good thing is you only gotta feed em half as much, Miss Gusa said. We went on back and forth like that for a long time, Papa said. I guess we just needed us a good laugh.

At Sun Down they gathered some sticks and built a fire then Miss Gusa fried some sausage in a skillet she had on the wheelbarrow. And a'course by then it was Dark and Mister Pegleg and his Family just went to singing all round, Papa said, and Oh I did like the sound a'that and it made me feel good and safe.

But that night he dreamt he was walking through the Woods and came up on this barn with a Coyote skin nailed to the door and he sat straight up because in his dream the dead Coyote skin was missing a front foot. Oh, he said and then Miss Gusa looked over from where she was sitting in front of the fire and said What's wrong with you. Papa got his breath and said I guess I just had me a Bad Dream is all. Well, she said, come on over here and set by me a minute I know all bout Bad Dreams. So I went over to the fire and set down by her, Papa said, and in a minute I was just a'shivering away at the Dream I had and Miss Gusa reached to hold my hand for it but I pulled it on away cause I didn't never wanna do nothing that'd make my Momma think I didn't Love her best.

ƝEXT MORNING WHEN THE SUN COME UP ON US we was already way on down the road, Papa said, but Miss Gusa was feeling puny and had to stop ever now and again and Spit Up on the side a'the road. You go on, she said, I'll catch up to you in a minute. But Papa would shake his head no and say No I ain't a'gonna walk off and leave you. And then they'd walk on for a while until Miss Gusa needed to stop and Spit Up again. I don't know what's wrong with me, she said. I ain't ordinarily like this. Papa found a jar of bees' honey in the wheelbarrow and spread some

Miss Gusa was feeling puny and had to stop ever now and again and Spit Up on the side a'the road . . .

on a piece of bread for her. Oh I was getting worried, Papa said. Here I was with a Sick Woman and didn't have no idea what to do. And then sweat just come a'running all down her face and she took to shaking, he said. Then Miss Gusa said I wanna go on and name my Baby. But it sounded all funny cause she was a'shaking so bad, Papa said, but I said Well what you wanna name your Baby and then Miss Gusa looked up at me her eyes just a'rolling and she said What Baby's that you say and then Boy Hidy she just fainted dead away. Papa covered her with the quilt because she looked like she was freezing to death, he said, then he splashed some water on her face because she felt like she was burning up and all this time he kept calling her by name to come on back to him from wherever she was. Miss Gusa Miss Gusa Miss Gusa, he said, Miss Gusa Miss Gusa Miss Gusa but She was just total gone out a'this World, Papa said, and I knowed I had to do something so I tumped the Wheel Barra over to empty everthing out but the water jar then went to lifting Miss Gusa up in it. She wadn't no little thing specially with her big belly, Papa said, and it like to a'wore me out a'getting her in but I did it then here we went on down the road me a'pushing her in the Wheel Barra with her legs bent at the knee and a'dangling over the front a'the bucket. Oh it was rough going on that bumpy o'dirt road, he said, and I near tumped poor Miss Gusa over moren once and to this day I don't have no idea how I didn't cause I was such a little Boy and she was such a big Woman at the time.

But Papa kept stumbling on down the road with Miss Gusa holding her belly in the wheelbarrow, stopping to rest a minute or two only when he felt like he'd fall over if he didn't. But the good thing was, he said, I knowed ever second where I was from all them walks I took in my head so when I pushed Miss Gusa in the Wheel Barra cross Cotton Mouth Creek I knowed wouldn't be long and we'd be at the Choats and that's what kept me a'going. Oh I was pooped, Papa said, just total wore out. Then Dark dropped down on us like a big rock and I thought maybe I oughta just lay me down here a minute for a little Nap and I might a'done just xactly that and fainted dead away like Miss Gusa did but just then I cocked my head and heard Band Music a'coming from way up the road and I went back to pushing Miss Gusa in that Wheel Barra hard as I could cause I knowed couldn't be from none other'n Fischer Hall right up ahead. And sure nough it was, he said, same place Old Karl took me off from in the wagon with them two Mexkins back when the Old Year was coming into the New.

64

Papa reached down and petted Miss Gusa's head then whispered Don't you worry Miss Gusa, we all but Home now. She opened her eyes a little bit then, Papa said, but I don't believe she seen a single thing in this whole World.

I PUSHED WITH ALL MY MIGHT

Papa said, and got Miss Gusa right up to the front doors a'Fischer Hall in the Wheel Barra but I couldn't push no further the steps was just too high and they was people dancing by inside not no five steps away but not a'one of em even looked at us. I seen Herman go a'stepping to and fro with a Girl then I seen Mister and Miz Choat a'bobbing up and down the way they always danced and I went to hollering Help Help Help Help Help Help but couldn't nobody hear me for the Poka Music. Oh to be that close to getting Help for Miss Gusa and still not get any made me feel like the whole World'd gone on and shut us out for good, he said. But finally the music ended and everybody in Fischer Hall heard him. They just poured out the door then, Papa said, and I told em Miss Gusa she's sick and somebody reached in the Wheel Barra to lift her out but drawed back and looked at they Red Hands and said Why that Wheel Barrow's full a'Blood and then here come Miz Choat right through the middle a'everbody and she's a'hollering Somebody get me some light over here then she give me a look to let me know she seen me there and got down to her knees in front of Miss Gusa in the Wheel Barra just when Herman shined a lantern. Oh she said Oh we got us a Baby coming here and I seen Herman bout to faint away. Then People just went to jabbering and one of em bent down and took a close look in Miss Gusa's face and said This woman is Dead. I couldn't believe it, Papa said, so I reached down and took Miss Gusa's hand like I wish I'd a'done last night when she was trying to be nice to me then Miz Choat said Everbody get a lantern and shine it here We gotta save this Baby. And everbody who had a lantern circled round and put the light on her And then, Papa said, Miz Choat pushed Miss Gusa's dress way up and reached up in there somewheres with both her hands and then in a minute here she come out with a little Blue Baby Boy wadn't hardly no bigger'n a Mouse. That Baby come way too early Somebody said. Oh poor thing. I kept a'squeezing Miss Gusa's hand, Papa said. I guess I was trying to bring her back to Life to see her Baby and think she give me just one little squeeze back but I never could be sure she did or not. Miz Choat stood that little Baby up in her hands just gurgling and grunting and a'fighting to get him a breath and then Miz Choat said Somebody run get me something to wrap this Baby up in and fore anybody else could do it Why Mister Choat took his coat and shirt off and Miz Choat wrapped that Baby up in em and then she put that tiny little Fella to her Heart and it looked to me like it just went right on in her. And then Miz Cooper I think it was said Oh Hattie that Baby wadn't in his Momma long nough to live. He's a Wet Lung for sure. People went to nodding at that and Papa heard some Man behind him say Hell that baby ain't big nough to bait a Fish Hook on. I didn't want Miss Gusa hearing nothing like that Papa said, so I reached over and covered her ears up with my hands even though I knowed she was already Dead and Gone Forever.

Then Miz Choat looked at all the People gathered round and said This Baby here come to us out of the Dark Night through his poor dead Mother for reasons I do not know and may not never know but I am here and now claiming him for my own and if anybody against it say it to me now otherwise I xpect you to be a good Friend and a good Neighbor to him all the days a'his Life and me and Mister Choat gonna raise him up to be the same to you all the days a'yours. Hattie, some woman started to say but Miz Choat cut her right off, Papa said. No Ma'am, she said, No Ma'am I will not hear this Baby was born too early to live, she said. I will not hear it. You come out to our Farm ten years from now when he's out there in the field a'stacking hay with Mister Choat and you tell me then he ain't a'gonna live. I didn't mean nothing by it the Woman said, Papa said. I know it, Miz Choat said. Then somebody else said You and Mister Choat raise him up like you said Hattie and we'll be his Aunt and his Uncle and his Cousin and his Friend and we'll all give a hand if Uh if. I just said he was gonna live, Miz Choat said, then she come over and pulled the coverings back to show me that itty-bitty little Baby Boy in her hand then whispered to my ear I don't know why you was chose to be the Bringer but you was. Then, Papa said, Miz Choat reached over and took my hand out from Miss Gusa's and touched it to that little Baby's chest and I seen under all the mess a Birthmark Bird with wings a'flying out his tiny little Heart.

MISTER CHOAT NAILED A WOOD BOX TOGETHER

and we put Miss Gusa in it and buried her right there next to Gilbert Lee on the Choat Farm, Papa said. But fore that, he said, Miz Choat and some neighbor Ladies stretched Miss Gusa's dead body out on the kitchen table and give it a good Soap Bath under a bed sheet where couldn't nobody see nothing. Reason I was there was Miz Choat said I was the only one could hold that little Baby and not no one other. By then she'd put three socks one inside the other then stuck Bird right down the middle to keep him warm as he could be. Bird that's what I called him for that Birthmark Bird he had coming out his Heart, Papa said, and in just a little while Why everbody else was calling him Bird too for the same thing. Well, Miz Choat said, I guess he just named his self with that Birthmark didn't he. Oh but he was little, Papa said, one lady a'washing Miss Gusa's body took her ring off and slid it all the way up Bird's arm past his elbow. Well she said, Papa said, Look a'here I never seen a human arm that small nor a human being neither one and for that Miz Choat give her a bad look and said Put your ring back on your finger Louise and keep it there we ain't a'gonna start doing tricks with him. And a'course all this time Bird was just there in my hands breathing so hard and fast as a little steam engine huh a'huh a'huh a'huh like that but faster and they wadn't nothing to do bout it Bird was just trying to clear all the water or whatever it was outta his little lungs Miz Choat said, so he could breathe. And they was two more things too, Papa said. One, Bird's eyes was still growed shut and Two, his Face went kind a'sideways like somebody maybe stepped on him one time. And maybe somebody did, he said. Maybe it was even Old Karl done it when he was arguing with Miss Gusa bout having a Baby anyhow and he just might a'put her to the floor in a fight and stomped on her belly. I wouldn't put it pass him, Papa said, but I can't say for sure he did it or not.

People came from all over Pleasant Valley to Miss Gusa's Funeral though not a single one of them except Papa even knew her name or what she had looked like in life. Miz Choat thought it was right that they came since in a way they had all more or less adopted Bird the night before same as she and Mister Choat had and didn't that make them a kind of Kinfolk too? Yes she thought it did, she said.

Somebody fetched o'Reverend Skeen from Cranes Mill, Papa said, and he preached a Goodbye Service over Miss Gusa. I don't remember everthing he said, he said, but I do remember he said One minute you are here and the next minute you are not here so Listen here Mister you better make Hay while the Sun is a'shining and then everbody looked round at everbody else and nodded back and forth like that was the truest thing they ever did hear in they Life. And I did too, Papa said.

That night Miz Choat set in her chair with Bird in her lap, Papa said, while Mister Choat and Herman and me just set there listening to Bird a'making all them Bad Noises with his fast breathing. And then all a sudden, he said, it started a'slowing down. Oh and in a minute you couldn't hardly hear but a breath ever now and then and then Oh you couldn't hear none at all and Miz Choat's eyes went to blinking back the tears cause she thought and I thought and we all thought we had maybe just lost our little Bird for ever, Papa said and we just set there like we was froze to solid Ice and then a tear come a'leaking down Miz Choat's face and she said to me I want you to reach down in this sock and tell me this dear little Baby here is still alive and breathing. Can you do that for me, she said, can you please please tell me he is still alive and breathing please. So I reached over and put my finger down the sock and give Bird just a little wiggle on his belly, Papa said, and then Miz Choat said Well? with just her eyes and Mister Choat and Herman went still as a rock watching me for a Sign. I wiggled my finger on Bird's belly again but didn't get nothing back and I guess my eyes said No I think he's done gone to Miz Choat cause she all but broke down but then I wiggled my finger on Bird's little belly again and then I wiggled it again one more time and then Oh. Oh then my little Half-Brother down there in the sock put his finger to mine and give it just a little wiggle back and I went to smiling for Joy same as Miz Choat started doing and then Mister Choat and Herman both come over and put they hand on that little Baby down in the Sock same as me and Miz Choat and then here we all went to laughing and crying both at the same time and you couldn't hardly tell one from the other.

WADN'T BUT A SINGLE DAY LATER

Papa said, and here come Old Karl a'riding up to the Choats on his Horse with a pistol to his belt. He Helloed the House and we all come out on the front porch, Miz Choat a'holding Bird up under her apron to where couldn't nobody see him. My Wife's here ain't she, Old Karl said. Yes she is here and she is here to stay, Mister Choat said. Same as these two Boys. We was they Family now, Papa said and I seen Mister Choat was ready to fight for us if he had to. Maybe even die for us but Old Karl he never even give me and Herman a look. I'd like to visit my Wife, Old Karl said, then we can have our talk bout them Boys there. Miz Choat give him an eye hot nough to burn a hole through a saddle blanket with. Go get your Shovel you wanna see your Wife she said. She's buried just over yonder in the ground. And as for these Boys here they're Choats now in ever way they can be cept in Name only and we just this minute had us all the Conversation bout em we ever gonna have from now to Kingdom Come. I seen the Snake Eyes come over Old Karl and I guess Mister Choat did too cause he stepped over in front a'Miz Choat to protect her from Old Karl if he had to and if he could. You ride on off Karl same way you come, he said. Your Wife she's dead and buried and these Boys here best I can tell don't want no more to do with you. It's all over and done with and let's not have no fuss bout it. I'll fuss you to god dam Hell and back, Old Karl said then put his weight to the stirrup and made to get off his Horse, Papa said, but just then somebody said Morning Karl and then somebody else did too and then we all looked over yonder behind Old Karl and maybe twelve or so Neighbors come a'walking out a'the Brush with they Bird and Squirrel Guns and they Hats pulled down tight on they heads. It was Mister Eickenhoff then I think it was, Papa said, who said What's a'going on here is it Trouble or is it a Visit? Your say which it is Karl, Old Man Tatum said, then we'll see where it goes from there huh. They didn't scare Old Karl a lick, Papa said, and he give em a smile and the Snake Eyes both at once. I come for my Wife and Boys and I reckon a Husband and a Father got ever right in the World, he said. Miz Choat looked over at Herman and said Herman run get me that sack I put down there at the back door and Herman went off to do what he was told then Miz Choat stepped off the porch and went over to look up at Old Karl there a'Horseback and I just naturally went with her, Papa said, but Old Karl no more give me a look than before. You say you want your Boys, Miz Choat said up to Old Karl on his Horse, You want this one here too? Oh and then, Papa said, she come out from under her apron with Bird in her hand and pulled the sock down to show Old Karl Bird's tiny little blue sideways Face no biggern some peach

69

you might pull off a tree somewheres. Oh and then Old Karl bent down from his saddle to have him a look at Bird and when he did Oh the Snake Eyes just went right off his face like somebody'd wiped em with a wet rag. I don't no way claim whatever that is there as my own he said, Papa said. Then Herman give Miz Choat the sack she wanted him to go get for her and she said Nor this neither I don't reckon then pulled the bloody dress Miss Gusa'd died in outta the sack and throwed it up in Old Karl's face. Oh, Papa said, that took the starch right out a'Old Karl and he put that dress to the ground like it was a Snake gonna bite him then kicked his heels to his Horse and went to galloping off through the Neighbors but then Old Man Tatum Hoohaaed him when he passed and that was the biggest mistake that Man ever made in his Life, Papa said, cause Old Karl looked back to see who it was Hoohaaed him and when he seen it was Old Man Tatum done it why he put him down on his List long with all them others he was gonna get Even with some day.

Including me and Herman now too I reckoned, Papa said.

IF EVER WAS A LADY PUT HER SELF TO A PURPOSE

Papa said, Why it was Miz Choat a'looking after little Baby Bird. Oh she'd set there all day and all night just a'petting his face didn't matter was it his good side or his sideways side, he said, both was Beautiful to her. Course Bird's eyes stayed shut like somebody's storm doors but even if he couldn't see a thing he always knowed when somebody stepped up to give him a Look cause he'd raise his hand like he wanted to say Hidy and be they Friend and some People'd wanna say Hello back and be his Friend but they was others couldn't barely stand to look at him cause his one eye and one ear maybe wadn't xactly in the right place on his head and they'd just turn round and go right on back Home. I helped Miz Choat all I could, Papa said. I was the one to mix the Cow Milk and Warm Water with just a drop a'Bee Honey and Miz Choat would stick her finger in it then let it drip off the end to Bird's mouth. I guess I got to be pretty good help, Papa said, cause one day Miz Choat told Mister Choat she thought her and Bird needed a Butler to get along and just wadn't no better one round than the one a'standing right here in front a'her and that was me. So after that, he said, Mister Choat'd

. . . then pulled the bloody dress Miss Gusa'd died in outta the sack and throwed it up in Old Karl's face.

take Herman with him ever morning to do the Farming and whatnot and I'd stay home and Butler Miz Choat and Bird. I liked it, Papa said, first time I ever was part of a Family all working together to make do.

Papa slept on a pallet at Miz Choat's feet so he'd be right there should she need anything at all in the middle of the night and when she needed to visit the Outhouse she'd trust Bird to him and go on out and then Bird would reach his hand up to Papa and Papa would put his face down to him so Bird could touch it and see Papa in his way. Oh Bird could see good as you and me, Papa said. But just not with his two eyes. Here's the proof, he said. If I was to reach to poke Bird on his Belly Why his hand'd be there fore mine would. Same thing with his Chin or his Nose or that Birthmark Bird on his chest, his hand'd be right there where I was thinking to poke him even fore I could do it. One day I said to Miz Choat Ain't that funny him able to do that, Papa said, and then Miz Choat said Don't tell nobody but I think Bird's learning to read off the Future and see what's a'coming. Oh she could get Spooky when it come to Bird, Papa said. And then she really did get Spooky when People went to seeing all kind a'different birds on that one little Birthmark Bird there over Bird's Heart. One person'd say Look a'there at that Dove a'cooing but another one'd say No that's a Mocking Bird see how it's a'flying home and then somebody else'd say Put your glasses on your face Maydell that's one a'them awful o'Blue Jays then somebody else'd say No that's a Song Bird cause I can hear her a'singing. Oh People seen ever Bird they was to see on the Earth right there on top a'Bird's Heart. Wrens and Sparrows and Bob White's Quail and Meadow Larks and Kill Dees and Wild Turkey and you just couldn't hardly name a Bird somebody or other didn't up and see, Papa said. Even Owls and Red Tail Hawks and some o'Ocean Birds but they couldn't never think a'the names. And, he said, the more Birds people seen there on Bird's Birthmark the more People they was a'coming to take a look for they selves and Miz Choat got to where she didn't like it a bit. I'm the one told Louise we wadn't gonna do tricks with him, she said, but now look I got a regular Medicine Show going on here. You know what I think, she said. No I don't know what you think, Papa said. I think you and me oughta sneak off down to the Colony with Bird and see what o'Jeffey got to say bout all this, she said. Oh Boy Hidy, Papa said.

People went to seeing all kind a'different birds on that one little Birthmark Bird . . .

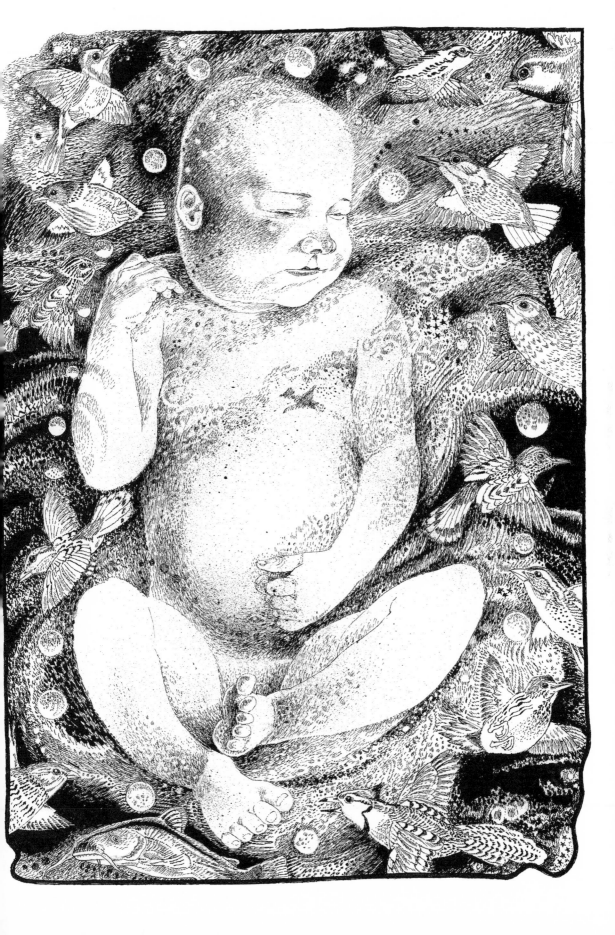

O'JEFFEY SEEN A FISH NOT A BIRD

Papa said, and Miz Choat was really put out bout it too. Now Jeffey, she said, everbody in the World look at Bird's Birthmark there and don't see nothing but Birds and here you go to seeing a Fish. A big one, o'Jeffey said, great big one, big as some o'Train a'coming through. See here it is, she said and went round Bird's Birthmark with her finger and for just a minute there, Papa said, I really did see a big Fish my self. Now Jeffey please, Miz Choat said, that ain't no Big Fish that's some o'Mother Hen a'setting on her Chicks. See, she said, then went round Bird's Birthmark with her finger and for just a minute I seen clear as day that Mother Hen setting on her Chicks she was talking bout, he said. Then Miz Choat squinted her eyes and give me a look. How bout you, she said. Tell o'Jeffey here you see the Mother Hen but not no Big Fish. I was a smart nough Boy to know I was in trouble which ever one I seen, Papa said, but when I went to looking at Bird's Birthmark I didn't see neither one. Well? Miz Choat said. I don't see no Fish, Papa said, but I don't see no Setting Hen neither. Well I swear Miz Choat said, don't see no Setting Hen. I reckon the whole World just up and gone Blind huh. And just at that second o'Jeffey give a fast look over her shoulder at some Ghost we couldn't see and said You stop poking me hear, I get to you when I'm ready to get to you—or maybe not get to you at all you keep a'foolin wit me. Hear. Then she looked at me, Papa said, and said Don't see no Big Fish huh, don't see no Setting Hen. Well Boy what do you see. Papa looked and he saw a bird running across the ground with his head and beak stretched way out in front of him and his long tail feathers stretched way out in back. Course it ain't nothing but a Road Runner Papa said, yall don't see him running through the Cactuses here. A Road Runner, Miz Choat said, you see a Road Runner. That's bad as seeing some big o'Fish, she said. O'Jeffey brushed somebody's invisible hand off her shoulder then smiled and reached down to tickle Bird under his little sideways chin but his hand was there before hers. Yall know what I think, o'Jeffey said. I think Mister Bird here is maybe a Mirra. You say a Mirror. Miz Choat said. Yes'm a Mirra, a Magic Mirra cause everbody who look at Bird see something different in that Birthmark from what everbody else see. Well that just ain't possible, Miz Choat said, everbody looking at the same thing. Looking ain't Seeing, Hattie, o'Jeffey said. I think what we got here is People look at Bird but don't see nothing but what they already got there inside they self. Now ain't that something, she said, ain't it. I see some Big o'Fish cause that xactly what I am. Big o'Fish a'swimming round in Spirit Water while everbody else a'walking round on everday land, that's me ain't it. Well ain't it. Miz Choat thought bout it a minute, Papa said, then got this funny look. Well you know they just might be some Truth in what you say Jeffey, she said. Me I never wanted nothing in this Life but looking after my little Baby Gilbert Lee. She went to blinking then, Papa said, and I knowed she was missing her little dead Baby over there in his Grave next to Miss Gusa. Well you got Bird now Miz Choat, Papa said, and you got me and Herman too ain't you. Yes I do Miz Choat said, got all three a'you now don't I, then brought Bird up to her face and give him a smile and a kiss and a hug. O'Jeffey laughed. Well now look a'there, she said, ain't that some o'Mother Hen for you. Then she looked over at me, Papa said, and said Course you still too little to know what that Road Runner you got in you is all bout But o'Road Runner he that Bird that just go to running on the ground here to there, there to here and even when he do fly it ain't hardly up off the ground. He just a Ground Bird ain't he and maybe that what the Inside You is trying to tell the Outside You that you just a Ground Bird. I don't know nothing bout being no Ground Bird, Papa said. Oh I reckon it just mean you gonna be a'running round in the Thorny Cactuses all your whole Life that's all. And gonna get poked a few times too I reckon, she said.

*T*HAT BOY I SEEN FIRST TIME I was ever over to o'Jeffey's was standing out there in front a'the house petting o'Molly when we come out to go Home, Papa said, o'Jeffey a'follering right long behind swatting at Spirits same way some body else might swat at Flies. Yonder that's my Granson Marcellus, o'Jeffey said. Marcellus, she said, bring yourself over to here an have a peek at this little bitty Baby Miz Choat got in her basket. Miz Choat pulled the covers back so Marcellus could have his peek, Papa said, and when he did his mouth made a big O on his face cause he never seen a human being so small in all his Life. Would it hurt I touched him, he said. No go ahead, Miz Choat said, just don't go to poking around on him. Marcellus reached to touch his finger to Bird's Nose, Papa said, and I thought sure Bird'd beat him there with his hand but No, he said, Bird let him touch his Nose then reached up and grabbed a'holt a'Marcellus' Finger. Oh and that made Marcellus smile, Papa said, and did me too and me and Marcellus couldn't help but grin at each other for it and I reckon in that Grin was our Friendship made though I didn't have no idea of such a thing at the time, he said. Why Marcellus I think that Baby already done like you, o'Jeffey said, look at him just a'holding on to your Finger there like some o'Snapping Turtle. Oh Yes Ma'am, Marcellus said then, Papa said, he reached down with his other hand to tickle Bird up under his chin and Bird grabbed a'holt a'that Finger too and helt on tight. Well just look at that, Miz Choat said, just one a'your Fingers ain't nough for Bird he wants the both of em don't he. Marcellus made like he was gonna pull his Fingers away, Papa said, but Bird wouldn't have it and just helt on to em for dear Life with Marcellus a'smiling down at him then Marcellus kind a'fell off in a Dream where he wadn't seeing nothing or nobody in the World but that little bitty Baby there a'holding on tight to his Fingers. I swear Marcellus, Miz Choat said, look like to me this Baby just wanna hang on to you from now to a week after Kingdom Come. Okay wit me if he do, Marcellus said, then Bird let go his Fingers and Marcellus got his hands back, Papa said, and then right quick he put em deep down in his pockets like he was hiding some Secret he just latched on to tween him and Bird.

PAPA RODE O'MOLLY BACK HOME

alongside Miz Choat and Bird in the buggy. O'Jeffey something ain't she, Papa said. You really think Bird is some kind a'Magic Mirra like she said. Well, Miz Choat said, o'Jeffey is just saying one Person look at Bird don't see nothing but a Pretty Baby, another Person look and might just see some o'ugly thing. Which one they see all depends on what they got in they self in the first place. Cept Marcellus, Papa said, I think he just sees a Friend. Like you huh, Miz Choat said. I reckon, Papa said and was glad of it, then he said I think Bird give him a Secret and Marcellus went and put it way down in his pocket. Yes Sir I seen that myself, Miz Choat said. I think they's something special going on tween them two. You notice them talking back and forth to one another the whole time Bird was a'holding his Finger, she said, but Papa shook his head No and said How they gonna do that, Bird ain't got him one Word yet that I know of. Well you don't know what a

Miracle is then, Miz Choat said, do you. It's something happens but can't no way happen, Papa said, that's what it is. So I don't guess you never seen a Miracle in your whole Life huh, Miz Choat said. No Ma'am, Papa said, Not never. Well Hon, she said, what you think this is you and me and Bird is a'riding through right now this very minute. If them Clouds and them Trees and that Hill yonder and you and me a'talking back and forth like this ain't no Miracle well then you just go on and tell me what one is. Papa thought about it a minute then said, No Ma'am can't do it. No Sir you can't do it, Miz Choat said. We all moving through one big Miracle here ever second a'our Life ain't we and don't you never let nobody tell you nothing other. Wadn't for Miracles like you and this little Baby here Why I'd go stark raving mad in this Life, she said.

*F*IRST THING WE SEEN WHEN WE GOT HOME Papa said, was Mister Choat a'laying up on the porch all whupped to a Frazzle. And not only that, he said, but Herman was gone. Miz Choat said one Word and I knowed she was dead right. Old Karl, she said, then went to running with Bird over to her husband. Oh Mister Choat he was a Bloody Bloody Mess his nose all broke on his face and his lips a'puffed up like pork sausages and his ribs broke so bad he couldn't even get his self up on his elbows. Where's my Brother Herman at. Papa said. Old Karl gone off to the Farm with him. He tried, Mister Choat said, but Herman said No Sir I'm a'staying right here where I am and not me nor my Little Brother neither one is ever going back Home with you. I'm your Daddy and you'll do what I say do, Mister Choat said Old Karl said, then he said Herman said, You had your chance to be a Daddy but you was mean and used us near to death instead and then you run our Momma off the place too and this here is what comes of it. I wadn't in it up to now, Mister Choat said, just listening and a'standing by. I was so proud a'Herman, Papa said, talking like Mister Choat said to Old Karl. Course Old Karl give him the Snake Eyes for it then quicker'n you'd think a big man could do it reached out and grabbed Herman up by the hair and went for the wagon with him just a'hollering. I said Karl you'll not go nowheres with that Boy, Mister Choat said, and when Old Karl didn't even slow down a lick I jumped on his back and pried Herman a'loose and told him to take off a'running then went to boxing Old Karl's ears hard and fast as I could. Oh Miz Choat was just a'crying cause she knowed what was coming next, Papa said. And then, Mister Choat said, Old Karl give a turn and I went a'flying then here he come and grabbed me up like a sack a'beans and went to work on me. Then Mister Choat looked up at Miz Choat and said Hattie I'm sorry Wadn't nothing I could do with him. Miz Choat touched her hand to his face and then kissed him on his cheek, Papa said, and said Oh my Darling Dear you set Herman free of that Monster is what you done and look a'here what all it cost you in the way of a Beating. Don't matter a shuck, Mister Choat said, I can grow me new skin and bone same as the next man but by god he didn't get Herman did he. No Sir by god he did not, he said, No Sir. I could see Beating or No Beating Mister Choat was proud to have saved Herman and I said Thank You, Papa said. I said Thank You for Herman and Thank You for me both then, he said, I asked him Which way was Herman a'running when he left the Country and Mister Choat pointed and said Yonder way and I reckon he's a'running yet cause it looked ever bit like his Pants was on Fire when last I seen him.

*I*T TOOK SOME DOING
but we finally got Mister Choat in the house and Miz Choat went to doctoring on him and I went to changing Bird's messed pants and making him some suppers with the milk and Bee Honey but all this time I couldn't think a'one thing but going off to find my Brother Herman and be with him. But Miz Choat said You don't have to worry about Herman he's a Big Boy and can make do on his own. No, she said, what we got to worry about is what if Old Karl comes back to here and wants to take it up again and Mister Choat his ribs so broke up he can't even rise from his bed. Well, Papa said, fetch me down Mister Choat's Bird Gun and I'll stand Guard at the winder. Oh now Hon, Miz Choat said, I'd never in this World ask you to shoot your own Daddy. No you just look after Little Mister Bird there and I'll pepper Old Karl myself if he's fool nough to come a'calling again.

Miz Choat pulled a chair to the winder and loaded up Mister Choat's double-barrel Bird Gun. I reckon I can get us a tail-feather or two with this if I have to don't you, she said. I knowed she was trying to say something funny cause she knowed I was scared, Papa said. And I was. They just wadn't nothing Old Karl wouldn't do once he put his Snake Eyes on you.

Papa pulled a little table up beside Miz Choat at the winder then set Bird in his basket on it where Miz Choat could put her hand on him whenever she wanted. Which was pretty much all the time, he said. Then Papa brought her a glass of warm milk from the stove and pulled a chair up beside her for himself. It was a Moon Night, he said, and they was so many shadows I thought I seen Old Karl a'creeping round tween the trees moren a hundred and fifty times but No it was just my eyes a'playing tricks. I think Miz Choat's eyes was doing the same thing cause ever once in a while she'd go to turning her head this way and that and putting her nose to the winder and a'holding on to that Bird Gun like it was somebody's Pet Dog. One time we heard Mister Choat make a groan and she went in there to check on him and I got to thinking Oh Mister and Miz Choat they so close to one another and care so much what happens to each other and my Momma and Old Karl never did, Papa said, so when Miz Choat come back to set down and take up the Bird Gun again I asked her how she xplained that, he said. Can't nobody xplain it, she said. That just the o'human Heart for you. Not never no telling where it might jump up and go. Sometime don't go nowhere at all, just set there like some o'Possum don't know if it's alive or dead. Another time might fly around everwhere they is like some o'crazy Bug and land on ever tree they is or maybe just on that one most special tree in the World and no other. That's the Lucky Heart. Only the Lucky Heart can do that, Miz Choat said. Only the Lucky Lucky Heart. That what you got I asked her, Papa said. The Lucky Heart. Miz Choat nodded. First time ever I did see Mister Choat my Heart just went in a Beeline to him. Bzzzz like that. Never seen the man before in my Life. Never met the man, didn't have no idea was he a Good Man or a Tin Horn Jackass or what but my Heart knowed, said Well Hattie there he is You see him and I said Oh Yes I do see him I do I do. So my Lucky Heart landed in just that one tree for all my Life and that's what I wish for you when your Heart goes to looking around for a tree to land in, she said and then I asked her Why was it my Momma's Heart landed in Old Karl's tree. I don't know why Hon, she said. Nature a'her people was to jump outta the nest pretty much fore you could fly. Just burning up to get out there in the World and go to Living. All the Criers was like that I'm told. Imagine the idea a'even coming to a place like Texas back in them old days anyhow Why everthing here was trying to eat you up, Miz Choat said. Inyins—Mexkins—Wild Animals. Wooo not me. No Sir, yall get it all settled up then post me a letter and maybe I'll come on down then that's what I say. But your Momma and her people—your people—was the Bark off the original Texas Tree and I think, she said, what happened to your Momma was she flew the coop fore her Heart had time to grow any Sense about what tree to land in so she just landed in the first one she come to and that was your sorry o'Daddy. No your Momma didn't have no Lucky Heart, she said. Course she was just fourteen years age and they's some might say that's right on the falling off edge a'being too young to marry anyhow. Me included but then I was a full sixteen before I ever married. Then, Papa said, Miz Choat cocked the Bird Gun and started whispering. Hon she whispered. Yes Ma'am I whispered back, Papa said. Let's us just set here real quiet now cause I see somebody a'moving yonder through the trees. And they a'moving this way, she said.

*M*IZ CHOAT PUT HER ARM ROUND ME

and I leaned to the winder and Oh Yes I seen that same Somebody she seen moving one tree to the next coming at us and no doubt about it, Papa said. He was a big thick man wearing a Farmer's Hat and Froze Ice went right up my back at the sight cause I knowed it was Old Karl come to fetch me in Herman's place. He's gonna get me I said, Papa said. And I tell you truly I was bout to Mess my pants at the thought of it. No Sir he most certainly ain't gonna get you, Miz Choat said, I won't let him. But now listen to me, she said, I want you to take this Darling Baby Boy here and get way up under the bed with him and don't come out for nothing. Not for nothing you hear. I said Yes Ma'am I do hear. I'm not worried and you don't be worried neither, she said, you hear me. I said Yes Ma'am I surely do. Ain't nobody in this World walking through me and this Bird Gun to get you, you know it. I said I do know it, Papa said. No matter what it is she said, I don't care even if it is General Robert E. Bob Lee his self they ain't a'coming through me. What's he doing now I said, Papa said. Miz Choat looked out the winder. He's just a'standing under that tree yonder, she said. Getting ready I reckon, maybe waiting for Sunup I don't know. Better not try to come in here at all I hope he knows, she said then looked at me and said Why ain't you and Bird in there up under that bed like I told you to. I couldn't tell her I wadn't never going up under that bed, Papa said, no moren I could tell her soon as I got my Spunk up I was going out there in the Dark and give my self over to Old Karl same way I done at Fischer so he'd leave everbody else alone and not harmed in no way especially the Choats and Bird all so dear to me, he said. And they was another reason too, Papa said, one that come a'rushing up on me and Oh it did surprise me what it was and that was Deep Down I didn't want Miz Choat to shoot my Daddy with that Bird Gun and maybe Lame him or leave him dead on the floor. No, he said, Mean as he was and Oh he was Mean and even if he was the one run both my Momma and my Brother Herman off I still didn't want no Bad End to come over him. Well Miz Choat said, are you a'going or not. I said Yes Ma'am I am a'going, Papa said, then I walked straight out the front door with her a'yelling Oh no Oh no Oh no, don't go out there Honey.

I didn't have no trouble in the Moon Light seeing him a'standing there cross the road under that tree, Papa said, I even give him a little wave to let him know I seen where he was and was coming on over. Ever step I took was bout ten years long and a couple a'times I admit I thought I might like it better to just let Miz Choat go on and shoot him with her Bird Gun but No I kept a'going, he said, then I seen Old Karl slip behind the tree but I knowed he was a'watching me ever second cause I could see his big o'Farmer's Hat a'sticking out the side a'the tree.

Boy Hidy I was scared, Papa said. I didn't have no idea what Old Karl was gonna do with me once he got me Home but I figgured he'd start off making me sleep out in the barn with the Mexkins. The only good thing might come of it, he said, was I thought I might catch sight a'Mister or Miz Pegleg trying to steal a Chicken one night if they was still up to it. I was to the tree and Old Karl went round to the other side where I couldn't even see him. I'm here I said, Papa said, but Old Karl didn't give nothing back not one Word and I thought Well maybe my eyes been a'playing tricks on me and he wadn't really never even there at all then I heard somebody a'moving round behind the tree like they was getting ready to jump out and get me. I was shaking but I kind a'brought my self up straight and said I'll go with you now but still didn't get not one Word back. I said I will go Home with you now I said, Papa said, and then here come back a voice from behind the tree that said Well I ain't a'going nowheres then who should step his self out to where I could see him in the Moon Light but o'Marcellus wearing a Farmer's Hat and Somebody's big o'coat made him look like a Bear.

O'Jeffey sent me he said.

Miz Choat was two ways bout it

Papa said. One she was glad to see Marcellus but Two she was some disappointed she didn't get to shoot Old Karl for what he done to Mister Choat. As for me, Papa said, I was so happy not to be going off with Old Karl again I could a'danced a jig on my own two bare feet. What you doing over here in the middle of the night for anyway Miz Choat said. Somebody was a'pulling on o'Jeffey the whole time you was over there wanting to tell her something, Marcellus said, but she was so busy a'talking to you she didn't pay it no tention til after yall was gone. Who was it, Miz Choat said, was it my own sweet Gilbert Lee trying to warn me. No Ma'am, Marcellus said, it was a Goose. A Goose, she said, o'Jeffey said it was a Goose tried to warn me. But I knowed who he was talking about, Papa said. It was Gusa wadn't it I said, Miss Gusa. I reckon, Marcellus said, any how o'Jeffey said Git you self over to there right quick now them People is gonna need some help and here I be. And we glad to see you Marcellus, Miz Choat said, but I do wish o'Jeffey come up with the news a little sooner, might a'saved Mister Choat that bad whupping he got. O'Jeffey say it hard to turn something away that already coming at you once it get to going, Marcellus said, then got down on his hands and knees and went to playing Finger Games with Bird in his basket, Papa said, then he looked up at Miz Choat and said Don't you worry too much about it Miz Choat, o'Jeffey say sometimes you just gotta have the Bad to chase up the Good. Oh that's what o'Jeffey said huh, Miz Choat said. Yes Ma'am she said it, Marcellus said. Well, Miz Choat said, Mister Choat's in there with his nose all smushed in and his ribs broke so I wonder did o'Jeffey give any hint a'what Good that might be a'chasing up but Marcellus had his head down in the basket and was a'blowing bubbles on Bird's belly to make him laugh and didn't hear a word of it, Papa said.

Papa said No you can sleep out on the front porch with me so the mice don't go to eating on your toes.

*M*ARCELLUS SAID HE'D GO FIND A PLACE TO SLEEP in the barn if he was allowed to but Papa said No you can sleep out on the front porch with me so the mice don't go to eating on your toes. I was still too little to see the harm in it, he said, and I wadn't xactly clear yet on how the World worked neither. We got down on my pallet and I just couldn't help myself and went to asking questions, Papa said. O'Jeffey really been talking to Miss Gusa, I said. Oh Yes Sir ain't nothing to it, Marcellus said, o'Jeffey she always talking back and forth like that to Somebody in them other Rooms. What other Rooms is that, Papa said. Well here now, Marcellus said, o'Jeffey say it work this way. We all in the same House but just in different Rooms is all. The Live Peoples is a'living in Rooms over here and the Dead Peoples is a'living in Rooms over there and they some people like o'Jeffey can talk back and forth tween the walls easy as you and me a'talking here. Wonder if they's anybody in one a'them other Rooms can tell me anything bout my Momma, Papa said. What's wrong with your Momma, Marcellus said. Nothing I know of I said, Papa said. I just don't know where she's at or my Brother Herman neither one. Well, Marcellus said, o'Jeffey say whatever you a'looking for in this World is somewheres out there in the World a'looking for you too. Papa felt a little wave of Joy pass over him at the idea that his Mother was looking for him just as hard as he was looking for her. You reckon that's so, he said. I don't have no reason not to reckon it's so, Marcellus said. But he said, Papa said, o'Jeffey said you got to be careful cause what you a'looking for is surely gonna pop up in front a'you one a'these days an when it does it just might not be xactly what you thought you was a'looking for in the first place.

*N*EXT MORNING ME AND MARCELLUS did all the Chores, Papa said, fed the Chickens and gathered the Eggs, run the Rats outta the corn bin, milked the Cow, slopped the Hogs, turned the Horses and Mule out to pasture and the Calves with they Mommas too, talked to o'Molly a minute and give her a pet or two, shoveled a Pile a'Horse Do outta the stall, then closed up everthing behind us and went out on the front porch to eat our bread and butter with Bee Honey on it. Wadn't but a few minutes and here come Miz Choat out to give Bird a neckid Sun Bath in the yard. Oh he was growing ever single day, Papa said, and you had to think back some to remember when he was Blue all over but, he said, poor little Fella still couldn't get his eyes open even a crack though there was his Eyeballs a'rolling round like marbles behind his lids. Marcellus, Miz Choat said after she'd let Bird take the Sun a bit, maybe you'd like to hold Bird here a minute or two. Oh you couldn't a'knocked the smile off Marcellus' face with a sledge hammer at that, Papa said, and then he built a Nest with his arms and made Bird a Home and course wadn't two seconds later and Bird had a'holt a'his Finger and I seen Miz Choat just a'smiling to see them two in they Friendship like that. Marcellus, she said, me and Mister Choat been talking this morning and we think if you'd like to stay on here for a time and you two Boys work the Farm while Mister Choat's a'getting healed up Why then we'd be glad to have you. Oh Yes Ma'am, Marcellus said, I been planning on a'staying here the rest a'my Life anyhow.

That was news to Miz Choat, Papa said, and she raised an eyebrow at him. Well Marcellus, she said, I'm glad you told me I wouldn't wanna run outta bread and butter on you. Oh No Ma'am, Marcellus said and give her a Thank You look, Papa said, then went back to letting Bird squeeze his Fingers. Miz Choat watched a minute, Papa said, then she said Marcellus is that Little Baby talking to you? Oh Yes Ma'am he is, Marcellus said. Well don't hog the information just for yourself Marcellus, she said, tell us what he's a'saying. Oh No Ma'am, Marcellus said, he wouldn't want me to yet.

OON AFTER THAT

Papa said, Bird grew him the funniest little Smile you ever did see that run straight cross his face then curled up at both ends like somebody's big o'mustache. Oh and he could make it curl and uncurl one end at a time like somebody a'winking they eyes. Miz Choat took Bird to show Mister Choat but it like to a'killed him it hurt so bad to laugh with them broke ribs he had. It was such a good Smile, Papa said, you just couldn't look at Bird and not feel good and happy no matter what was your troubles. And Oh, he said, I did so wish my Momma and my Brother Herman both could a'got a good dose a'that Smile though they was no where round to be seen or heard. Miss Gusa too, Papa said, but if Marcellus was right bout ever body being in the same House then maybe Bird was smiling through the walls at my Momma ever day and making her feel better. Oh and the people who come to look at the Birds flying out a'his Birthmark just couldn't get nough a'his Smile too and fore long his little sideways face all but disappeared to they eyes for the Smile.

Bird is a Blessing to us all, Miz Choat said one evening at the supper table when he was big nough to feed off a spoon. He is a Blessing come to us out of the Dark, she said, then reached over and touched my cheek. And so are you who brung him, she said then reached over and squeezed Marcellus' hand. And so are you a Blessing Marcellus, she said, for now and always ever. Marcellus just looked down in his plate, Papa said, but he was shining at the Words. Then, Papa said, Miz Choat said Mister Choat, and Mister Choat said from the bedroom Yes Miz Choat I hear you, and she said Mister Choat You are the biggest Blessing to me in all my Life and he said back to her And you are to me in all a'mine too Miz Choat.

O'JEFFEY COME A'RIDING UP ON HER MULE one day, Papa said, and me and Marcellus helped slide her on off to the ground so that poor creature could stand up straight from all the pounds. Marcellus you been a'minding your self over here, she said. Oh Yes Ma'am I sure has, he said, and Oh Yes Ma'am he sure has I said right behind him, Papa said, then Miz Choat come out of the house with Bird in her hand. A surprise and a pleasure both to see you Jeffey, she said then just naturally give Bird over to Marcellus. Maybe not no pleasure, o'Jeffey said, then Papa said Miz Choat could see they was something wrong and said Well why don't we find us a shady spot to set in if they's something you wanna talk about. Yes Ma'am Miz Choat they is o'Jeffey said, Papa said, so we went over and set on the edge a' the front porch. Maybe you'd like a glass a'Grape Juice from the vines down yonder on Dry Creek, Miz Choat said. Well that's the trouble Miz Choat, o'Jeffey said, you being so good to offer Grape Juice and I hear it Marcellus been a'sleeping out on the Front Porch with this Boy here and a'eating in the house both. Why yes that's true Jeffey, Miz Choat said. Well we can't have it no longer Miz Choat, she said, White People round here is a'getting to think we think we good as they is and when the Paying Work come around they ain't gonna be a penny's worth for me and mine.

Miz Choat set her jaw and said, Now Jeffey I won't hold back on an ordinary everday Kindness to Marcellus or to anybody else just to suit some Pea Brained Ignoramus just happen to come in to this world White. Moren one Pea Brain what gots me worried, o'Jeffey said. What I won't do for one Jackass, Miz Choat said, I won't do for no ten thousand and ten other Jackasses neither. Yes'm o'Jeffey said, Papa said, but you ain't the one be a'paying the Piper neither huh. I would if I was to violate my own Heart on it, Miz Choat said, and I know you ain't a'asking me to do that are you Jeffey? O'Jeffey didn't say nothing just kept a'watching Marcellus play his Finger Game with Bird and I could see she was bout to cry, Papa said. Jeffey, Miz Choat said, you come to take Marcellus back Home with you didn't you. I had to get holt a'my self at the thought a'that, Papa said. Next to Mister Pegleg Marcellus was my Friend and I didn't have no idea where I might ever find me another one. Yes Ma'am Miz Choat, o'Jeffey said, that surely is in my mind Yes Ma'am it is. Miz Choat was bout to cry her self and said Bet everbody wondering where that Grape Juice went to I was talking about then, Papa said, Miz Choat went in the house and come out with the Grape Juice and we all had us some and all this time o'Jeffey was watching Bird work his smile back and forth one side his mouth to the other. Mister Bird he's a Smiler ain't he, she said. Now look at that, make you Smile too don't he. Yes Sir o'Bird he a Magic Mirra and a Magic Smiler both ain't he. Then, Papa said, o'Jeffey kind a'lost her own Smile and looked over at Marcellus wiggling his Finger in Bird's hand and Bird just a'holding on like they was born together. Well Marcellus, she said, look like to me I done lost you Heart and Soul over to this little Baby here and I wouldn't take that from you or him neither one. Then, Papa said, o'Jeffey went to waddling back to her Mule but Marcellus said Wait Granny then give Bird over to Miz Choat and went with o'Jeffey to help her back on her Mule and they said they Goodbyes and give each other a hug and then she rode on off her poor o'Mule bout to fall over from the pounds ever step he took.

*A*ND FROM THEN ON
Papa said, a whole World was made round Bird and Marcellus and they was the only ones in it. Why if Marcellus come in the door from outside some-

where, he said, Bird was already a'reaching up for him from his basket and his little Smile would start a'going side to side fast as a Whip Saw. I never seen nothing like it, Mister Choat said when he was up and round and out and bout again. It wadn't that Bird didn't pay no attention to the rest a'us, Miz Choat said, it was just that what him and Marcellus had tween em Why they just wadn't no Word for it. Course some people who come over to find they special bird in Bird's Birthmark Bird didn't like it worth a bean, Papa said. I won't name her, he said, but they was this one woman said Listen Hattie I don't know bout you letting that little Nigger Boy there get so close to Bird, he gonna grow up to thinking they ain't a lick a'difference tween em. Oh, Miz Choat said, I'm afraid it's done too late, the Great Lord God Almighty His self already done give him that idea.

Then one day, Papa said, Mister Choat come back from Fischer with a letter in his hand for me. It was from Herman and we all gathered round to see what he said. He said, Papa said, Here I am and am okey-dokey. How are you and ever body else Good I hope. Guess what I seen Momma's Horse today but wadn't Momma riding her. Please Do not tell our Daddy about me here. Herman. Momma's Horse, Papa said. Momma's Horse Precious right there where Herman is and maybe Momma too but No he didn't say one word more bout her.

Papa asked Miz Choat if she could tell from Herman's letter where he was and she looked at the postmark and said Herman mailed his letter from New Braunfels Texas and he is either there or was just passing through. Well I said, Papa said, I have to go see if my Momma is in New Braunfels Texas. If Precious is there Why she must be there too. Oh now Hon, Miz Choat said. No I have to go I said, Papa said, I don't care even if it is on the Moon. Yes he has to go, Mister Choat said, you don't want him being sorry all his Life he didn't. Yes I know you are right Miz Choat said but it breaks my Heart for him to go then she hugged me tight and said You are a Road Runner ain't that what you told o'Jeffey. A Road Runner he goes Here to There, Here to There remember. I said Yes I do remember, Papa said. Well she said If you can go Here to There, Here to There then you can go There to Here, There to Here just as easy too so you please come on back to us with your Brother and your Momma both or just by yourself if such is the result of your trip.

Early next morning I give Bird a Goodbye Kiss on his nose and when I did, Papa said, he reached up and took a'holt a'my ear and it didn't look to me like he was ever gonna let it go so I said Now Mister Bird you be a good Boy and let go a'my ear and then he did and Miz Choat picked him up and her and me went out to the pen where Mister Choat and Marcellus was a'waiting with o'Molly and a sack a'eats and a map to New Braunfels Texas that Mister Choat had drawed up for me. Mister Choat shook my hand, he said, and said Careful as you go and always keep a Eye out for Trouble and I said I would then Miz Choat give me a dollar and another Goodbye Hug she had for me and I said Thank You and after that I got up on o'Molly then seen Marcellus a'looking at me. Well Marcellus I said, Papa said, and Marcellus give me a nod and said Well right back and off I went on down the road to find my Momma and Brother in New Braunfels Texas even if they was something in me already knowed I'd never in my Life find a Family better'n the one I was leaving behind me right that very minute.

*I*T WAS SLOW GOING ON O'MOLLY

Papa said, and I got to thinking bout what o'Jeffey told Marcellus and then Marcellus told me which was Sometime you get the Bad cause it's the Bad what chases up the Good. I said to myself that just might be true, Papa said. Just look, he said, here I was going off down the road to find my Momma and Brother both and all cause Old Karl had tried to grab Herman up and take him back to the Farm but No Mister Choat had jumped on his back and then Herman'd run all the way to New Braunfels Texas where he seen our Momma's Horse Precious and the only reason I was able to go try and find him and her now was cause o'Jeffey seen the Trouble coming and sent Marcellus to the Choats to give a hand and now look he is there forever to help Mister Choat at the Farming and the Chores and everthing else but even moren that there he is to be a Friend and a Brother and a Helper to Bird for all his whole Life. If I had my worries bout leaving the Choats and Bird Why they all went Woosh when Marcellus put his Roots down on the Choat Farm. So in Life one thing just naturally follers long behind another don't it, Papa said, I guess that's what I learned that day he said. Good follers Bad. Up follers Down. Night follers Day. Wet follers Dry. And then I thought a'poor o'Miss Gusa and I added Dead follers Live to my list and then I thought a'Old Karl and added Mean follers Nice. Course my list could

a'gone on forever cause everthing is always turning into something else ain't it even when you wadn't planning on it. And here's the proof a'what I just said, Papa said, I hadn't gone no moren a mile and here was this skinny little Dog wadn't nothing but skin and bones just a'setting out there in the middle a'the road with his chin to the dirt where I reckoned somebody'd just run off and left him. I got down off o'Molly and said Come on here to me you little fritz but he couldn't do no moren just set there and shiver so I picked him up and give him a good look all over and didn't see no harm to him and then I give him a hand full a'Miz Choat's corn bread and a drink a'water then stuck him in my shirt and went on off down the road with him already a'sleeping. See that's what I mean, Papa said, one minute there I was just a'riding down the road all by myself and now look a'here the next minute I got me a little Friend to take care of if he wadn't already too far gone.

I DID LIKE THAT LITTLE DOG

Papa said, and went on and named him Fritz since that was the first thing ever I called him. Soon as we got to a Creek I give him a bath and me one too while o'Molly was a'nibbling on grass all round then after that he set up in front a'me on the old hull I had for a saddle, Papa said, and I never in my Life seen a Dog no prouder. And not only that, he said, but he went to grinning bout it too and saying Heh Heh Heh like that. I don't know how he done it but ever now and then he'd be setting up there on o'Molly with me and he'd just go to grinning and saying Heh Heh Heh like some o'Loonie. He did it one morning when I was asking directions to New Braunfels Texas from some o'Farmer I seen on the road and the Farmer said Did your little Dog just talk or am I hearing Things in my head. Well I said, Papa said, I think he's trying to learn to talk but so far all he can say is Heh Heh Heh. The Farmer said Well he wadn't surprised to hear it cause he had him an o'Dog one time said Howdy Howdy Howdy to everbody he met but never got no further with it than that but he knowed all you had to do to get a Bull Frog to talk was just ask him How deep is the water in the Creek and he'd tell you Knee-deep Knee-deep Knee-deep ever time. Oh and o'Molly went to loving little Fritz ever bit much as I did, Papa said, and ever time he'd go to take a nap the o'Swayback'd sneak up on him then give him a quick push with her

I did like that little dog Papa said,
and went on and named him Fritz . . .

nose and flip him over like you would a Flapjack and then Fritz'd go to yap-ping and running round like the Sky was falling in on him. Oh it was a Laugh to see, he said, but then Fritz got smart bout it and just played Possum like he was napping and when o'Molly'd come a'sneaking up on him and reach to turn him a flip Why then o'Fritz'd jump up and bite her on the nose and then it'd be o'Molly who'd go to running round in circles and snorting like something was bout to get her. Oh I laughed til my side hurt, Papa said, and I thought I was the most lucky Boy in the World to have Friends like these two Idgits here.

*W*ADN'T BUT MAYBE THREE DAYS LATER Papa said, when I come up to this place on the River where maybe bout a hunderd People was having a Picnic and eating Watermelons. Oh I wanted me one, he said, so I rode over to where they had a stack of em and of all People on Earth there was my Brother Herman a'cutting em up in Slices with a Butcher Knife and handing em out for Money. Herman I said, Papa said, it's me your very own Little Brother and Herman said I ain't got time to talk to you right now I got to sell these Slices many as I can then Fritz looked down at him and said Heh Heh Heh then Herman looked up at him on o'Molly and said What'd that little Dog just say to me, and I said He said Heh Heh Heh. He's grinning at me too Herman said. Yes he's a Grinner I said then said where's Momma's Horse Precious at You said you seen her. Yes but just that one time and I ain't seen her since. What bout Momma. Herman shook his head No, Papa said, and I had to look off somewheres else to keep from crying. Help me sell these Watermelons, Herman said, a nickel the Slice then he reached over and give o'Molly a Hello pet and said How's the Choats and Bird but don't tell me now lets go on and sell these Melons while everbody ain't had too much to drink yet and still wants one. So, Papa said, I went to selling Watermelon Slices with Fritz a'tagging long behind. Watermelon I'd holler, Papa said, Watermelon right here you want one or not. And just bout everbody did, he said, and then when I'd hand em a Slice and they'd pay me the nickel and then Fritz'd set down right in front of em and grin and say Heh Heh Heh and they'd laugh and most ever time they'd buy another Slice just to see o'Fritz do it again and by Sun Down we had just one Slice left and me and Herman eat that one up our self then give the rine to o'Molly and after that Herman divided the Money up with the Man hired Herman to sell his Watermelons in the first place and then we went over and bought us some sausages and bread for our suppers and I give half a'mine to Fritz, Papa said. Then, he said, we all four found us a Spot down there by the Comal River where they wadn't no couples spooning and laid down on the grass to go to sleep under all them stars just a'sparkling up there in the Sky like the Nickel Conchos on my Momma's Saddle and I was just bout to get sad bout it, Papa said, when here come o'Fritz to give me a look in my face and they just wadn't no way you could stay sad with him a'grinning down at you like that and a'saying Heh Heh Heh.

OH IT WAS SO GOOD to be with my Brother Herman again, Papa said, and next morning we went riding double on o'Molly in to New Braunfels Texas. I guess you could say we went Triple, he said, if you count Fritz a'setting up there in front a'me with his chin on the saddle horn. Papa asked Herman if he was sure the Horse he seen was their Momma's and Herman said Yes couldn't a'been no other Horse in the World. Something ain't right, Papa said. If Momma was going over to see her Folks in Fayette County she'd need her Horse Precious to ride on wouldn't she. I know it, Herman said. Maybe something Bad happened to her along the way. Papa covered his ears with his hands. I don't wanna hear nothing like that, he said, you just hush up right now if that's all you got to say. No you hush up, Herman said, You ain't half big nough to boss me round yet. What, Papa said, I can't hear you.

They went back and forth like that a minute or two then decided to go to every Horse Lot and Livery in New Braunfels and ask if anybody'd seen their Momma's Horse with the Lazy S2 brand on it. First Livery we come to, Papa said, the Man thought we was there to sell o'Molly. Sorry boys, he said, you couldn't pay me to take that o'Nag or that little Pissant of a Dog neither one. They ain't for sale Mister, Herman said, and even if they was we wouldn't sell em to some o'Potbellied Jackass like you. Listen to that, Papa said, o'Herman hadn't lost none a'his sass since I last seen him but the Man didn't mind it too much and asked us what we wanted anyway and we told him we was looking for a Horse with the Lazy S2 brand on it and had he seen it and he said he seen lots a'Horses in his day but No he didn't believe he ever seen that particular one. Then he said, Papa said, What's so special bout that Horse anyhow that you're a'riding round on this o'Pile a'Bones here a'looking for it and I said It's our Momma's Horse Precious and we can't find it nor our Momma neither one. The Man took his hat off then, Papa said, and said Yes I lost my own Momma here just this last month on the Tenth and People come up to me at the Grave and said Well your Mother was ninety-three years of age wadn't she and had her a good long rich full Life didn't she and you can't ask for no moren that can you But you know what I say to that, he said, I say So the god dam Hell what if she did Live to ninety-three years of age and had her a good rich full Life a'doing it, she's still gone now ain't she. Gone forever god damit and I want her back. I want my Momma back don't matter if she lived to age six hunderd and three I want my Momma back, he said, I want her back. Oh and then, Papa said, he set down on a bucket over there by the fence and went to crying bout it and me and Herman and Fritz just kind a'slipped on away which was pretty much all you could do on the o'Swayback anyhow.

❦

*T*HEY WAS A BAND STAND RIGHT THERE in the middle a'Town, Papa said, and a Horn Band just a'tooting away up there on it for all the People standing round. And most ever one a'them had a Fat Belly, he said. Where'd all these Fat Bellies come from, Papa said, I bet any two of em'd sink a boat. That's what a Pork Sausage'll do to you, Herman said. That's all they eat round here then warsch it down with some Beer. Come on I'll show you, he said. So, Papa said, me and Herman went cross the street and they was this Saloon full a'more Fat Bellies and I set Fritz up on the bar but the Man come over and said sorry Son we don't serve no Dogs in here and I said Well he don't want nothing to drink anyhow and the Man said No that was just a little Joke I was playing on you I didn't never really think you was trying to buy a Beer for your little Dog there. And then, Papa said, Fritz grinned up at him and said Heh Heh Heh and the Man said Yes Sir everbody comes in here got em a Talking Dog don't they then Herman put a coin down and said We'll take us two Beers please and the Man said Okay but I don't want no gunplay.

So, Papa said, that was the first Beer I ever did drink in my Life and wadn't but a few minutes and that Beer wanted him a Beer too and Why then that second Beer wanted him one too and wadn't long and here the whole World just went to wobbling all over the place and the Man picked me up off the floor by the seat a'my pants then carried me outside and hung me over the hitching rail and Oh then, he said, I went to Urping up on my feet and making a puddle in the street til I was bone dry and wadn't able to do no moren go Uhhh Uhhh and make sick faces at everbody who come up to take a look at the poor little Drunk. This is a bad road you on here Son, one Man said, even your own little Dog there don't want no more to do with you. It was true, Papa said, Fritz went over and set down by o'Molly like he didn't even know me. Well, Herman said, let's go find someplace to chunk you in the River and I tell you, Papa said, that sure did sound good to me.

HERMAN DID XACTLY WHAT HE SAID

he was gonna do, Papa said, he took me out to Landa's Pasture and chunked me in the Comal River and it was so cold I shriveled up like a wad a'paper. How bout I go get you another Beer, he said, or you think you done had nough for the next twenty–thirty years or so. I splashed water at him and he jumped in then Fritz did too. We needed us a good bath anyhow, Herman said, then dove down in the water and come up with a Inyin Arra Head in his hand. Look a'here, he said, we're taking us a bath in some o'Inyin Camp ain't we. I went down to take a look, Papa said, and sure nough they was big Inyin Arra Heads just all over the place down there and something else too a'poking up outta the bottom that looked to me like a tree stump but Herman took a look and said No a tree stump don't have no teeth on it and whatever that is does. So, Papa said, they wadn't nothing to do but dig it up outta there and see what it was. So we went down under the water and started a'digging with both our hands and sticks, he said, and wadn't long and we seen Whatever It Was was upside down and had him two big long rows a'pointy teeth. What is that thing, Herman said when we come up to

get some air, I ain't never seen nothing like it. Me neither I said, Papa said and we went to trying to dig it out again and all this time Fritz and o'Molly was napping over yonder on the bank like they was on some Special Holiday then we come up outta the water again and Why here was this Cowboy a'setting there Horseback a'looking down at us. What'd you boys find down there in the mud you working so hard to get it out, he said. We told him it was something had teeth on it but we didn't have no idea What. He grabbed his rope off his saddle and give Herman the loop end and said Well tie me on and we'll take us a look. So, Papa said, me and Herman went back down under the water again and looped it round that thing then come up and give him a wave and he turned his o'hammer-headed Horse and said Heeyaa Firefoot Heeyaa Heeyaa then give him his heels and a little slap with his quirt and then Oh his Horse bent way forward and went to pulling with all his Might and Oh then here come that Whatever It Was up out the water and up on the bank. That thing's long as you and me put together, Herman said, but I don't no way know what it is. That's just his head, the Cowboy said. No telling how big the rest of him was. But what is it I said, Papa said. Why what's wrong with you Boys, he said, you don't know an antique Rock Aligater Head when you see one. I bet you that thing's least a thousand years old and maybe more yet. You don't find one a'them things ever day a'the week I can tell you that. Herman wanted to know what they should do with it and the Cowboy said he thought if we could find the right Man interested in such things Why he might buy it off us at a good price but if we just left it there on the bank somebody else was gonna come along on a Mule one day and just drag it off somewheres and also, he said, he learned his self it ain't always a good idea to go a'running off with things don't belong to you and we might consider that before somebody puts us in the Jail House or hangs us up by the neck off a tree somewheres for stealing they Aligater Head. We didn't want none a'that, Papa said, so me and Herman got it back down to where we found it and when we come back up out a'the water the Cowboy said You boys come on with me now and I'll cook you some beans for your suppers. And then he rode on off to lead the way and when he did I whispered over to Herman. Herman I whispered, Papa said, I believe I have seen that Cowboy somewheres else in my Life but I don't remember when or where it was neither one. Well then, Herman said, you still just as stupid as you ever was ain't you.

Why what's wrong with you Boys, he said,
you don't know an antique Rock Aligater
Head when you see one.

HIS NAME WAS CALLEY PEARSALL

Papa said, and to this day he cooked the best plate a'beans I ever did eat and Herman said the same thing too. Course, Papa said, I ask him right off had he seen our Momma's Horse Precious with the Lazy S2 brand on her and he said On the Right Hip is it. And me and Herman both jumped cause that was xactly where Precious had her brand on. Well yes he said I did see a Lazy S2 Horse here no moren a week or two ago. Was our Momma a'riding her, Papa said. I don't believe I know your Momma, Calley said, But No Sir wadn't nobody a'riding this Horse. She just come a'galloping out a'the Brush and run on past me like a'wiff a'smoke then stopped and throwed up her head to say Come On Boys Come On and course o'Firefoot lit out after her and there's me just a'hanging on for Dear Life and that's the whole story a'me a'getting here to New Braunfels Texas. I seen her in town myself, Herman said, then wrote my Little Brother here a letter bout it. And I come a'running I said, Papa said. He wants his Momma, Herman said. Wouldn't surprise me to see him go to crying bout it here in a minute or two. Oh I've had me many a good cry myself over one thing or another in this Life, Calley said, They ain't nothing I know of better to wash a Hurting Heart out with he said then reached over and give Fritz a roll over on his back and scratched his belly. Bet he's some kind a'Nitwit huh, he said, chases Grasshoppers and Doodle Bugs and such I reckon. You still a'looking for our Momma's Horse, Papa said. I wadn't never looking for your Momma's Horse in the first place, he said. Like I said, he said, it was more like she was a'looking for me when she come a'blowing out a'the Brush like that and got me and o'Firefoot to chasing her cross the Country. Might be she'll come a'looking for you again, Papa said. Nothing'd surprise me bout that Horse, Calley said. Never seen nothing like her. Maybe we can ride along with you, see if she does, Papa said. We got our own Horse so it ain't no trouble to keep up. Calley looked over at o'Molly. Yes Sir, he said, I seen your Horse when I first rode up she's a Dandy ain't she. Well can we, Papa said, I don't know that it'd hurt any. No but the thing is I got other Fish to Fry, Calley said, but let me sleep on it and I'll give you my answer first thing when you wake up in the morning. Then, Papa said, he went over and made him a pillow with his saddle and Herman give me a look and said If he says we can ride long with him we ain't. What you mean We Ain't, Papa said. I mean I ain't and you ain't neither, Herman said, that's what I mean by We Ain't. I need me a Helper selling Watermelons and you're it. Besides our Momma ain't out there no wheres to be found, he said. Oh don't say that Herman, Papa said, she's out there somewheres just a'waiting for us to come find her. No she ain't, Herman said, you just a stupid little Boy a'dreaming. If Momma'd a'wanted us to find her she never would a'left. Well I'm a'going anyhow I said, Papa said. No you ain't, Herman said, now just hush bout it.

*F*IRST THING WE SEEN NEXT MORNING Papa said, was Calley Pearsall wadn't nowhere round to be seen but they was four hard Bisquits he left us on a flat rock for our breakfasts. Well, Herman said, Cowboys is just like that ain't they Here one minute and gone on down the road the next like some o'crazy wind a'blowing through. I was sorry Calley was gone, Papa said, I was hoping I might could get him to help me find Precious and my Momma too. You know what I think, Herman said, I think when you get right down to it o'Calley rode on out a'here in the middle a'the night cause somebody's after him and he'd just as soon they not catch him. Who not catch him I said, Papa said. Wouldn't surprise me not one bit it was the Sheriff a'Comal County or somebody else, Herman said, somebody like that wears him a Badge and got a big long Pistol a'sticking down his pants. Boy Hidy, Papa said, what's got in to you to say something like that bout our Friend Calley Pearsall. I'm older'n you, Herman said, and just know a lot more about things is all. Well how bout this then, Papa said, here we are a'eating these Bisquits he left us for our breakfasts, wouldn't no Out Law do that I reckon. Herman looked over to see Fritz rolling around trying to bite a hold on his Bisquit but not having much luck with it and said Well Yes I'd have to say that is in his favor all right but my advice to you and me both is just keep one eye on him. If he ain't a Out Law he's least half a'one. I guess I seen it in his eyes, he said, and you just gotta trust me on that okay.

We rode back to town in a little while, Papa said, and Boy Hidy people was coming from ever which direction all up and down the street and running over to this big glass winder in the Dry Goods Store where the rest a'the town was already pushing and shoving to get a look at something inside. Let's go see Herman said, Papa said, and I give o'Molly a little kick and we bounced on over with Fritz a'leaning out over the saddle horn and pointing the way with his nose and him all this time just a'howling away like some-body was a'pinching his Hiney with a pair a'pliers. Oh and then, he said, we got down on our hands and knees and crawled up tween everbody's legs and then come up and looked through the big glass winder and Why there was that great big o'Antique Rock Aligater Head me and Herman found in the Comal River. Well I reckon you believe me bout o'Calley Pearsall now don't you, Herman said, wouldn't nobody but a Out Law go and steal a Aligater Head off a couple a'poor little o'Boys like us would they.

Herman was fit to be tied

that Calley Pearsall had gone and stole our Aligater Head, Papa said, and went jumping through the door just a'hollering Who owns this place Who owns this place and a Man with a big mustache come up and said Well I do and I bet I can guess who you are. Course they was people all over, Papa said, and when one Lady reached to see what a rock Aligater Head feels like why Herman pushed her hand away and said Don't touch it, that things older'n you and your o'Granma both then he looked back at the Store Owner and said What'd you say. And the Store Owner said I bet you the two Boys found this Curiosity in the Comal River is that right. Yes Sir your Agent said you'd be along this morning sometime. What's a Agent I said, Papa said. Some-body who goes and steals your Aligater Head that's what a Agent is, Herman said, and maybe everthing else you got he can walk off with too then Her-man seen some little Kid just a'rubbing away on the Aligater Head with his hand and Herman said You better find you something else to do with that hand there Mister Pee Wee fore I bite it off and feed it to my Piggies. Oh and then that little Kid run off just a'yelling for his Momma, Papa said, and then the Store Owner reached over and handed Herman a invelope. This is from that Cowboy he said, as you can see he wrote something on it to you. And Yes he did, Papa said, and Herman read it out loud and it said To the Boys. Here don't be mad at me. Adios Calley. Well open it up the Store Owner said and then Herman did, Papa said, and Oh Boy Hidy wadn't nothing in there but Ten Dollars. Ten Dollars just pretty as you please. That's Five Dollars a piece the Store Owner said, I give him Fifteen Dollars for that thing and I see he split right down the middle with you two Boys. That's a Square Deal if ever I seen one ain't it. A surprise too I reckon, he said. Well Herman I said, Papa said, I'll sure be glad when I'm old as you are so I can tell if somebody is a Out Law or not like you can.

We went on back outside then, Papa said, and seen where Fritz was setting up on o'Molly and just a'grinning at people and saying Heh Heh Heh and I know I could a'sold him for maybe another Nickel or two but course I'd a'never. Well here, Herman said, here's your half a'the money then he folded some dollars up and stuck em down in my pocket. You gonna be a Rich Man here fore long ain't you, he said, what with all that Watermelon Money you gonna make. I ain't got nothing to do with Watermelons, Papa said. I don't know what you a'talking bout. I told you you was gonna be my Helper, Herman said, I can't make no Money less I got me a Helper. I'm gonna go find our Momma, Papa said, I ain't got no time to be your Helper. Oh then he give me his Snake Eyes and said Well you either gonna be my Helper or you ain't gonna be my Brother no more. Well Yes I am too your Brother, Papa said, And don't you never say I ain't. No you ain't, Herman said. I don't have me no Brother. He wadn't all that sad bout it, Papa said, it was just something he decided right then and he was sticking to it. What if I still wanna be your Brother even if you don't want me to be one, Papa said, what bout that. No a Brother is Family and a Family helps one another, Herman said. I ain't got no Family, he said, I ain't got no Momma and I ain't got no Daddy and now I ain't got no Brother neither one so just Hush bout it he said then, Papa said, he give me a Look like he didn't care a lick if he never seen me again or not in his whole Life and went on off down the street and never even give me a look back and Oh I never did feel so all alone and sad as I did right then so I got up on o'Molly with Fritz and bumped on off down the street the other way and when I come by the Saloon the Man from yesterday come out and seen me then raised him up a make-believe Beer and took him a big long make-believe Drink then slapped his knee and went to laughing at me like some o'crazy Loonie but I couldn't get o'Molly to go no faster to get on by.

I WADN'T NO MOREN MAYBE A MILE OR TWO on down the road from New Braunfels Texas, Papa said, when here come the Sheriff a'Comal County a'riding up right behind me with three other

Fellas and all with they Pistols and Guns ready for a fight. I didn't do nothing I said, Papa said, I'm just a'riding down this road here a'looking for my Momma. We're not after you Son, the Sheriff a'Comal County said, we're after Jack Ivey the Third and his Partner Calley Pearsall. I know you and your Brother both done had dealings with Calley Pearsall over something yall stole outta the Comal River down yonder in Landa's Pasture so let's not start our business here together with you a'fibbing about it. Yes Sir I said, Papa said, then I said No Sir, he said, and the Sheriff a'Comal County said Well which one is it Yes Sir or No Sir and I said Well Sir it's Yes Sir me and my Brother Herman is the ones found that Antique Rock Aligater Head in the Comal River all right but No Sir we wadn't the ones hauled it off down to the Store and sold it. I don't wish no Jail Time on you and these Men here with me don't neither, he said, but we been sworn to fetch those two Bandits and bring em in for they dose a'Justice and we'd be forever in your debt Young Sir for whatever you can tell us regarding they Whereabouts. Last I seen a'Mister Calley Pearsall he was spooning down a mouth a'beans and making his saddle to go to sleep on and I ain't never even heard a'Jack Ivey the Third in my Life. I wanna believe you Son I truly do, the Sheriff a'Comal County said. Yes Sir you can believe me I said, Papa said, then the Sheriff a'Comal County said Did Calley Pearsall share with you the proceeds of his rustling that Aligater Head you Boys found in the Comal River. You mean what he got for it down at the Store, Papa said. You ain't about to start a'arguing with me about it now are you Son, the Sheriff a'Comal County said. No Sir I ain't, Papa said, he left us Five Dollars each down at the Store for our troubles. Five dollars, the Sheriff said, Oh my. And I knowed right then Herman hadn't told him not one word bout his Five Dollars and I was more or less sorry I already had bout mine. Well, the Sheriff a'Comal County said, I'm gonna have to ask you for that Five Dollars he give you for it is illgotten money and as such rightfully belongs to the County and not to you or no other person. So I give him the Dollars from down my pocket, Papa said, and he counted em up and said Why Young Sir you short a Dollar here this ain't but four. So I reckoned Herman missed his count when he give me my part so I reached down my other pocket and come out with the Dollar Miz Choat give me and give it on over to him and the Sheriff said Being that you was Co Operative with me I'm gonna let you go this time but you ever commit a Criminal Act in Comal County Texas again Why then Mister Boy you better give Jesus Henry Christ your Heart cause I sure as Hell gonna get your little red Hiney my self. Then, Papa said, the Sheriff a'Comal County give me a little smile for a Warning then touched his hat like he was General Robert Everett Lee and rode on off down the road with his Men a'stringing out behind him one after the other.

Wadn't a second later and o'Fritz grinned over at some bushes on the side a'the road and out come a'riding none othern Mister Calley Pearsall his self with a big o'Pistol in his hand. I come a quarter inch from shooting that Son of a Bitch for a'taking your money, he said, but I'd a'had to shoot the whole god dam Bunch if I had and I didn't wanna leave a mess a'bloody meat out here in the middle a'the road for somebody else to trip over when they hadn't done nothing I know of to provoke me.

COWBOY CALLEY PEARSALL stuck his pistol back down his pants, Papa said, then seen the look on my face and said You ain't a'scared a'me are you. Yes Sir I am I sure am I said, Papa said. Yes Sir Mister Pearsall said I reckon I might be scared a'me too if I was you then he give me a wink that made it easy to be a'setting there on o'Molly in his company. Look a'here he said I got something for you then he put his hand way down his pocket and come out with his Five Dollars and give em over to me, Papa said. Now you back to even where you was ain't you and no harm done huh he said and I said Well I do thank you for these Dollars and for them other Dollars back at the Store both. No that's okay, Calley said. I like to travel with my Rich Friends when I can then he said Heeyah Heeyah to his Horse Firefoot and went to riding on up the road and I give o'Molly a touch a'my heels too and went a'bumping along to catch up and when I did he looked over and seen o'Fritz just a'grinning at him and saying Heh Heh Heh like that. You know, Calley said, when I was just a Squirt like you I had me a little Dog too Best Friend I ever did have and it like to a'killed me when the Tonks come up to the house one day Dark a'night and stole him out from under the porch where he made his bed. How'd you get him back I said, Papa said. Oh I never, he said, it was a hard time in the Country back then and I reckon they just cooked him up in they Cook Pot that night and ate him for they suppers same as you might have to do one day with o'Smiley there. I said Whoa and jerked o'Molly up to a'stop, Papa said, then hugged Fritz up close as I could. Why I'd never do that in my Life I said, Papa said, then I said Don't you never say nothing like that to me ever again. Listen here, Calley said, I don't wish it on you but you ever get to where your own Family is a'starving to death right there in front a'your eyes you'll do just any god dam thing in this World to get em a bite to eat and don't think for one minute you won't. No I won't, Papa said. Not Fritz No Sir Not Ever. Calley thought bout it a minute then said No I reckon if I'd a'had a say on it I'd a'just let the whole god dam Tonk Nation starve to death one and all fore I'd a'let em eat my little Dog. I don't wanna talk bout it no more, Papa said, it makes me sad to think it. Yes Sir this o'World will do that to you it sure will, Calley said. How far you a'riding with me anyway. Just til I find my Momma or my Momma's Horse Precious one. And then I asked him when he seen her was they a Mexkin Saddle on her had Nickel Conchos just a'sparklin on it, Papa said. No, no such saddle nor any other, Calley said, I'd a'rememberd that. It was my Momma's Saddle, Papa said, and then my eyes just went to swimming at the thought and Calley said Let's just leave this subject alone for the rest a'the day okay but Listen here I liked it you bristled up at me here a minute or two ago for what I said about eating your little Dog. That just come out, Papa said, I didn't mean nothing by it. No, Calley said, it come out cause you love your little Dog there and I wouldn't wanna ride no ten feet down the road with a Man who didn't. Then he reached over and give Fritz a good scratch on his head and said Don't you worry Amigo, ain't nobody gonna put you in the Cook Pot long as I'm around and got my Pistola here in my britches. That scared me a little, Papa said, cause I could see he meant it ever word.

*T*HAT NIGHT CALLEY PUT HIM SOME DRY BEEF in the Beans and it sure made for good eating, Papa said, then I worked myself up and said You Fried them Other Fish you got to Fry yet. What Other Fish to Fry is that you a'talking about Calley said. The other night you said you had some Other Fish to Fry. Oh you mean o'Jack I reckon he said. No I ain't Fried him up yet but you can set your Hat on it I'm gonna Fry him up good when I find him. Oh and then I looked over at him there in the Fire

Light a'wearing his Big Hat, Papa said, and I seen Why this is one a'them Out Laws tried to steal Old Karl's money that night when I played sick but this is the one kept the other one from a'shooting us. What'd o'Jack do to you make you wanna Fry him up like that I said, Papa said. He shot a man dead out a'Foolishness and cause I was there with him when he done it they a'wanting to hang me for it too, Calley said. They's a lesson in that for you ain't they. I don't know why they would be, Papa said, I ain't never shot a man dead in my Life. The Lesson ain't about shooting a man dead, Calley said, lots a'men do that. No Sir the Lesson is bout being Careful what Company you keep in your Life. Like the Company you a'keeping right now, he said. You understand. Yes Sir I believe I do, Papa said. You a'saying you are a Bad Man and a Out Law both and if I ain't careful it's gonna rub off on me too. Yes Sir that's right, Calley said, So maybe you and your little Dog there better ride on off while you still got your good Reputations. I don't believe you such a Bad Man as you say Mister Pearsall, Papa said. You don't huh, Calley said. You must know something bout me I don't. I know you ain't no Bad Man I said, Papa said, I know that. You know a Lot for somebody ain't even eighty years old yet you know it, he said. Yes Sir I reckon, Papa said, I wadn't bout to tell him how I knowed it in case I was wrong bout him and he went to shooting at me for tricking em out a'finding the money that night with that cough a'mine. You saying you don't wanna help me find my Momma's Horse or my Momma neither one, Papa said. I'd like to help you find em both, Calley said, and if I wadn't already a'looking for Jack Ivey the Third and if the Sheriff a'Comal County wadn't already a'looking for me Why then I'd just throw my saddle up on o'Firefoot there and we'd go to looking for your Momma together til Hell froze over and all the Little Childrens was out there a'skating on the Ice.

That night when I went off to sleep, Papa said, here come all them Shimmery People and Boy Hidy I was surprised to see em I reckon cause it'd been so long since I had. What yall want now I said in my Dream and they stepped back to show me they was a Fork in the road up ahead and they went to pointing to the Fork that was a'going that way and not the other and I took that to mean if ever I was to come to a Fork in the road like that I was to go that way and not the other and then the very next day me and Calley come to just such a Fork in the road and Calley said Well now I reckon o'Jack went one way or the other but I don't have no idea which. That one I said, Papa said, and pointed to the one a'going that way. What makes you pick that way over the other way, Calley said. I seen it in my Dream last night, Papa said, just clear as Day. Well if you are Right, Calley said, I'm gonna hire you out for a Sooth Sayer and go to San Franciso on all the Money I make then he took the way I pointed to and went on up the road with me and Fritz just a'coming long behind on o'Molly. What if it turns out I'm Wrong bout it I said, Papa said. Wrong's just the other side a'the same o'Coin, Calley said. Sometimes it leads you to find what you didn't even know you was a'looking for in the First Place. Yes Sir I said, Papa said. So you a'saying you understand what I'm a'saying huh, Calley said. No Sir, Papa said, not a Lick of it.

ME AND CALLEY COME A'RIDING IN

to Lockhart Texas, Papa said, and first thing Calley seen was o'Jack Ivey the Third's Horse right there in the Horse Lot on the Public Square. Well Bessa my Coola that's o'Jack's Horse a'standing right yonder, he said. And then I looked, Papa said, and Why standing right there next to o'Jack Ivey the Third's Horse was my very own Momma's Horse Precious. That's my Momma's Horse I said, Papa said, and was bout to give o'Molly my heels to go over and give her a hug but Calley signed me back to stay where I was and said Something's wrong here it ain't like o'Jack to raise up a flag he's in town then he looked over cross the street to Siddons Longhorn Saloon and seen people going in and coming out and a Man guarding at the door. That's one a'the men was a'riding with the Sheriff a'Comal County yesterday am I right or am I wrong, he said. I took me a look and sure nough it was and I said Yes Sir you are right. I don't like it, Calley said. I bet they caught poor o'Jack and the Sheriff a'Comal County got him chained up in there for Cause. Gonna hang him too I reckon he said and not a god dam thing to do about it but blow o'Jack a Kiss Goodbye and wave him Adios Amigo. I gotta go over there and ask him how he happen to come by my Momma's Horse, Papa said, Maybe he knows where my Momma is too. I'd go with you, Calley said, but that o'Sheriff might try to drop me off a limb with a rope round my neck. I know it, Papa said, and I don't hold it against you that you a'looking out for your self then, he said, I went to walking cross the street with Fritz tagging long behind and went up to the Man guarding the door. I'd like a visit with Jack Ivey the Third Please Sir I said, Papa said. The Man give me a little smile and said Oh you would huh. Yes Sir I would I said, then he said Well Jack Ivey the Third's in there with the Sheriff but they had em a long day and they both pretty much all talked out I reckon. Well I still need to talk to him I said, I think he might know where my Momma is. Oh now I remember you, the Man said. You that little Boy was on the road yesterday a'looking for his Momma. Yes Sir, Papa said, Thats me and I still am. Well they ain't nobody in there can tell you where your Momma is so you and your little Pooch there might just as well run on along now. Well maybe if I talk to the Sheriff a'Comal County he'll let me talk to Mister Ivey the Third a minute or two, Papa said. No I don't believe he would, the Man said, Now run along fore I lock you up in the Jail for being a'Public Nuisance. That's when I remembered I had the Five Dollars Calley give me in my pocket, Papa said, so I pulled it out and said Well tell the Sheriff a'Comal County I'd give him this Five Dollars here if he'll let me talk to Mister Ivey the Third and the Man sucked that Five Dollars right outta my hand and said Well I don't guess it'd hurt to ask him would it and away he went to ask the Sheriff could I talk to Jack Ivey the Third bout my Momma or not then here he come right back out again and said the Sheriff said he was gonna Allow it and Thank You for the Five Dollars then the Man stepped back and pointed cross the room to a door way in the back where people was lined up to go in. Go on, the Man said, the Sheriff a'Comal County and o'Jack Ivey the Third is both in there a'visiting with everbody. So, Papa said, I picked Fritz up to me and got in line with them other People then I accidentally turned and got me a look back out the front door and Boy Hidy there went o'Calley Pearsall just a'galloping off down the street on Firefoot and Oh he had my Momma's Horse Precious tied on a long rope behind him and she was a'running off down the street too.

I DIDN'T KNOW WHAT TO DO

Papa said, course I didn't have no choice neither I couldn't a'made o'Molly run fast nough to catch em even if I'd a'put a Firecracker up under her tail and lit it afire. Then, he said, the Man come up behind me and said It's your turn now but just remember to talk loud cause they both gone a little Hard a'Hearing here lately. And so I stepped in, Papa said, and Oh wadn't no-

body in there but four feet a'sticking up out from under some bloody o'bed sheets. Which one you wanna talk to first, the Man said, then pulled the coverings back to show me the dead neckid bodies a'the Sheriff a'Comal County and Jack Ivey the Third with bullet holes all in em both and liquids just a'oozing out ever one a'them holes to the floor so you had to watch where you stepped it was so slick. Ask em any o'thing you like the Man said, just remember Talk Loud. How'd they come to this Bad End, Papa said. Oh wadn't nothing to it, the Man said, the Sheriff come over here to get him a Refreshment and there was o'Jack standing there at the bar a'getting him one too and the Sheriff said Jack you gonna have to come with me for Criminal Acts and Jack said No I won't do it and the Sheriff said I ain't a'asking you Jack I'm a'telling you and Jack said You must have a Wast Nest in your god dam ear you Son of a Bitch you don't hear me a'saying No and the Sheriff said I got three armed men standing cross the street yonder I can call over here if I have to and Jack said If you don't put no more value on they Life than that Why then go on and call em on over but I'm thinking I maybe better go on and shoot you right now anyhow fore the odds go to stacking up against me with them other three coming in here. Well let's us just talk bout this a minute the Man said the Sheriff said but o'Jack said No let's just go to shooting I'm tired a'fooling with you you Sorry Son of a Bitch and everbody else in this World like you and so they just went to shooting back and forth at each other and then went to running and hiding over be-hind chairs and tables and doors and People just a'fleeing in ever which di-rection them bullets a'hitting so close all around then o'Jack fell down dead over there by the Foot Rail to the Bar and the Sheriff his self just a'bleeding stepped over to him and said Well Jack I reckon you learnt your lesson now huh but if not I still got me a bullet or two in my Pistol for you then he give him a little kick just to be mean about it and when he did o'Jack raised up in a Big Surprise and let pop with his last bullet and it went in here under the Sheriff's chin then come out up here the top a'his head in a big mess a'blood and goo. Anyhow, he said, that's what the Bartender seen it all said. And one more thing, the Man said, if it don't matter to you I'm gonna give over your Five Dollars to the Sheriff's handsome Widder as a Gift when I go pay respect but fore I could answer, Papa said, he said I'll ask you to pull them sheets back up over they dead faces when you done your looking then he give me a smile and a knock on my head and went on out the door and I

. . . just remember to talk loud cause they   *109*
both gone a little Hard a'Hearing here lately.

did what he asked me to do then me and Fritz went on out too and that was the last time I ever did see o'Jack Ivey the Third the man who might could a'told me where my Momma was but he was dead now and I was sick about it. Course it was a mystery to me too, Papa said, where o'Calley Pearsall had got off to with my Momma's Horse Precious but they just wadn't no way to know so I give my heels to the o'Swayback and me and Fritz went a'riding on out a'Lockhart Texas feeling Bad bout just everthing they was in the World to feel Bad bout.

*M*E AND FRITZ WOKE UP NEXT MORNING Papa said, and Why there was o'Calley Pearsall a'cooking up a pot a'Beans on the fire and Oh there was my Momma's Horse Precious a'standing right there behind him. Mister Pearsall I said, Papa said, You ever do anything in your Life ain't a Surprise. No Sir I don't believe I ever do, he said. They was both dead wadn't they the Sheriff and poor o'Jack both. Yes Sir and that was another Surprise to me, Papa said. And so was you a'running off down the road with my Momma's Horse. Well I knowed o'Jack had to be dead if they had him over there in the Saloon otherwise they'd a'had him in the Jail House and I knowed if Jack was dead he hadn't a'gone off to his Maker without him a'taking the o'Sheriff a'Comal County long with him. He did didn't he, he said. Oh Yes Sir he did I said, Papa said. Anyhow I didn't figgur neither one of em had no more use a'your Momma's Horse so I took her cause I knowed you'd maybe have notions a'that being stealing or something was you to take her yourself but me I didn't give a god dam even if it was. Papa stepped over and gave Precious a hug around the neck and a kiss on her cheek. They ain't a prettier Horse in the World, he said. Well Firefoot ain't so pretty I'll give you that, Calley said, but they ain't a Horse in Texas can out run him. I don't understand how Precious come to be here, Papa said, I know my Momma would a'never sold or traded her away neither one. A Horse like that No Sir I don't reckon she would, Calley said. Well anyhow she's back in the Family now ain't she. It took me a minute or two fore I knowed what he was saying, Papa said, then I said You mean you a'giving me my Momma's Horse. She wadn't never mine to give Calley said, but I want you to have her so you don't use up too much a'your Life a'hunting for something just might not be there for you to find anyhow. I don't have no idea what you a'saying, Papa said. Calley took him a bite a'Beans and said I'm saying that Horse there might be close as you ever gonna get to finding your dear sweet Momma and maybe you just oughta thank your Lucky Stars you got her then go find something else to occupy your mind and not just finding your Momma but I am not saying Forget bout her No Sir I'd never say that but I am a'saying Life is chock full a'many interesting things and xperiences and you oughta grab you up all you can and not lose the World for just one thing no matter the Hurt. No Sir, Papa said, I'm gonna find my Momma even if it takes me to Kingdom Come. Well, o'Calley said, all I'm a'saying is just don't lose your own Self a'doing it cause sometimes it's hard to get it back if you do.

CALLEY WAS SURPRISED I DIDN'T WANNA RIDE Precious when we was making to go, Papa said, but I said No Sir she's my Momma's Horse and I'm a'keeping her fresh for when I find her. You oughta ask your o'Swayback there what she thinks bout that, Calley said, she ain't xactly no Spring Chicken you know it. I hadn't thought bout that, Papa said, but Calley was right o'Molly was a'getting up in years in fact was already up in years when I was first borned. How bout this, Calley said, you ride on Precious and let Fritz ride on the o'Swayback what about that. Well I said, Papa said. And here's something else you got to think about, Calley said, you got four Mouths to feed now counting your own and Five if you count me but I'll be a'cutting off from here fore long so that was just a Joke me being Number Five. Where you a'going, Papa said, that's another Surprise you just gonna ride off ain't it. Well I was a'looking for o'Jack Ivey the Third, Calley said, but he's dead now so they ain't no purpose to that is they but I got other Fish to Fry now anyhow. But, he said, the thing is you gonna need to inherit bout a thousand dollars or Hire Out to somebody one if you're gonna feed all these other mouths we was talking about. Hire Out, Papa said, I don't wanna Hire Out to nobody I told you I'm a'looking for my Momma. Well then Calley said here's my advice to you. Sell your Creatures or give em away one cause if you ain't got no Money you can't get em nothing to eat and you just gonna starve em to death. No I ain't, Papa said, I'd never. It don't have to be no Forever Job you understand, he said, just one for now. I might even know a'one. It ain't in no Town is it, Papa said. Oh No, Calley said, I wouldn't do that to you. Is it in the direction a'Fayetteville, Papa said, Miz Choat said maybe my Momma went there. Well I don't know, Calley said, which Direction is Fayetteville in. Papa pointed out cross the Country and said More or less in that Direction there I reckon but I can't say for sure. This is a good Sign, Calley said. That job I might know about is off in that Direction too.

So we went riding off in that Direction, Papa said, me a'riding Precious and Fritz perched up there on o'Molly like he was keeping a eye out for Trouble.

WE GOT OFF DOWN THE ROAD A PIECE

Papa said, and here a chilly little Wind come a'blowing up even if we was in the middle a'Summer Time then Calley pulled up and I seen Fritz sniffing at the air. We about to get us some Weather here, Calley said, maybe moren we want if you ask me. I didn't have no idea what he was talking bout, Papa said, so I said I don't have no idea what you a'talking bout. Calley's eyes was up on the Clouds and he said This is a nice little Wind we got here but if it stops for a minute all of a sudden then takes to blowing like Hell from some other place why then we most likely got us a god dam Whirled Wind coming and who knows what else to boot. Well, Papa said, when he said that I went to studying them Clouds too and Oh Boy Hidy they was just a'twisting and a'turning and a'folding back in on they selves like Miz Choat was up there a'stirring em with her big spoon. I don't like it I said, Papa said, and Calley said Get your little Dog over to you and hang on tight so I give a slap on my knee and Fritz jumped off o'Molly then run over and jumped up to me and I could tell he didn't like this Weather no moren me and o'Calley did. Now listen, Calley said, it's gonna come a god dam big giant Storm here in just a minute but we ain't a'waiting for it No Sir we're right now gonna make for that o'Tin Shed we seen out there in somebody's cow pasture about a mile back yonder you remember. I said I did, Papa said, and right then the Wind stopped dead and wadn't a blade a'grass moving no where in Sight and Calley said Don't be fooled This is the Quiet fore the Storm and Oh he barely got them words out his mouth then here come a Mighty Wind just a'whistling and a'roaring and a'blowing us and everthing else in a circle and sideways too and then Oh this rain a'Ice Balls big as your fist come right long with it knocking the whole Country Side down flat like maybe somebody was smearing it with a board. O'Calley said Run Run Run Run for your Life but me and Fritz and Precious was already a'running for our Life fast as we could go and Oh them Ice Balls a'hitting us all three and making us yelp ever time. It got so bad, Papa said, I could just barely make out o'Molly a'running long side and then somebody's o'Cows went to bellering but then I lost em all to sight they was just too many Ice Balls to see through but o'Calley he was always right there on my side him a'putting his hat to the Ice Balls and a'pointing the way through the Ice and Wind Storm to that o'Tin Shed we'd passed by bout a year ago and Oh when we got there o'Calley knocked the door down with his shoulder then pulled me and Fritz and Precious on in then slapped Firefoot's hind end with his hat to get him on in too and there we was all inside that Tin Shed but them Ice Balls was just a'peppering down and knocking off pieces a'the tin roof and walls like somebody was out there with bout ten thousand hammers sounded like this DingDangDingDang-DingDang and course you couldn't hear a word even if you'd a'tried cause it was the End a'the World but I went to yelling for o'Molly when I seen she was lost somewheres out there in the Storm and not to be seen. Then I made to go find her but o'Calley grabbed me up at the door and I went to fighting and yelling to let me loose but No No No he wouldn't have it and squeezed me like in a vice to hold me back and I just went to crying cause they was no Hope for my o'Swayback out there in that Storm a'Ice Balls all by her self with no Friend anywheres in the World to offer her a Helping Hand.

OH THAT STORM JUST WOULDN'T QUIT Papa said. DingDangDingDangDingDang it went on that Tin Roof like that til you was almost crazy with it and the Wind a'going WeeeWhoosh Weee-Whoosh and I think me and Fritz would a'both blowed away cept o'Calley pulled us in a heap then bent down over us like some o'Mother Hen and helt us to him with the Whole World just a'going DingDangDingDangDing-Dang then after bout six years it went more like DingDang Ding Dang Ding Dang Ding Dang Ding Dang and then Calley looked up through what was left a'the roof and said Well Bessa my Coola if that wadn't a Storm come through here wadn't it. Then we went outside, Papa said, and Why the whole Country was beat bare a'ever single leaf on ever single tree and they wadn't nothing left far as you could see but stobs a'sticking up that'd once been trees and Oh them Ice Balls was piled up everwheres you looked in some places up to your knees but No Sir that wadn't all. Then here the Sun come out and fore you knowed it this Fog started a'rising up off the ground like a upside down cloud but the worse thing was ever where you looked was some poor o'dead Cow been beat to death by the Storm and I all but went to crying cause Oh No I thought that's what's happened to o'Molly too, and I could see Calley was thinking the same thing, he said, cause he pointed and said You go look yonder ways and I'll go look yonder and Oh me and Fritz and Precious went to looking everwheres and ever time we seen a Bump sticking up out there in the Fog somewheres we'd run over to see was it a Cow or my poor o'Molly and ever time it was somebody's Cow most always a dead one but sometimes one just been beat down so bad by the Ice Balls she just couldn't get up no more and then the Fog started a'swirling over the ground and you'd a'thought you was a'walking on that Cloud and some-times you could see everthing they was to see in front of you and the next minute you couldn't see nothing at all not even your own two feet and then of a sudden Fritz jumped out a'my arms and went running off in the Fog to where I didn't have no idea where he'd a'gone to and Oh Boy Hidy I went to yelling Fritz Fritz Fritz and running and stumbling through that Cloud af-ter him but Oh he was just gone then I looked way way out there and I seen this Horse a'coming through the Fog and I looked and then Oh I seen it was the o'Swayback just a'walking toward me like they wadn't nothing wrong then I seen somebody was a'riding on her and I looked and I seen they was wearing a hat same as me and then I looked and I looked and I looked and then I bout had me a Heart Attack cause the Person riding o'Molly out there through the Cloud wadn't nobody in the world but Me. Me, Papa said, and o'Fritz a'riding right there on the saddle with me.

. . . ever where you looked was some poor o'dead
Cow been beat to death by the Storm . . .

OH AND THEN THE FOG SWIRLED

Papa said, and I lost that Other Me to sight and I thought No I never seen that Other Me in the first place but No then it swirled again and there I was coming at me through the Fog on o'Molly again with little Fritz there on the saddle in front a'Me and something else now too, he said, a Man riding just behind that Other Me with a big gun cross his saddle and carrying some weight on him but not nough for you to call him a Fat Man. Then that Other Me pulled up in front of me and Why it was like I was looking in the mirra at my self we was so close in our faces, Papa said, and I said I do believe I know you don't I and then this Other Me took they hat off and this bunch a'hair just come a'flopping out from under neath all the way down past they shoulder and Oh I seen No wadn't some Other Me at all but was some o'Girl looked just like me. This your Nag and little Dog here, she said. Where'd you find o'Molly I said then jumped off Precious and give her a big hug round the neck, Papa said. She come a'running in our barn outta the Storm and went straight over and put her nose in the feed bucket like she owned the place. I guess she's smartern she looks huh, she said. Well, Papa said, it peeved me she said that bout the o'Swayback after all her troubles in the Storm so I said Yes and I hope you are too and at first she just looked at me then she went to smiling and said That was a funny thing for you to say to me and I said Well I meant ever word of it and then she couldn't help but go to laughing. Was you born with that Funny Bone, she said, and Papa said I didn't know I had me a Funny Bone. Well you do she said Look a'here even your little Dog is a'laughing and sure nough Fritz was going Heh Heh Heh like he sometime did and I said He does that don't matter if something's funny or not. I'm Annie Oster, she said, but you might wanna call me Annie O cause I got me a cousin named Annie Bunton and everbody calls her Annie B and me Annie O to tell us apart when they a'talking bout us. And then, Papa said, we give each other a smile and it was like I'd a'knowed Annie all my Whole Life and Oh we was Friends from then on out and ever after. Maybe even Brother and Sister was more like it at that time, he said. Then her Pa rode up and so did Calley and they give us looks back and forth and Calley said They kinda look like Pete and Re Pete don't they and her Pa said Yes they do but I hate to hear all these Cows a'bawling they been hurt so bad in the Ice Storm and Calley said Yes Sir I do too then he pulled his Lever-Action out his saddle scabbard and said I reckon if we can get em up on they feet they gonna Live but if we can't then they done for it and best thing to do for em is go on and put em out a'they misery. So, Papa said, we spent the rest a'that day and way up in the night trying to get them poor o'beat up Cows back up to they feet again and some we could but some we couldn't and them we couldn't was shot dead and butchered for the Larder. And evertime a gun went Boom, he said, me and Annie looked over at each other with the same o'hurt eyes but they wadn't no help for it that we could see.

*I*T WADN'T FAR BUT IT WAS LONG PAST MIDNIGHT by the time we stumbled through all them Ice Balls and made us a bed in they barn, Papa said, and you could see the Moon and Stars right up through what was left a'the roof too. These People here gonna need some help, Calley said. Gonna be a month a'Sundays to come out from under this business. I know it, Papa said, looks like some body's Giant Feet just tromped round on everthing don't it. Well everbody's safe and our Animals is too that's the good thing, Calley said, and I thought Yes Sir, Papa said, and I got me a Sister outta the deal too but what I said was You know Mister Calley we might oughta stay here a day or two and help these People if we can. That's a good and decent thought, Calley said, and it don't surprise me you had it. Then he said How much you been around Girls in your Life and I said Some but not Much, Papa said. Well, he said, you guard your self. Girls ain't like Boys. What're they like, Papa said. Nobody knows, Calley said. Sometime you think you do then you find out you don't. Just be on your guard, he said, that's all I know to tell you. Come a time you'll see what I'm talking about Calley said, but when you do won't be nobody there to help you. Okay, Papa said, but I didn't have no idea what he was talking bout. I'm glad all our Animals is safe he said, its different with your Animals they always gonna be there with you ain't they. I reckon so, Papa said, then I pulled Fritz a little closer and looked over at Precious and o'Molly both a'sleeping on they feet. You know a lot don't you Mister Calley, Papa said. Yes Sir, he said, and dam me to ever lasting Hell if I didn't learn it all the Hard Way too but I ain't a'complaining. Here's the thing to remember bout Bad Times, he said, you a'listening. Yes Sir I said, Papa said, I am. They pass, Calley said. Don't matter how Bad a Time is the one thing you can count on is it's gonna pass.

I bet you old nough to already learned that for you self by now ain't you. Yes Sir, Papa said, then I thought bout my Momma and me and Herman in the Creek with the Little Bay Mare that last day fore Momma rode off and I said In my Life I found that to be true a'the Good Times too. No, o'Calley said, you let the Bad Times just run right on through you like water out a drain pipe but you dam up the Good Times to where you can always go back to em in your Memory when you need a Good Feeling. Is that what you do, Papa said and Calley said Well that's what I try to do then he turned over and went off to sleep.

I WOKE UP NEXT MORNING with Annie a'wigglin my big toe, Papa said, then she reached up and took Fritz to her. If I had some money I'd buy this little Idgit off you, she said. No you wouldn't cause he ain't for sale, Papa said, then I looked over to see if o'Calley had run off on me again but No there he was a'sleeping over there on his saddle. Go wiggle his toe you wanna wiggle somebody's toe, Papa said. Annie got this look like she just might do it and said You don't think he'd shoot me for it do you. I don't know, Papa said, then o'Calley opened one eye and said Oh Yes Ma'am I would and it surprised Annie so bad she jumped up and run over behind the o'Swayback to hide and Calley said No you don't have to worry it's way too early in the morning for me to go to shooting People and then Annie looked over at me and said He's just like you ain't he, he got him a Funny Bone too.

Me and Calley fed the Horses and o'Molly and talked to em a minute or two then went on up to the house, Papa said, Course it was just awful to see the whole Country Side all beat down like that by the Ice Balls far as you could see in ever direction you looked.

Annie's old Granny was at the stove cooking up steaks for breakfast, Papa said, and Boy Hidy she was a Corker if ever they was one. I hope you like steaks, she said, that's all we gonna have to eat around here for the next two-three hunderd years if you ask me. Where you from anyway. Up on the Blanco River I said, Papa said, then I lived for a time with the Choats there round Fischer somewheres. How bout that Cowboy there, she said, and pointed her cooking fork at Calley. Tell her I don't tell People where I'm from cause ever time I do they want me to go on back down there quick as I can he said, then Granny Oster said Ask him Why's that and Calley said Well tell her she's just gonna have to wait and find out for her self one a'these nights when I go to howling at the Moon and a'shooting my Pistol off. Oh I do like me a Tease she said and give Calley the first steak come off the stove then Calley caught Mister Oster's eye and said Me and my young Amigo here'd like to stay and help you with your patching up if you'd have us. Mister Oster nodded and you could see how relieved that made him. We'll have you and be glad of it, he said, then Annie smiled and nodded too then reached under the table and pinched my leg so hard I bout jumped outta my chair. What's wrong with this silly Boy here Granny she said, he can't even set still in his chair can he. Keep your hands to you self Annie, Granny Oster said, you ain't a'fooling nobody.

*A*FTER BREAKFAST Papa said, Mister Oster and Calley went to nailing the house and barn back together and it was our job to get what was left a'the Cows to grass somewheres that hadn't been all beat down by the Ice Balls and Granny Oster said That may be many miles away or may be hardly no miles at all just ain't no way to know where the Storm played out til we get there. Annie wanted to ride Precious but I said No, Papa said, she's my Momma's Horse and can't nobody ride her but me but you can ride o'Molly there if you want to. Well if I have to ride that o'Swayback Horse then Fritz has to ride with me, Annie said. You gonna get something you ain't gonna like here in a minute you keep a'talking to the company like that, Granny Oster said, now be Civil or get up here in the wagon with me one. But Annie swung up on o'Molly easy as any body might a'done it, Papa said, and off we went a'looking for fresh grass with Granny Oster leading the way in the wagon and me and Annie follering long behind the Cows to make sure we didn't lose us no Strays. And Oh, Papa said, I forgot to mention the air was just full a'Buzzarts and they was hopping round everwheres you looked a'pecking on them poor o'dead Cows and Coyotes was everwheres eating on em too. You ever seen anything like this in your whole Life, Annie said and I said No I never, Papa said, and I hope never to see it again neither. I seen a lot a'dead Animals in my Life, Annie said, but never no dead Person. Well I did, Papa said. Two of em both shot all to bits over in Lockhart. How'd that make you feel, Annie said. Well, Papa said, it made me feel Bad cause one of em might could a'told me where my Momma is but he was dead as a bisquit and didn't say a word. I didn't know you was a'looking for your Momma, she said. Well Yes I am, Papa said. Ain't you too old to be a'looking for your Momma, Annie said. No I ain't, Papa said, and you don't need to say nothing like that no more. I might mention I don't see your Momma no wheres round here neither. No my Momma's gone she said but my Pa said we ain't gonna dwell on it. How'd she go, Papa said. I just told you, Annie said, we ain't gonna dwell on it. Okay, Papa said, I was just asking. Some Men come up to the house one day when my Pa was down yonder a'working in the field and when they rode off Why my Momma'd already lost her self and couldn't do no moren gurgle and jabber and then next day she just died a'the Horrors and that's when Granny come to move in here so we'd had somebody to look after Little Baby Me. I don't need to know nothing else, Papa said. I never knowed my Momma a single minute I can remember, Annie said, but I miss her I do. Papa looked over and saw Annie was squeezing her eyes shut. You can come over here and ride with me on Precious for a minute or two if you want to, he said. So Annie slipped off o'Molly then handed Fritz up and climbed up on Precious behind me. Then she wrapped her two arms round my middle and put her cheek to my back, Papa said, and that's how we went for a good long while and then, he said, Annie said I like you and I said Well I like you too Annie and then we rode on a ways more and she said No I mean I really like you and then, Papa said, I said Well Annie I really like you too You like a Sister to me I reckon and then she squeezed me and pushed her cheek up against my back and said No I don't mean like no Sister. And I thought bout it a minute and then, Papa said, I said Okay me too Annie.

*B*Y NOON TIME THE WHOLE WORLD'D TURNED to mud for that hot Sun a'melting down all them Ice Balls, Papa said, and seemed like Granny Oster couldn't go no ten feet without her a'getting the wagon stuck. At first me and Annie thought it was funny to have to get down off Precious and go to prying the wagon out with long poles but didn't take but a time or two a'falling face down in the Mud and we'd had bout all the fun we wanted. Granny, Annie said, if you can't drive that wagon no bettern this we gonna have to set you up on the o'Swayback and send you Home. And I'd be glad to go too, Granny said, don't you think for one minute I wouldn't. But wadn't long, Papa said, and we started to seeing less Ice Balls and more Green Grass a'sticking up tween em and Why by suppertime it looked like we'd gone all the way to China or somewheres for all the grass they was and leaves in the trees too and Boy Hidy we had us some happy Cows then. And we was happy too, he said, cause we was where the Storm'd played out.

That night Granny and Annie fried some steak for our suppers, Papa said, and we was all four a'us counting Fritz just setting there eating it and Annie said Granny they's something we wanna tell you but we don't want you to fall over dead when you hear it. Okay I'll try not to, Granny said, but I can't make no promises. Me and him is probably gonna up and get married here fore too long. I almost spit out my suppers at that, Papa said, I hadn't heard nothing bout it. Well I'm not surprised, Granny said, when that o'Love Bug bites you they just ain't much you can do to get away from it. Where you reckon yall gonna settle she said. She was talking to me, Papa said, and course I didn't have the first idea bout it. Well, I said, Papa said, but Annie jumped in and said Well we was hoping you and Pa'd build us a room on the back a'the house and we'd just live in there. I like that idea, Granny said, that way we'd always have us somebody handy to do the chores and whatnot then she reached over and shook my hand like she was pumping water and said Welcome to the Family Mister we gonna come visit you ever chance we get and Annie said What in the World you talking about Granny I just said we was gonna be living right there with you and Pa. Yes Ma'am you are, Granny said, soon's they let you outta the Jail House. The Jail House I said, Papa said. Yes Sir the Jail House, Granny Oster said, you go to marrying too young they gonna throw you way back there in the Jail House for a'Robbing the Cradle. No they ain't, Annie said. They's People all over the place married not much oldern us. I'm just telling you, Granny said, course you can always run off and hide in the Woods somewheres to keep em from catching you and hope the wild Inyins don't get you instead. Yeah we'll do that then, Annie said, won't we. No, Papa said, not til I find my Momma. Oh, Annie said, I forgot about your Momma. Well then it's settled, Granny Oster said, First Things First. I'm glad you two is so smart bout things like this.

*B*Y THE THIRD DAY THE SUN'D PRETTY MUCH licked all them Ice Balls down to just little puddles running off all over the place, Papa said, and Granny Oster said Let's turn these o'Cows back round and go home I had just bout all this out door Life I want for maybe three-four years. Not me, Papa said, I liked ever minute a'being out there just easing long with the Cows like some o'timey Cowboy with his Horse and his Dog and his Sweetheart right there the side a'him and course in the pitchurs I was making in my head Granny was the Cook and was following long behind on the Chuck Wagon. And Oh, he said, they was times I'd look out over the Country Side and see a Tribe a'wild Inyins just a'whooping and a'yelling and a'coming to murder us with they bows and arras and some other times it'd be Mexkins with they big Pistolas and long knives but which ever one it was I'd pull Fritz and Annie and Granny Oster up on Momma's Horse Precious with me and away we'd gallop cross the Prairie like our Pants was on Fire and Annie'd hold on tight to me and we'd look back and give em a laugh over our shoulder cause wadn't no Inyin or Mexkin born could catch us long as we was riding Momma's Horse Precious and, he said, in the pitchurs I was making in my head they never did. Then that same morning we come up on this o'one-eyed Inyin Man had his wagon out there in the middle a'the Creek then unhitched his Horse from it and let it go. Well that's a silly thing to do ain't it Annie said, Papa said, then that o'Inyin climbed up on his wagon seat and put his hands on his knees and went total still like he was froze solid there and his Horse went off to eat some grass on the other side a'the Creek. What's he doing, Annie said. Granny made a eye shade with her hand and said He's a'getting ready to die. They do that. What's he gonna do just fall over dead in the Creek one a'these days, Papa said. I don't know, Granny Oster said. Well I'm gonna go talk to him Annie said, Papa said, then wanted me to come long with her so we waded out there knee deep in our bare feet and Oh that water was so cold from all them Ice Balls floating down in it. Good morning, Annie said, you want something to eat. That o'Inyin didn't even look at her out his one good eye, Papa said, and not at me neither. Are you lost, Annie said, where's your Wife and Children at but that o'Inyin just kept a'looking straight out there somewheres, Papa said, like we wadn't even in the World. Well listen I said, Papa said, we gonna be crossing our Cows right over yonder here in a minute You just holler you need something then we waded back over to Granny and she said Bet you

. . . but that o'Inyin just kept a'looking
straight out there somewheres, Papa said,
like we wadn't even in the World.

123

didn't get one word outta that Old Man did you and Annie said No not one. No and you won't never, Granny Oster said.

We crossed our cows in little bunches

at a time, Papa said, and you could see how that Creek was coming up higher and higher each trip we made from all the Ice Ball melt. Wadn't long and the Creek was just a'gushing and that poor o'one-eyed Inyin was still a'setting out there in the middle of it in his wagon and me and Annie was getting worried for him and so was his o'Horse a'watching from the other side and just a'crying. That Water's gonna get him if he ain't careful Granny, Annie said. Yes it is, Granny said, and you better go on off somewheres you don't wanna see it. I'm gonna go fetch him back, Papa said. Ain't no power on this earth can fetch that Old Man back, Granny Oster said, he got his mind set on the Beyond and you can go out there and whack him on the head nine times with a fence post it ain't gonna make no difference. And all this time we was talking, Papa said, that Creek was coming up Higher and Higher and Higher and in just a minute it was half way up on his wagon and still a'coming up some more and I said I better go get him now or he ain't gonna be there to get got. Hurry, Annie said, we don't wanna lose him to the Water. He's already lost to the Water Granny said then give me a squinty look, Papa said, and said I wouldn't go risking my Life on something already decided. But Papa took a rope, tied one end to Granny's wagon and the other end around his waist and waded on out and Oh it was cold, he said, and that Water running way harder and fastern it looked like from the bank and it was all I could do to keep my feet under me so I wouldn't go to washing on off down the Creek with all them Ice Balls and sticks and whatnot but I got to the wagon and that o'Inyin was just a'setting there on the seat with his one eye and his hands on his knees all calm to where you would a'thought he was setting out there on the porch somewhere just a'smoking his pipe. We need to go back now I said, Papa said, this Water's gonna come up here and get you in a minute if we don't. He didn't even look at me, Papa said, so I reached up and took a'holt a'his sleeve and went to pulling on it. Hey I said, Papa said, Hey Hey Hey but he didn't take no notice a'that neither so I pulled on his sleeve harder and went to hollering Hey Hey Hey Hey Hey

124

loud as I could but the Water went past the wagon so loud now he couldn't a'heard it thunder I reckon and then I looked over and seen Annie and Granny and Fritz just a'jumping and a'hollering for me to get on back over there right now but when I went to take the rope from round my middle and tie it on to the Inyin's wagon to pull it out Why that Water reached up and took holt a'me like they wadn't nothing to it and sent me off down the Creek like a Fish but the other end a'the rope was still tied on to Granny's wagon so when it got to the limit it curved me over to the bank and Annie run over there and pulled me out just a'choaking and a'sputtering and Oh she was scared and a'crying like a Baby and Fritz was jumping all over me too. And then, Papa said, Granny Oster hollered Look Look Look and we looked and the Water come up to that o'Inyin's chest then here it come up to his chin and all this time him just a'looking straight out yonder from that one eye a'his like he didn't have no care in the World and then of a sudden the Water come all the way up over his head and then Oh, Papa said, Oh and then that Water rolled him and his wagon both Over Over Over Over and took em on down the Creek with it and now we stood there like we was froze solid from what we just seen and that Inyin's poor o'Horse on the other side a'the Creek did too.

OH WE LOOKED AND WE LOOKED

Papa said, and then we looked some more all up and down that Creek for maybe a mile or two and never did find no moren a piece or two a'the wagon but not one hair off that o'Inyin's head and all this time, he said, his Horse was a'running up and down the Creek Bank on the other side a'looking too. He's a'looking for his Friend ain't he, Annie said, and then that Horse went to crying the way Horses go to crying some time and then so did o'Molly on our side a'the Creek and they just stood there looking at each other and a'crying back and forth like two Little Lost Children then here Annie went to crying too and Granny went off behind the wagon so we couldn't tell if she was a'crying or not. Oh don't cry Annie I said, Papa said, I'll go over there and get that Horse for you and fore she could say one word to talk me out of it I went to wading on across and maybe ten steps out that Creek reached down and knocked me off my feet and away I went on down the

Creek again but this time wadn't no rope to curve me back Home and On On On down the Creek I went and the only thing I seen when I come up for air a time or two was Annie and Fritz and Granny just a'hollering and a'chasing down the Creek Bank after me but then I bumped on something stuck under a log and loosed it and then off I went a'riding it on down the Creek like a raft but I looked down and Oh No wadn't no raft at all but Oh was that poor o'dead Inyin Man just a'looking up at me out his one eye but I didn't dare let go a'him cause I'd a'drowned too same as him then the Creek took a turn and when it did I grabbed a'holt a'some tree roots growing out the bank and helt on and here in a minute Annie and Granny pulled me out and then we all three pulled the o'dead Inyin out and he still had his hands on his knees which was both cocked up like he was still a'setting there on his wagon seat and no matter what you did you couldn't make him flatten out and lay down. We just gonna have to bury him setting up like this ain't no way round it I can see, Granny said. So, Papa said, we went to get the shovel back at the wagon and when we got there we seen o'Molly had got her self through the flood and was over there now cross the Creek making Friends with the o'dead Inyin's Horse. Well would you just look at that Annie said, Papa said, but Granny said Look later we got us a Grave to dig now fore it goes to getting Dark on us I don't wanna have to bury some o'one-eyed Inyin in the Dark if I can help it No telling what might come a'flying up outta the hole when the Sun goes down. So, Papa said, we went on back and picked a pretty spot under a Oak Tree and dug a Grave big nough to where that o'Inyin could set up in it and that's how we buried him. Then, he said, when we got back to Granny's wagon Why there was o'Molly back over on our side a'the Creek again and standing there right next to her was the o'dead Inyin's Horse which she'd swum the Flood to go get and bring back no matter the risk to her own Life.

NEXT MORNING I TOLD ANNIE

she oughta ride that Inyin Horse back to Home it was her Horse now, Papa said, but Annie said No that Inyin Horse had him a hard day yesterday and she thought she oughta ride with me and Fritz like always and, he said, I said Yes I reckon so too. So, Papa said, we just eased long toward home on

Precious with the Cows and the o'Swayback and now the o'Inyin Horse too a'eating whatever grass they could find long the way behind Granny's wagon and Annie talking the whole time. You think you gonna find your Momma or not she said, Papa said, and I said Yes I am and she said What if you don't you still gonna come back and see me and she was squeezing me so hard round the middle I couldn't hardly breathe but I said Yes and then she squeezed me even harder and I said You bout to kill me Annie.

We went like that for three days I think it was, Papa said, and I reckon it was one a'the best Trips I ever did take and at night the Coyotes'd just go to howling and yipping and I'd get homesick for the Peglegs and in my mind send em a Hello. I sent Hellos like that to my Momma and to Herman and to the Choats too, he said, and I ask Granny Oster if she thought they'd get em and she said she thought they most likely would cause her old Granny had told her when she was just a little Girl that she had to be careful what she was thinking cause Thoughts was real things same as a Red Wast was and they could fly up on you and sting you if they wadn't the right kind a'Thoughts to be a'thinking so you had better be careful. And then, Papa said, Annie said I don't believe that for a second. How can a Thought be real if you can't even see it and Granny Oster said Why course you can see a Thought and you can taste one too. Oh now Granny, Annie said, then Granny said Close your eyes both a'you and we did, Papa said, and then Granny said Now don't open em but Look a'here in your mind I got a Lemon in one hand and a Sharp Knife in the other you see em and now here I am a'cutting this Lemon in two and now open your mouths in your minds and see this Lemon here in my hand and now I'm a'putting half of it in your mouths each one and now I'm A'SQUEEZING THAT LEMON in your mouth and Oh, Papa said, I could taste that Lemon as if she really did squeeze it in my mouth and Annie could too cause we opened our eyes and we both had our faces all scrunched up it was so sour. See, Granny Oster said, what'd I tell you. Now here's the thing to remember, she said, You go to thinking Good Thoughts you gonna feel Good. You go to thinking Bad Thoughts you gonna feel Bad. What if you can't help what kind a'Thoughts you a'thinking I said, Papa said. Why then, Granny Oster said, You just like me and ever body else that's all but you gotta try any how. Take Annie's Mother there for xample, she said, When she passed over the Whole World went total black on me for a hunderd and fifty years but when I reached back in Memory to where my little Daughter was still just a Baby I could find a smile cause I was so glad to have had her in my Life in the first place.

CALLEY AND MISTER OSTER WAS ALL BUT DONE with they patch work on the house and barn when we come a'riding up with the Cows and now the o'Inyin Horse too, Papa said, and Calley said Well I see you increased the population a'Animals round here and I'm glad to see they ain't nobody a'chasing you to get this o'Nelly here back. It took Granny and Annie and me all three a'us to tell em the whole story a'that poor o'one-eyed Inyin Man a'drowning his self in the Creek and for once o'Calley couldn't come up with a Joke bout it. You wouldn't think a Man's Life could get so hard and empty he'd just throw it away in the Creek like that would you, he said. Well it can, Mister Oster said, it dam sure can and then, Papa said, I seen his jaw go tight and he went to looking off somewheres else and Granny Oster took his hand and give it a squeeze and he said A Man lose somebody close to him he'll go to looking for a door to get him the god dam Hell outta his own Life I can tell you that. I'm sorry I didn't know I was bringing up Sad Things, Calley said. Was Sad, Mister Oster said, still is Sad by god. Calley squinted at him, Papa said, and I knowed he was placing him. Yes Sir I heard you found those two Men hurt your Wife. Found em, Mister Oster said, Yes I god dam sure did find em and then Annie said Pa you said we wadn't gonna dwell on it remember. No we ain't gonna dwell on it, Mister Oster said, I was just saying I can see how a Man might get so low he'd drive his wagon off down in the Creek somewheres like yall say that o'one-eyed Inyin did and let harmful things come to him from the Water. Granny squeezed his hand again, Papa said, and said I'm glad you never done that Son that would a'broke my Heart in two. I know it Mister Oster said then Annie stepped over and put her arms round em both and then, he said, Calley took a'holt a'my arm and said Come on I wanna show you some work we done down yonder on the barn and when we got off a ways he said That's a private Can a'Worms I didn't mean to open there and we don't need to be standing around like a'couple a'Bohonks when they go to crying bout their Sad Story. You know that Story huh, Papa said. Everybody in the Country knows that Story, Calley said, I just didn't know it was they Story til a minute ago. What'd Mister Oster do shoot em for hurting his Wife I said, Papa said. No not at first, Calley said, first he tied em to a tree then took his knife out and cut the bottom a'they feet off so they couldn't run off on him if they was to get a'loose when he wadn't looking then he reached tween they legs with his knife and went to whittling on they Sticks and what he whittled off he cut up in little parts and made em eat em ever single one. Oh, Papa said, I don't wanna hear nothing like that Oh No Sir I don't but Calley wadn't through with the Story yet. Then Mister Oster set down to have him a drink a'water right there in front a'them Men and he said Well I reckon you Sons a Bitches is just bout sorry for what you done to my Wife now ain't you then he took this old Shot Gun he had with him and sent em both on off to Burning Hell where they belonged. I just set there, Papa said, trying to get them pitchurs he'd been a'making outta my head. But Calley still wadn't done with it. Next day, Calley said, a couple a'Cowboys come a'riding up and seen them two dead bodies Mister Oster'd whittled on then they come up on Mister Oster setting down there by the Creek a'trying to shoot his own head off but all he could get outta his o'gun was Click Click Click. Anyhow the way I heard it was it took him bout five years to get right in his self again but he wouldn't never talk bout it even though Granny Oster moved in to help with Baby Annie and the house but now look they all three over there just a'crying and a'talking and maybe now he's a'getting it all out on the table to where he can look at it and if he can look at it Well maybe that means it's all coming out of him now and when it does maybe he can just shoo it on off the table like you would some dam o'pesky fly. And then o'Calley thought bout it a minute, Papa said, and said And then again something like that Well no maybe not never.

I COULDN'T SLEEP THAT NIGHT Papa said, for Mister Oster's Sad Story a'running back and forth through my head like some crazy o'Loonie and was just a'twisting and a'turning ever which way to where o'Fritz went off somewheres else to catch him a wink. What's wrong with you, Calley said from over there where I was keeping him awake too. I keep a'seeing that Story you told me bout Mister Oster in my head and it won't let me go to sleep I said, Papa said. Why'd you go and tell me a Story like that anyhow. I think that was the first time in my Life I was ever mad at Calley Pearsall, he said. Calley got up on his elbow and lit the lantern then squinted over at me. I've found in my Life a person who ain't heard Sad Stories about other People don't have no idea what to do with it when the Sad Story is they own, he said. I was just trying to do you a favor. You saying you think I'm gonna have me a Sad Story some day, Papa said. Well you a'breathing air ain't you, Calley said. Yes Sir I believe I am, Papa said. Well then Amigo, he said, they ain't no doubt in my mind but that you gonna have you a Sad Story or two here one a'these days. I ain't gonna be able to sleep for sure, Papa said, now that you got me thinking some o'Sad Story gonna land on me too. Yes Sir and give it nough time gonna be moren one land on you, Calley said, it's just the way the World works but listen here, he said, Good Stories gonna land on you too. They travel in pairs the Good and Bad together and depending on what you do with em they gonna steer your Life one way or the other. Huh, Papa said. That's what Stories are for, Calley said, believe me I know. They was something bout the way he said it, Papa said, made me wanna know more. You got your own Sad Story huh Mister Pearsall, I said. I got more Sad Stories'n you can shake a god dam stick at Calley said. But Good Stories too huh, Papa said. Well the Good Stories is just up the road and a'heading this way I reckon he said. I know what my Sad Story is Papa said. You do huh, Calley said. Yes Sir I do, Papa said, it's if I don't find my Momma here fore too long. Wait a minute, Calley said, you still got your Momma there in your Heart ain't you. Yes Sir I do, Papa said, I sure do. Well then, Calley said, she ain't lost to you. You don't really lose nobody til they gone total outta your Heart, he said, and then, Papa said, o'Calley got him the saddest look you ever seen in your Life there on his face in the lantern light and he said Or til you done gone total out a'theirs.

I GUESS I FINALLY GOT OFF TO SLEEP
Papa said, cause of a sudden I was back home in the Creek and Momma and Herman was both out there in the water a'riding the Little Bay Mare and just a'laughing and a'carrying on and waving at me to Come on in. So, he said, in my Dream I just jumped in clothes and hat and all and went to

swimming to em but hard as I swimmed I couldn't make a inch then I felt something had a'holt a'my foot down under the water and was pulling me down so I kicked and I kicked and then this big o'Fish come up outta the water with his mouth wide open to swaller me up and Oh it wadn't no fish at all but was Old Karl his self and he had me by the toe and was just a'pulling me Down Down Down under the water and then somebody said Get up outta that bed you o'Lazy Bones and I opened my eyes and Annie was there a'wiggling my toe the way she did in the mornings and Boy Hidy was I glad to see her. What's wrong with you, she said, you was having a Fit. I thought somebody was after me I said, Papa said. Granny Oster's whats gonna be after you you don't come on to Breakfast. Go away and I'll put my pants on, Papa said, but I knowed she'd go hide over there somewheres and try to get a peek so I said Sic her Fritz Sic her and Fritz run over there a'barking and Annie run on out the door and up to the house.

What're you doing up so early, Granny Oster said when I come in the house, Papa said, Why I was gonna serve you your breakfast in bed this morning. He's just o'Lazy Bones ain't he Granny, Annie said then patted the chair next to her for me to come set down in so I set down, Papa said, with o'Calley and Mister Oster setting right there cross the table from me and we all just went to eating and didn't nobody say nothing for a long time then o'Calley looked at me and said he and Mister Oster'd been a'talking this morning and Mister Oster'd come up with the idea that I just might like to stay here and move in with them course I'd have to do chores and whatnot to earn my keep. A Boy oughta have a Home and Family Granny said, Papa said, and Annie locked her eyes tight on me to see what I was gonna say and so did ever body else. You don't have to answer while you're a'eating your Breakfast, Calley said. You gonna stay too, Papa said. No not me I can't, Calley said. Remember, he said, I told you I still got some other Fish to Fry. Can I go with you, Papa said. Well I don't know you'd like it where I'm going, Calley said. Well can I go with you anyhow, Papa said, I don't have to like it do I. You'd like it better right here Annie said then Granny Oster said Annie just hush you don't wanna go to nagging on the Boy like that. I seen Calley was watching me, Papa said, so I said You ain't a'saying I can't go with you are you and Calley said No I ain't a'saying that. Well then, Papa said, I'm a'going with you. I won't never find my Momma just a'setting here in one place I don't reckon. Then Annie slapped her fork down on the table and said Well I hope you happy with your self now Mister Calley Pearsall you just helped this Boy here break my poor o'Heart you know it.

SINCE I WAS GOING

Papa said, I wanted to just go on and go right now cause I knowed it was gonna be hard to say Goodbye Annie. And it was, he said. She come down there to the barn when I was putting my o'hull of a saddle on Precious. You really going ain't you, she said. Yes I reckon I am, I said. To find your Momma that's why ain't it Annie said. I give her a nod then she went over to where Fritz was setting up on o'Molly over there side by side next to the o'Inyin Horse and she give him a itch under his chin and he went Heh Heh Heh at her. I guess you a'taking little Fritz here with you to break my Heart in some more places ain't you. Be nice Annie, Papa said. I'm not sure I'd just go to riding off down the Country with Mister Pearsall, she said, I bet he's got him a Secret or two you don't know about. Maybe three or four. I don't care if he does, Papa said, me and him're Amigos. You find your Momma then you'll come back and see me won't you, Annie said. Yes I will, Papa said. What if you don't find your Momma and you get tired a'looking for her, Annie said, will you come back and see me then too. Yes I will, Papa said, But I ain't never gonna get tired a'looking for her til I find her. Some day you and me gonna get Married ain't we Don't you think that's True, she said. I don't know nothing bout getting Married, Papa said, but I reckon we can say that's True less it turns out it ain't True later. No, Annie said, I want you to say its True forever cause I won't have nothing else to go on once you ride off from here if you don't. I come close to just staying there with the Osters, Papa said, that's how many feelings I had for Annie even back then but of a sudden Calley come in and said You ready we need to get on if we're a'going and I said Yes Sir I am ready and got up on Precious and give o'Molly a little whistle to come on but she just stood there with the o'Inyin Horse beside her and wouldn't do it. I give her a couple more whistles and said Come on now Molly Come on but she just stood there then Fritz jumped off her back and run over and jumped up on Precious with me. That o'Swayback ain't a'going, Calley said, she wants to stay right here with her Friend don't she.

Let her stay, Annie said, it won't hurt nothing. Boy Hidy, Papa said, I was happy and sad all at the same time. Happy o'Molly had her a Friend of her own now and a Home to boot but Sad she wadn't gonna be with me no more like she'd always been for all her life and mine too. Then she tossed her head two-three times and winnied and the o'Inyin Horse did too and Calley said They a'saying You go on now they gonna be fine here together and Good Luck to you. I knowed he was right, Papa said, so I got down off Precious and give o'Molly a hug round the neck and the o'Inyin Horse one too then climbed back up on Precious and rode out the barn with Annie a'follering and Fritz crying back at o'Molly then here was Mister Oster and Granny both a'standing there to give us a Goodbye Wave and me and Calley give em a Goodbye Wave back then put our heels to our Horses Precious and Fire-foot and went a'riding on off and the last thing I heard Annie say was Don't you dare forget me and I looked back over my shoulder at her and said Don't you worry any Annie I won't.

*W*HAT BOUT THESE OTHER FISH YOU GOT TO FRY Papa said as they rode along, you never did say what they was. Well they went and changed on me, Calley said, before they was one kind a'Fish I had to Fry then I run across you and now theys a whole nother kind a'Fish I got to Fry. What kind a'nother Fish, Papa said. O'Calley give me a little smile then and said Well I'm gonna help you find your Momma that's what kind a'nother Fish. Oh that did make me happy Papa said, then Calley said I got a few thoughts on where we might go to looking for her but course it's your Momma we gonna be a'looking for so you'd be the one to call the shots if that suits you. I said I guess it did suit me, Papa said, then o'Calley said No don't guess on it You either the Inyin or you the Chief now which one you gonna be. Okay, Papa said, I'll be the Chief. Okay Mister Chief, Calley said, then I'll be the Inyin how's that. Papa said he thought that was fine then reached down and gave Fritz a scratch and Fritz said Heh Heh Heh and then after they rode a while Calley said Where you leading me to Chief and Papa said Well I thought this was the Direction you wanted to go in. No, Calley said, that ain't being the Chief. If you gonna be the Chief then you gotta be the one tells us Inyins which Direction we wanna go in. I don't know what Direction, Papa said. Then you better ask one a'your Inyins if maybe he knows what Direction to go in but what you don't never wanna do if you're the Chief is just set there and say I don't know. Okay Inyin, Papa said, you got any idea what Direction we oughta go in. Yes Sir Chief as a matter a'fact I do, Calley said. I think we oughta back track to where your Momma's Horse Precious come out a'the Brush from in the first place then just ask around and see if anybody round there can tell us where it come from. That was over there toward Kendalia somewheres as I recall, Calley said. That where you wanna go Chief. Yes Sir I reckon it is, Papa said. Okay Chief, Calley said, lead on I'm right behind you. Course I didn't have no idea in the World where Kendalia was at so I said What Direction you reckon Kendalia is in and Calley pointed and said I believe it's yonder ways Chief and I said Well come on you o'Inyin I reckon we a'going this way here and I give Precious just a touch a'my heel and off we went with Calley a'follering long behind. Now you're a'Chiefing he said.

*T*HEY WAS DEER EVER WHERES YOU LOOKED Papa said, and big o'Turkey Gobblers too and Calley pulled out his Lever Action and handed it over. I bet you been thinking it'd be good to have us some meat for our suppers tonight huh Chief, he said. Course they wadn't a Boy born in Texas couldn't shoot a gun so I took it and went off and popped us a nice fat Turkey pretty as you please and Oh we did eat good that night when we made us a camp and o'Fritz did too and after that I had a pile a'Dreams but I only remember one and that was when all them Shimmery People was standing on top of a little hill way off out yonder somewheres and they was all waving at me to come on and it seemed like I took just a step and I was already there and then they went to pointing again and I looked and way out there cross the World was that Limestone Bluff with the Cave in the side of it and growing out the Cave was that same o'curved Cedar Tree just like they'd showed me in earlier times. I see it I said, Papa said, what yall want me to do bout it and then of a sudden we was all standing there at the bottom a'the Bluff looking up at that Cedar Tree a'growing out the Cave and then when I looked round I seen all them Shimmery People just go to blinking out like they wadn't no moren a bunch a'Lightning Bugs and Boy

Hidy I did not like it one little bit cause I was sudden standing there all by myself, he said, and then I looked up and Why there me and Fritz was way up there in the Sky like we was birds looking down and what I seen when I looked down from way up there in the sky was me and Calley Pearsall and Fritz a'standing down there on the ground and we was a'looking at some poor o'dead Horse at the bottom of the Bluff had something way down in its mouth but such a Bad Sick Feeling come over me I didn't stay in my Dream long nough to go down there and see what it was.

*T*HE NEXT MORNING we was just riding long and of a sudden o'Firefoot went to snorting and throwing his head round and then Calley took him a squinty look over his shoulder and said I think they's somebody a'follering me and I don't like who I reckon it is. Neither one of em in fact, he said. Why would somebody wanna foller you I said, Papa said, you ain't done nothing wrong. Well maybe you don't think so, Calley said, but they's some people might not agree with you. Well they'd be wrong, Papa said, ain't that right. Well Yes and No, he said, depends on how you look at it. Yes to me I ain't done nothing wrong but No to them others think Yes I dam sure did do something wrong. Boy Hidy what a puzzle, Papa said, I didn't have no idea what in the World o'Calley was talking bout. Okay, I said. Okay what Chief, Calley said. Okay I don't have no idea in the World what you a'talking bout, Papa said. Well maybe it's time I tell you the whole Story, Calley said, you wanna hear a Story. Yes Sir I do, Papa said. Okay, Calley said, here one night not too long ago me and o'Jack Ivey the Third remember him come a'sneaking up on this o'Horse Trader and his sick Boy in the Dark thinking we might just get us a easy Dollar or two if you know what I mean but they was a complication the Boy was bad sick and just a'coughing away so we just went on our way and no harm done but then o'Jack got to thinking about it and said I bet you that dam Boy wadn't no more sick than I am and all that coughing was just a Trick to keep us from finding they Money and I say we go back and shoot the Man and the Boy both for they dam Joke but I said No we already done gone from there now so let's just keep a'going but o'Jack had his Horns Up and said I don't know about you but I ain't gonna be able to sleep tonight without I first rob somebody Then here in a minute we come up on this little Place on the road where some men was a'drinking and a'playing cards and o'Jack said Well here we are at the Money House ain't we and I said You go in there with your Horns Up like this Jack and you gonna get you self shot to Death and maybe me too so let's just keep a'riding on but Jack said No I told you I ain't a'going to sleep tonight without first I got Somebody's Money a'jingling in my pocket and he went on in and I just set there on Firefoot thinking maybe I oughta just ride on off from here right now but thinking too maybe I oughta go in there and knock o'Jack on his head with my Pistola fore he gets his self shot dead for Bad Behavior. O'Calley stopped talking then, Papa said, and went to looking off out there somewheres like maybe somebody was coming on behind us and I waited a minute or two then I said I bet you went in there to help your Friend ain't that what you done. O'Calley took him a long breath and I knowed this was one a'his Sad Stories. Yes Sir that's what I done, he said, but when I was a'going in o'Jack was a'coming out and he had his pistol in one hand and everbody's Money in the other and then somebody in there pulled a gun out and took a pop at Jack and maybe at me too I don't know but it didn't hit nobody but Jack didn't like it worth a dam any how so he aimed his pistol on the man and said I'll thank you not to shoot at me no more you Son of a Bitch then shot him one right through his Heart or close to it best I could see and then away we went in the Dark but next morning I told o'Jack This ain't the Life for me Jack and Jack said Yes but you too god dam late for that now ain't you and here's the Sad part, Calley said, o'Jack was right bout that and ever since then theys people been looking to get me same way that o'Sheriff a'Comal County got o'Jack for shooting that man dead in his Heart. Oh I felt bad that o'Horse Trader and his sick Boy Calley was talking bout wadn't nobody in the World but me and Old Karl, Papa said, and it like to a'broke my Heart we hadn't just give over our Money that night and then they wouldn't a'been no reason for o'Jack Ivey the Third to go a'robbing and shooting somebody else and then get his self shot to death for it and now maybe my friend Calley Pearsall too but, he said, I was fraid to say Anything bout it cause I didn't wanna lose my Friend over it. I wish that o'Horse Trader and his poor little o'Sick Boy had a'just give you they money, Papa said, wouldn't a'been all this other and you'd be without a care in the World. Well it was my own doing, Calley said, people get placed by the company they keep I wadn't ignorent

136

a'that. But you didn't do nothing, Papa said, just tried to help your Friend is all. No, Calley said, o'Jack wadn't never no Friend a'mine not even for one day a'his sorry o'god dam Life was he a Friend a'mine and also Jack Ivey the Third wadn't never his real name neither No Sir he took names on and off him like some people do they dirty underpants. His real name was Umpton Plum but that name didn't have nough sass to suit him so he throwed it off and put him on another one. Oh, Papa said, well what was you doing with him if he wadn't your Friend. I was trying to keep one eye on him for my sister Eurica, Calley said, o'Umpton was her third husband and one a'them other Fish I got to go Fry when I can get round to it, he said, is ride over there to her place and tell her she better get to looking for Number Four.

WE HADN'T GONE BUT MAYBE ANOTHER MILE or two, Papa said, when o'Calley pulled Firefoot up and said I know I told you you was the Chief but now I got to ask you to be the Inyin instead and let me be the Chief okay. Okay but what'd I do wrong, Papa said. Nothing, Calley said, but they's Men after me and I don't want em to place you by being with me the same way I placed myself by being with o'Jack so I got to run you off. Yes Sir, Papa said, but I thought we was Amigos. Yes Sir we are Amigos, Calley said. Well then, Papa said, I'm a'staying with you Amigo even if they get me for it. Didn't we just say I was the Chief and you was the Inyin, Calley said, didn't we just say that. I don't remember, Papa said. Calley give me the Eye then, Papa said, and said You don't remember that or you don't wanna remember that which one is it. Both, Papa said. No, Calley said, when you was the Chief you got to tell us Inyins what to do but now I'm the Chief and I get to tell you Inyins what to do ain't that what we said. What if I say I don't care what we said, Papa said. Then, Calley said, I'd say If you can't keep your Word to me I wouldn't wanna ride with you no how cause being able to count on a man's Word is the most important thing they is or was or ever will be in this World. I didn't say I Didn't Care what we said, Papa said, I said What If I didn't care what we said. Well now just hold on a minute, Calley said, I didn't never think for one minute you wadn't gonna keep your Word to me cause I know you are good for ever Word you say to me ain't you. Yes Sir I am, Papa said. Okay, Calley said, Who are you then.

I'm the Inyin, Papa said. Who you think is a'looking for you anyhow. I know who's a'looking for me, Calley said, it's the Pardee Brothers Barnell and Udell mean god dam Peckerwoods the both of em that's who. What they want with you, Papa said. It was they brother Udo Pardee o'Jack shot and killed that night funny names they got huh and like I said I got saddled with the Act right long with Jack cause I was there with him and now they wanna shoot me for it. Where you gonna go, Papa said. Oh nowheres in particular, Calley said, probably just ride round the Country with my head down til they get tired a'looking for me. What if they don't get tired, Papa said, what if they just keep on a'coming on. Well then, Calley said, I reckon I'll just have to ride on down there to Mexico and go to cooking Beans for my Living. You reckon I'll ever see you again Mister Pearsall, Papa said. You go on and keep a'looking for your Momma like always and if somebody don't put bout sixteen-twenty bullet holes in me I'll sneak up on you when you ain't looking one a'these days and give you a Surprise Howdy Do how's that. You give me your Word on that, Papa said. Yes Sir I do, Calley said, then he put his finger to his hat and rode on off, Papa said, then here in just a minute he was out a'sight and gone and I said to Fritz, Fritz, I said, you reckon it'd hurt any if we was to just foller long behind in case our o'Amigo is to need a hand with them Pardee Brothers coming after him and o'Fritz grinned and said Heh Heh Heh.

$\mathcal{S}$O WE FOLLERED CALLEY'S TRACKS Papa said, and I seen where they went in the Creek but I couldn't see where they come out the other side so I figgured o'Calley just went a'riding right on down the middle a'the Creek so he wouldn't leave no Tracks for them Pardee Brothers to foller so I went a'riding down the middle a'the Creek too thinking when I seen where Calley come out Why then I'll just foller him on Dry Land but I rode and I rode and I rode and still didn't see no Tracks a'him coming outta the Creek then a Voice said Why you a'riding down the middle a'the Creek like that it ain't no road and I looked over and setting there on a old Mule was a Boy bout my size. You talking to me I said, Papa said. You the only one in the Creek ain't you, the Boy said. If you gonna be a Smarty Pants bout it I'm gonna just keep on a'going, Papa said. No I ain't, the Boy said, I just don't know how to talk to People is all and my Momma says I ain't gonna get very far in Life if I don't learn how. My name's Arlon, he said. You didn't see a Man come riding by here in the Creek did you Arlon, Papa said. Why you ain't looking for somebody are you, Arlon said. Well I'm a'looking for my Momma, Papa said, but I need to find this other Man I'm looking for now to help me with it. No I ain't seen a Man but I only been here a short while, Arlon said, I'm on my way over to my Granma Nettie's place where my Aunt Mary lives with her then I'm just gonna ride round the Country for maybe a year or two to see what I can see. Ain't you got a Home, Papa said. Yes but I left my Home behind, Arlon said, I already seen it my whole Life and don't reckon I need to see it no more. You ain't got no Home neither huh, he said. Home's where ever my Momma is, Papa said, that's why I'm a'looking for her. Well, Arlon said, you can come with me over to my Granma Nettie's place if you want to maybe her or my Aunt Mary seen this Man you looking for come a'riding by there and they might could tell you which way he went on to. You're a good Friend and I thank you, Papa said, then I rode up outta the Creek and when I got over to Arlon on his Mule he reached out to give Fritz a pet and said Your Dog ain't gonna bite my arm off is he. Probably your arm and your leg both, Papa said, then we went to laughing cause that would a'been hard for Fritz to do he was so little. Once I settle down somewheres I'm gonna get me a Dog too, Arlon said, maybe even eight or six of em I ain't sure yet. This little Dog here and my Horse is the best Friends I got in the World, Papa said. I know it, Arlon said, then turned his o'Mule and we rode on off for his Granma Nettie's place and in just a little bit it turned Dark on us and we still wadn't there. You do know where your o'Granma Nettie lives out here in the Dark don't you I said, Papa said. Well I never been there in my Life, Arlon said, but I reckon it's out here somewhere if I can just find it.

$\mathcal{S}$EEMED LIKE WE RODE ALL NIGHT LONG

Papa said, then we come up on this Farm with a lantern light in the winder and Arlon hollered Hello the House Hello the House and here come this woman out the door just a'crying and a'moaning like some o'Loonie and Arlon said That's my Aunt Mary there but I believe they's something wrong don't you so we went over to her and Arlon said Aunt Mary what's come over you you ain't gone loco on us have you and his Aunt Mary went a'running in the kitchen and Oh they was a Dead Woman on the floor with a spoon in her hand and a pot a'beans spilled out all over the floor. Why that's my Granma Nettie ain't it, Arlon said then went to pulling on her to get that poor o'Dead Woman back up on her feet. Get up Granma, he said, Get up Get up Get up but o'Granma Nettie wadn't no moren a sack a'potatoes so Aunt Mary and me give a hand and we all three got her up and put her flat on the kitchen table, Papa said, and then I got her dress down so couldn't nobody see nothing. Oh My Goodness Gracious Sakes Alive Arlon, Aunt Mary said, we got to run go tell Floyd and Erma we got us a Death in the Family so somebody can get to digging a grave over yonder next to Daddy's. Uh oh I thought, Papa said, I hope she ain't planning on leaving me here with some o'Dead Woman. I'll go with you, Papa said but Aunt Mary said No you stay here I don't want the Varmints to get in the house and go to eating on my Mother while we're gone. When you reckon you'll be back, Papa said. I'd guess sometime tomorrow or the next day, she said, I'm not sure which. Papa said he thought tomorrow'd be best for him and Aunt Mary said she'd try but she couldn't make no Promises cause sometime it was hard to get away from Erma she liked to talk so much. And all this time, Papa said, Fritz was over there eating beans up off the floor. You better watch your little Dog there eating all them beans, Aunt Mary said, that's what Mama was doing when she fell down dead on the floor. I think she might a'put too many hot Chili Peppers in there that's why, she said, but she wouldn't never listen to me about it or nothing else neither. Fritz I said, Papa said, Fritz get away from them beans but it was too late, he said, all the beans was gone and now Fritz was over there in the corner just a'licking away on his little Behind I reckon cause a'all them Chili Peppers in the beans he ate.

*A*RLON AND HIS AUNT MARY RODE ON OFF Papa said, and there I was all by myself with poor o'dead Granma Nettie and they wadn't nothing to do but just pull up a chair and wait til they got on back. And that's what I did, he said, but then the candles started a'flickering like somebody was trying to blow em out and then Oh I heard somebody go a'walking back and forth cross the wood floor in they bare feet and I looked over at Granma Nettie to make sure she wadn't the one a'doing it and when I did Why she give me a big Wink then grinned and went to wiggling her toes the way you might your own fingers. Oh Boy Hidy, Papa said, I didn't wanna see nothing like that so I squeezed both my eyes shut and just set there but then here in a minute the Possums and the Coons and I don't know What All Else went to scratching on the doors and winders and even up there in the attic trying to get in I reckon for a little snack on Aunt Mary's Momma but Oh that wadn't all, he said, right there in the middle a'all them Varmints trying to get in they was this little Putta-Putta-Putta-Putta sound like that but just to where you could hardly hear it but I tell you it was a Toot for sure so I opened up my eyes and first I thought Why that must be o'Fritz tooting over there where he's still a'licking on his little Hiney in the corner and I said Fritz what's wrong with you you eat too many a'them beans up off the floor tonight but then, Papa said, all of a sudden here come that Putta-Putta-Putta again and Oh I like to a'jumped out a'my pants this time cause wadn't o'Fritz a'doing it at all No Sir it was poor o'dead Granma Nettie just a'laying there flat on the kitchen table and Tooting away like some o'Freight Train. Oh listen here, Papa said, I run in the other room quick as I could and grabbed up a quilt off the bed then went back in there and covered her up head to foot with it and Whew I didn't hear no more Toots outta her but then, he said, it got so quiet I started just a'singing away to keep myself company but then, Papa said, Granma Nettie started joining in so I went to singing loud and fast as I could to get her to hush but No she wouldn't and so I stopped singing and just went to hollering loud as I could but she did too and wadn't but a minute and we was both just a'hollering away so loud the dishes went to rattling and I seen a mouse go running in a hole and then Fritz went to barking and going in Circles and then of a sudden Oh they was this great big Knock Knock Knock on the door and I come up out a'that chair like my Pants was on Fire.

I OPENED THE DOOR

Papa said, and they was these two Men a'standing there. I knowed right away who they was, he said, They was the Pardee Brothers and they had em each one a pistol in they hand. Who else there in the house with you, the older one Barnell said. Nobody, Papa said, just one o'dead Granma Lady.

Dead is she, Udell said, how'd she ride a Horse to here then. She didn't ride no Horse to here, Papa said, she was already here dead on the floor. We just tracked two Horses to here, Barnell said. Was you a'riding one of em, Udell said. Yes Sir I was, Papa said, if you mean from over yonder at the Creek. And who was you with, Barnell said, and don't go to storying bout it. I was with a Boy bout my size name a'Arlon, Papa said. You was huh, Barnell said. Yes Sir I was, Papa said. No you wadn't, Udell said. Yes Sir I was I said again, Papa said, How you know anything bout it anyhow. Well where is o'Arlon then, Barnell said, I don't see him no wheres. He and his Aunt Mary rode off to go tell the kinfolks Granma Nettie is dead and get em to go to digging a grave over yonder next to Somebody or Other. So you telling me Calley Pearsall ain't here in the house with you, Barnell said. Who, Papa said. Don't go trying to pull the Wool over our eyes Mister, Udell said, we know they was a Boy a'riding with Calley Pearsall when they had o'Jack Ivey the Third on Show over there in that Lockhart Saloon and that's you ain't it. Was me then, Papa said, ain't me now. I hear you saying Calley Pearsall ain't here in the house with you, Barnell said, is that what I hear you a'saying. No Sir he ain't, Papa said, just poor o'dead Granma Nettie. I reckon we gonna have to see that for our self Mister, Udell said. Yes Sir, Papa said, well come on in but it ain't Calley Pearsall and he didn't have nothing to do with shooting your brother Udo neither I hope you know that. He was with Jack Ivey the Third that night, Udell said, that's Guilty nough for us. Papa stepped back and pointed to the kitchen. See her on the table in there, he said. I put a quilt on her cause she kept a'grinning at me. Barnell and Udell raised up they pistols, Papa said, and Barnell said O'dead woman was a'grinning at you huh then they give each other a nod and creeped on over to the kitchen door and looked in. So that's o'Granny there on the kitchen table is it, Barnell whispered. Yes Sir, Papa whispered back. You sure that ain't o'Calley Pear-sall just playing Possum on us. No Sir it ain't, Papa whispered, take a look you don't believe me. We'll do what we dam well please Mister, Udell whis-pered, now do you self a favor and go hide under the bed or somewheres. And then, Papa said, the Pardee Brothers pointed they pistols on Granma Nettie and went to tip-toeing at her one little step at a time and when they got right close Barnell give Udell a sign and Udell reached to pull the quilt back but just when he did poor o'dead Granma Nettie let go a big PUTTA-PUTTA-PUTTA-PUTTA and Oh them Pardee Brothers was so surprised by

Boy Hidy they some people sure gonna be mad at you two for shooting up they poor o'dead Granma like this.

it they just went to hollering and jumping and shooting off they guns and Fritz let off a'licking his Hiney and went to barking and running round in circles again and Oh I run over there behind the door to save my Life and when they was done shooting off all they bullets Barnell said Well I reckon that SonofaBitch done had bout all a'that he wants huh and Udell said Yes I reckon he's one dead Possum now ain't he. It ain't Calley Pearsall like you think it is, Papa said. Boy Hidy they some people sure gonna be mad at you two for shooting up they poor o'dead Granma like this. And then, he said, Barnell and Udell went to laughing at me and Barnell said The Hell you say. Yes Sir I reckon the Hell I do say, Papa said, then they eased over there and Udell pulled the quilt back and Oh they like to a'fell over dead they self cause wadn't no body under there but poor o'dead Granma Nettie. See what I tolt you Papa said.

BARNELL AND UDELL PARDEE

couldn't neither one of em find they tongues for bout a year, Papa said, then Barnell said Udell I think we in some trouble here for Murder. Murder, Udell said. Murder. This dam Boy said o'Granma here was already dead didn't he. How can you Murder some body if they already dead, he said. What got me worried, Barnell said, is Was she already dead. You heard her make that noise same as me didn't you. Udell went to thinking bout it a minute, Papa said, then said Uh Oh. But maybe dead people do that too, Barnell said, I don't have no idea. Well I reckon the Sheriff'll know, Papa said, or go find him somebody that does. The Pardee Brothers just went total Froze when I said that, he said, and Udell said Barnell I don't like it what this Boy here just said and Barnell said No I don't like it neither We didn't mean to do nothing wrong did we. O'Calley Pearsall didn't mean to do nothing wrong neither, Papa said, but yall was sure nough ready to shoot him for it any-how wadn't you and now I reckon some o'Sheriff or other gonna feel the same way bout yall too huh. This little Booger likes to talk don't he Barnell, Udell said. Yes but what's wrong, Barnell said, is this little Booger here just might be right. I wish to Hell we'd just a'stayed to home. Well No we had to do right by our Brother Udo didn't we, Udell said. Ain't that what you said. That's fore it all come to this, Barnell said. Now I don't believe I'd a'said that No I know I wouldn't then Barnell set down there at the table, Papa said, and went to praying I reckon and in a minute he reached up and took a'holt a'Granma Nettie's hand and closed his eyes like he was trying to talk to her in his head and then after a time he opened his eyes up and said What we got to do now is patch this Old Woman up like we didn't never shoot her in the first place and won't nobody ever know we did what we did. What about this Boy here, Udell said and pointed his gun, He knows. No I don't believe he does know, Barnell said then raised up a eye brow at me, Papa said, and said Do you Mister. It took me a minute but then I seen the bargain he was wanting to make with me and I said No Sir I don't know nothing bout it a'tall Just long as you ain't a'looking for o'Calley Pearsall no more for some-thing he didn't never do no how. Alright then we ain't, Barnell Pardee said. Why don't we shake on it, Papa said, and stuck out his hand. Why you a sneaky little Booger ain't you, Udell said, but Barnell give him a poke in his ribs, Papa said, and we all three shaked hands on it.

ALL THAT SHOOTING

Papa said, and turned out them Pardees didn't put but one bullet in poor o'dead Granma Nettie anyhow and that one was up there round her Belly Button and they cleaned the little hole up and her dress covered over the top a'that. But Oh, he said, they was bullet holes just bout ever wheres else you looked in the walls and the floor and even up there in the ceiling and they went to carving plugs outta a oak stick they found then hammered em in to where you couldn't hardly see nothing less you knowed just where to look and Udell said Maybe we oughta go in the Business but his brother Barnell said This ain't no time for jokes Udell now run go get the Horses we got a long ride to Home and when they was a'climbing in the saddle Barnell looked down at me and said You give me your Word you ain't gonna tell nobody. No Sir and I ain't, Papa said, I'm good for ever Word I say. Well, he said, I'm gonna send out the News that we ain't a'looking for Calley Pearsall no more so he can sleep at night. He's lucky you come along to save him. Well if I did, Papa said, I don't have no idea how. I don't neither, Barnell said, but I got this feeling however it was might a'just saved me and Udell here too. I'm sorry bout your brother Udo, Papa said, I reckon he was a nice man huh. Well it varied a great deal Barnell said and then they rode on off to

Home, Papa said, and I went on down to the barn and done the chores like I knowed Arlon's Aunt Mary'd want me to then here she come with a Man and a Wood Box in a wagon long bout Sun Down but no Arlon. Where's Arlon I said, Papa said, and Aunt Mary said His Momma and Daddy is watching him so he don't go running off somewheres again. Arlon got him a bad habit a'doing that and they just about decided they got to tie him down to keep him Home. Well tell him goodbye for me when you see him, Papa said. You ain't gonna go back with us to the Grave, she said. No Ma'am, Papa said, I'm a'looking for my Momma and I'm hoping to find her just up the road a'piece. Well you go on then, Aunt Mary said, you been a good Friend to look after my Mother for me while I was gone. I hope it wadn't no trouble to you. Oh No Ma'am wadn't no trouble at all, Papa said, didn't seem like you was gone no moren a minute or two the whole night long.

O FF ME AND FRITZ WENT AGAIN ON PRECIOUS Papa said, but we hadn't gone a mile down the road when here come Arlon on his old Mule. Surprised to see me ain't you, he said. I reckon your Momma and Daddy gonna be surprised too ain't they I said, Papa said, when they find out you gone off again. I reckon so, Arlon said but didn't seem much troubled bout it. So where we going, he said. I'm going up this road to find my Momma, Papa said, I don't have no idea where you a'going. With you if you let me, Arlon said. But don't worry bout it if you don't want to. He looked all sad bout it like Fritz did that day I found him in the road. Well it's okay with me so long as you ain't got another o'Granma out here in the Woods somewheres. Why what happened, her o'ghost didn't get after you did it, he said. No, Papa said, but your Granma Tooted and then two Men come a'running in a'shooting off they pistols at her. Tooted, Arlon said. Yes Sir, Papa said, Tooted. Dead people don't Toot, Arlon said, do they. Your o'Granma did, Papa said, almost took the roof off the house with it too. Naw you just saying that, Arlon said. That's not something I'd say if it wadn't True, Papa said, you know me better'n that don't you. Arlon shook his head like he just couldn't believe it, Papa said, and said I'd a'liked to a'seen that. Wadn't nothing to see, Papa said, but you sure had to hold your ears shut to keep from hearing it. Arlon all but fell off his old Mule a'laughing at that,

Papa said, and in a minute I was laughing too and then o'Fritz couldn't help his self neither and went to going Heh Heh Heh and we rode on down the road for a while all three of us just a'laughing away. What's your Momma gonna do when she sees me with you, Arlon said. She ain't gonna run me off is she you don't reckon. Well if she don't I might, Papa said, but Arlon didn't see no Joke in it and I knowed right then he had him a Sad Story. You ain't had a Happy Life huh Arlon I said but he didn't say nothing back. You ain't alone, Papa said, everbody's got em a Sad Story if they a'living and breathing, he said. Mine's if I don't find my Momma. Mine's if my Momma finds me, Arlon said. That don't make no sense, Papa said. It would if you knowed her like I do, Arlon said, but I ain't gonna say nothing bad bout her. Okay you don't have to, Papa said, we just talking here anyhow. You are, Arlon said, but I ain't talking no more. Okay, Papa said, they ain't no law says you have to. You must Love your Momma to wanna find her so bad, Arlon said. Yes Sir I do, Papa said. She didn't never whup you ever day a'your Life with a leather strap huh, Arlon said. No she'd a'never, Papa said, but my Daddy might. My Momma don't care, Arlon said, wadn't nothing for her to go a'whupping my Daddy too. And he didn't do nothing bout it, Papa said. Took him another pull on his Jug is all, Arlon said, and then went to crying like some little o'Baby. Boy Hidy you do have you a Sad Story don't you Arlon, Papa said. Yes and when I grow up, Arlon said, I'm gonna go back and shoot the both of em for it when they ain't looking.

We WAS JUST RIDING ALONG

Papa said, and Arlon give me this look and said You ever take things don't belong to you. Why No I never, Papa said, that's stealing. Well that's how I make my living, he said. If somebody ain't watching they shoes I'll steal em right off they feet. They'll put you in the Jail House for that, Papa said, did you know that. Put you in the Jail House and throw away the key. Feed you too, Arlon said. It ain't all bad. So you been in the Jail House before huh, Papa said. Yes Sir been in the Jail House and been in there moren once too, Arlon said, and I reckon I'll be a'going back in there again here one a'these days. Now why would you say something like that, Papa said. It's just how I feel in me that's all, Arlon said. Not me, Papa said, I don't want no part a'the Jail House and listen you just better not go to stealing nothing from me you hear. No I ain't, Arlon said, you the only Friend I got. I ain't big, Papa said, but I'm big nough to fix you if I have to. I said I ain't, Arlon said. Yes but some people that steal can't tell the Truth neither, Papa said. I wish you hadn't a'told me bout you stealing things now I reckon I got to keep my Eye on you don't I. It probably wouldn't hurt to, Arlon said. Maybe I better keep my eye on me too. Okay I said, Papa said, and then Arlon said Okay too and we rode on a ways and then he said After you find your Momma what you gonna do. First thing'd be to go get my Brother Herman back from over there in New Braunfels, Papa said, then we could have us a Family again. And then what, Arlon said. Nothing, Papa said, I don't believe they'd never be nothing no better'n that and if they was I don't know what it'd be. Maybe I could come over there and help you with your chores sometimes, Arlon said. Well you could if you want to, Papa said, you'd be welcome. Arlon didn't say nothing for a long time, Papa said, then he said You reckon I could come over there and Live with you and your Family too. I don't see no reason why not, Papa said, course you'd have to quit all your stealing for good cause my Momma just wouldn't have it in the Family. Oh and then Arlon just went to Dreaming a'way, Papa said. Would they be room for my Horse too, he said. You ain't got no Horse, Papa said, that's a Mule you got there. I know it but if I was to get me a Horse, Arlon said. How you gonna get you a Horse, Papa said, you ain't planning to go steal one off somebody are you. I thought you told me you done give up all that stealing. I did, Arlon said. So what Horse you talking about then, Papa said. Well okay if I ain't got no Horse, Arlon said, you reckon they'd be room for just my Mule then. Well we'd just have to make room for your Mule if they wadn't, Papa said, and then Arlon reached down and give his old Mule a pet on the neck and said, You hear that Colonel we got us a Family and a Home.

*S*O NEXT DAY WE WAS JUST RIDING
on down the road to Kendalia again, Papa said, and here come this o'Farmer up behind us in his wagon but they was more to it than that cause setting in the back a'the wagon was Old Karl's two Mexkins Pepe and Peto. I give the Farmer a Good Morning, Papa said, and Arlon did too then I said Where'd

148

you get them two Mexkins you got here in your wagon and the Farmer said
They come walking up to my place here a couple a'months ago a'looking for
Work and I took em in. Never seen no better Workers. Why you know em,
he said. Yes Sir I do, Papa said, then looked over and seen Peto take his shoe
off and hold his foot up at me the one with the missing big toe on it so I'd
know him and I put my hands up under my arms and went to flapping my
elbows like a chicken and going Puck-puck-pa-kuck Puck-puck-pa-kuck so
he'd see Yes I knowed him too and he give me a mean ugly look for it. Where
you think he lost his big toe, Arlon said. I know where he lost it, Papa said,
I chopped it off for him with a Grubbing Hoe one night that's where he lost
it. So where you Boys headed for, the Farmer said. Kendalia I reckon, Papa
said, you know how far that is. Still a ways, the Farmer said, that's where
I'm a'taking these two Fellas here. I don't know why you would, Papa said.
They got em a bunch a'Brothers and Sisters and god knows what all round
there somewheres, the Farmer said, and I told em they do good Work for
me for one month Why I'd just ride em on up there in my wagon and let em
visit a day or two for Pleasure. They tell you anything bout where they was
working fore they got to you, Papa said. They said for some old Cabron, the
Farmer said, it's a bad word they got means Shit Head something like that
don't it. I reckon it does, Papa said, they was talking bout Old Karl and them
words just bout fits him like a glove. Well they been a'doing good Work for
me, the Farmer said, and I don't see no harm in keeping my Word to em.
Well I don't think you'd owe a Mexkin nothing, Arlon said. He's talking bout
keeping his Word Arlon this ain't bout no Mexkins, Papa said, ain't that
right. I've known a lotta men in my Life, the Farmer said, and far as I can
see these Mexkins here is good as any. I might could say the same bout some
Coloreds I know too. Well No Sir I don't think you could, Arlon said, that's
why god painted em black and turned em a'loose over there somewheres
where they ain't no White People. Africa, the Farmer said. Well you might
be right, he said, I don't xpect they's a smarter Boy n'you in the whole World
from the look of you. Oh Arlon just went to beaming at that, Papa said, then
the Farmer said we was welcome to ride along with him and the Mexkins if
we liked and I didn't see where it'd hurt any if we did so I give him a nod and
said Thank You and we went on up the road with Arlon just a'smiling away
to his self at being the smartest Boy in the World.

149

THE FARMER GIVE ME AND ARLON AND FRITZ

some boiled potayto for our suppers, Papa said, and the same for Pepe and Peto and we all set there round the fire a'eating together. You ain't a Preacher are you, Arlon said, letting these Mexkins set here with us like this. Eat your supper the Farmer said and be glad I'm a'letting you set here too. Arlon was still just a Boy like me, Papa said, but he already had him some Snake Eyes and he put em on the Farmer. You saying I don't belong here, he said. No Sir, the Farmer said, I was just trying to say Go on and eat your supper and don't worry bout no body else. Well what if I don't wanna eat with no Mexkins, Arlon said, what if it's against my Religion. Well then, the Farmer said, I'd have to tell you to go off over yonder somewheres else to eat your supper cause this is my Table I set here and I'll be the one says who can eat at it. Arlon they ain't no call for you to go to acting this way, Papa said. Why don't you just be quiet and eat your suppers. Cause I don't like eating with no Mexkins that's why, Arlon said. Well I don't neither, Papa said, but it don't mean we gotta eat with em ever day the rest a'our Life. I believe you just bout smart as your Friend here ain't you, the Farmer said. Now why don't we all just leave off talking and go to eating. So we went to eating, Papa said, and Arlon put his Snake Eyes on the Mexkins and here in a minute Peto got him some Snake Eyes too and he put em right back on Arlon and they just set there doing the Snake Eyes on each other and then Arlon said If I had me a Grubbing Hoe I'd come over there and chop your other big toe off for you What would you think bout that. But course Peto couldn't understand a word of it, Papa said, and Arlon laughed and said Look at that Mexkin he's so dumb he don't even understand a Word I say. Tell him in Mexkin then, the Farmer said. What's that, Arlon said. I said Tell him in Mexkin what you wanna tell him, the Farmer said, so he can understand you a'saying you gonna come over there in a minute and chop his toe off for him. I would, Arlon said, but I don't speak no Mexkin. Well I speak a little, the Farmer said, you want me to tell him he better look out you gonna come over there in a minute and chop his toe off for him with a Grubbing Hoe. I don't speak a lot a'Mexkin but I can probably get that much over to him for you, he said. Oh and then, Papa said, Arlon took his o'Snake Eyes off Peto and throwed em over on the Farmer like you might a rock or something. You a'trying to Joke me ain't you he said. What if I was to get my Grubbing Hoe and come over there and chop your toe off with it. Son, the Farmer said, you might not know it yet but you gonna go to Hell in a Hand Basket you keep a'behaving this way and then he give me a Look to see if I was listening too and went on over there and put Fritz down in the Dish Water and give him a good warshing long with ever thing else. Arlon, Papa said, you ain't a'making us no Friends here. Then for just a snap a'your finger, he said, Arlon put his Snake Eyes over on me and I seen xactly what the o'Farmer was talking bout.

PEPE AND PETO DIDN'T SAY NOT ONE WORD the whole trip, Papa said, but then we started going up this little hill and they stood up in the wagon and went to jabbering back and forth then we started down the other side and Oh they started a'laughing and a'pointing cause just down the road a ways was all these Mexkin shacks and running out from em was just a whole bunch a'little Mexkins a'all sizes and then, he said, Pepe and Peto couldn't wait no more and they jumped out the wagon and run on down there to meet em and then just all of em went to hollering and hugging and laughing and crying and the Farmer said That's they Family there. Oh and then here come some Mommas and Papas and Brothers and Sisters and Cousins and I don't know who all else and wadn't but a minute and Pepe and Peto was each a'hugging on some Mexkin Lady and little Mexkins was just a'jumping all over em and then some Old People come a'walking up and went to hugging on em too. They all glad to see each other ain't they, the Farmer said, ain't nobody believes in Family moren a Mexkin does you know it. Yes Sir, Papa said, I never seen nobody so glad to see each other in my whole Life and then Pepe come back to the wagon with bout a hundred little Mexkins hanging on him and said something to the Farmer and the Farmer said He's a'asking Don't we wanna stay and eat supper with em they gonna cook a Goat and while they was talking here come all them little Mexkins over to me and Fritz setting there on Precious and Oh they just went to petting on Fritz and laughing they liked him so much and Fritz liked them too and put his big grin on. I don't believe I'd let em pet my Dog like that, Arlon said, you don't know what they got But I didn't see no harm in it, Papa said, and figgured if I was one a'them little Mexkins why I'd wanna pet o'Fritz too. They can pet on Fritz all they want to I said,

Papa said, I don't see no reason Why Not. Your little Dog up and die on you from all them Mexkins petting on him you gonna see Why Not, Arlon said. Well if you so worried bout it, Papa said, don't let em pet on your Dog then. I don't have me no Dog, Arlon said. Well when you get one don't let em pet on him then. No Sir I won't, Arlon said, now you ready to get on. I was, Papa said, but then I looked over and here come Pepe with all them little Mexkins a'hanging on him and he said something to me but I didn't have no idea what. He's asking you and your Friend there to stay for a supper on that Goat, the Farmer said. Not me, Arlon said, I don't want no part a'eating with a bunch a Mexkins. How bout you, the Farmer said, this fella here just trying to show you some Good Manners is all. That struck me funny, Papa said, cause long as I a'knowed Pepe and Peto they never tried to show me no Manners at all that I could remember and then, he said, it come to me that No I never did them neither. Let's go on, Arlon said. And I might a'done it too, Papa said, but right then here come this music up from them shacks down there and it was a Horn and a Guitar coming together and the music from it was like a rope tied round my neck just a'pulling me to it and they just wadn't nothing I could do bout it. You go on, Papa said, I'm gonna stay here and have some suppers on that o'Goat with all these Mexkins.

I TURNED O'FRITZ A'LOOSE

Papa said, and away he went a'running down the road with them little Mexkins just a'laughing and a'chasing him to them shacks down there and I went too, he said, and when I got down there I climbed off Precious and follered the music and come up on these two Mexkin Men just a'setting there under a tree with a Horn and a big o'fat Guitar and Oh it was so pretty to hear I bout fell over dead on the ground a'listening but then here come all these other Mexkins with Milking Stools and benches and whatnot to set on and I set on one of em too and next thing they was little Mexkins in my lap and all over me and Peto and that Farmer both setting down right there next to me and over yonder three Mexkins cooking that Goat but I couldn't hardly see it I was so swallered up by the tune. You like music don't you, the Farmer said, I never seen Nobody so taken by it. I wish I could play me a song, Papa said, I'd like to be a Horn Man like that fella there someday. The

152

Farmer said something to Peto in his language and Peto looked over and give me a smile and a nod, Papa said, and it was like we was old Friends bout it then here come some more Mexkins with they own Horns and Guitars and Fiddles and one had him a Drum and I don't know what all else and they went to making music too and then more Mexkins come from ever which direction to listen and then here Fritz jumped up in my lap with all them little Mexkins and you just never seen or heard nothing like that music in all your Life, he said, and the smell a'that o'Goat just a'cooking over there on the fire didn't hurt nothing neither. But the big thing, Papa said, was this old old Mexkin Man come out there in front a'everbody else on his walking stick and went to singing this sad sad song and ever Mexkin there went to crying or was bout to and I asked the Farmer What's that song bout to make all these Mexkins cry like this and he said He's a'singing bout his Lost Home back across the River over there in Mexico and he's singing If something bad happens to him over here in Texas somewheres and he should die from it just say No he ain't dead he's just a'sleeping and then take him on back to Mexico that he loves with all his Heart and bury him in the ground over there. That's a sad song ain't it, Papa said. Yes it is, the Farmer said, and all these other Mexkins here'd sing you the very same song I reckon. And the more I listened to that Old Mexkin sing bout his Lost Home over there cross the River, Papa said, the more I got to thinking Why I must have a little Mexkin in me too cause I was always crying to my self bout my Momma and my own Lost Home same as him.

*T*HEY KEPT A'COOKING GOATS AND PLAYING MUSIC way up in the Night, Papa said, and everbody just a'dancing and a'singing and a'hanging on to everbody else and passing a bottle a'something or other round tween em but I just set there listening to all that music they was making and just couldn't get nough to fill me up it was so pretty. You better get on to bed, the Farmer said, you gonna still be setting here when the Sun comes up if you ain't careful. I just ain't never heard nothing like it, Papa said. Well, the Farmer said, I've heard it said Color is the Luxury of the Poor but I reckon that's true a'Music too don't you. I nodded, Papa said, but I didn't have no idea what Luxury was or where you might could

get you some. I'm glad to see you having such a good time, the Farmer said. You didn't look so happy when I first come up on you yesterday. I reckon I'm gonna be happy when I find my Momma, Papa said, that's who I been a'looking for. You think she's in Kendalia huh, the Farmer said. I hope so, Papa said, that's where somebody got her Horse Precious off her but I got her now but not her Saddle. Her saddle, the Farmer said. Yes Sir, Papa said, her Daddy took it off a dead Mexkin in the Battle had big bright Conchos all over it. Conchos, the Farmer said, was it Nickel Conchos and square skirts and single rigged. Oh I just come alive at that, Papa said, and I said You seen my Momma's Saddle huh. Well maybe but not round here no wheres, the Farmer said. Where then, Papa said. I ain't saying it was your Momma's Saddle, the Farmer said, but I seen one like it in back a wagon parked front of the Hardware Store over yonder in Sadler I think it was. Sadler, Papa said, Why that's way over there close to Home where I come from. Whose wagon was it. Oh don't have no idea whose wagon I reckon was somebody who went in the Hardware Store that's who. And you didn't never see who come out and went off in the wagon huh, Papa said. No the Farmer said, that was some time ago I'm talking about. Boy Hidy, Papa said, my Momma's Horse Precious and now her Saddle too but right then, he said, this Mexkin come up and kicked dirt on me and went to hollering and cussing and shaking both his hands at me and I was bout to take off a'running but I wadn't gonna leave o'Fritz behind so I just set there like a Knot on a Log and him a'going at me like a Loonie. Don't say nothing back to him, the Farmer said down low, that man's drunk on something. Why don't he like me, Papa said, I didn't do nothing. Cause you're White the Farmer said, why you think. Then that Loonie kicked dirt over on the Farmer too then went to kicking more and more on both a'us to where it looked like he was dancing a jig but wadn't funny cause here some others started a'doing it too and I could see they ever one had they Snake Eyes on and I was scared what they was gonna do to us but the Farmer kept a'whispering Just don't say nothing Just don't say nothing but them Mexkins they went on with it to where I thought Oh they gonna murder us for being White but then of a sudden somebody come a'pushing through em and a'hollering something or other and Why it wadn't nobody but Peto buttoning up his pants and his Wife there with him and then here come Pepe too with a bunch a'little Mexkins a'follering and they went to hollering and shooing all them other Mexkins back to where

I just set there listening to all that music
they was making and just couldn't get nough 155
to fill me up it was so pretty.

they come from and then went to talking at the Farmer and the Farmer said They a'saying they's some White People here in Texas treats Mexkins like Throw Away People and they had em too much to drink tonight and wanna make us two pay for it and we better go on and go right now and not come back. I looked up at Peto, Papa said, and whatever part of a Friend I seen in him here just a few minutes ago was all gone now.

*W*E GOT ON OUTTA THERE QUICK AS WE COULD Papa said, and I was glad to do it but o'Fritz kept a'looking back and crying bout it and I said No Fritz we ain't welcome there no more and we just gotta go on. And then here in a bit, he said, we seen this little fire by the side a'the road and it was Arlon just a'setting there all by his self. How'd you like that Goat, he said, was it good eating. Yes it was, Papa said, I wish I'd a'brought you some. No I told you I don't wanna eat no Mexkin Goat. Well I figgured you get hungry nough you'd change your mind, Papa said. Took yall long nough to get here I reckon, Arlon said. You know how long I been a'setting here. You was welcome to stay, the Farmer said, it was your own choice to go. Well I didn't have no idea yall was gonna be this long, Arlon said. You got anything in that wagon I might can eat. I could tell Arlon was rubbing on the Farmer, Papa said, but he reached in his wagon box and come out with a couple a'boiled taters and give em over to Arlon. If them don't fill you I can find you something else I reckon, he said, and Arlon just went to eating without even a Thank You and I thought Boy Hidy I don't know I want this fella here to move in with me and my Family or not then I looked over and seen him give Fritz a push away cause o'Fritz was wanting to get him a bite a'that tater too. Get on away from here, he said, then give him another mean push and for just one second I could taste that same o'Copper taste in my mouth I tasted that night everbody in the World was trying to kill poor o'Mister Pegleg. Arlon I said, Papa said, you give o'Fritz one more mean push like that and I'm gonna come over there and fix you right quick you hear me. And, he said, I reckon I had me some Snake Eyes on too cause Arlon went to looking scared like some poor little o'lost Baby out there in the Woods somewheres then he put his head down tween his legs and just went to shaking all over like he was freezing to death and I went from being

156

mad at him to being sorry I talked so bad at him. Arlon I said, Papa said, but Arlon got up and went off out there in the Dark somewheres. I was just gonna tell him I was sorry, Papa said. He don't want you to be Sorry, the Farmer said. He wouldn't have no idea how to get along in a World where they wadn't nobody mad at him.

ARLON WAS THERE ON HIS BED ROLL next morning, Papa said, and it was like wadn't nothing happened the night fore bout them Mexkins and whatnot and I kept a'going back and forth on what I thought bout him. Yes I like him No I don't like him Yes I like him No I don't. But whichever one it was, he said, I was more less stuck with him any how so I just pushed it outta my head and we went a'riding on off to Kendalia just up the road a piece now the Farmer said. What you gonna do you find the Man had your Mama's Horse, Arlon said. I'm gonna ask him how he got her and where my Momma is. Maybe he stole her, Arlon said, they ain't nothing but Horse Thiefs in this Country any how. Who told you that, the Farmer said, who told you they wadn't nothing but Horse Thiefs in this Country. Nobody, Arlon said, I just knowed it. Yes Sir but how you know it, the Farmer said. You just accused the whole population a'being a Horse Thief, he said. How you know that. I don't know, Arlon said, I reckon I was just born a'knowing it. Like you know the Sun goes round and round the Earth, the Farmer said, same way you know that huh Just born a'knowing it. Yes Sir, Arlon said, one day I was born and the next day I already knowed it. Well Sir you just one a'the lucky ones ain't you, the Farmer said, just born already a'knowing everthing they is to know. No wonder your Momma and Daddy didn't never send you to School. Yes Sir they never, Arlon said. You ever feel like you wish they had the Farmer said. Arlon give him a look like he just hit him in the head with a rock but fore he could say anything back the Farmer said Here's another thing bout going to School You can make a Friend or two there might last you your whole Lifetime. I already got me a Friend right here, Arlon said, I don't know what I'd do with another one. He was talking bout me, Papa said, and I liked having me Friends like my Brother Herman and Mister Pegleg and Marcellus and Bird and the Choats and little Fritz here and o'Molly and now Precious and course o'Calley Pearsall and Annie Oster but Boy Hidy I just didn't know bout putting o'Arlon on my list. I mean, he said, they was a little Bell just a'ringing away in my head going DingDong DingDong DingDong like that but what it was a'saying was Look Out Look Out Look Out but, Papa said, I didn't wanna go and hurt Arlon's feelings no more so I just give him a little nod and I could see he took it for a Promise I was his Friend like he said and then that little Bell in me went to ringing again and this time it was a'saying Uh oh Uh oh Uh oh but I didn't pay it no attention at the time.

*W*E GOT TO KENDALIA

Papa said, and wadn't much to it Just a'couple a'Stores and a Saloon cross the street and a Horse Lot over yonder under that Bunch a'Oak Trees where ever body put they Horse when they come to Town on Saturday and Oh they was a fella over there had him a Store next to that Saloon where People come to get they Pitchur took and I wanted to go over there and have a look but I had other Fish to Fry bout my Momma's Horse first and wadn't no two seconds later and here come this Man outta the Saloon with smoke just a'blowing out his Nose and his Ears both and he said What the Hell you a'doing with my Horse there Boy. No Sir this ain't your Horse, Papa said, this is my Momma's Horse Precious. No you are a lying little Son of a Bitch, the Man said, that is my Horse and then the Farmer jumped down off his wagon with a Hammer in his hand and he said You go to talking to this Boy that a'way and I'm gonna split your head wide open for you like a Watermelon with this hammer I got here and then, Papa said, here come the Sheriff and a bunch a'other Men from out the Saloon too and he said Hold on Hold on and the Man said This is my Horse here he stole it and Papa said, No Sir this ain't his Horse it's my Momma's Horse Precious and I don't know but what its this Man here might a'stole it off her. If that Horse is your Horse, Marvin, the Sheriff said, where'd you get it from Let's clear that up first. Off some o'Horse Trader over there round Sadler the Man said, that's where. Sadler, Papa said, Sadler. Why that's where you seen her Saddle in the back a'that wagon too ain't it I said to the Farmer, Papa said. What d'you know about that o'Horse Trader, the Farmer said, what'd he look like. Big Fella, the Man said, kind a'onery. Wouldn't trade less he got him a little something extra To Boot. Oh, Papa said, Oh Boy Hidy that is Old Karl the Man was talking bout and nobody else in this World but Old Karl. Old Karl had my Momma's Saddle that the Farmer seen in the wagon front a'the Hardware Store and now Old Karl had my Momma's Horse Precious too and he traded her to this Man here over in Sadler not a day's ride from Home and I reckon that's where Old Karl was them first few days after Momma rode off and me and Herman was looking after our self. That's my Daddy you a'talking bout had my Momma's Horse, Papa said, but I can't xplain how he come to have her. Well how'd you get your Momma's Horse, the Sheriff said, can you xplain that. So I told him bout Calley Pearsall and Jack Ivey the Third and how Calley got my Momma's Horse when I went over there cross the street to have a Look in the Saloon at the dead neckid bodies a'Jack Ivey the Third and the Sheriff a'Comal County, Papa said, and the Sheriff said Yes he already knowed most a'what I said cause the Sheriff a'Comal County was a dear Friend a'his and he near cried his eyes out when he heard o'Jack that Dirty Son of a Bitch shot his Friend up under the chin and blowed his brains out the top a'his head. It's still my Horse, the Man said, I don't give one Fart of a Fat Brown Donkey bout the Sheriff a'Comal County. That riled the Sheriff, Papa said, and the Sheriff said Yes Sir Marvin if this is your Horse just show me the Bill a'Sale and we'll go back to our game a'cards. No I ain't got one, the Man said, it was a Hand Shake Deal. That ain't no proof, the Sheriff said. Well you got my Word on it, the Man said, ain't that good nough. I just got your god dam word on my Friend the Sheriff a'Comal County too, the Sheriff said, and No Sir your Word on it ain't worth a Donkey Fart nor a Big Fat Donkey Shit neither one to me. And while they was going back and forth on it, Papa said, I looked cross the street and seen Arlon a'coming out the Saloon even when I didn't never even see him a'going in but I didn't pay it no mind cause my head was busy a'churning away on how it was Old Karl got my Momma's Horse Precious and her Saddle both in the first place and where she was at.

$\mathcal{S}$O THE SHERIFF give me my Momma's Horse Precious back, Papa said, and when him and all them other Men went a'walking back to the Saloon the Man leaned over at me and said That's my god dam Horse there Mister and I'm a'gonna get her back and you just better look out. I didn't argue with the Man, Papa

said, I just wanted to go off somewheres where I could settle my head. Your Friend just went in that Store over there cross the street where they'll make a Pitchur of you, the Farmer said. For a minute I didn't even know who he was talking bout, Papa said, that's how fogheaded I was bout Old Karl and Momma's Horse and Saddle. Well I'm gonna go on, the Farmer said, you was good company. Yes Sir, Papa said, you was too. You be careful with that other Boy, he said, he got the Devil's Hand on him if ever I seen one. Well he had him a hard Life, Papa said. Yes Sir and I reckon it's gonna get a lot harder here fore long just watch it don't lap up over on you too while it's at it. The Farmer drove on off in his wagon then, Papa said, and me and Fritz went on cross the street and looked in that Store and there was Arlon looking at a Pitchur of his self on a piece a'tin. Look at this, he said, you ain't never seen nothing like it. I looked, Papa said, and Why there Arlon was on that piece a'tin just like in Life even the buttons on his shirt. Come on, he said, I want one a'you and me together and he just wouldn't have it no other way so him and me went over there in front a'this sheet the Man had painted with a Big Lake and some Sailing Boats on it and I set down in a chair with Fritz there on my lap and Arlon standing there behind me and the Man said Be Still now Be Still and then he took the lid off something he had pointed at us and counted to seven or eight or twenty or something like that and then Arlon said Make us another one so we each got us a Pitchur of our self and the Man said Can you pay for this many and Arlon said Yes Sir I can pay and don't you never doubt me again and the Man said Keep your little Dog still this time He ain't gonna be much moren a Smudge in that first one. And then we seen the Pitchur here in a few minutes and sure nough o'Fritz looked like a Smudge and Arlon said We don't want that one do us another one and the Man did, Papa said, and then we each had us a Pitchur with Fritz just a'grinning back at you but now he was a'setting the other side a'my lap I reckon by some magic in that box the Man had and I showed it to Fritz and I said Look a'here Fritz it's you on this piece a'tin forever and then, Papa said, I looked over there and Arlon come out his pocket with a hand full a'coins but I swear I didn't have no recollection a'him ever having even a penny there in his pocket fore then.

*B*OUT THE TIME WE COME OUTTA

the Pitchur Store, Papa said, all them Men and the Sheriff too come out a'the Saloon next door and they was just a'jumping all over this one Fella for something wrong he done but I didn't know what. Let's see what this is all bout I said, Papa said, but Arlon was already up on o'Colonel and just a'kicking his way off down the street. Bout then, he said, one Man give that Fella a good lick and put him down to the ground with it and ever other Man there cept the Sheriff went to kicking on him and hollering Thief Thief Thief and I went over to the Sheriff and said What'd that poor man do to earn all them kicks. He stole money off the poker table when we all come over there a minute ago fooling round with you and your Momma's Horse. Somebody see him steal the money, Papa said. He was the last man outta the Saloon, the Sheriff said, couldn't a'been nobody else. Well Yes Sir it sure could a'been somebody else I thought, Papa said, it could a'been o'Arlon done it when wadn't nobody looking cept me when I seen him come out the Saloon but I didn't say nothing. You look like you about to Spit Up, the Sheriff said. I know it, Papa said, maybe it was that Goat I et on last night and then, he said, that Fella they was kicking got up to his feet and run off down the street with all them others a'hollering Thief Thief Thief at him. Well he's ruint for Life round here ain't he, the Sheriff said, and then all them other Men went back in the Saloon and the Sheriff was just bout to go too but he looked over and seen that Pitchur in my hand. Got you a Pitchur huh. How in the Hell you figgur they do that. I don't have no idea how in the World, Papa said. Look at this. My little Dog here wadn't even setting on that side a'me fore that Man made this Pitchur. The whole thing's a wonder to me, the Sheriff said, then pointed at Arlon standing there behind me, Papa said, and said Who's this fella here in the Pitchur with you. Oh, Papa said, that's just Arlon. A Friend a'yours huh, the Sheriff said. Well, Papa said, kind of a'Friend I reckon Yes Sir. I don't remember seeing him over there when we was all talking bout your Momma's Horse. Well we rode in to town together, Papa said, and that Farmer in his wagon too. Oh yes, I remember now. Had him a hammer in his hand. Yes Sir, Papa said and then the Sheriff reached over and give Precious a little pet and said Take good care a'your Momma's Horse. Yes Sir I will, Papa said, then the Sheriff looked at the Pitchur another minute or two and I thought Uh oh he's a'studying on Arlon but then he give it back over to me and said I'll be dam if your little Dog there in the Pitchur don't look like he's just a'grinning back at you.

O H I FELT BAD BOUT NOT TELLING THE SHERIFF I seen Arlon coming out the Saloon when me and everbody else was still cross the street talking bout Momma's Horse Precious, Papa said, but that would a'been like saying Arlon stole the Money off the poker table and I didn't know he did or he didn't. But course, he said, I figgured he did moren I figgured he didn't but I didn't know that for sure No Sir not for certain sure I didn't so I thought Well I'll just wait til I come up on him again here in a little while and see what he got to say for his self bout it then tell him to go take the Money back fore the Sheriff comes a'looking for him and maybe me too with his Pistol out. And then, Papa said, I got to thinking bout Old Karl having my Momma's Horse Precious and her Saddle too and how it was he come to have em and ever time I'd try to figgur it out that little Bell in my head'd just go to ringing again and I couldn't tell what it was a'saying but it just wouldn't stop ringing and that night when me and Fritz closed our eyes to sleep it was still a'ringing and then of a sudden there we was in my Dream a'standing at the bottom a'that Bluff again with the Cave up there and that Cedar Tree a'growing out it and, Papa said, I looked down at Fritz and Oh he had growed him some Feathers and a Bird Beak and then Oh I seen I had me some Long Feathers too, he said, and then a Big Black Shadow come by me Whoosh like that and went to carrying something big up that Bluff like they wadn't nothing to it then went on in that Cave to where I couldn't see no more but that was okay with me, he said, cause that place really give me the Squirms ever time I stood there in my Dreams and I didn't want no more to do with it if I could help it. I think they was some more to that Dream, Papa said, but it went right out a'my head when Fritz went to licking my face and I opened my eyes and Why here come Arlon a'riding up outta the Dark Night on his Mule. Arlon I said, Papa said, I wanna ask you bout what you was a'doing over in that Saloon. Oh, he said, I was just stealing me some Money off the poker table is all.

I COME RIGHT UP OFF THE GROUND AT THAT

Papa said. Arlon, I said, They's a Man back there in Kendalia took him a good Whupping for what you stole and now they all calling him Thief Thief Thief. Yes Sir, Arlon said, I know my self how it is to get a Whupping for some thing you didn't never do. Well you gotta go give that money back. Why's that, Arlon said, ain't nobody knows I took it. Well I know it, Papa said, and I don't want no part of it. You already a part of it, Arlon said, you got a Pitchur come out a'that money ain't you. I give him a Look then, Papa said, and he was just a'grinning back like maybe he was kin to o'Fritz here. You was trying to lock me to you when you bought me that Pitchur with stole Money wadn't you, Papa said. Well it come out that way didn't it, Arlon said. No Sir, Papa said, I ain't no Thief and I don't wanna be placed for one for something you done but not me. Well I ain't a'taking the Money back, Arlon said, they wadn't very smart just a'leaving it out on the table like that was they. What got me, Papa said, was o'Arlon just went to giggling when he said it. We ain't Friends no more, Papa said, you just gonna have to go you own way and me go mine. Arlon's giggling dried right up, Papa said and he said No you and me're Friends locked tight for Life we sure are. No Sir we ain't, Papa said, not no more. I got other Fish to Fry and I don't wanna get in trouble being no wheres round you. Okay I won't do it no more, Arlon said. That's a Promise how bout that. I shook my head No, Papa said, I could just bout see the Devil's Hand wiggling its fingers on Arlon's shoulder like the Farmer said. You turning me away ain't you, he said. Yes Sir I am, Papa said, next time it might be me taking a Whupping for something you done like that Man back there in Kendalia ever body thought stole they Money. Arlon put his head down like he was bout to cry, Papa said, and he said Okay how bout I just ride back over there and give em they Money back even if they gonna put me in the Jail House for it. I thought you told me you liked being in the Jail House, Papa said. Ain't that what you said. I don't know if I did or not, Arlon said, I say all kind a'things. Yes Sir and some of em ain't nothing but Ball Headed Lies. Papa said. Here you go a'talking ugly to me again, Arlon said. You better be careful with your mouth or I might have to come over there and close it up for you. I wadn't scared a'him yet, Papa said, so I give him a little wave the back a'my hand like I was shooing off a fly and said Arlon you better just go on fore we start a'fighting. What if I wanna fight, Arlon said, and he come out with that Farmer's little cooking knife that I didn't even know he had. Where'd you get that knife, Papa said. That o'Farmer give it to me that's where, Arlon said. No he didn't, Papa said, it's some thing else you stole off somebody ain't it and now here you a'lying bout it too. He had him another knife, Arlon said, he didn't need him two of em. You're a Thief Arlon, Papa said, you're just a plain o'Sneak Thief ain't you. Well I told you I was didn't I, he said. Yes Sir you did, Papa said. I don't know what I had in my ears not to been a'listening. So you just a'running me off like you might some o'mangy Dog huh, he said. Yes Sir I am, Papa said. I don't want no more of you. Arlon got up on his old Mule and went to riding off in the Dark, Papa said, but he give me his Snake Eyes and said I'm gonna return the favor here one a'these days and then the Night swallered him up.

ARLON WAS GONE Papa said, and I was glad to be shed a'him and now wadn't nothing to do but ride to Home and ask Old Karl how it was he got my Momma's Horse Precious and Saddle off her and did he know where she was a'living now that I might ride over there and tell her how much I been a'missing her all this time. Course I was scared to death a'Old Karl, he said, but wadn't no help for it so I went to gathering up my things to go and then here come this voice outta the Dark said Put your hands up over your head Mister and don't you move a wisker so I put my hands up in the air, Papa said, and here come the Sheriff from Kendalia and another Man with him and the Sheriff said Where's that Boy was with you in town. I don't know, Papa said, he rode off somewheres on his o'Mule. Yall in cahoots stealing money ain't you, the Sheriff said. No Sir I ain't no Thief, Papa said. I didn't xpect you to confess you was, the Sheriff said, then the other Man went to digging in my pockets, Papa said, but course couldn't come up with nothing. What'd yall do with the Money, the Man said. I ain't never had none, Papa said, and still ain't. Your Friend got it huh, the Sheriff said, took it right off the poker table when we was all over there cross the street talking bout your Momma's Horse is that it. Yes Sir I reckon, Papa said, but I wadn't no part of it or I'd own up. You know what we do with Boys that steal things round here, the Sheriff said, anybody ever whisper it in your ear what we do. No Sir, Papa said, but I don't reckon I wanna hear it no how. We cut they little

Nuggets off and feed em to the Pigs then we run em Butt Neckid through the Prickly Pear Cactuses bout a week or two, the Sheriff said, how you like that. I never stole nothing, Papa said, I was over there cross the street with you the whole time and didn't know nothing bout it. Well that's true you was over there with us wadn't you, the Sheriff said. Yes Sir I was, Papa said. I don't deserve to go running through the Prickly Pears for something I didn't never do. No I don't blame you for feeling that way, the Sheriff said. But listen here's the Bad Part, he said, Even if you wadn't the xact one stole the Money you was riding with the one that did and I reckon that puts you two in the very same o'Pickle Jar don't it. I was bout to cry, Papa said, then here come a Man outta the Dark had Arlon all tied up on his Mule and then here come two more Men behind him on they Horses but one of em was a'laying belly down on his cause he was D-E-A-D-dead. Good Lord God in Heaven, the Sheriff said, what befell o'Marvin. The Man reached over and pinched Arlon's ear hard as he could, Papa said, then said Why this little Nit here stabbed o'Marvin three maybe four times with this little Cook Knife he had up his sleeve when we went to tie him up but Hey it was big nough to do the job I reckon. Then, Papa said, the Sheriff looked over at me and shook his head like it was the saddest thing he ever come cross in his whole Life. Well, he said, I don't reckon this bodes much good for you neither does it Sonny Boy.

*T*HEY PUT MY HANDS UP BEHIND MY BACK Papa said, and tied em tight. I'm gonna lay First Dibs on his little Dog there, one a'the Sheriff's Men said but the Sheriff said No we just gonna throw him in the pot next time we a'dealing the cards and Winner take all. His Horse then, the Man said. No I might need that Horse my self, the Sheriff said, for Sheriff work. To lose my little Dog Fritz and Momma's Horse Precious too in one lick just bout broke me down, Papa said, but I looked over at Arlon and said Arlon you a'holding the Truth here Now you gonna let em set me Free with it or you gonna Lock me up with a Lie for bout a hunderd years which one is it. Arlon give me the Snake Eyes then, Papa said, and my Heart just went to bumping cause I knowed certain which way he was gonna go.

You run me off he said. Yes Sir I did, Papa said, I reckon you had it coming to you. Oh Arlon's eyes just went Cold Cold Cold at that, he said, and then Arlon looked over at the Sheriff and said No Sir Sheriff he didn't do nothing. Oh I all but fell off Momma's Horse when he said that, Papa said, but then here he come right back behind it with But he's the one told me how to do it. Oh, Papa said, Oh Boy Hidy I was lost forever now wadn't I, but then, he said, the Sheriff said When. What, Arlon said, When What. When'd he tell you that, the Sheriff said, When'd he tell you How to do it. Well When we was all just standing there that's When, Arlon said. You mean When we was all standing over there cross the street talking bout his Momma's Horse, the Sheriff said, that When. Yes Sir that When, Arlon said. I don't remember him even talking to you, the Sheriff said. Well he was just a'whispering it, Arlon said, I couldn't barely hear it my self. What'd he whisper to you, the Sheriff said. He whispered Go get the Money off a'the poker table they ain't no body a'watching, Arlon said, that's What he whispered to me so I just went on over there and got it like he said. Tween the two a'us he's the one says What to do and I do it. How'd he know they was Money on the poker table, the Sheriff said, he whisper some thing about that in your ear too. You don't believe me do you, Arlon said. No Sir Not one god dam word of it, the Sheriff said, not one. Yes Sir that's how it was looking to me too, Arlon said. What you reckon yall gonna do with me. You a Thief and a Liar and a Cold Blood Murderer it ain't gonna be Home Sweet Home for you for a good long while and maybe a lot longer, the Sheriff said, I can tell you that much for sure. Well it wadn't never no Home Sweet Home for me any how, Arlon said. What bout him he said and pointed at me. The Sheriff reached over to make sure my hands was still tied tight, Papa said, then said We just gonna have to wait and see what o'Judge James T. Nemeyer wants to do with him but if you Boys the praying kind I'd urge you to go to praying now that the Judge is getting him a good night's sleep cause if he ain't it's gonna be Bad Pookie for you two tomorra. Arlon looked over at Papa then and said You don't hold this against me do you. Yes Sir I reckon I do, Papa said, that wadn't no way to treat a Friend. You wadn't no Friend, Arlon said. I ain't never had a Friend to me in my whole Life and then, Papa said, the Sheriff and them other Men went a'riding off with us in the Dark.

167

the next day, Papa said, and they was all in town to see the Sheriff come a'riding in with the Dead Man Marvin and us two Criminals with our hands tied up behind our back and, he said, I thought Oh Boy Hidy I'm glad my Momma ain't here to see me now unfair that it was but what was my Big Worry now was here come bout half a'Kendalia a'hollering and a'shaking they fist at me and Arlon and a'trying to pull us off our Horse and do us Bad Harm even fore o'Judge James T. Nemeyer could get a lick in and only thing saved us, Papa said, was the Sheriff bumped em back ever which way with his Horse then went to shooting his pistol off in the air to show he wadn't no body to fool with and then he put us in the Jail House where a'couple a'o'Fellas already in there went to Hoohaaing us like they was big Loonies and Oh Yes Sir they was. When you gonna get me some Breakfast, Arlon hollered at the Sheriff, I'm bout to dry up and blow away in here. You just better Hush, the Sheriff said, I don't wanna hear nothing more outta you. Least a Bisquit, Arlon said, what makes you so Mean. You gonna see some Mean here in a minute or two when the Judge gets a'holt a'you, the Sheriff said. You reckon he'll gimme a Bisquit, Arlon said, then him and them two Loonies just went to laughing away at they Joke, Papa said, but it was all Gloom to me cause the Good Times a'my life was all behind me now and Oh how I wish I a'listened to my o'Amigo Calley Pearsall bout being careful who you get you self placed with cause it could come to this like it did to him for being with o'Jack Ivey the Third. You Boys tuck your shirts in now, the Sheriff said, and lets go see what the Judge got to say bout your Future.

Oh the Court Room was packed to the ceiling with mad people, Papa said, and the Sheriff and another Man marched us right down front through em and had us set down and the Sheriff tapped Arlon on the shoulder and said If you got any sense at all you won't ask the Judge for a Bisquit cause he ain't gonna think it's funny then Judge James T. Nemeyer come in and said Anybody here wanna speak for these Boys. Nobody did, Papa said, but then the Sheriff pointed at me and said Well Judge this one here is just a Victim of the Circumstance to my mind and I'd give him another chance if I was you but course I ain't. Well Sheriff come on up here and let's talk bout it, the Judge said, and the rest a'yall just set tight while we at it. So the Sheriff went on up there, Papa said, and wadn't even a cough from nobody else while they was talking bout what to do with me then the Sheriff come back and said Stand up and see what the Judge got to say to you. So I did stand up, Papa said, but I had to take a'holt a'my chair I was shaking so bad. You got any thing to say for your self Son, the Judge said. Yes Sir Judge I was just a'looking for my Momma, Papa said, I don't care nothing bout stealing money and stabbing people. I believe what the Sheriff said about you, the Judge said, You just got caught running with the wrong Crowd didn't you and I ain't gonna throw you in that Hell Hole over yonder in Gatesville for it. Oh I bout fell to the floor I was so happy, Papa said, but then the Judge said Course I can't just let you go Free neither so we gonna have to find somebody to look after you here in your formative years and— But fore he could finish somebody way back there in the back hollered Judge I'll take the job and be glad to do it and when I looked Why wadn't nobody in the World but that o'Farmer led us here to Kendalia in the first place.

*T*HE JUDGE AND THE SHERIFF and the Farmer talked bout it a good long while, Papa said, then the Judge whistled me up there with em and said I'm a'ordering you to go live with this Man here for no less'n two years and you got to help him on his Farm ever way you can and he's gonna give you Clothes to wear Food to eat a Place to sleep and in all ways possible be good to you and you can't ask for no better Deal than that can you. No Sir, Papa said, and I thank you for going easy on me for something I didn't never do no how. Yes Sir and see you don't never do it from here on out neither. Yes Sir I said, Papa said, and then me and that Farmer went to walking out and Judge James T. Nemeyer said Stand up and I looked back and seen Arlon stand up and then the Judge said You got anything to say for you self Boy and Arlon said Yes Sir I do You reckon they's somebody could run get me a Bisquit I'm bout to dry up and blow away here and didn't nobody laugh at his Joke but o'Arlon his self and then we was gone on out the door to where the Farmer's wagon was and o'Fritz was a'setting up there on Precious and Boy Hidy I was glad to see em and give em both hugs and scratches under they chin and round they ears to let em know it. We got a Stop to make, the Farmer said, then we be off to Home bout three days down the road. His name was Benno Armke, Papa said, and I found him to be just bout good or bettern any other Man on this

Earth. What you reckon that o'Judge gonna do with Arlon, Papa said. Send him to Gatesville Reformation School in Coryell County I reckon, Mister Armke said. Is that a good place for him, Papa said. Well it's gonna either be a Dumping Ground or A Child Saver one or the other, he said, ain't nothing but Time gonna tell us which one. I'm Lucky I ain't going long with him, Papa said. I reckon you saved my Life Mister Armke. Well when I left my Home in Kentucky my Momma looked me in the eye and said Benno You do least one good thing while you out there in the World and don't you never come back Home again til you do, Mister Armke said, and now I'm thinking maybe you the Good Thing I'm gonna do so I can go back to my Home in Kentucky again. You sound like that Old Mexkin Man a'singing bout his lost Home back in Mexico the other night you know it, Papa said. Oh you mean Old Crecencio, Mister Armke said. That's his name huh, Papa said. Crecencio Salas, Mister Armke said. That's the Stop we gotta make Old Crecencio's coming home with us and course so is Pepe and Peto and now all them others too. All them other Whats, Papa said. Why all them other Mexkins, Mister Armke said, eight or ten or what ever it is of em counting they Wifes and all they little Beans.

AND YES SIR

Papa said, there they was a'standing out there in the Road with they bundles and whatnot when we come a'riding up and wadn't but a minute and Pepe and Peto had Old Crecencio and his wife Old Lupita loaded up in the wagon and all them little Mexkins too cept one had the name a'Pedrito and Mister Armke put him up in front a'me on the saddle and took Fritz over to play with all them other little Fellas in the wagon and I could see Peto didn't like it his little Pedrito setting there with me. Mister Armke I said, Papa said, what in the World you gonna do with all these Mexkins you got here. Why give em a Home and teach em the King's English so they can get along better with people over here in Texas. You reckon you can do such a thing, Papa said, I ain't never heard a'teaching a Mexkin nothing in my Life. I don't see no reason why not, Mister Armke said, and I hope you don't neither cause you the one gonna do the Teaching what you think about that. I don't know what I think bout that, Papa said, I ain't even got one grade a'School my self and here you wanting me to go teaching Mexkins. You just put your Mind to it and you'll do fine, Mister Armke said. Well, Papa said, maybe we can find some body to teach me how to teach some body else. Why I can teach you how to teach right now, he said. Okay, Papa said. Okay, Mister Armke said, show this little Squirt your Hand. So I showed little Pedrito my Hand and said Here Pedrito look at this. Okay, Mister Armke said, now show him your Hand again but this time tell him what it is. So, Papa said, I put my Hand up to his little face and said Hand Hand Hand but he just looked at it so I went to shaking my Hand close in his face like maybe I had a Snake in it and said HandHandHand HandHandHand like that and Oh Pedrito went to crying and then here come Peto a'running over there and grabbed him away from me. Well I reckon that's nough lessons for one day, Mister Armke said and I was just bout to say maybe he oughta go a'looking for him another Teacher, Papa said, when here come this little Girl's voice from over there in the wagon said Hand and we all looked over there and Why it was Peto's little daughter Graciela there in the wagon laughing and saying Hand Hand Hand like that. Well I reckon you a Teacher after all ain't you, Mister Armke said, and then, Papa said, I rode Precious over there and raised up my Hat to show her and said Hat Hat Hat and she come right back at me with Hat Hat Hat then I raised my Hand up again and she said Hand Hand Hand and it made me so happy at being a Teacher you'd a'thought I just found a Treasure down there in my pocket some where so I give Graciela a little smile and a poke on her belly with my finger then set my Hat on her head and it went way down past her ears to where she couldn't hardly see nothing out from under it and Oh it looked so funny me and all them other little Mexkins just went to laughing like Loonies bout it but then, he said, here come o'Peto again just a'cussing at me and he yanked my Hat right off her head and she went to crying and run over there to her old Granma Lupita and Old Crecencio give Peto a look and said One Word to him and whatever that One Word was it was like a trap just went shut on Peto's tongue and he didn't have no more to say so he and Pepe went on off in the Woods and all them others just set there in the wagon a'looking scared and crying. What'd I do wrong, Papa said. You didn't do nothing wrong, Mister Armke said, Peto just fraid you gonna teach his little Chilren moren he knows his self and then they won't have no more use for him. And that'd just about break his Heart, he said.

OH I FELT BAD BOUT COMING TWEEN PETO
and his little Chilrens, Papa said, and I worried so hard bout it I couldn't
sleep a wink that night and then we wadn't on the road no moren two minutes the next day, he said, when here come Hilario and Graciela and little
Pedrito too with something in they hand for me to name in English and Oh
there was Pepe and Peto over there just a'watching me and ready to get mad
for teaching they little chilren some English. Well Boy Hidy I said to myself,
Papa said, how in the World you a'gonna get out of this one here cause on
the one hand Mister Armke said it was my job to teach these little Mexkins
how to talk English and on the other hand if I did Why it was just gonna
break they Daddy's Heart. What them kids had in they hand, Papa said, was
a Horny Toad Lizard and they went to jumping up and down a'wanting me
to give em a name for it and then it come to me of a sudden what I could
do to both give em a name and not break nobody's Heart at the same time
so I made signs for em to stay where they was at and went walking to Pepe
and Peto to tell em my idea but when I did they went to throwing rocks at
me not to come over there but I did any how and when I got there I closed
my hands up together like I had something in em then opened em and said
Horny Toad Horny Toad Horny Toad but they wadn't really no Horny Toad
in my hand and Pepe and Peto didn't have no idea what I was talking bout
and made a sign at me with they long finger to say Thank You Anyway I
reckon and walked off but then, Papa said, here come all them little Mexkins
a'wanting me to give em the words for what they Horny Toad was in English but what I done instead, he said, was go to pointing at they Daddys
like theys the one could tell em the name and not me. So, Papa said, they
all run over there to they Daddys and opened up they hand to show em the
Horny Toad Lizard they got then just stood there a'looking at they Daddys
and waiting for em to name it. But, he said, Pepe and Peto didn't have no
idea what was going on here and they was bout to run them kids off but
then Peto looked over at me and I said with just my lips but not my mouth
Horny Toad Horny Toad Horny Toad and then Peto's eyes of a sudden come
alive and he looked down at that Horny Toad they had there in they hand
and said Horny Toad Horny Toad and then all them little Mexkins went to
hollering Horny Toad Horny Toad Horny Toad like they was singing a song
bout it and Pepe and Peto did too and then Peto give me a look to say Thank

You for what I just did, Papa said, so I give him that same sign back with my long finger that he give me a minute ago to say Okay You Welcome.

*T*HAT NIGHT

after all them little Beans was asleep, Papa said, here come Pepe and Peto over to me when I was giving Precious her Goodnight Hug. What yall want I said, Papa said, and both of em touched they Nose and first I thought they was smelling something bad but then they touched they Ear then they Mouth and they Chin and they Arm and they Leg and then it come to me, Papa said, they was wanting me to name each part for em in English so I touched my Nose and said Nose and they touched they Nose and said Nose then I touched my Ear and said Ear and they did too and then I just kept a'touching ever part a'my body and naming it in English and Pepe and Peto follered right along Touching and Naming Touching and Naming just pretty as you please Foot Toe Leg Knee BellyButton Chest and so on right up to the Hair the top a'my Head then come back down the body again to name they Neck Shoulder Back Hiney Heel for em and then, Papa said, I give em a Test to see how much they learned. I'd point to something like my Eye and see could they name it in English and Yes Sir most times they could but other times No they couldn't but, he said, I'd just stay on em til they could and then one time I pointed to my Ear and Pepe said Hiney and I just went to falling over a'laughing cause it was so funny the Pitchur a'your Hiney being there on the side a'your head in place a'your Ear but Pepe and Peto didn't think it was funny cause they was there to learn and not for no Jokes. Next morning, Papa said, we stacked all them little Mexkins up on Precious one behind the other Pedrito then Graciela then Hilario then Lalo like that and Pepe and Peto went to walking long side em and here in a minute Peto touched his Nose and said Nose and then ever one a'them little kids touched they Nose and said Nose and then Pepe and Peto went up and down they body like that Touching and Naming ever part and them little Mexkins Touching and Naming em right back but then they got tired a'all this learning and wadn't paying no attention til Peto touched back there and said Hiney and then, Papa said, Oh they just come wide awake and all but fell off o'Precious a'laughing so hard at the word Hiney and just couldn't quit even when Pepe and Peto went to hollering at em for it and then, he said, when it was time to get down off Precious and everbody go pee in the Bushes Why them little Mexkins run up behind one another and give a swat back there then holler Hiney Hiney Hiney and run off fore the other one could swat em back and that was funny too til Hilario hollered Hiney Hiney Hiney and run up behind his old Granma Lupita and give her a swat while she was doing her business there in the Bushes and she fell over in her own mess and it took Pepe and Peto and Mister Armke all three of em to get her back up to her feet and she was so mad bout it she told em they wadn't never to say Hiney again for the rest a'they whole Life.

*T*HAT NIGHT AFTER SUPPER Papa said, Mister Armke come over to me and said he been a'talking to Pepe and Peto and they was bout ready to give up the Teaching it was so hard and would I take the Job back but they wanted to learn English too and I said, he said, Yes Sir I will and Mister Armke said Yes Sir I thought you would but keep them kids away from they old Granma Lupita she still mad as a Hornet bout the Hiney word. This is how I done it, Papa said, I put one a'them little Mexkins up on Precious and the rest a'us'd just walk along and the one up on Precious'd point to something out there in the World and I'd name it in English then everbody else'd have to name it too one at a time even Pepe and Peto. It was like we was a Walking Schoolhouse, Papa said, and I teached em everthing we passed by in English and all the one setting up on Precious had to do was point at it. Graciela was the first one and she pointed at a Tree and I said Tree and then all them others said Tree then she pointed at a Rock and everbody learned Rock but when it was Hilario's turn up on Precious he pointed at his old Granma Lupita over there in the wagon and all them others said Hiney and then course they all went to laughing til they was bout to fall over but Peto pulled Hilario off Precious for it and give him a little Whupping. Then it was Lalo's turn but he just set up there on Precious like a Knot on a Log and wouldn't point to nothing in the World even when his Daddy went to hollering at him and made him get down off Precious and when he did, Papa said, I reached over there just for fun and give him a little knock on his head like it was a door or something and said Hard Nut to Crack Hard Nut to Crack and it made him so mad he went to swinging at me and I felt bad bout teasing him. Then, Papa said, Pepe got up on Precious with Pedrito in his lap cause they was all fraid he'd fall off up there just by his self he was still so little and he just went to pointing at everthing they was and then when his turn was over Why then here come Mister Armke with Old Crecencio and Mister Armke said Old Crecencio wants him a turn up on Precious too if it is okay and I said Yes Sir it is okay, he said, and then Pepe and Peto helped Old Crecencio up on Precious and then this look come over his face like he wadn't a Old Man no more but was somewheres back there in his head when he was just a Young Man again and then, Papa said, he got Lalo up there on Precious with him and them two rode on off out there in the Country somewheres and didn't come back by Sun Down so Pepe and Peto and Mister Armke and me went a'looking for em and where we found em was up top this little Hill just a'setting there on Precious and Old Crecencio was a'looking way off out yonder toward his First Home back in Mexico and he was a'shaking the reins and a'giving Precious little kicks to make her Go but they was big tears in his eyes, he said, I reckon cause she wouldn't take him back to Mexico like he wanted her to. He don't know much about Precious if he thought he could get her to run off and leave you behind does he, Mister Armke said.

I THINK OLD CRECENCIO

was a'missing his Mexkin Home back down there cross the River bout as much as I was a'missing my Momma, Papa said, but They ain't no help for it Mister Armke said, less they's somebody can take him back down there to it and I don't know who that might be do you. No Sir I don't, Papa said, but maybe he'll get over his Home Sickness when he starts him a new Life at your Farm. No Sir I don't believe he will, Mister Armke said, he's Old Old Old and now his mind is turning back to his early Life when he was just a Squirt a'living down there in Mexico with his Family all together on some little Farm they had already been a'living on for a hunderd years and more. He told you this huh, Papa said. Yes Sir he been a'telling me his whole Life Story ever day there in the wagon Said it was a Hard Life but it was a Hap-

py Life til one day here come a bunch a'Mexkins riding up from they own Goverment said Git off this land and don't you never come back on it again It don't belong to you no more and Crecencio's o'Daddy went after em with a Pitchfork for it but them other Mexkins shot him down dead right there in front a'him and his Momma and all his little Brothers and Sisters and I guess ever body else who was round there at the time, he said, then they took the two biggest Boys and put em to working in some Mexkin Mine way down South and Old Crecencio was one of em but his Brother Juan the Other One died from the work it was so hard and they wadn't hardly nothing to eat neither the whole time but one day bout ten twelve years later Crecencio and this other Fella there with him hit somebody in the head with a Pick Ax they had and run off from there and course first thing Old Crecencio did next was go to looking for his Momma and all his Brothers and Sisters but he couldn't find not a one of em his whole Life til just here lately. Where'd he find em, Papa said. Oh they just come a'walking up outta the Dark the other night to see him Mister Armke said. And they was all these other people with em too. What'd they want, Papa said. They said they wanted to tell him they was waiting for him back yonder at the Old Home Place cross the River and they said they'd stay there didn't matter how long it was til he come on back over to be with them. I thought they lost they Old Home Place to them other Mexkins for ever, Papa said, when they come a'riding up and shot his Daddy down dead. Well it ain't that kind a'place no more, Mister Armke said, it's more a Spirit Place now like the kind people carry round in they Heart from where they was the most Happy in they Life. You mean it ain't really there no more, Papa said, it's just a Ghost Place now is that what you a'saying. You mean you can't see it no more. They's other ways to see things than just with your Eye, Mister Armke said. At night when Old Crecencio sees his Family come a'walking up to him outta the Dark he ain't seeing em with his Eye he's a'seeing em with his Heart. I had to think bout that a minute, Papa said, then said You reckon I can find my Momma that way. Well, Mister Armke said, sometimes that's the only way they is.

OLD CRECENCIO TOOK BAD SICK THE NEXT DAY,

Papa said, and everbody just went to crying bout it cause they figgured he

Old Crecencio was a'looking way off out
yonder toward his First Home back in Mexico . . .

was gonna up and die on em right then and there. Everbody but not Lalo, he said, Lalo just set right there beside his old Granpa and helt on to his hand and wouldn't let go for nothing. They say him and Lalo was always the closest a'the bunch, Mister Armke said, no matter the years tween em. Then Old Crecencio started crying a little the tears just a'leaking out his eyes one and two at a time and ever time one of em did Why Lalo'd squeeze Old Crecencio's hand and go to leaking tears too. This is how close them two are, Mister Armke said then squeezed his hands together to show me a tight knot. Is Old Crecencio crying cause he hurts so bad, Papa said. No, Mister Armke said, he's crying cause now he knows he won't never live long nough to get back down to Mexico to die there and be put in the same ground as all his People was put before him and he's afraid his Spirit just gonna have to go walking round over here in Texas for all time to come without Friend nor Family. That's the saddest thing I ever heard in my Life, Papa said. Yes Sir I know it, Mister Armke said. Makes me cry too just a'thinking about it. What if I was to take him back down there on Momma's Horse Precious, Papa said, I don't think it'd hurt nothing. You're a Good Boy and that's a Kind Thing to offer, Mister Armke said, but I don't believe he'd last moren a day or so on a trip like that. I was just trying to figgur a way to get him under the Mexkin dirt so his Spirit wouldn't have to go walking round Texas all day just by its self, Papa said. I know it, Mister Armke said then looked over and seen Lalo a'watching everthing we said so Mister Armke told him in Mexkin what it was we was saying and when he was done telling him Lalo dried up his eyes and looked over at me his head just a'spinning with some Idear he just got but at the time I didn't know it was cause a'something I said, Papa said. Anyhow, he said, the next morning Lalo was gone and didn't leave no sign behind to say Why or Where To.

*W*E LOOKED AND WE LOOKED

Papa said, but Lalo was just no wheres to be found not even a Foot Print to see. Oh and them others had a fit bout it, he said, and I thought they was a'losing they mind all cept Old Crecencio who was still breathing but had fell into some kind a'Hiber Nation like a Bear and didn't have no idea was Lalo there or not Or anybody else in the World neither. Mister Armke said

Lalo's Daddy even had the idea maybe some o'Inyin come a'sneaking in that night and stole him for a Slave it'd be just like em but Mister Armke said No all the Inyins was just Slaves they selves these days and that wadn't it. He just run off that's all they is to it, he said, and his o'Granma Lupita said Lalo had his own mind moren any the others did and it wadn't no surprise to her he did and then that poor o'Woman just bout went down bout it like everbody else. I didn't know what it was to lose me a Child, Papa said, but I figgured it was bout as bad as losing you a Momma like I did so I told Mister Armke if he'd allow it me and Precious and Fritz'd just go to looking for Lalo right now and bring him back a'Live if some o'Wild Animal or something else hadn't already eat him up. Yes Sir you go on and do that, Mister Armke said, and you sure gonnna make a lot a'people Happy if you do find him but I doubt you ever will cause the Country is so big and wild and you don't even know what direction to go in. No Sir but I got somebody who does, Papa said. And who is that, Mister Armke said. Why little o'Fritz here, Papa said. I didn't know he was a Track Dog, Mister Armke said, I reckon that's a surprise to me. I know it, Papa said. Then when I was all ready to go, he said, all them Mexkins ever one come up all round me with big tears in they eye and put they hands on my leg up there on Precious and made Church signs Head Chest Heart Chest something like that at me and Estella the Mother rubbed on some beads she had there in her hand and Peto the Father was saying Please Find Him Please Find Him Please Find Him with just his eyes and I never thought I'd ever feel sorry for a bunch a'Mexkins in my Life but I did them and then when me and Fritz went a'riding out Why I looked over and seen Old Crecencio just a'snoozing away over there and I thought, Papa said, Well I reckon he's the Lucky One don't have no idea in the World little Lalo just might be lost and gone forever.

I WAS WRONG BOUT O'FRITZ

Papa said, he wadn't no more a Track Dog than some o'Toad you might find in the dirt somewheres and ever time I put him down to go a'Tracking Lalo he'd just set there and lick on his Hiney til I let him back up on Precious again. You ain't much of a Track Dog Fritz I told him, Papa said, but then the second day he stuck his chin out and went to barking in a different direction and I hollered Lalo Lalo Lalo and steered Precious off in that direction but come the Dark and we still hadn't seen a hair on his head but next morning Fritz went a'barking like before and off we went in that direction again. Course, he said, I didn't have much faith o'Fritz was really and truly Tracking Lalo but I didn't have no idea what other direction to look in so I just said Lead on Fritz Lead on and follered along and I guess we might a'gone all the way to China like that but the fourth morning I think it was I seen where some body or some thing been in my sack a'Beans during the Night and took em a hand full or two. Well Fritz I said, Papa said, you wadn't no Track Dog before and now you ain't no Guard Dog neither are you But that night I put my hand on my sack a'Beans so I'd know if any thing or any body come up outta the Dark and tried to make off with em and wadn't two seconds and I was to sleep and in my Dream here come all these people a'walking up the road to me and first I thought Well here is all them Shimmery People showed me that Cave with the Cedar Tree a'growing out it but No, Papa said, it was a whole different bunch a'Shimmery People this time and I said Who are you people any how and what you want with me and then the one in front carrying the Pitchfork pulled his old ragged shirt up and Why they was Bullet Holes all in him where some body'd been a'shooting him up and down and I knowed he must be Old Crecencio's Daddy from the Story and all them others with him wadn't nobody but Shimmery Mexkin Kin Folks. Any a'yall speak English can tell me where Lalo is and why he just up and run off like that I said, Papa said, but they just laughed like it was the funniest thing they ever heard in the World then Crecencio's Daddy come out from behind his back with my sack a'Beans and I said Hey what you doing with my sack a'Beans Here give em back but he just put em round behind his back again so I grabbed a'holt a'him to get my Beans back and when I did here come a big Yell and a Holler and I waked up and Why there I had Lalo in my hands for trying to steal my Beans and Fritz went to licking on his face he was so glad to see him.

LALO FOUGHT LIKE A LOONIE

Papa said, and it was all I could do to hang on to him but I did then he settled some and I cooked him up a bowl a'Beans and said Here eat these Beans and Oh he did eat em right up then made signs he wanted some more but I made signs to say No you already et so many Beans you gonna be Tooting like a'little Steam Train as it is and Where in the World was you a'going anyhow you got any Idea how worried ever body is bout you. Course he didn't understand much a'what I said, he said, and just closed his eyes and went off to sleep but I didn't trust Fritz to stay awake and keep him from running off again so I stayed up my self all night long with my eye on Lalo and then next morning I said Well Lalo let's get on back Home and pointed my finger back to where we come from but he shook his head No and pointed his finger in the direction he was a'going in yesterday. Then I pointed to Home again and he pointed the other direction again and we just went to pointing back and forth like that, he said, Me a'pointing Him a'pointing Me a'pointing Him a'pointing and I said Lalo you are a Hard Nut to Crack you know it and then Lalo said something in Mexkin took bout a week to say it but all I got out a'it was Mexico. So I pointed to where he was pointing, Papa said, and said No Mexico No Mexico but Lalo nodded his head and said Si Mexico Si Si Mexico but I shook my head No again and said No Sir No Mexico and Lalo jumped up and took off a'running again and I like to never caught him but when I did he had this big tear in his eye he wanted to go to Mexico so bad so I made a sign he should climb up on Precious with me and Fritz but he wouldn't do no such thing til I pointed in the direction he wanted to go in and said Yes Mexico Yes Mexico and then Oh Boy Hidy, Papa said, here come a bunch more tears out his eyes and down his face but them new tears was Tears a'Joy cause now he knowed we was riding on down to Mexico like he wanted to but I didn't have no idea What in the World for.

*T*HE LONGER WE WENT THE HUNGRIER WE GOT Papa said. My beans and corn bread was the first to run out what with three a'us a'eatin on it counting o'Fritz. Precious was happy just eating on the grass and wadn't no bother but fore long Me and Lalo was chasing Lizards and picking Berries to get our suppers but then one day we come up on this big bunch a'Prickly Pear Cactuses three four times over your head and far as you could see and they was these big red Berries a'growing out the top of em and Lalo went after em with a long stick and knocked em down and once you got the stickers off Why they was good eating and we et so many of em we was bout to pop then filled our sack up full and went on and all this time, Papa said, me and Lalo was getting to be Friends without even a'knowing it and wadn't nothing for him to grab up something off the ground then bring it over to me so I'd name it in English for him. That's a Tumble Bug or that's Rabbit Do or that's a Flint Rock or whatever it was then o'Lalo'd name it just to his self and lock up what he just learned in his head so he could find it later. And sometimes, he said, we'd just be setting there at the fire eating some o'lizard or something for our suppers and o'Lalo'd look up at me and say Red Spider and I'd say Red Spider back to let him know he was saying it right then here he'd go just a'naming everthing else he had there in his head to make sure he was naming em right and almost always he was but it near wore me out cause Lalo was bout a Ten New Words to the Mile Man and them words added up in a hurry and fore long we could even talk a little back and forth cause not only did I name everthing we seen, Papa said, but everthing we did too like I'd say Look a'here Lalo now we giving o'Fritz a scratch on his head or Look a'there Lalo how far we come since we left our Home but when I said that, he said, I turned and pointed back over our shoulder and Why here come a whole bunch a'Men a'riding after us fast as they could go and Lalo said Snake Snake Snake which was his word for Bad Bad Bad and Oh Boy Hidy, Papa said, it sure nough was.

*T*HEM MEN PULLED THEY HORSES UP all round us, Papa said, and it was like this big Dust Storm come up over us and you couldn't hardly see you hand in front a'you face and then, he said, this Man come a'stepping outta the Dust Storm to view and he had two big Ears on him looked like handles on some o'jug you might find in the kitchen somewheres and Fritz didn't like him one bit and just went to barking like he was gonna eat him up and Jug Ears said If that little Dog there don't shut up I'm gonna wring his god dam neck for him and pitch him in the Cactuses. He ain't doing nothing, Papa said, You just let him alone. And I might do the same god dam thing with that little Yeller Belly Mexkin you got there too, he said. I told Fritz to shush, Papa said, but they wadn't much I could do to keep Lalo from being a Mexkin. We just passing through, Papa said, just leave us alone and we be on our way but Jug Ears just give a laugh at that and said to them others We might could use us a couple a'Boys like these here for Fun don't you reckon and it wouldn't surprise me even that god dam little Dog there. Oh I didn't like this one bit, Papa said. I didn't know what he was saying at that time a'my life but I knowed it was No Good for me and Lalo and Fritz. Just go on, Papa said, yall ain't gonna do nothing. No Sir you dam sure wrong bout that Mister Jug Ears said then climbed down off a'his Horse and come a'walking up with all them others right there with him and fore I could do anything he grabbed o'Fritz outta my hands and chunked him over yonder somewheres like they wadn't no more to him than a clod you might pick up in the Corn Field then when he turned back round to us Lalo give him a slap cross his ugly face so hard it took his hat off and made his eye squint and all them others went to laughing they thought it was so funny but not o'Jug Ears He took his knife out his belt and said Ever body just watch I'm gonna show you how you skin a little Mexkin and eat his dam guts for you Breakfast and when he grabbed for Lalo I jumped at him and he throwed me away like he did Fritz then come at me with his knife and Oh he would a'sliced me up in little pieces for sure but right then Oh they was this big bloody red hole come up sudden on his chest and Oh he went a'flying back with both his arms and his legs a'going out like a great big X and then they was this sound a'Gun Shot come from way off out yonder somewheres on the other side a'the World and then I looked, Papa said, and Why here come a Cowboy in a big hat just a'whooping like some o'crazy wild Inyin and a'spurring his Horse with his Big Gun in his hand ready to shoot somebody else if he decided to and then, he said, I like to a'fell over dead cause I seen that Cowboy in the big hat just saved our Life wadn't nobody but my o'Amigo Calley Pearsall his self and Firefoot was bringing him on so fast his feets wadn't even touching on the ground.

OH THEM OTHERS SCATTERED like they Pants was on Fire, Papa said, but not o'Jug Ears his scattering days was over for ever. He didn't hurt you did he, Calley said then picked Fritz up outta the Bushes and give him a good look all over then he seen Lalo standing over there by o'Precious. Whose your Friend there, he said. That's Lalo, Papa said, he's bent on going to Mexico and they just ain't no turning him

183

from it. Well I was bound that way my self for reasons of Life or Death when I come cross your tracks, Calley said. If you a'talking bout them Pardee Boys No Sir they ain't a'chasing you no more, Papa said, then I told him bout the o'Tooting Granma and all the rest of it and said Mister Pearsall you just Free as a Bird in the Air now I reckon and Calley said You remember that time you asked me Did I have any Good Stories in my Life and I said I thought the Good Stories was maybe just now coming up the road to me You remember me a'saying that. Yes Sir I do remember you a'saying that, Papa said. Well, Calley said, I reckon maybe it was you was that Good Story I was talking bout coming up the road to me but I didn't know it til just this minute. Then o'Calley reached over and took my hat off then put his own Hat on my head in its place like a Daddy might do his Son and I never been more proud a'nothing in all my Life. Course now I need me another one ain't that right he said then went over there and picked up that big o'Mexkin Sombrero o'dead Jug Ears didn't need no more and set it smartly down on his own head and run the stampede strap down under his chin and said Well I reckon all them Fancy Girls up in San Antoneya gonna think I'm some o'Billy Goat now huh. Yes Sir and we got us another Billy Goat right here I said, Papa said, then I picked up my old flop hat off the ground and set it up on Lalo's head and said Cowboy Cowboy and he just went to grinning from one ear to the other and then he said Vaquero Vaquero which I figgured was Cowboy Cowboy in Mexkin. Well, Calley said, I reckon this is just Hat Day all round ain't it then he took him a look over at o'Jug Ears' Horse just a'standing there but it was the Saddle Bag and not the Horse grabbed his eye and he went over there and run his hand down in it and come out with bout a'gallon bucket a'Gold Coins and the same thing on the other side. Oh Gold Coins just ever wheres, Papa said, even down there in o'Jug Ears' pockets. I reckon you know what this means don't you, Calley said. Yes Sir I reckon I do, Papa said. It means you can go buy you self a Cow and a Farm now if you want to. No sir, Calley said, it means all them other Sons a'Bitches gonna be a'storming back in here fore you know it to get they Money back and I say Let's us mount up and whup it the god dam Hell on down the Country fore they do. Then, Papa said, o'Calley grabbed Lalo up off his feet and set him down on top a'o'Jug Ears' Horse and said Here Senor Lalo you got you your own Horse now and I believe he is a good one from what I can tell just by looking. And then, Papa said, I hefted Fritz up on Precious and me and Lalo squeezed our Hat down

. . . that Cowboy in the big hat just saved our Life wadn't nobody but my o'Amigo Calley Pearsall his self . . .

185

on our head til our ears went down double and off we went a'chasing cross the wide open Country after my Friend Calley Pearsall who saved me and Lalo's Life that day and would again here fore long.

We RUN ALL THAT DAY

Papa said, and o'Precious never give out a lick nor Lalo neither but my poor little o'Behind bout fell off from the bouncing Up and Down and first Creek we come to Why I just set my self down in the cool mud and went to wiggling it for relief and so did Lalo his. I didn't have no idea I was running with a couple a'Mud Ducks, Calley said, then squatted down there by me and went to twirling his spur and keeping a sharp Eye out. You reckon they still after us, Papa said. Oh Yes Sir I do reckon it, he said, Yes Sir I god dam sure do. O'Jug Ears bout scared me to death, Papa said. It was your courage that I seen, Calley said, and that little Lalo's too. Course it's a wonder that Son of a Bitch didn't cut your ears off for it, he said. I never seen you scared Mister Pearsall, Papa said, I wish I knowed your trick. Oh they ain't no trick to it Calley said, I'm scared three four times a day and another six seven times on Sunday. Then he give me a look and said You scared a'something else you ain't told me about yet too ain't you. Maybe, Papa said, I don't know. Well if you don't know this is gonna be a short Conversation, he said. Old Karl got my Momma's Horse and now I know he got my Momma's Saddle too, Papa said, but what I don't know is how he got em but I do know my Momma wouldn't a'never just give em to him. And now you wanna go ask your mean o'Daddy about it but you scared a'him is that right, Calley said. And where my Momma is too, Papa said, I wanna ask him that. Calley took o'Jug Ears' Hat off and run his finger round and round in it to think then put it back on his head and justed the chin strap. What if your mean o'Daddy tells you something about where your Momma is that you don't really wanna know, he said. Even if deep down inside you maybe already do know. Oh and when he said that I just couldn't help my self no more, Papa said, and went to crying my eyes out and when I did Calley Pearsall reached over and put his hand down on my shoulder and then here in a minute Lalo come over and he did too even if he didn't have no idea in the World what we was even a'talking bout, he said, then when I was all cried out Calley brung me up to my feet and give me a swat and then Lalo one too and said You Mud Ducks better get mounted up now We got Bad People a'riding to here wanting to shoot us for they Money.

SO WE WENT A'RIDING ON OFF AGAIN

Papa said, but now I knowed in my Heart my Momma was gone forever and I knowed in my Head Old Karl was the one who done away with her. Course I reckon I knowed that all along like Calley said but just didn't wanna say it to my self. But what I didn't know, he said, was how I was gonna get him back for it cept kill him hard as I could I knowed that much. I thought I might hide in the barn and Pitchfork him dead one morning the way Pepe and Peto tried to do Mister Pegleg or get up in the hay loft when he was a'milking the Cow and drop something big on top a'his head to squash him or maybe push him in one of them Brush piles when it was all on fire and watch him worm round like them Snakes usted to then hit him with a stick ever time he tried to get out til they wadn't nothing left a'him but a little pile a'ash and then I'd kick them ashes over and let the wind take em somewheres far far away to where you couldn't never find em no more. That was my favorite way, Papa said, cause I thought that's what the o'Devil would do with him anyhow when he got him down there in Hell and it made me feel good to see him suffer like that. But, he said, it was hard a'holding that Pitchur a'him suffering like that cause that little Bell in my head just went to ringing again and what I heard it saying was Oh No Oh No Oh No and then here come this new Pitchur over on top a'the old one and this new Pitchur was of Me and my Momma and my Brother Herman out there in the Creek a'playing with the Little Bay Mare that time fore we was all broke a'part and I couldn't help but go to smiling at it even as we was riding along then of a sudden Calley said Let's give our Horses a rest and eat us some suppers. And then after we done that, Papa said, Calley come over to me and Lalo with some rope he had and said he reckoned we might probably be riding all night long and he was gonna tie us on our Horse so if we went to sleep while we was riding along we wouldn't fall off in a big pile a'Donkey Do or something and then,

Papa said, he tucked Fritz up under my shirt and buttoned it up to where only his nose was a'sticking out and Fritz liked it so much he grinned and said Heh Heh Heh like he did sometimes and I seen Lalo pull his hat way down tight so he wouldn't lose it if we should have to go a'running some-time in the Night to get away from something or somebody.

THE MOON COME UP BRIGHT AND ROUND

Papa said, and they was a Man in it looked just like Old Karl to me and I figgured he was up there waiting to get me cause a'what I'd been a'thinking bout getting him But then here in a minute it wadn't Old Karl up there in the Moon no more but was now my Momma a'watching me, he said, and I never felt such a Peace come over me as did then and I wadn't fraid a'Old Karl no more nor a'them Men a'chasing after us neither one. I reckon that's what a Momma's Love is ain't it, Papa said, it's just being watched over by your Momma's Love Eye and feeling safe bout everthing they is in the World and then I went off to sleep just a'riding along on Precious like that and then I looked over and Why there was my Momma a'riding right long side me on that Little Bay Mare and then she smiled at me and reached out her hand and I give her a smile back and reached out my hand to touch hers but they was something funny in my Dream us trying to touch hands but we just couldn't do it no matter how hard it was we tried but it wadn't no trouble at all for her to reach over and give o'Precious a pet and when she did Why Precious give her hand a big Blubber Kiss back. And then, he said, Momma rode over to Lalo a'sleeping there on o'Jug Ears' Horse and leaned over and give him a hug round his neck and touched her head to his head and whispered something to his ear but I don't know what it was she whis-pered to this day. Anyhow, Papa said, I didn't see how she could whisper something to Lalo but couldn't even touch my hand. That didn't seem right to me. Then, of a sudden, he said, Momma reared that Little Bay Mare up on her hind legs and throwed me a Smile and a Kiss then waved her Hat up in the air to say Goodbye and went a'whooping and a'running off in the Dark and I Tried and Tried and Tried to foller but o'Precious just wouldn't turn to it and then Somebody said Wake up you Mud Ducks we here. So I opened my eyes, Papa said, and Oh they was this Great Big River in front a'us and on the other side wadn't nothing but Cactus. That's Mexico over yonder ain't it I said, Papa said, and Calley said Yes Sir that's Her and if you ain't careful she'll eat you up and spit you out fore you know it then he looked over and seen Lalo untying the rope helt him on to his Horse. Where's he think he's a'going to, Calley said. Mexico I reckon, Papa said, that's what he come all the way down here for. What's he want over there in Mexico, Calley said. I don't have no idea, Papa said, he's a Hard Nut to Crack. Well warn him they's Sink Holes all out in that River and they'll swaller you and your Horse both right up and the harder you kick to get out the deeper down you go til they ain't no ever getting out again Tell him that, Calley said. Lalo I said, Papa said, Mister Pearsall said they's Sink Holes all out in that River and— He ain't a'listening, Calley said, and then I looked, Papa said, and sure nough there went Lalo just a'kicking and a'hollering at his Horse to get him on cross that River to Mexico quick as he could.

$\mathcal{C}$ALLEY PULLED HIS BOOTS OFF Papa said, then his shirt and his pants too. I don't trust that River, he said, not one god dam bit. I didn't neither, Papa said, they was Swirls all in it but nothing scared Lalo and he just kept a'going the Water getting so deep his Horse couldn't walk on the bottom no more and we give out a breath when he come up the bank on the other side then jumped down off his Horse and give us a big wave and I waved back but Calley was a'looking way off out yonder somewheres in a different direction and squinting his eye to see what it was he was a'seeing but I seen right quick it was that bunch a'Men chasing us for they Gold Coins and I said Its Them Mister Pearsall. Yes Sir it's Them, he said, it god dam sure is. Then, Papa said, we both went to hollering and signaling at Lalo to come on back over here on our side but he seen em too and was already trying to get up on his Horse but his hands was all clenched up over something he had in em and he couldn't grab a'holt a'the reins and was just a'stumbling round like a Loonie and them Men was just a'coming on so Lalo and his Horse both jumped in the River trying to swim over to us but it was hard for Lalo to swim with just his Fists and not no hands. Take a'hold a'his Horse when he comes out, Calley said, I'm a'going in for Lalo then he took him a jump in the River and went to swimming for Lalo who was beating at the Water with his Fists and going Up and Down in the water but it looked like to me it was more Down than Up and then I seen this big Swirl take him and then Oh I didn't see him no more and I went to hollering Lalo Lalo Lalo but No he was Gone just Gone Gone Gone but then o'Calley Pearsall took him a dive down in that Swirl and here in bout a hunderd years he come up with Lalo and went to swimming to me with that Swirl just a'trying to pull him and Lalo both back down under again and bout that time I grabbed holt a'Lalo's Horse and seen them Bad Men coming on fast and Boy Hidy I thought we was Deaders for sure but Calley come up outta the River with Lalo there under his arm and he grabbed bout five hand fulls a'Gold Coins outta o'Jug Ears' saddle bag and chunked em ever which way high up in the air to where them Men could see em shining in the sun then he hefted Lalo up in his arms and I did Fritz in mine and Calley's clothes too and away we went fast as we could Lalo's Horse a'follering and I looked back and seen them Men rein up and go to fighting over them Gold Coins Calley throwed all over the place but Calley hollered Don't You Linger Boy and I give Precious my heels and there we went and I seen Lalo in Calley's arms still had his hands all clenched up over something in his Fists but I couldn't tell was he drowned dead or still a'living.

WE RUN AND WE RUN AND WE RUN

Papa said, and we didn't stop til we couldn't run no more then we put Lalo down on the ground and he opened his eyes up but you could tell he didn't have no idea bout nothing. What's come over Lalo I said, Papa said. He lost his Mind when the swirl got him, Calley said. It ain't there in his body no more. How's he gonna get it back, Papa said. I don't know, Calley said. I never seen nothing like it. We gotta get him to his Momma, Papa said, she'll get it back for him. What's that he's got there in his Fists he's holding on so tight to, Calley said. I don't know, Papa said, then I tried to pull Lalo's fingers open to see but they was clamped shut so hard you couldn't a'opened em with a Number One Jonson Pry Bar. Least he's alive and breathing, I said, I was fraid we was gonna lose him in the Sink Hole. Yes Sir but he's in some kind a'State, Calley said, then touched Lalo's cheek and said Lalo look a'here at me We gonna take you on Home to your Family now You ready to

*. . . then I seen this big Swirl take him
and then Oh I didn't see him no more . . .*

go. And then, Papa said, Lalo got right up on his feet and went over to his Horse and just stood there cause he couldn't climb up on the saddle without his hands to help him do it so Calley went over and said Lalo I'd feel better bout everthing if you'd ride double with me so you don't fall off your Horse and hurt you self and Lalo never even looked at him but went right over and stood by Calley's Horse Firefoot and Calley said Look at that He understood ever word I said I reckon that's a good sign don't you. Yes Sir I hope so, Papa said, but I was worried sick maybe Lalo wadn't never gonna get his Mind back again and I said to o'Calley when he was putting his pants and boots back on What you reckon was down there in that Sink Hole to take Lalo's Mind like that and Calley said I don't have no idea what but I've heard it said that a Sink Hole don't never take nothing outta this World but that it gives something else back in return. You reckon that's what Lalo's holding there in his Fists, Papa said, something the Sink Hole give him back for taking his Mind. No I don't reckon so, Calley said, Lalo already had his Fists round something he got over there in Mexico fore the Swirl took him. Well what you reckon then, Papa said. I don't know, Calley said, but if that Sink Hole really did take Lalo like we been a'saying Then maybe that ain't even Lalo standing over there by my Horse but Somebody Else the Sink Hole give us back in trade.

*L*ALO WADN'T NO TROUBLE RIDING TO HOME

Papa said. We give him water to drink and he drinked it We give him Beans to eat and he et em Course he was still in that State like he come outta the Sink Hole in and the other thing was he couldn't speak a word a'English no more. I pointed at a Tree and said Lalo what's that there and he said Maria Luisa and I said No Lalo that's a Tree don't you remember it and he said Armando and I said No Lalo that's a Tree Tree Tree and Lalo said Luis Alejandra Gustavo Rosa and then I looked over at Calley, Papa said, and I said Mister Pearsall I think poor o'Lalo come outta that Sink Hole a Loonie don't you but Calley said I don't know Let's just listen to him here a minute and see what all he says. So we just rode along a'listening to Lalo and he said Elisa Valeria Nacio Miguel Sandra Rodrigo Fabiola Jose Angelica Mario Juana Eva Tomas Javier like that and just wouldn't quit for nothing. So who is all these Names he's a'talking bout here, Papa said. I don't know, Calley said, but he's about to wear me out with em ain't he you. Yes Sir he is, Papa said, then I said Lalo why don't you just say them Names to you self a while We don't need to hear em no more but Lalo just kept on a'going with it Adriana Oscar Liliana Beto Javier Juana Silvia Antonio and On and On and On til my head was bout to fall off and even little Fritz went to barking at him to Hush but No he wouldn't and even when we was trying to sleep that night he was over there mumbling Names Daniela Eduardo Santiago Elisa Aurelio all night long and then three four days later here we come a'riding in at Mister Armke's Farm and Oh here all them Mexkins come a'running to see we got Lalo back and they went to crying over him and trying to hug him and kiss him and whatnot but he just kept a'naming Names Paulina Ricardo Manolo Sofia and then o'Granma Lupita put her hand up to her face in a Big Surprise and went to crying like somebody hit her with a stick and Mister Armke went over and said something to her and she said something back and then He come over to me and Calley and said Old Lupita says All them Names Lalo been a'naming is of Family People going back ever bit a'two three hunderd years and she says they all ever one come outta that Sink Hole with Lalo. I ain't surprised to hear it, Calley said, One thing don't go in a Sink Hole but what Something else don't come out but I wouldn't a'guessed it'd be so many Dead Mexkins at a time. Then we looked over and everbody was follering Lalo round to the back a'the barn where they was a new Grave just covered up with Old Crecencio in it and Lalo went right over to it and opened his Fists up and Why out come two handfuls a'Mexkin Dirt he been a'holding on to all this time and that Mexkin Dirt fell down on top a'Old Crecencio's Grave. Oh and then Old Lupita just went to wailing bout it and so did all the rest of em and Mister Armke said they was all so Happy cause now Old Crecencio was buried under Mexkin Dirt like he always wanted to be and his Spirit wouldn't just have to walk round in Texas til Kingdom Come. And then, Papa said, Lalo closed his eyes and dropped down Dead.

OH POOR LALO Papa said, he made that whole trip down there to Mexico and back to get him two handfuls a'Mexkin Dirt for his o'Granpa and then Oh Boy Hidy there he went right outta this World his self. La Vida Brinca Old Lupita said and Mister Armke said it means Life Jumps and Yes Sir it sure did for Little o'Lalo didn't it, Papa said, and I never felt so sorry for nobody in my whole Life like I did for all his Family and specially for his Momma and Daddy Estella and Peto. They just stood there a'holding hands and crying like two little lost Childrens and then Old Lupita and Pepe's Wife went to giving Lalo a bath and dressing him up and combing his hair for his Trip to Heaven. And then, he said, they even set the Hat I had give him on his belly cause they said he always wanted to be a Vaquero moren anything and now my Hat made him one. But the very last thing they done fore they nailed the box shut over him was put some Saint round his neck to protect his Soul on his Trip but Mister Armke said He thought Lalo must a'already been a Saint his self for what he done for Old Crecencio's Soul and at such a young age too and Calley said Yes Sir I do believe he was for sure a Saint that come down here to Earth from Above to help his Family in ever which way he could and here's another way he helped em, he said, then went over there and give them Mexkins half a'the Gold Coins outta o'Jug Ears' Saddle Bags and said This is another Gift from Lalo to you but what's left is for me and him. He pointed at me then, Papa said, and when he did Mister Armke said Do you want to say anything to the Family bout Lalo here at his Funeral so, he said, I told em bout trying to get o'Lalo to come on back Home and not go to Mexico at all but Lalo just wadn't gonna have it no other way but go to Mexico to get that Dirt for his o'Granpa no matter what. He was a Hard Nut to Crack I said, Papa said, and when Mister Armke told em what I said in Mexkin they all just went to nodding and crying again cause they said that was just xactly what o'Lalo was like all his whole Life wadn't it Then after they covered him up there next to Old Crecencio the Family ever one of em come up to me and Calley and give us a hug for bringing Lalo back to them all that way from Mexico and when it was Peto's turn he give me a long hug right close to him and now it wadn't only I could see the tears in his eyes but now I could feel his Heart a'Breaking right there next to mine too and I don't know what come over the two a'us but from then on out me and Peto was Friends for Life and Ever More.

Mister Armke Told Pepe and Peto

they might wanna consider buying they own Farm with all this money they had now, Papa said, but Peto said No Senor the First Money they was gonna spend was to the Wood Carver bout six miles away and Mister Armke said Okay go on and go but mean while me and Pepe gonna start building you a House right here on this Farm but then Pepe said No Senor he wanted to go too so the House would just have to wait til they got back from the Wood Carver so Mister Armke looked at me and said Mean while would you please keep a'teaching these little Mexkins here all the English you can and I said Yes Sir I will, Papa said. And then, o'Calley said, Why then I'll teach em everthing they is to know bout a Horse and Saddle and whatnot since they gonna need to know that too ain't they if they gonna have they own Horses and Cattle here one day soon but I don't know that little Girl over there needs to learn it. Oh Yes she does, Mister Armke said, Graciela needs to learn everthing them little Boys learn and you just watch she'll do more with it in her Life Time than they will. Well then, Calley said, maybe we oughta set up School for they Mommas too and put Old Lupita in there with em. No you can't teach an Old Woman nothing, Mister Armke said, after bout fifteen years a'age they just ain't teachable no more but what they do learn after that generally goes against you. You sound like you was some o'Married Man one time, Calley said, am I right. Yes Sir I was a o'Married Man one time, Mister Armke said, but she up and died on me when we was walking to Here from off the Boat in Galveston where I got her. Oh I am sorry Calley said and I am too I said, Papa said. Well she was a First Wife that's all, Mister Armke said, and I never found me another one knowed so much bout everthing they was to know as she did or was so willing to tell you about it ever minute a'the Day and Night. Well I reckon that was some thing being married to a Book like she was huh, Calley said. Oh Yes Sir she was a Book all right, Mister Armke said, Big o'Fat Book stayed wide open all the god dam time. Then Mister Armke looked over at me, Papa said, and said What's your Intention for all that money you got now. I ain't even thought bout it, Papa said. How much is it anyhow. It's nough to keep you in Vittles a good long while, Calley said, I can tell you that. Well if its that much I'd like to go give some of it to Mister and Miz Choat for all they kindness to me in the Past, Papa said, and some more to Bird and Marcellus too and then the rest of it to my Brother Herman I reckon. Woo you gonna be Stone Cold Broke fore you know it, Calley said. Well, Papa said, I ain't gonna need no money where I'm a'going anyhow. And where's that, Mister Armke said. Why over to Old Karl's place, Papa said, to ask him to his Face what he done with my Momma and her Saddle.

I SNUCK DOWN THERE to the graves that night, Papa said, and took me just a little hand full a'that Mexkin Dirt off a'Old Crecencio's Grave and put it over on Lalo's in case he wanted to go walking round Mexico with his o'Granpa sometime Then bout three days later, he said, here come Pepe and Peto back from the Wood Carver with this Box they had and they set it on back a'Mister Armke's wagon where everbody could see and opened it up and Oh they was this little wood statue a'Lalo bout yay high wearing my Hat and a'holding his two Fists out in front a'him like he did all the way back from Mexico with that Mexkin Dirt in em. Saint Lalo, Calley said, ain't that something They went and carved a Saint outta him. And look what else, Mister Armke said, then run his fingers over some words carved in Mexkin all round the bottom. You got any idea what that says he said. No Sir I ain't got no idea I said, Papa said. It says Hard Nut to Crack, Mister Armke said, I reckon you give em they Family Motto and from here on out, he said, won't nobody in the Family ever give up on nothing cause Saint Lalo never did even if it killed him not to. Oh and then, Papa said, they all went to touching Saint Lalo like he was a Live Living Person and Mister Armke said You just watch By tomorrow Old Lupita'll have a pair a'pants and a coat for him then Peto handed Saint Lalo to me so I could get a good look at what he was carved out of and I nodded cause it was Mesquites and Mesquites was the hardest wood they ever was and Saint Lalo would last For Ever. That little Saint Lalo just lifted this Family up about six notches, Calley said. They ain't nothing they can't do specially now with all them Others here helping em too. What Others you talking bout, Papa said. Why all them Mexkin Ancestors that come outta that Sink Hole with Lalo that's what Others, Calley said. Lalo brung em back here to Texas with him same as he did that Mexkin Dirt he put on o'Crecencio's Grave and I reckon now theys a'kinda Lalo Road tween Here and Mexico for the Living and the Dead both ain't they. Yes Sir, Papa said, but that's a lot a'Mexkins ain't it. Well, Calley said, Texas been Home to Mexkins all the way back to when Adam was just a sneaky little barefoot Winder Peeker and they just ain't no such thing as Texas anyhow, he said, less you got a bunch a'Mexkins in it.

EVERBODY WENT TO BUILDING A HOUSE

for all them Mexkins, Papa said, and they propped Saint Lalo up over there on the fence to keep watch so wouldn't nobody hit they finger with a hammer or saw off a leg or something and fore long everbody just naturally went over and talked to him three four times a day bout this and that and when the first Cold Blue Norther come a'whupping in Why Old Lupita made a little Quilt and wrapped it round Saint Lalo to keep him warm. I asked Calley one day Did he really think Saint Lalo was watching over everbody, Papa said, and Calley said Yes Sir I do believe it and I believe all them Ancestors come outta the Sink Hole with him is watching too. You ain't telling me we working here with a bunch a'Ghosts all round us are you, Papa said. Don't tell me you a'telling me that. I'm telling you what I think about it my self, Calley said, I ain't a'telling you what you oughta think bout it you self But they Ghosts all round here whether you like it or not and if I was you I'd be glad of it. No Sir they too scary for me, Papa said, and I don't want nothing to do with em. They's probably bout a hundred of em watching out for you ever second a'the day cause you was Saint Lalo's Special Friend. I hope they are for me too. Well I don't know bout that, Papa said. Well, o'Calley said, if something Bad happens to me First Thing I'm gonna do when I'm a Ghost is tap you on your Noggin to let you know me and them Mexkins is all a'looking out for you. You already been a'looking out for me, Papa said, if it wadn't for you o'Jug Ears would a'got me for sure. They's somebody else gonna get you for sure too if you ain't careful, Calley said. You know who I'm talking about don't you. Yes Sir I do, Papa said, You talking bout Old Karl ain't you. Here's my advice, Calley said. You wait til you got another fifteen-twenty years on you fore you go a'knocking on his door to ask him what he done with your Momma and her Saddle. Maybe a century or two fore you do that okay Cause I'm afraid that old man'll gobble you up and pick his teeth with your bones. No Sir I cain't wait, Papa said, It just ain't in me to wait. It

197

ain't in you to listen to Good Sense neither is it, Calley said. You just told me a minute ago you wadn't trying to tell me what to think, Papa said. That was about something else Amigo, Calley said, This here is about your own dear sweet young Life. Well I'm a'going anyhow, Papa said. Yes Sir, I can see that, Calley said, Well then I reckon I'm a'going with you and if o'Mister Good Sense should come a'riding up and try to talk us out of it, he said, Why then we just gonna pull our guns out and shoot that Son of a Bitch right off his Horse.

A COUPLE A'TWO THREE DAYS LATER Papa said, Mister Armke come back from the Saw Mill with the last load a'Sawed Boards for the new House and Oh something else too a Announcement they was gonna have The First Annual Bird Dance over at Fischer Hall and everbody was invited to come but you couldn't get in less you was dressed up like the Bird you seen you self to be when you looked at that little Birthmark Bird there on Bird's chest. Course, he said, I xplained to Mister Armke and Calley Pearsall where Bird come from in the first place and how his Momma Miss Gusa died in the Wheelbarra that night and how the Choats took him in to raise as they own and how everbody else round Fischer took a Oath they'd help raise him up too cause really he was pretty much Everybody's Little Boy who come out of the Dark that Night. I reckon you'd like to go to that Shindig wouldn't you, Mister Armke said. Yes Sir I would, Papa said, but I got other Fish to Fry. Wait a minute, Calley said. I'd like to go to a Dance sometime where they wadn't nobody dancing but a bunch a'Birds. Well you'd have to be a Bird a'some kind you self fore you could go, Papa said. They ain't gonna let nobody in but Birds. Well I ain't gonna be a Chick A Dee or nothing like that, Calley said, I don't wanna go that bad. I'm a Road Runner, Papa said, just think a'some o'Bird you'd wanna be if you was a Bird. Maybe I'll be a Lion, Calley said. I kind a'see myself a Lion don't you. It's a Bird Dance Mister Pearsall, Mister Armke said, not some o'Animal Dance. I could a'been happy a Road Runner, Calley said. I'd make a pretty good Road Runner just a'running like Hell cross the Country Side. Well go on and be one then, Mister Armke said, I don't see nothing wrong with they being two Road Runners at the same Bird Dance I don't reckon. I don't neither, Papa said, and we can stick a beak and a couple a'tail feathers on o'Fritz and he can be the Little Baby Brother Road Runner. Mister Armke said something to Old Lupita and she nodded at it and said something back then Mister Armke said, Papa said, Old Lupita says she can make Bird Suits for you Boys but she's gonna need some sticks to make Wing Bones with and maybe some Horse Tail Hair to make a Bristle Hat that looks like a Road Runner's Top Knot. How bout Cow Tail Hair, Papa said, I ain't cutting Precious' Tail off just to go to a Bird Dance. Well No Sir who would, Calley said, and then Mister Armke said Okay bring her some Cow Tail Hair and she'll just have to make Do with that. And then later, Papa said, when we was nailing them new Sawed Boards on to the new House Calley said I'm glad you give up Going to Old Karl's Place and is a'going to the Bird Dance instead. No Sir I never, Papa said, they both on the same xact road. I just wanna say Goodbye to the Choats and Bird and Marcellus fore we go on to Old Karl's. You mean you wanna say Hello, Calley said, not Goodbye. I didn't say it, Papa said, but No I did mean Goodbye cause I didn't think they was gonna be nothing left after Old Karl got through with me.

*W*E FINISHED THE LITTLE HOUSE

for the Mexkins, Papa said, and bout that same time the Mexkins finished a little Wood Church with a pointy top for Saint Lalo and his Granma Old Lupita and his Momma Estella was always going over there with a Tamaley or something and Graciela put Colored Rocks and Flowers in it and one time she found a Turtle Shell and she put that in there too, he said, so I reckon o'Saint Lalo had bout all he needed. And by now, Papa said, they was nough English going round to where we could talk a little back and forth so when it was time for me and Calley to go I went over there and knocked on they door with Fritz and Calley and said Well we gotta be going on to the Bird Dance now and Oh everbody give me a big hug and Fritz and Calley one too and Graciela took a'holt a'one a'my legs and Hilario the other one and Oh they went to crying bout us leaving and a'hollering Tree Dog Rock Possum but what they was trying to say was Stay Stay Stay but just couldn't think a'the right word for it and then Pepe and Peto come out to the Horses with us where Mister Armke was waiting and offered out they hands and me and Calley shook each one of em and then Peto said Son Nove a Beech and Calley said I reckon he's talking about your mean o'Daddy ain't he and fore I could say anything back, Papa said, Pepe nodded and said Jess he ees talking a bout heem that Son Nove a Beech and then Peto made that sign with his long finger. You look after this Boy, Mister Armke said to Calley. Then here come Old Lupita with our Bird Outfits and Calley took em and said Thank You Senora I wish you could see us when we are out there on the Dance Floor a'flapping and a'dancing away with all them other Birds and Old Lupita said Jess Son Nove a Beech cause she just heard Pepe and Peto say it and she didn't know what else to say and then Oh here come Estella out the House with Saint Lalo in her arms. She wants him to Bless your Trip and bring you back Home again, Mister Armke said. I ain't never had a Saint Bless me in my Life, Calley said, but I don't mind if he does and I Thank Him for it. I reckon I feel the same way, Papa said, and I Thank Him too. Then, he said, Old Lupita leaned over at Saint Lalo like she was listening to something he was saying and Oh her eyes got big as a Supper Plate and she said something and Mister Armke said Old Lupita said that Saint Lalo just said You Boys better keep your eye out for the o'Jaybird at that Bird Dance cause that o'Jaybird is the meanest Bird they ever was or ever gonna be.

IT WAS A CHILLY RIDE

Papa said, not freezing cold but cold nough you could see smoke a'coming out you mouth and out o'Fritz's too, he said, but Fritz didn't have no idea where that smoke was coming from and kept a'trying to bite it and fell off Precious doing it but then jumped right back on again and I blowed my Smoke Breath at him and he went to barking and trying to bite that too. You can't live on just Smoke, Calley told him, you can eat about a Cloud and a half of it and you still ain't gonna get a Toot's worth. It was bout then, Papa said, that Precious went to acting funny and throwing her head this way and that and poking her chin out like they was something up ahead somewheres she didn't want no part of. What you reckon's wrong with Precious I said, Papa said. I don't have no idea, Calley said, but I'd keep a tight seat if I was you and pay my attention. Animals know a Hell of a lot more bout Things than us o'Cowboys do. You reckon, Papa said. Why Hell yes I sure do reckon, he said. Take your Regular Cow for xample A Cow won't sleep down by the

Creek when she knows it's gonna come a Big Rain cause she don't wanna get caught in a Flood and get washed on down with houses and trees and whatnot No Sir a Cow always goes to High Ground to sleep when its gonna come a Big Rain You just watch. Well, Papa said, I seen Cows that drowned down by the Creek when it come a Big Rain cause they didn't go up to High Ground. Yes Sir I know it, Calley said, but them ain't the Cows I'm a'talking about here. Course Turkeys is altogether different, he said. A Turkey'll just stand there with his beak wide open and look up in to a Rain Storm til he drowns his self to death and then you gotta go pump him dry fore you can cook him for your suppers. Is that right, Papa said. Oh Yes Sir, Calley said, one a'the best Turkey Dinners I ever et was one drowned on flat ground over in Gonzales County bout a mile or two from the San Marcos River in a Rain Storm. I'd a'liked to seen that, Papa said. Well the good thing bout that one, Calley said, was after he drowned a big o'Bolt a'Lightning come down out the Sky and blowed all his feathers off and cooked him for me both at the same dam time.

OH YOU COULD HEAR THE POLKA MUSIC
coming from way off, Papa said, and I seen Calley go to bobbing his head in time with it. You a Dancer even on o'Firefoot ain't you Mister Pearsall I said, Papa said. Yes Sir I do like to Dance, Calley said, I dam sure do My Feet was borned for the Dance Floor and once they out there on it Why the rest a'me just has to hang on for the Ride. I made a Pitchur a'that in my Head and went to laughing, Papa said, and right then Precious shied at something and I all but went a'flying out the saddle. You sure they ain't a Burr under her tail, Calley said, I never knowed Precious to be so finnikey in all my Life. Maybe it's just this Chilly Weather got her so jumpy, Papa said. Or maybe that music just got her wanting to Dance too, Calley said. Like it does you I reckon huh, Papa said. Yes Sir I'm gonna have to get my rope here in a minute and tie my feet on so they don't go Dancing off down the Country somewheres by they self. And right when we was a'laughing at that Precious stopped dead in her tracks and wouldn't go no further, Papa said, and Calley said I reckon they's Something bothering that Horse but she ain't gonna tell us what it is Is she. Maybe a Horse just don't wanna go to a Bird Dance

I said, Papa said, and Oh Calley just went to laughing at that and said You getting funny here in your Old Age ain't you And then I went to laughing at what he just said cause I really wadn't even trying to be funny when I said that bout Maybe a Horse don't wanna go to a Bird Dance It just come out funny and I wadn't even close to being Old Age like he said any how. You a Funny Bird I said, Papa said, then the both a'us went to laughing at that so hard we all but fell off our Horse and Fritz went to howling at the Moon and Calley said Well I didn't know Fritz was a Coyote, I thought he was a Little Brother Road Runner didn't you and then Oh here we went to laughing all over again at that til o'Calley swatted at me with his big Hat and said You quit it If we a'going to the Bird Dance we better go on and get our Bird Suits on or they ain't even gonna let us in So, Papa said, we unsaddled our Horses for they Relief and turned em a'loose to eat what grass they could find then started to laugh all over one more time at the memory a'all them Funny Things we been a'saying up to now.

*W*E PUT FRITZ'S ROAD RUNNER BIRD SUIT on him, Papa said, and first thing he done was go to licking on his Hiney but his pointy Bird Beak poked him right there on the Spot and Oh he took off a'yipping and a'running round in circles his Tail Feathers just a'kicking up a Dust Storm so much it all but killed us. You gotta learn to be more careful where you put your Beak in Fritz, Calley said. If you'd a'Tooted it'd a'blowed both your ears off. And if that wadn't funny nough, Papa said, then me and Calley put on our Bird Suits and we looked bout as funny as anything you ever seen what with our Road Runner Hats made outta Cow Tail Hair and them long Wings Old Lupita made outta sticks and old Croker Sacks and, he said, course we had long Road Runner Beaks too that covered our face up all but just our eyes. You're a Bird if ever I seen one, Calley said, then off we went a'walking through the Woods to the Bird Dance and here in a minute we seen the lights coming out a'Fischer Hall like it was on fire and Why they was Horses and Wagons all over the place and even a regular little Town a'Tents over there for the Birds who was gonna stay the night but the thing that bout made me fall over was all them Birds going in and out Fischer Hall and the ones inside that come a'dancing by the door when we was stepping up to go in. Oh, he said, they was a Sparrow dancing with a Chicken Hawk and a Red Bird Cardinal dancing with a Rock Wren and two Turkey Gobblers a'dancing together with they big tails fanned up and then I seen this o'Mother Hen a'dancing with a Banty Rooster and I knowed it was Mister and Miz Choat cause they was dancing Up and Down in one place like they always done. I'm gonna grab me a Pretty Bird and go to dancing my self Calley said then grabbed a Bow Legged Yeller Bird might a'been a Canary I reckon when she passed by and they went a'dipping and a'whirling on cross the Dance Floor like something you might see in one a'them Shows down in San Antoneya they always talking bout and course all this time Fritz was over there in the corner tween a couple a'Mornin Doves and a Red Wing Black Bird trying to figgur out how to lick his Behind without poking it with his Pointy Beak again. And then, Papa said, I looked cross the Dance Floor and way over yonder was this Giant Bird Nest made out a'Leaves and Sticks and Why setting up in it pretty as you please with Flowers all round him was my Little o'Half Brother Bird his self and even if his eyes still wadn't open yet he was a'pointing his finger right straight at me like he knowed all along I was gonna be there and I could see his Eye Balls a'rolling round and round and side to side behind his little thin blue Eye Lids like always, he said, and standing right there holding his other hand was this tall skinny o'Sissertail and I knowed it couldn't be nobody but my Friend Marcellus a'looking out for Bird like he always done and then he seen me too and come a'hurrying toward me through the Dancing Kill Dees and Ducks and then a Barn Owl a'dancing the Polka come by with o'Fritz in her arm like he was a Baby Doll then out the corner a'my eye I seen Bird just a'jabbing his finger cross the Dance Floor to where this big o'Jaybird was pushing past some little fat Tit Mouse I think it was then stepped in view for bout half a'second just when Calley and that Pretty Bow Legged Yeller Bird was a'going out the Front Door to the Woods in a tight hug then I lost that Jaybird outta view behind a King Fisher and some other Birds but my Blood run cold like Froze Ice any how cause I knowed that Jaybird had him another name when he wadn't in a Jaybird Suit and that name was Old Karl and then I seen Old Karl stretching his wings out to swoop down on little Bird setting there in his Nest without o'Marcellus or me or nobody else in this World to protect him in this time a'terrible Danger coming.

203

I POINTED MY FINGER OUT AT HIM

Papa said, and went to hollering Jaybird Jaybird Jaybird but couldn't nobody hear me what with everbody making the sound a'whatever Bird they was as they Hopped and Danced round the Dance Floor going Caw Caw Hoo Hoo Cheep Cheep and a lot of em was whistling too Why they was such a racket you'd a'thought you was up a Tree with all the Birds in the World setting there on the limb with you and then Marcellus come over to me just a'grinning in his Sissortail Suit and I pointed at that Jaybird a'shoving his way through bout six Wood Peckers and I said That's Old Karl there in the Jaybird Suit going after Bird you see him but No he didn't cause they was other Dancing Birds covering up the view again. No I don't see no Jaybird at all, Marcellus said, you sure you ain't talking bout that o'Goose there with the gimp leg. And just then, Papa said, the view opened up and there was that Jaybird pushing other Birds out the way again so he could get to Bird over there in his Nest and then we couldn't see him no more for all the Birds and then Oh here he come in view again but Oh now the Nest was Empty Empty Empty and Bird was Gone. Then Marcellus pointed and hollered Yonder he goes making off with Bird. Oh and then, Papa said, Marcellus went a'running to catch him fore he got out the Front Door with Little Baby Bird and I did too and we run through all them Dancing Birds a'knocking em over ever which way and a'hollering JAYBIRD JAYBIRD JAYBIRD but couldn't nobody hear nothing and ever second that o'Jaybird was getting closer and closer to getting away with Bird but then, Papa said, Marcellus took him a jump through the air at Old Karl in his Jaybird Suit and Old Karl give him a Lick right in his face hard as he could with his fist and put him down like a sack a'flour but now ever Bird in there stopped dancing and looked to see what was a'going on and they seen Bird there in the Jaybird's claw and seen he was bout to make off with him out the Front Door and then Oh you never heard such a'Anger coming up out a bunch a'Birds in your Life and then there they went a'moving at Old Karl like one big giant Mad Bird and they was Blood in they Eye and he seen it too and grabbed out his Knife and pointed it to Bird's Birthmark Bird there on his little chest then put his Snake Eyes on everbody and said This is my property here and you Sons a Bitches done making all the Fuss over him you ever gonna make and if a'one a'you reaches you a hand out to take him from me Why I'm gonna stab my knife right through his Core and on down to Hell and Back.

And Oh Boy Hidy, Papa said, that stopped all us Birds there like somebody just knocked us back with a Hammer and we didn't have no idea what to do next cause we was scared a'bringing Bad Harm on Bird. And then, he said, I looked back there past the Band Stand and I won't never in my Life forget what I seen next cause Oh now here come my Momma's Horse Precious just a'walking in the Back Door then she raised up her head and looked way down yonder cross the Room to where Old Karl was a'holding his Knife to Bird and then, Papa said, Oh and then here come these Red Hot Burning Fires up in her eyes and she put em both right on that o'Jaybird and you couldn't a'pulled em off with a'Logging Chain and a'Team a'Mules.

AND THEN

Papa said, Precious went to walking cross the Floor direct at him and I said Why Precious what you doing a'walking in here like this You aint a Bird but she went on by me like I wadn't even borned yet and ever Bird in there stepped back out her way to make a Road for her to pass. And Oh, he said, Old Karl seen her coming too and his mean o'Snake Eyes went Wide Wide Wide with ever step she took at him and in a minute them Snakes was all gone out his Eyes and in they place now was Fear Fear Fear, Papa said, I reckon cause he knowed they was something Bad he done one time and Now Precious was coming to get him back for it And Oh that Jaybird just went stiff as a Cedar Post and that's when Calley and the Pretty Bow Legged Yeller Bird Girl come back in the door from out in the Woods behind him and Calley seen that Jaybird a'standing there with his Knife to Bird and knowed something Bad was bout to happen so he just kind a'reached round Old Karl with two light fingers and took the Knife right out his hand like he was just out there in the Corn Field picking him a weed. Thank You Sir, Calley said, Now if it don't matter to you I'm gonna take that Little Baby Boy too I know he must be a'getting heavy on you at a time like this. And Old Karl was so Froze by Precious a'coming at him he didn't make no protest so that's xactly what o'Calley done and then he give Bird over to Miz Choat then Precious give Calley a hard push with her nose to get out the way and stepped up to Old Karl close as you and me a'standing here together right now. Oh and then, he said, Precious' eyes went to burning holes in that Jaybird like she was trying to decide Should he Live or Should he Die and didn't

205

me or nobody else dare make a sound or nothing and then when we was all just bout decided Precious was gonna stand a'looking at him like that til the end of the World Why of a sudden she let out a Scream scattered all us Birds then quickern a Rattle Snake she struck out her big Horse Teeth at him and locked his Head up in her mouth and clomped down hard as she could and Oh Blood come a'squirting out Old Karl's ears and you could hear his Head Bone go Crack Crack Crack and Oh, Papa said, Oh and then Precious took a jump out the Front Door with Old Karl just a'hollering and a'flapping his wings there in her Teeth and run on off with him out yonder in the Dark a'Night somewheres.

 OH AND THEN

Papa said, everybody went over there to Miz Choat a'holding Bird in her arms to make sure he was okay and he was so she put him back in his Nest and even big o'rough Farmers and Ranchers come over with tears in they eyes and cooed over him they was so glad to still have him in the World with em. And then, he said, they come over to hug Calley and Marcellus for they part in saving Bird and they did me too, Papa said, but just a little bit and some of em give me Looks and shied away I reckon cause it was my Daddy was the Bad Jaybird and they didn't know but what maybe I was gonna grow up and be a Bad Jaybird too and if that was true why then they didn't want no more to do with me even now and it made me feel so alone I went over there and set down in the corner where couldn't nobody see me and then here in a minute when I couldn't help it no more Why I just went to crying like some Little o'Lost Baby. And I might be still a'crying yet, he said, but this Hand come down on my shoulder and give it a little squeeze and I knowed it was my o'Amigo Calley Pearsall without even having to look up to see and then Calley come down on one knee and he said I'm sorry you wadn't spared seeing all this tonight particularly that part a'o'Precious chomping down on your mean o'Daddy's Head but remember what Old Lupita said. What'd she say, Papa said, I can't remember nothing right now. La Vida Brinca that's what she said, Calley said, Life Jumps and you either Jump with it or you just got to get the god dam Hell out a'the way and let it pass you by. You hear me he said. Yes Sir I do hear you, Papa said. Well then you a'Jumping or you just a'Setting there a'letting Life go by, Calley said. I don't know which one,

. . . she let out a Scream scattered all us Birds then quickern a Rattle Snake she struck out her big Horse Teeth at him . . .   207

Papa said. Well listen here, Calley said, I want you to know it don't matter a Lick to me how Bad your Life gets or how much Bad they is in it I'm always gonna be right here by your side a'Jumping with you, he said. Long as you a'Jumping too huh. Well Yes Sir I'm a'Jumping too then, Papa said. Oh you don't know what its like to have a Friend like o'Calley Pearsall at a Time like that in your Life, he said, but I do.

WE CHUNKED OUR BIRD SUITS IN THE BRUSH Papa said, then rode triple me and Calley and Fritz on o'Firefoot and here in bout a hour come up on all them other Birds still in they Bird Suits but most all they beaks was gone now. Yall found anything a'Old Karl, Calley said. No Sir nothing, Mister Choat said, not a sign a'that o'Jaybird nor Mandy's Horse Precious neither one but we figgur maybe she carried him on back to Home and that's where we a'going. Well Mister Choat she ain't the same Horse she usted to be, Papa said, might not even remember where Home is. Yes Sir something got in her all right Dam sure did, Mister Calhoun the o'Wood Pecker said, That was a sight wadn't it. I never seen the like of it neither, Old Man Grimes said, if I had to xplain it to somebody wadn't there I'd say a Haint got in that Horse and wouldn't come out til she done what she come to do. It ain't all that unusual, he said, Haints getting in People I mean. That's xactly right, somebody in a Barn Swaller Outfit said, Hell I had me a Brother-in-Law got tooken over by a Haint one night and jumped off the god dam Roof thought he could fly and by god he dam sure could. But just for bout a second or two, he said. Oh everbody just went to laughing at that, Papa said, and some other Bird said I reckon a Haint wadn't all that got in to your Brother-in-Law that night was it if he went to jumping off a Roof. He might a'had him a Snort or two I reckon the Barn Swaller said. It wouldn't a'surprised me. Yall need to hush your joking and get back to looking for sign, Mister Pullins said, I hate the idear a'that SonofaBitch being free and a'loose in this Country if he's still alive after half his head got eat like that by a Horse. You need to put a clamp on your lip if you gonna talk like that Mister, Calley said, his Boy here don't need to hear it. Well he'll hear any god dam thing I decide to say Mister Pullins said and o'Calley reached over and swatted his Hat right off his o'Ball Head and said Well don't decide to say it then. Oh Mister Pullins was mad then, Papa said, and he said Who the Hell you think you are to knock my Hat off my Head like that and Calley said Keep talking Mister and you gonna find out who the Hell I think I am here in bout half a shake a'this little Dog's tail. And then Mister Choat said Let's leave off a'this and go to talking bout something else okay And Mister Grimes said Some a'yall acting like you don't believe in Haints but a Haint ain't nothing but a Ghost and they ain't a Man here don't believe in Ghosts. I don't, Mister Phelps said, Don't count me in on believing in Ghosts. Yes you do, Mister Grimes said, You dam sure do believe in Ghosts. No Sir I dam sure as Hell do not believe in Ghosts and don't you never say nothing like that about me again in your Life to where I can hear it. Well you go to Church don't you, Mister Grimes said. Yes Sir I do go to Church, Mister Phelps said, and you know it. And you believe in Jesus Christ don't you, Mister Grimes said. Why Yes I do believe in Jesus Christ, Mister Phelps said, who the Hell you think I am. Well then you ignert o'Fool, Mister Grimes said, you do believe in Ghosts cause Jesus Christ is The Holy Ghost and a Holy Ghost is still a Ghost ain't he. And right then, Papa said, Mister Choat rode his Horse up tween them two and said Okay let's find us something else to talk about here for a'while fore yall go to shooting one another.

ME AND CALLEY AND FRITZ RODE OFF to the side by our self, Papa said, reason being everbody kept a'looking at me like I was from Arkansas or something cause I was Old Karl's Boy and Calley didn't wanna have to swat somebody else's Hat off for it and I ask him, he said, what he would a'done if that Man he swatted the Hat off of would a'talked back to him. I'd a'taught him some Manners or got myself whupped one, he said. I don't believe they's anybody in the whole World can whup you, Papa said. Oh Listen here, Calley said, they's maybe one or two can do it. Not no moren that, Papa said. No I don't reckon so, Calley said, but you don't never know til you a'crawling round there on the ground somewheres a'looking for your Teeth. That never happened to you, Papa said. Might one day though, Calley said, I doubt it but it might. We ain't riding off to a Picnic here are we, Papa said, You reckon they mean Bad Harm on my Daddy if we find him. Yes Sir they do, Calley said, and you need to know I mean Bad Harm on him too but only if he's still alive which I don't reckon how he could be. You think he's already dead then, Papa said. Dead Dead Dead, Calley said. Yes Sir Dead and gone to Hell but not fore your Momma's Horse Precious give him a ride to somewheres she wants him to die at or already be dead at. You talking like you think she's a Person not a Horse, Papa said. You didn't never hear me say I don't believe in Haints did you, Calley said. No Sir I didn't hear you say that, Papa said. You think bout that long nough Why you'll know xactly what I figgur happened last night at the Bird Dance. I don't have to think bout it long nough, Papa said, I already know you think my Momma's Ghost went in Precious last night so she could come out and get Old Karl for whatever Bad he done her ain't that what you a'thinking. We need to leave go a'this, Calley said, this is your Momma and Daddy we a'talking about here and I don't wanna make you feel Baddern you already a'feeling. Old Karl ain't my Daddy no more, Papa said. If I got a Daddy in this World now Why it's you. Whoa there now, Calley said, I ain't Nobody's Daddy. I don't mean no Blood Daddy, Papa said, I ain't a'saying that. Well what kind a'Daddy you talking about then, Calley said, I wanna get this straight. Same kind a'Daddy you already been to me That kind, Papa said. It's a lot a'work being your Daddy you know it, Calley said. How bout I be your Brother. I already got me a Brother, Papa said. Okay a Uncle then, Calley said, o'Uncle Calley how about that. You don't wanna be my Daddy, Papa said. I don't wanna be Nobody's Daddy, Calley said, I don't wanna have to stay Home at night if I don't want to. Okay, Papa said, I won't say no more bout it. Did I hurt your feelings, Calley said. Yes Sir you did, Papa said. Well I'd rather hurt your Feelings than be a Bad Daddy to you, Calley said, like this last one you had was.

WE WAS STILL A MILE OR SO

from Old Karl's place, Papa said, when ever Man there went to pulling out they guns and squeezing they beaks on tight to get ready. Look at these Bohonks, Calley said, they just a'itching to shoot somebody ain't they. Yes Sir, Papa said, I reckon they are. Oh Yes Sir and you can bet they gonna too, Calley said. Hell might shoot two or three of em here fore the Night's over but won't a dam one a'em be Old Karl cause he's already a Gone Goose somewheres else but No Sir not here. Anyhow, he said, when they go to shooting you and me and this little Pooch here just gonna go jump behind a tree to get outta the way Okay. Okay, Papa said. You don't want a bullet in you somewheres do you, Calley said. No Sir, Papa said, I don't. No Sir me neither, Calley said, we'll just get us the god dam Hell out the way ain't that right. Yes Sir, Papa said, that is right. If a stray bullet was to get me, Calley said, where you reckon you gonna bury me You wouldn't just leave me on the ground for the Bugs to eat would you. I'd have to get somebody to help me, Papa said, You too big for me to haul off just by myself. Somebody'd help you, Calley said, You don't have to worry bout that. One a'you grab my hands and the other one grab my feet and start a'hauling. You ain't planning on getting shot tonight are you, Papa said. No Sir I ain't planning on it, Calley said, but you don't never know do you. Well why don't we just wait til somebody shoots you and talk bout it then, Papa said. What if I'm already dead and can't say nothing about it What about that, Calley said. Well, Papa said, I reckon I won't say much neither then. Oh and then, Papa said, Old Karl's House come in view and somebody yelled There He Is and Mister Choat yelled No No No they ain't nobody in there but everbody else went to hollering and charging they Horses at the House and a'shooting off they guns fast as they could pull the trigger but, he said, o'Calley took a'holt a'Firefoot and kept us from a'going with em so we just set there behind a tree and they blowed out all the Winders and the Jugs on the front Porch and o'Fritz wagged his tail he liked it so much then here come Mister Pullins with one a'his arms just a'flopping like a wet rag and a'dripping blood. See what I told you bout these Bohonks, Calley said, Well I hope he gets Home fore he bleeds to death. And then the shooting stopped and me and Calley and Fritz rode careful up to the House just as Mister Calhoun the o'Wood Pecker was coming out the front door. They ain't No Body in there, he said, I say we burn the god dam thing down so he can't never come back even if he wants to and he was just striking a match on his boot to do it when Mister Choat stepped over and pinched the fire out right there tween his fingers. Ain't nobody gonna burn this House down, he said, it belongs to this Boy here now and his Brother too I reckon so why don't yall line up and tell him I'm Sorry for shooting out all your Winders And then tell him what you gonna do to replace em ever one. No Sir that's okay I said, Papa said, but Calley leaned back to me and said No you need to let em say they I'm Sorrys so they won't go off to Home feeling Bad bout what they done to your property here tonight.

SO I STOOD UP THERE ON THE PORCH

Papa said, and all them Men in they Bird Suits come a'walking by and give me a Hand Shake and a'I'm Sorry like Mister Choat told em to do but Oh Boy Hidy they didn't like it one bit saying it to Old Karl's Boy and give me a Look ever time but Calley said Oh don't worry bout it Hell they just being Human is all then Mister Choat said You Boys come on Home with me and Miz Choat'll fix you some good Hot Coffee and some Bisquits fore we go to looking for Old Karl again and they all went a'riding off with him just as the Sun come up over the Hill and Calley said Well I hope you ain't Sleepy are you. No Sir why would I be sleepy I said, Papa said. Well you ain't had no sleep for bout a hunderd and fifty-two years that's one reason why, Calley said, but good thing you ain't cause we still got Fish to Fry and they in just about the Worsted god dam place they is in the World to get to. I don't have no idea what you a'talking bout, Papa said. I seen Blood Drops and Hoof Prints back yonder a'leading off from Fischer Hall, Calley said, and they was a'leading off in the direction a'The Devil's Backbone. The Devil's Backbone, Papa said, Why they ain't nobody ever went in the Devil's Backbone that ever come back out again. Oh I did, Calley said, Two-three times. It ain't nothing but a sliver of a Path bout wide as your foot winds round the top a'Canyons and Gullies and Holes and Cactuses and Rattle Snakes and whatnot and if you was to slip and fall Why its Adios Muchacho to you for Ever More. You didn't tell nobody else bout them Hoof Prints did you, Papa said. No Sir didn't then and wouldn't now, Calley said, To them all this is just a dam Side Show. But to you it's Family. Yes Sir I reckon so, Papa said. That don't mean The Devil's Backbone gonna be easy, Calley said. They's gonna be Skins and Bruises all up and down you fore we're done You know it. Yes Sir I know it I said, Papa said, and then Calley said And most likely they gonna be some Tears too.

Papa said, Fritz a'leaning out over the saddle horn in front a'Calley to point the way then me behind Calley with my hands stuck down in his back pocket to hang on to by and o'Firefoot didn't make no complaint and kept up a good pace all day long til of a sudden we was going Up Up Up and that Path was a'getting Skinney Skinney Skinney and in a minute Why we was up so high you could see the whole World stretching out all round you in ever which direction and then Oh the ground went to slantin straight down on both sides a'that little sliver of a Path and ever time o'Calley leaned out from the saddle to get him a better look down the side a'the Canyon why then poor o'Firefoot'd have to do a little Tippy-Toe Dance just to keep from falling off and I'd squeeze my Eyes shut and hang on tight. How you liking the Devil's Backbone, Calley said, I told you they wadn't much to it. Yes Sir I said, Papa said, I remember you a'saying that. You keeping a good eye, Calley said, I think we might see something down there somewheres here in a minute if we just keep a'looking. I'm a'looking, Papa said, but the Truth is I was so scared I pretty much had my eyes shut down tight the whole time then here in a minute I guess I just went off to sleep cause next thing I knowed Why they was all them Shimmery People a'walking on the Air all round us like they wadn't nothing to it and Oh more a'coming from ever which direction and Oh Boy Hidy there was Miss Gusa over there and Lalo a'riding Piggy Back on his old Granpa Crecencio and Why there was Gilbert Lee just a'grinning and a'wearing some o'Farmer's Straw Hat and a'smoking him a Pipe like that o'Catfish did that time and way back yonder, he said, I think I seen that o'Inyin got drowned in the Creek and Why ain't that the Sherriff a'Comal County over there behind him and they was all a'walking so close to us they just wadn't no way we was ever gonna fall off the Devil's Backbone so I give em a wave and hollered Thank Yall for a'keeping us safe here then one of em come a'riding out from behind all them others then reared up her Horse to where I could see who it was and Oh, he said, Oh Oh Oh it was my very own Momma was who it was and she was a'riding on her Horse Precious and the Little Bay Mare was just a'dancing long behind em in the clouds and Oh there was Mister Pegleg a'hobbling fast as he could on his three legs to catch up and then here Momma waved and come a'riding through all them others to get to me and she was smiling at me and I was a'smiling back at her and right then o'Fritz went to Barking Barking Bark-

ing and I come back awake just when he jumped off o'Firefoot and went a'running and a'tumbling end over end down in that Canyon til we couldn't see him no more. He knows they's something down there somewheres, Calley said, or Somebody. Well I'm a'going down there with him I said, Papa said, then stepped off o'Firefoot lightly as I could. Careful as you go, Calley said, Me and Firefoot gonna pick us a way down and see you at the bottom. Then he give Firefoot a easy touch and there they went a'Tip-Toeing on cross the Devil's Backbone looking for a place to go down without getting kilt a'doing it. And then just when they went out a'view, Papa said, here come this Noise up from way down yonder in the Canyon and it was o'Fritz just a'Howling and a'Crying like he lost his Best Friend in the World and his Heart was breaking in two cause they just wadn't no way he was ever gonna get over it.

I'M COMING FRITZ I HOLLERED

Papa said, I'm coming, but they wadn't no easy way down the Canyon that I could see so I took me just one little step and Oh off I went a'slipping and a'sliding down that Canyon and they wadn't nothing to grab on to no wheres and Down Down Down I went Faster Faster Faster and I knowed if ever I was to hit bottom a'going that fast I was gonna break my self in a hunderd places and then Oh Boy Hidy I bounced off a rock or something and then off a'something else and now I was a'going Head over Heels Faster Faster Faster bout a mile or two on down then just fore I hit bottom Why this Hand come a'reaching out from the Canyon Side and grabbed a'holt a'me to slow me down then let me go again and next thing I knowed I hit bottom but it wadn't no hard rocky Bottom like I reckoned it was gonna be but was something bounced me up like maybe I landed on a Hay Stack but when I looked Oh No it wadn't no Hay Stack at all but was my Momma's dead Horse Precious I landed on with Old Karl still a'sticking out her mouth there, Papa said, and Fritz setting right there beside her crying. Then I looked up to see who it was reached out from the Canyon Side to save me and Why it wadn't nobody at all but was that o'curved Cedar Tree a'growing out a Cave up there just like them Shimmery People been a'showing me all them times in my sleep.

Why we was up so high you could
see the whole World stretching out   *2/5*
all round you . . .

Calley and Firefoot come a'stumbling down bout two hours later, Papa said. Calley took one look up at the Cave and said I'd reckon that's where he put your Momma huh. I'd reckon it too, Papa said, but I ain't climbed up there yet to look. No Sir you leave the Looking to me, he said, then went over there and grabbed Old Karl by his Boot Heels and tried to pull his head out from in Precious' mouth but he just couldn't do it. Precious ain't gonna let him go is she, Calley said, she brung him here to stay for All Time just like Old Karl done your Momma. That's what killed her too I reckon, he said, o'Precious'd a'rather choaked to death on that sorry o'Son of a Bitch than let him go. Yes Sir, Papa said, I'm gonna miss her. Yes Sir miss her your whole entire Life, Calley said, That's the kind a'Horse she was But be glad you was blessed with her like you was even for a'short time in your Life cause They ain't many ever come around like her. I can say the same thing bout o'Firefoot here too, he said, I reckon you know that huh. Yes Sir I do I said, Papa said, then I reached over and took Fritz off from Precious where he was still a'crying and said Fritz it's gonna make you sick you keep a'crying like this but there I was a'doing the same xact thing myself. Then Calley said I know we been a'putting it off but I reckon I better climb on up there and take me a look in that Cave fore it gets too Dark to see anything and it's already bout to.

*S*O CALLEY CLIMBED ON UP Papa said, then went deep in the Cave to where I couldn't see nothing of him no more then here in a minute he poked his head back out at me and Fritz and said No Sir your Momma ain't in here They's just some o'Husk of a Human Being but they ain't nobody in it no more. And then it come to me I already knowed my Momma wadn't in there, Papa said, cause it wadn't but maybe three-four hours ago I seen her a'riding her Horse Precious up in the Air a'long side me. Oh No Sir my Momma ain't in there I said, he said, my Momma is out here a'riding round on Precious somewheres a'keeping a Eye out for me and always will be I reckon. Yes Sir that's how I see it too, o'Calley said, and then he went to filling up the Door into that Cave so couldn't nobody ever get in again and then, Papa said, he come on back down and we went to piling Rocks up over Momma's dead Horse Precious with Old Karl a'sticking out her mouth til you wouldn't never know they was down there under all them Rocks like that for Ever and Ever and Ever.

WE RODE OFF FROM THERE EARLY NEXT MORNING
Papa said, and Calley said Them was hard Fish to Fry wadn't they and I said
Yes Sir they was for me. I wish I could relieve you of the Hurt, he said, I
know it ain't easy both your Momma and Daddy like that now. I just wish I
had my Momma's Saddle with the Conchos on it to remember her by, Papa
said. Why then we'll just go to hunting for it Calley said, Hell we ain't got
nothing else to do So we cut for Old Karl's place and right away we seen
somebody beat us to there and was inside Ram Sacking everthing. Hello the
House Hello the House, Calley said, then let go a couple a'Pops up in the air
with his Pistola to let who ever it was know we wadn't fooling around. And
then, Papa said, the Front Door come open and Why my Brother Herman
come a'stepping out with his arms full a'all kind a'things. Who's a'doing all
that shooting, he said. Why it's me your Brother and our o'Friend Calley
Pearsall I said, Papa said. We found where our Daddy put Momma after he
murdered her. She irritated him that's why, Herman said. You don't know
where that o'Son of a Bitch hid his Money Box do you. No I never give it a
thought Papa said, I come looking for our Momma's Saddle You ain't seen it
have you. I thought I just told you I'm a'looking for Old Karl's Money Box,
Herman said, what would I want with some o'Saddle.

So, Papa said, me and Calley went walking down to the Barn and first
thing I seen was this big pile a'ashes where Old Karl'd had him a Burn Pile
over there by the Pens but I didn't think nothing of it at the time and we
went on in the Barn and everwheres I looked I seen something from the
Past in my head. I seen my Momma over there brushing Precious down and
I seen Miss Gusa holding her fat Belly and a'gathering the eggs and then
there was my Brother Herman pitching hay down from the loft to the Little
Bay Mare and Oh yonder was Mister and Miz Pegleg a'nawing on a Chicken
and Pepe and Peto was over there a'cooking em another one on this little fire
they had And then, Papa said, I looked over behind the Corn Crib and Why
there I was myself when I was just a Little Boy and I was digging a hole in
the ground and when I finished digging it Old Karl come over and dropped
his Money Belt down in it and covered it up then set him a fire on top like
he usted to make me do when we was out on the Road a'trading Horses so
wouldn't nobody think to look there if they was meaning to steal his Money
And then, he said, I looked round but now Momma was gone and so was
Precious and the Little Bay Mare and Miss Gusa with her fat Belly and my

Brother Herman and Mister and Miz Pegleg and Pepe and Peto and Old Karl and me too when I was just that Little Boy all a'us Gone now Gone Gone Gone just me left a'standing there bout to cry over Lost Times but then I looked out there by the Pens and seen that Burn Pile again and I said Mister Pearsall I know xactly where my Daddy hid his Money Box so I grabbed up a shovel and Calley did one too and we went to digging under that Burn Pile and here in a minute we seen this big o'Canvas Sack down there in the hole and I reached down and opened it up and Oh here come bout a million Sparkles up out a'that sack and they was all from them bright Nickel Conchos there on my Momma's Saddle that she gone a'riding off on that Black Morning and after that, Papa said, I never did see her alive again even one more time in my Whole Life but there she was when she come a'riding up on Precious with all them other Shimmery People to keep me and o'Calley safe on the Path cross the Devil's Backbone.

*W*E PULLED THAT CANVAS SACK out the hole, Papa said, then pulled Momma's Saddle out a'that. That's a good Saddle, Calley said, I ain't never seen one no better. Her Daddy got it after that Fight they had with the Mexkins then he give it over to her sometime after that, Papa said. I reckon you'd have to call it a Air Loom Saddle then wouldn't you, Calley said. I'm just gonna call it Momma's Saddle, Papa said, and I'm gonna ride it all the Days a'my Life. I would too, Calley said, a Saddle like that Yes Sir I sure would. And then, Papa said, o'Fritz went to digging away at something in the bottom a'the hole. Must be something important, Calley said, or else he'd be over there somewheres else a'licking on his little Hiney wouldn't he. Well lets have us a look, he said, then jumped down in the Hole and went to digging with the shovel and in just a minute he said Why they's a Big Tin Box buried down here under where your Momma's Saddle was. I knowed what it was, Papa said, it couldn't a'been nothing but Old Karl's Money Box. So I stepped down in that hole with Calley and we lifted it out but it wadn't easy. Then we looked over and here come Herman just a running down from the House. That's it he said, Papa said, that's Old Karl's Money Box ain't it then he dropped down on his knees and pulled the lid open and Why they was Money Money Money in it all the way up to the top. They's moren a Thousand Dollars in there if they's a penny Calley said, and they's something else in there too. Then, Papa said, Calley reached way down deep under all that Money and come out with a pair a'Bran New Shoes. Sticking a pair a'Shoes in there with his Money Why that don't make no sense at all does it, Herman said, then chunked em over there out the way so he could go to counting the Money but, Papa said, I went over there and looked and Oh them Shoes was just xactly my size when I run off from Home that Day long ago when Old Karl wouldn't buy me none.

WE CARRIED OLD KARL'S TREASURE BOX up on the porch, Papa said, so Herman could keep a'counting it then me and Calley went in the House to cook some Beans for our suppers but I couldn't hardly eat a Bite for dwelling on them Shoes Old Karl had in there in the Box with his Money. Did he buy em the same time he bought them other two pair for Pepe and Peto then not give em to me out a'Pure Meanness or was it he bought em later after I run off from Home thinking to give em to me to say I'm Sorry if I was ever to come back again. I didn't know which, Papa said, but I sided with the Meanness over the I'm Sorry. Them o'Shoes is walking all over you ain't they, Calley said, I can tell. Yes Sir they a Puzzle to me, Papa said. Well ever Man oughta do at least one Good Thing in his Life I reckon, Calley said, even Old Karl though I doubt One Good Thing is gonna be nough to keep him outta the Hot Flames. You figgur he's already burning in Hell then huh, Papa said. Truly I do so believe, Calley said. In Hell with his Pants on Fire for evermore. Them Men think I'm gonna be just like him when I grow up don't they, Papa said. Yes Sir I reckon they do, Calley said. I don't wanna Live round People think like that bout me, Papa said. No Sir it ain't a good way to Live, Calley said, Believe me I know. Some People think Bad bout you Mister Pearsall, Papa said. Not just Some People, Calley said, a whole god dam Bunch a'People. Cause your Daddy was a Bad Man, Papa said. No cause he was a Drinking Man, Calley said, that's a different kind a'Bad Man than your Daddy was but it's Bad nough. What'd he do, Papa said. They's other Things we can talk about, Calley said, it don't have to just be about my Daddy you know it. Okay, Papa said, then here in a minute Calley said, my Daddy got to drinking in town one day and wanted to show his little Son how fast he could drive his wagon down the street so he went to whooping and a'hollering at his Horses and they throwed they ears back and away they went fast as they could go on down the street and he was a'holding his Little Boy close to him and they was just a'laughing and then of a sudden they was all these People crossing the street and they Horses run right over em Five in all and killed ever god dam one of em, Calley said, Two Mommas and two Babies and a little Foot Walker about three years of age I reckon. Calley put his head down almost in his bowl a'Beans so I couldn't see his eyes, Papa said, then he said They Tarred and Feathered that Drinking Man and run him out a'Town and ain't Nobody never seen him in this World since. You was that Little Boy in the Wagon, Papa said, wadn't you. Yes Sir I was, Calley said, and still am by god.

*W*E ATE OUR BEANS

Papa said, then come out on the Porch where Herman was still down there on his knees a'counting the Money up. You better warsh your Hands good when you get done handling all that Money, Calley said, they say it'll give you a Itch you can't never get over. Herman didn't even look up so we got us a drink a'water and just set there on the Porch a'watching him. Herman I said, Papa said, I guess you heard me say Old Karl did away with our Momma didn't you. What, Herman said. Your Daddy murdered your Momma then stole her Horse and Saddle, Calley said, ain't you a'listening. Yes Sir I heard that, Herman said. But he didn't one time look up from a'counting the Money when he said it, Papa said. You better go over there and give your Brother a kiss Adios Goodbye, Calley said, I think that Money's got him Lock Stock and Barrel course he been a'living in the City ain't he. I'm at three thousand dollars, Herman said, and still a'going strong. They ain't no hurry Herman, Papa said, it's all yours anyhow. Oh Herman looked up then, Papa said, his eyes going wide as one a'them Silver Coins in the Box. You don't want no Share, he said. Just some for Bird and the Choats and Marcellus, Papa said. What about this Farm here, Herman said, you gonna want your Share a'it ain't you. No Sir not one Clod of it, Papa said. It's all yours. Well this is a Surprise to me It sure is, Herman said. But I would like to have Momma's Saddle, Papa said. Maybe we'll draw lots for it, Herman said, that'd be fair.

What in the god dam Hell would you know bout Fair you greedy little Son of a Bitch, Calley said and give Herman a look that made him turn his head over there to the Woods for a minute but when he looked back he had his Snake Eyes on and he said Mister Pearsall I've whupped moren one Man talked to me like that over in New Braunfels and you better know it. Well Son if you wanna whup me you just come on with it any o'time suits you to and I'll see what I can do to protect my self and Oh Herman took a jump at Calley fore the words was out his mouth and caught him one right there on his Nose and the blood just come a'leaking out and Calley said Okay now its my turn I reckon and then, Papa said, he give Herman a quick Whupping all over his Nose and Mouth and his Eyes and Ears to where it looked like Herman got his Head stuck up in a Hornet Nest somewheres and couldn't get it out. Well now, Calley said, how's that for a Thank You after you hit a man on his Nose. Herman still had his Snake Eyes on even if he couldn't hardly see out em Papa said, and he said I'm gonna pay you back for ever lick you give me one a'these days so you just better watch out Mister. Oh I will watch out, Calley said, and when you see me Watching Out you god dam sure better be a'Watching Out too.

*T*HEN CALLEY WALKED OFF

Papa said, and Herman looked over at me and said I can remember a Time when you'd a'jumped in and helped me in a Fight like that. You the one sassed him, Papa said, I figgured you was looking for a Fight like always. How was I to know he was gonna be so Mean, Herman said, they ain't a One can whup me like that over in New Braunfels. Well they is here ain't they, Papa said. You just Hush, Herman said, you seen what I done to his Nose. Yes Sir and I seen what he done to your whole Face too, Papa said. You better be careful, Herman said, I just might tell you and your Friend both to get the Hell off my property here in a minute or two. Well why don't you, Papa said, I'm starting to think I don't want no more to do with you anyhow. Get off my Property then, Herman said, You and him both How you like that. What bout Momma's Saddle, Papa said, how we gonna decide who gets it. Gimme a dollar for my half and take it I don't care, Herman said. I give him a dollar outta my pocket, Papa said, and I told him I'd bring it back by here some day so he could look at it again if he wanted to. No I don't wanna see it again, he said, and not you neither. I went down to the Barn then where o'Calley was fooling around with Fritz and Firefoot and said Well my Brother Herman just run us off from here. I'm not surprised, Calley said, not after that Licking I give him. It's not just that, Papa said, I think he's gone and turned into Somebody Else and I don't know how to turn him back to who he was. No Sir People like your Brother don't never turn back around to who they was, Calley said, No Sir they just keep a'going yonder ways to who they gonna be from now on out and don't let it surprise you the next time you see him your Brother Herman done turned into the god dam Devil or Somebody just like him.

ME AND CALLEY RODE UP TO THE CHOATS

bout suppertime with Momma's Saddle, Papa said, and Why there was Bird setting in his little wagon at the Yard Gate a'pointing his finger right at us. I reckon he knowed yall was coming, Miz Choat said, he been out here a'pointing his finger like that for bout an hour ain't that right Marcellus. Yes Ma'am Marcellus said then Miz Choat said Come over here and give me a hug and tell me bout your Momma I know it ain't good. So, Papa said, I told her everthing they was to tell bout Momma and the Devil's Backbone and Old Karl a'sticking out Precious' mouth dead like we found him and Oh we stood there a'holding one another and cried bout it then Miz Choat said Well I see you got Mandy's Saddle back I know she'd be glad a'that then she give Calley a hug too and said I remember you saving Bird from Old Karl's grip the other night but I don't recall what kind a'Bird you was. Well I was a Road Runner at the Bird Dance, Calley said, but I just made that up cause my Young Friend here was one. Well we gonna see what kind a'Bird you really are here in just a minute she said and then, Papa said, when we got in the House Miz Choat layed Bird down on his bed and pulled his shirt up to show Calley the little Birthmark Bird there on his chest. Okay what Bird you see there on his chest, she said, and Calley bent way down to have a Look then scrunched up his face and said Oh I see a whole flock a'Birds and they all the same kind And then this frown come over him, Papa said, and he said Buzzards they all Buzzards Oh Lordy they all Buzzards ever one. You the first one to ever see a Buzzard Miz Choat said. Not a Buzzard Ma'am, Calley

And then this frown come over him,
Papa said, and he said Buzzards
they all Buzzards . . .

said. Buzzards A whole sky full a'Buzzards flying round in a circle. Don't yall see em, he said. Buzzards just ever where. And right then, Papa said, Mister Choat come in the door and said Uh Oh it looks to me like Mister Pearsall's seeing something in Bird's Bird there ain't he. Buzzards Miz Choat said. And that ain't all, Calley said. Oh No Sir that ain't all, he said. And then, Papa said, Bird's eyes just went a'going round and round and side to side behind his eye lids and Miz Choat said Tell us what else you seeing there Mister Pearsall We ain't a'having no secrets. Calley squinted his eyes and got right down close to Bird's Birthmark Bird and then he said Why they's a Little Man a'walking round under all them Buzzards and he's got a old rotten Hang Man's Noose hanging round his neck and Oh they's Death in his Eye if ever I seen it and his Hair is White Oh just White as White can be all over his head but he don't look like no Old Man to me. And then, Papa said, Mister and Miz Choat got over there close as they could to one another and said to where you could just barely hear em say it Oh No Oh No it's o'Pelo Blanco a'coming. Pelo Blanco, Calley said, Pelo Blanco. Then he touched his hand to his big o'Pistola there in his pants and went over to the winder to see if they was anybody a'coming up the Road and for the First Time in my Life, Papa said, I seen he was a'scared a'something in this World. Is o'Pelo Blanco coming to do you Bad Harm Mister Pearsall I said, Papa said, but Calley just shaked his head No and give me this Long Sad Look like he was bout to cry and Oh right then I knowed it wadn't Him o'Pelo Blanco was coming to get—

No Sir, he said, it was Me.

And thus ends

THE DEVIL'S BACKBONE

Book One of The Papa Stories

ACKNOWLEDGMENTS

My Grandfather was a good Storyteller and some of the stories in this book were inspired by some of his.

In the last couple of years of the War my Mother—recently divorced from my father who simply could not walk past a bottle of beer—ran the local telephone office in Edna, Texas, which was also our home. The Tom Callaways lived just down the street and around the corner by the First Baptist Church and every evening after supper and just about the time the Lightning Bugs started winking in the yard Mister Callaway would sit down in his big chair on the side porch and start telling stories to whoever was there to listen, as my big brother Jim and I always tried to be.

If you went down the street and around the corner from the telephone office in the other direction you'd pass the old Hill Cotton Gin then look both ways before you crossed the railroad tracks to the Hardware Store on the other side where that good and generous man Mister Gus Westoff would always give you a few scrap boards and some nails to go build something with—and usually he'd tell you a good story to boot, even if you were just five or six years old and still in short pants. It was Mister Westoff who told me a story about an escaped slave woman who ran wild for years through the Navidad River Bottoms without the locals ever being able to chase her down, even from horseback. For a while, Mister Westoff said, they found the barefoot tracks of a small child alongside hers on the river banks but then one day, he said, the child's tracks disappeared forever and I worried for months what might have happened to that child and how heartbroken the Wild Woman must have been at the loss of her little son or daughter.

A few years later an Aunt who worked in the Book Department at Foley's in Houston sent me a copy of J. Frank Dobie's *Old-Time Tales of Texas* for Christmas and in that book was Mister Dobie's version (he said a good story belonged to whoever could tell it best) of The Wild Woman of the Navidad. So here was that same story I had first heard from Mister Westoff in his Hardware Store back in Edna in the 1940s but now here it was made

Eternal in a Book . . . in a Book! Even at that young age the idea that stories right out of your own life could be made into books just set me afire and I suppose I've never really gotten over it.

A lot of Friends helped me with this one, none more so than my pals Steve Harrigan and Bill Broyles, who set their own work aside at various times to read and give perceptive comments on mine. That was true also of Pat Carter . . . and Jack Watson . . . and Barbara Morgan . . . and Connie Todd . . . and Dr. George Siddons . . . and Julie Speed . . . and Van Ramsey . . . and Dyson Lovell . . . and Alice Worrall . . . and DJ Stout . . . and my son Reid . . . and of course, and as always, my wife Sally.

The Devil's Backbone is the fourth book I've published with the University of Texas Press. I like it that my books are published here at home in Texas where my publisher Dave Hamrick, a man with a passion for books and publishing and Texas, is now bringing a whole new vision to the Press. And thanks also to my editor Casey Kittrell, who made the publishing of this book such a fun and congenial journey, as did Ellen McKie, my most talented design partner on at least a half-dozen other books before this one. And certainly thanks to all the other good folks over there at the Press who in one way or another had a hand in the making of this book, most especially Lynne Chapman . . . and Jan McInroy . . . and Nancy Bryan . . . and Theresa May . . . and Gianna LaMorte . . . and Victoria Davis . . . and Brian Contine . . . and Regina Fuentes . . . and Brenda Jo Hoggatt . . . and Dawn Bishop.

It was a great blessing to work with Jack Unruh, one of the most celebrated of all American illustrators. Jack's drawings always surprised, always delighted, always illuminated, and I am grateful that his work is forever a part of this book. Thank you, Jack.

I also want to thank my two spunky assistants—Amanda Buschman (now Utter) and, when Amanda left for Baby Wyatt, Kate Bowie (now Carruth). No writer ever had better company on a daily basis than I did with these two jolly ladies. Thank you, Amanda. Thank you, Kate.

Until January 16th of this year my pal Ocho (born December 8, 1998) was here with me every day too—and sometimes I think he still is.

Bill Wittliff
April 14, 2014